NO PRINCE CHARMING

SECRETS OF STONE: BOOK ONE

ANGEL PAYNE & VICTORIA BLUE

NO PRINCE CHARMING

SECRETS OF STONE: BOOK ONE

ANGEL PAYNE & VICTORIA BLUE

WATERHOUSE PRESS

Sometimes, fate is the coolest thing.

Who knew two Facebook friends would find a writing home with each other?

On behalf of us both, THANK YOU to the fans, readers, family, and friends who have supported this project—and believed in Killian and Claire from the moment they burst to life in our imaginations. We do it for all of YOU and hope you enjoy the beginning of the Secrets of Stone series.

PROLOGUE

Claire

April...

Oh my God.

The words sprinted through my head, over and over, as I prodded at my lips in assurance I wasn't dreaming. Or hopping dimensions. Or remembering the last half hour in a *really* crazy way. Or had hours passed, instead? I didn't know anymore. Time was suddenly contorted.

Oh. My. God.

What the hell had just happened?

Forget my lips. My whole mouth felt like I'd just had dental work done, tingling in all the places his lips had touched moments ago—which had been everywhere.

My mind raced, trying to match the erratic beat of my heart. "Christ," I whispered. My voice shook like a damn teenager's, so I repeated myself. Because *that* helped, right?

Wrong. So wrong.

It was all because of that man. That dictatorial, demanding...

Nerve-numbing, bone-melting...

Man.

Who really knew how to deliver a kiss.

Hell. That kiss.

Okay, by this age, I'd been kissed before. I'd been *everything* before. But after what we'd just done, I'd be awake for long hours tonight. *Long* hours. Shaking with need... Shivering with fear.

I pressed the Call button for the elevator with trembling fingers. Turning back to face the door I'd just emerged from, I reconsidered pushing the buzzer next to it instead. The black lacquer panel around the button was still smudged by the angry fingerprints I'd left when arriving here not more than thirty minutes ago—answering his damn summons.

Yeah. He'd summoned me. And, like a breathless backstage groupie, I'd dropped everything and come. Why? He was my hemlock. He could be nothing else.

I was even more pissed now. At him. At me. At the thoughts that wouldn't leave me alone now, all in answer to one tormenting question.

If Killian Stone kissed like that, what could he do to the rest of my body?

No. That kind of thinking was dangerous. The tiny hairs on the back of my neck stood up as if the air conditioner just kicked on at full power.

It had been a while since I'd been with a man. At least like...that.

Okay, it had been a long while.

For the last three years, career had come before all else. After the disaster I simply called the Nick Years, Dad had fought hard to help rebuild my spirit, including the doors he'd finagled open for me. Wasting those opportunities in favor of relationships wasn't an option. My focus had paid off, leading to a coveted position at Asher and Associates PR, where I'd quickly advanced to the elite field team for Andrea Asher herself. The six of us, including Andrea and her daughter, Margaux, were called corporate America's PR dream team. We were brought in when the blemishes were too big and horrid for in-house specialists, hired on a project-by-project basis for our thoroughness and objectivity. That also meant the assignments were intense, ruthless, and very temporary.

The gig at Stone Global was exactly such a job. And things were going well. Better than well. People were cooperating. The press was moving on to new prey. The job was actually ahead of schedule, and thank God for that. Soon, I'd be back in my rightful place at the home office in San Diego and what had just happened in Killian Stone's penthouse would remain no more than a blip in my memory. A very secret blip.

I shook my head in defiance. What was wrong with having lived a little? At twenty-six, I was due for at least one heart-stopping kiss with a man who looked like dark sin, was built like a navy SEAL, and kissed like a fantasy. *Sweet God, what a fantasy.*

"You didn't do anything wrong," I muttered. "You didn't break any rules...technically. He consented. And you sure as *hell* consented. So you're—"

Having an argument with yourself in the middle of a hallway in the Lincoln Park 2550 building, waiting on the world's slowest damn elevator.

I leaned on the Call button again.

While *still* trying to talk myself out of pouncing on Killian's buzzer too. Or perhaps back into it. If I could concoct an excuse to ring his doorbell before the elevator arrived...

No. This is dangerous, remember? He's dangerous. You know all the sordid reasons why, his and yours.

Maybe I could just say I accidentally left my purse inside.

And that'll fly...how? One glance down at my oversize Michael Kors clutch had me cursing the fashion-trend gods, along with their penchant for large handbags.

I leaned against the wall, closing my eyes and hoping for a lightbulb. I was bombarded with Killian's smell instead. Armani Code. The cologne was still strong in my head, its rich bergamot and lemon mingling with the spice of his shampoo and the Scotch on his breath, like he'd scent-marked me through the intimacy of our skin...

My fingers roamed to my cheek, tracing the abrasion where he'd rubbed me with his stubble. My head fell back at the impact of the recollection.

In an instant, my mind conjured an image of him again, standing in front of me. Commanding. Looming. Hot...and hard. I felt his breath on my face again as he yanked me close. The press of his wool pants against my legs. The metallic scrape of his cufflinks on the wood of his desk as he shoved everything away to make room for our bodies. Then the wild throb of my heart as he tangled his hands in my hair, lifted my face toward his, and...

Yes.

The memory was so vivid, so good. I used the flat of my palm on my face now, thinking I could save the magic if I covered it. Protecting it from the outside world. Our perfect, shared moment in the middle of all this chaos.

Whoa.

"Get a grip." I dropped my hand along with the furious whisper. It was one kiss. Incredible, yes, but I guaranteed *he* wasn't still thinking about it like this. Behind that majestic door, Killian Stone moved again in his world, already focused on the next of his hundred priorities, none of them bearing my name. And he expected me to get back to mine, cushioning his company from that big, bad outside world I'd just been brooding over. *You've been hired to help clean up the Stone family's mess, not add to it.*

The elevator finally dinged.

At the same time, Killian's condo door opened behind me.

I locked a smile on my face, trying to look like I had been patiently waiting for the elevator the entire time.

"Miss Montgomery?"

Not Killian. I didn't know whether to curse or laugh.

"Yes?" I managed a Girl Scout-sweet reply.

A kind face was waiting when I turned around. The man wore such a warm expression I was tempted to call him Fred. *Not* Alfred. Just Fred. The man was too handsome for a full Alfred.

Fred handed me a small ivory envelope and then stepped over into the elevator. He held the doors open while I got into the car with him. We rode in silence down to the lobby. I squirmed while Fred smiled as if it were Saturday in the park. Did he know what his boss had just done with me?

I winced toward the wall. Technically, Killian was *my* boss right now too.

Mr. Stone. Mr. Stone. Mr. Stone.

He can never be "Killian" again.

The sooner you remember that, the better.

I was dying to open that little envelope but carefully slipped it into my queen-size clutch for when I was alone again in the cab on my way back to the hotel.

"I'll call the car round for you." Like his employer, Fred made it obvious the subject wasn't up for debate, so I forced a smile and followed him across the gleaming lobby to the building's front awning. In less than a minute, the black town car with the Stone Global logo on its doors appeared. I climbed in, all the while yearning for the anonymity of a city cab instead.

Chicago was a great city, but the traffic was insane, even as evening officially blended into nighttime. Nevertheless, Killian's building was swiftly swallowed by the lush trees of the neighborhood. I was on my way back to the hotel. Back to real life—and all the dangers that waited if anyone on the team ever learned where I'd just been.

For just a few more seconds, I yearned to remember the fantasy instead. Perhaps the treasure in my purse would help.

I pulled it out, running reverent fingers over it again. Nothing was written on the outside. Killian—Mr. Stone—had simply expected it would be delivered straight to me.

The elegant handwriting inside, dedicated to just one sentence, dried out my throat upon impact.

I must see you again.

He left no signature. No phone number. Not even an email address. But the strangest part about it all? I wasn't surprised. He was Killian Jamison Stone. And he kissed like *that.* Things—and people—came to him, *not* the other way around.

But did I have the strength to be one of those people, knowing I'd never see him again after three months?

CHAPTER ONE

Killian

March, one month earlier...

"Have a seat."

I tried to be diplomatic about it. Trey's stoned eyes and clammy skin were evidence enough of how he'd tried to self-medicate the nightmare away last night. But this mess—*his* mess—wasn't going away anytime soon. I'd closed the shades, blocking out the panoramic view of the river and skyline, to force him to see it. All ten monitors on my office wall blared the headlines from the major news carrier websites.

Stone's At It Again—Times Two

Throwing Stones? Looks Like He Did

Stones, Sex, and Politics—They Really Do Mix

Senators' Daughters? He'll Take Two, Please—At Once

Oh, Trey! Come and Play the Washington Way!

The titles progressed in creativity from there.

Trey didn't sit. Instead, while taking a surly trip to the

sideboard, he snarled, "Turn that crap off."

I parked my ass against my desk and braced my legs. "Not happening."

"Where the hell's all your booze?"

"Forget it. Also not happening."

"All you have here is coffee."

"Because it's nine in the morning." I glanced at the monitors again and clenched my jaw. A blonde and a brunette this time. One of them was still in her school uniform. The other had waved hello to eighteen just last week. Yes, *that* was our single ray of hope. At least one of the girls was "legal."

"I hate coffee."

"Drink it. You're going to need it."

"I'll gack."

"Good. It'll save me the money from having your stomach pumped."

Trey hurled the coffee mug, thankfully still empty, past my head and into one of the monitors. "You know what? Fuck you, Killian!"

The hatred he flung from those bright eyes, now visible through a tangle of hair, hadn't changed since we were kids. Neither had the stake of sorrow it drove into my gut. But unlike then, I wasn't willing to share my Lego for a chance at his love. Because since then, I'd learned it wouldn't make a difference. How'd the ditty go? *What doesn't kill you makes you stronger.* I could work with that.

"Sorry," I drawled, "you're not my type, brother. Besides, I'd have thought you were a little weary of fucking by now."

"Nice," Trey sneered. "I see the asshole factor of this office is seeping into you with no problem."

"Probably true. But right now, my 'asshole factor' is

keeping *your* ass from being nicknamed gerbil bitch by prisoner two-fifty-six before dinner tonight. So sit."

Watching the color drain from his pretty-boy cheeks was an odd relief. Maybe the dumb shit had started to comprehend how much trouble he was really in. He finally dropped into one of the room's new conference chairs. The white leather didn't do anything for his pallor.

Against my better instincts, I gave in to a moment of sympathy and sat across from him. Sympathy? That proved it—I had to be five kinds of fucked up. His trip down Idiot Avenue was costing market share for Stone Global by the minute. My lunch with the Melbourne investors, carefully orchestrated for the wow factor of the sitting at the chef's table at Alinea, would have an appetizer course of paparazzi flashbulbs. My real workday would end long after midnight.

But the way Trey's hands shook, dragging through his hair, ripped my goddamn gut out.

"So how long is this shit gonna take? I've got plans for Mardi Gras, Kil. I'm supposed to leave tomorrow."

So much for compassion. I surged to my feet. "You know the term jailbait, Trey? They call it that for a reason. You slept with a pair of senators' daughters."

"No." The protest was as snide as the Mardi Gras hall pass request. "I slept with *one* senator's daughter. The *legal* one."

"So she brought her friend along for fun?"

"Ashley's a curious kid! She wanted to watch."

"In her bra and school skirt? With the movie option going on her phone?"

"Her sweater made her hot. And she wanted to capture everything as a memento."

I gave in to pinching the bridge of my nose. It wasn't a

move I indulged in often, knowing Trey and Lance loathed its similarity to Father's signature stress pose, but right now I prayed it made Trey's goddamn eyes bleed.

"Memento," I repeated. "You really believed that?"

Mirth gleamed in my brother's eyes. "You want the real answer or the one we're gonna fork over to the PR department?"

I almost gave in to the urge to laugh. "You really don't get it, do you?"

"Come on, Kil. Of course I do. Hell, I get Christmas cards every year from the team down in PR. With the bonuses they make because of me, they're buying cars for their kids and taking vacations to Bora Bora."

"Better tell them to research economy models and a few days in a forest yurt."

"Huh?"

I leveled my stare, hard and unyielding, across the room. "You haven't just spilled the milk this time, Trey. This is a world-class oil slick, meaning things are going to get stickier before they get better." I stopped there. He didn't have to be told the entire story. Not yet, at least. I still had trouble believing it myself. Despite Senator Wooten's enraged call for a press conference later today, no doubt designed to paint Trey as a predatory pervert, could "little" Emily Wooten have actually been acting with the full green light from her father? I'd turned down the housing development deal from Wooten's cronies over a year ago. It had looked like beneficial low-cost housing on the outside, but the structures wouldn't have lasted through their first exposure to a brutal Chicago winter.

It was very possible that Wooten had done his homework and unearthed the weakness in Stone Global's massive hull. And now we had an oil slick.

"What the hell are you talking about?" Trey demanded.

I folded my arms and stated, "No in-house PR. Industrial-sized slicks require big guns for cleanup. Andrea Asher is on her way from California, and she's bringing her best team with her." I checked my watch. "We have five hours until they arrive. Great timing. They'll get here just before Wooten gets up on his soapbox."

"Fucking great." Trey looked like a man on his way to the gallows again. "Should I order beer and corn nuts?"

"No beer," I snapped.

"Cold fish."

I rose and crossed to the door that led to my private bathroom. "Sounds like a perfect temperature for your shower. Wash your hair and shave too. Then get some goddamn sleep. I've had Britta pull out the sofa bed in the anteroom for you."

Trey closed the door on me with a furious *whomp*. Again, nothing I wasn't used to. The filthier pieces of our family dynamic took up a lot of space under our rug. It was simply my job to carry a very big broom. The task had always been manageable, but I was smart enough to know when to ask for help. I was also smart enough to seek the best, and that meant Asher and Associates. Though it was the first time I'd used the woman's number, I wasn't saving the digits to speed dial. This effort would be massive and expensive, and I expected this PR dream team to put the fear of God into Trey at the same time they commanded his reputation to rise up, be healed, and walk from the grave. After they performed that small miracle, we could all live happily ever after on our respective sides of the country.

And as long as they didn't discover the darkest, dirtiest secrets under the family rug, we'd all get along fine.

CHAPTER TWO

Claire

"You're going down." I threw the taunt at Chad as we deplaned. Sure, we were teammates, but that didn't mean a little good-natured competition wasn't in order. Besides, traditions were sacred, and this one had sprung to life on one of our trips over a year ago. Points were assigned for varying degrees of horror experienced during our coach-class flights—a game we used to smile through the pain. Or acknowledge our masochistic sides. There was a difference, right?

The answer could wait. I finally had the drop on Mr. Chad Lerner, my geek-cute yet all-too-cocky teammate. I was sure of it this time.

"No damn way." Chad laughed and readjusted his new Kliik eyeglasses as we strolled the jet way to the terminal. "Did you see the nightmare I was stuck with? You're delusional to think you're winning this one, little girl."

From several feet behind us, Michael joined his laugh with Chad's. He knew why we teased each other, though he'd been so far back in the plane, we didn't know if he was still in today's running. I glanced to where his head of thick gold waves appeared over the sea of other passengers. From this distance, the guy could be mistaken for Ryan Reynolds, especially when the top half of his handsome face became animated by a gloating waggle of brows.

I volleyed with a deep pout. "Damn." The guy racked up automatic points for being stuck in the last five rows of the plane. Throw in a screaming kid or a gossipy seatmate and he'd have this sewn up, at least for today. Our final teammate, Talia Perizkova, was scheduled to join us in a few days, after wrapping up a job for the firm down in New Orleans.

Our little competition never included the other two members of the team because they always sat in first class while we were herded to coach with the other cattle. Andrea was the owner of the leading PR fix-it firm in the nation, so she never sat in coach. Neither did her princess-zilla daughter, Margaux.

Okay, maybe the princess-zilla thing was overkill. Margaux *had* been my classmate at USD, even my pseudo-roomie for a couple of months, and I remembered a few people who'd strained to see her softer side despite the friendship-through-intimidation routine that'd served her well through life. I'd personally given up on the quest halfway through sophomore year, especially after the events of senior year, but that had been three years ago. Maybe it was time to give her a fresh chance.

Or maybe it wasn't.

We passed the plane's flight crew as we entered the terminal. The attendant who'd been serving the first-class cabin wore a tear-stricken gaze, gripping a wine glass rimmed with Margaux's signature berry lip stain.

While giving the girl a sympathetic smile, I prayed Margaux had limited herself to *one* glass of wine before accompanying her mother to one of the most important meetings in Asher and Associates' history.

There was no sign of Andrea and Margaux at baggage claim. They were likely outside already, watching as Stone Global's driver loaded their bags into the company's limo. That meant Michael, Chad and I would have to postpone a final points tally while hurrying through baggage claim and then hustling our asses to the curb.

Watching the carousel vomit luggage was strangely calming. The *thunks* of the pieces as they touched down were predictable and steady, the last of life's elements I could count on for the next few months. We were headed into a public relations DEFCON One situation. Trey Stone was a monumental embarrassment to his family's company. Before the plane tickets had been purchased for Chicago, we'd all agreed this newest fiasco was likely a scrape on the surface of what the playboy was capable of. Experience had shown us how the drill went in situations like these. They usually turned worse before they got better.

Trey had two brothers, as well. Lance, eleven months behind him, was the dream-prone artist. The youngest was Killian, Josiah Stone's hard-ass heir apparent as ruler of the empire—and the face that flashed into a million women's minds in the greater Chicago area every night when they closed their eyes to sleep. The men's labels meant nothing. We'd throw open *their* closets of secrets too. Yank up their rugs until no dust ball or spider web was concealed anymore.

No doubt about it. We were in for a hell of a ride with these billionaire boys.

The baggage beast finally spewed my bright-orange suitcase. I tried to elbow my way in to grab it but missed. I swiftly caught Michael's eye above the crowd, gave him my best puppy-dog look, and pointed at my bag. With a charming wink and a gleaming smile, he grabbed it off the belt.

"Handsome, tall, *and* strong?" I joked as he set the bag in front of me. "I don't know how you haven't been snatched up, my friend."

Surprisingly, his grin fell. A strange darkness entered his eyes. "Yeah. That's me. Oh-so-snatchable."

I wanted to press him on the moment of melancholy, but he reverted to smartass mode, bumping my shoulder. Bags in tow, we headed outside, starting anew with the debate about who would win this round of our friendly competition.

Michael threw a smirk at Chad and me. "You know I have you both beat, right?"

"*Pffft.*" Chad shook his head. "Back of the plane doesn't mean squat. You *do* remember the time I sat last row but collected two phone numbers by the end of the flight?"

I nodded. "Instant disqualification if digits are exchanged. You know the drill, Mikey."

As we stepped into a frigid Chicago morning, Michael patted his overcoat pockets. "Not a thing here except dried baby drool."

"Egghhh." Chad grimaced. "I'd say that takes the trophy."

"Not so fast, fancy pants," I broke in. "The woman next to me had three white rats in her purse." They stared at me like I was about to hit them with the punch line. "I'm not joking. Rats. Three. In her purse."

"*Flowers for Algernon*, anyone?" Michael smirked.

I tossed a mock scowl. "I can't believe it. A geekier comeback than Chad."

Chad swept a deep, chuckling bow. "I concede. You win this round, *mademoiselle*."

"Agreed," Michael added.

I curtsied in return.

We sobered upon seeing Andrea and Margaux waiting by the car, scowling at our antics. They were dressed in nearly identical St. John Knits ensembles, tapping their Louboutins in tandem. I did my best to ignore whatever Chad mumbled under his breath about the ice queen and her minion, following Michael out to the stretch town car.

We had about thirty minutes to travel from O'Hare to the Stone Global building in downtown Chicago. Andrea used the time to update us on information that had been leaked to the press since we'd left San Diego that morning and how the facts affected our handling of what many outlets had already labeled *Treygate*.

Michael was the first to speak up. "Maybe we need to get him out of the country."

"No. Running and hiding makes him look guilty. I say we face it head on." Andrea always favored a fortress approach and had the battering-ram personality to prove it. In this case, I admitted to walking the fence about agreeing to the tactic, though I wasn't sure Michael's approach would work either. There was so much we didn't know about the machinations of the Stone empire. Something told me we wouldn't be able to repair anything until we knew everything.

"He needs an image cleanser. Can we get a diversion in there?"

I nodded approval to Chad's suggestion prior to my own response. "We find a squeaky-clean girl for him to be seen with a few times a week, release a few statements that she's good for him, and in a month or so, he's a changed man. Slow and steady, controlling the narrative by making them stick with nice, boring activities." It wasn't innovative, but sometimes the wheel didn't need to be reinvented.

Margaux clucked her tongue. "The press will see right through it. This is big-time news, Claire, not local gossip-rag stuff. We need to take every piece seriously."

She punctuated by grimacing like she just ate something sour. I played neutral with my outward response but formed an inward retort. I *was* taking it seriously. "Boring news day" was an approach we used all the time, and it usually worked. The press, more fickle than thirteen-year-olds, would move on if Trey Stone didn't give them any more newsworthy behavior. *Voilà*. Mission accomplished.

"Excellent point." I managed a diplomatic tone for my reply, a feat made easier by the promise of inserting a zinger at the end. "Maybe you have a strategy of your own to share, Margaux? We'd love to hear about it."

I relished the squirm that would cause, if only for a few seconds. It never happened. Instead, Margaux gazed out of the window with a slow smile. "I only have one declaration to make right now. First—and only—dibs on Killian Stone. That man is fine and all mine."

"Dibs?" Andrea issued the reproach. "Darling, grown women don't call *dibs* on men like Killian Stone."

She rolled her eyes. "God wept in his wine, Mother. You know what I mean." One of her gel-coated, French-manicured fingers circled at the rest of us. "And the rest of you do, as well. I have blackmail-worthy secrets on all of you."

Michael and Chad sent soft chortles at the wink she added to soften the message. I didn't join them. My secrets, while never my choice, would also send me to jail for a long time. Margaux's extra glance my way served as confirmation that she hadn't forgotten either. In exchange, I simply had to declare my libido a no-fly zone for Killian Stone. Done and confirmed.

The limo lurched to a stop in front of a huge skyscraper. The Stone Global building was one of the hugest monoliths of the Chicago skyline. At first approach, the place seemed like a hundred other corporate buildings in the country, but as we neared, the tight security detail was obvious. I wasn't sure if the Fort Knox mentality was due to the current scandal or if they typically ran such a tight ship.

After being processed through the metal detectors at the front door, we were directed straight to an elevator and then whisked sixty-seven floors up. The ride took less than a minute, but we rode in silence to our destination. A woman with Grace Kelly refinement waited when we stepped off and guided us to the conference room at an efficient pace.

Killian and Trey Stone were already waiting there for us.

Though they were both about the same height, one of them had stiffer posture and a more precise cut to his thick, near-black hair. And a *much* better-fitting suit. It was he who turned the moment our escort walked into the room.

"Mr. Stone, Andrea Asher and her team have arrived." After finishing the announcement with a serene nod, our escort left the conference room.

He turned toward us.

I froze in place as the tower of my self-control toppled over—and burned to ashes.

Talk about presence. The man was stunning and glorious, forbidding and beautiful, intoxicating and commanding—and dear God, scary as hell—in the most sexy, toe-curling ways I'd ever experienced. My body throbbed in places it hadn't in a very, *very* long while.

Shit. Shit. *Shit.*

This wasn't good. At all. Margaux had already all but jammed her homing beacon into the man. The more important factor—I was here to work for him. To *work*, period. To dig him out of a public-relations nightmare, *not* to plunge my hands into his pants. Or run them all over his gladiator-sized shoulders. Or lose them in his black satin hair...

Get your head back in the game, Claire. Now.

Andrea stepped forward, perfectly manicured hand outstretched, to introduce herself. The rest of us fell in behind her—except for Margaux. She strode up next to her mother, turning on the charm in ways I hadn't seen from her since the last project we'd tackled with one of Hollywood's favorite bad-boy hunks. I couldn't decide whether her girl-balls irritated or impressed me. I supposed it didn't matter, since her maneuvers yielded the same results here as they did in Hollywood. Stone hardly glanced at her after his perfunctory courtesies.

A small army of his colleagues filed into the room in our wake, and he introduced Andrea to all of them. His voice was velvet on the air, as if he hosted a wine tasting instead of a PR crisis summit. The innate strength of the sound made me stroke my forearm, thinking I should have worn a sweater instead of a short-sleeved shift. The dress had seemed practical at the time, but suddenly I had goosebumps. Lots of them.

Finally, Killian pivoted to the man of the hour. The action required him to face us again, making the hair on my arms dance. Rubbing them didn't help this time either.

"And this is my oldest brother, Trey."

"It's a pleasure to meet you," I murmured when Trey came to me at the end of the receiving line. We clasped hands, but then he wouldn't release me. His persistent hold made the creeps set in. I tugged away as he sneaked in a little wink.

"Enough."

One word. Steady, hard...and thoroughly arousing. For a moment, I had trouble believing the order had actually come from Killian. Then the man himself stepped up. "My apologies. He's out of control, and this is exactly why we need you all here."

"It's— Ummm—" Heat rushed my face. Mortification clutched my chest. "It's— It's all right. It's been a rough day for everyone, Mr.—errr—"

"Stone." Andrea practically hissed it.

The man quelled her with a glance. "As stated, Ms. Asher, it's been a rough day for everyone."

He slid his hand against mine. His skin appeared lightly suntanned. His grip was equally warm. Unlike his brother's clammy shell of a clench, I wished *his* hold would never end.

"Let's try this again. Killian Stone. And you are?"

"My name..." *What's my name again?* "C-Claire. Claire Montgomery." Next to him, I felt small, fragile, and breathless. To my horror, it was wonderful.

His thick fingers wrapped around mine, seeming to swallow my skin with his. "It's a pleasure to meet you, Miss Montgomery." His slight emphasis on the *pleasure* had to be my sleep deprivation at work, though there was no mistaking how his dark, *dark* stare delved into me. He kept searching my face, although for what, I wasn't sure. Or perhaps I didn't care. This man likely got anything he wanted from any woman he chose—and could give her anything in return.

Right. And toads could be kissed into princes. And pumpkins became carriages. And insecure princesses never held on to disastrous secrets as relationship collateral.

I'd given up on fairy tales a long time ago and never once regretted the choice. Now certainly wasn't the time for change.

"It is *Miss* Montgomery, isn't it?"

"Please, no. I mean yes. It *is* Miss, but Claire is fine. J-Just Claire."

Andrea stepped forward. "Claire's one of the junior members of our team, Mr. Stone. She's a whiz with reports and analysis."

It was Andrea's version of dictating this would be the first and last time I spoke directly to the man. Could I blame her? I kept stammering like an idiot. I needed to pull myself together. I never acted this way around clients, whether they were Adonis brought to life or not. The job was our primary objective, not eye-fucking the man who had his hand on the checkbook. And wondering what his hands would feel like in other places on my body...

"Mr. Stone, I'm Chad Lerner. I'll be handling the social-media portion of the campaign." Chad gave Killian a solid handshake, not a bit intimidated by the man who stood almost a foot taller than his five-foot-five. For some men, size really didn't matter. Chad was a social-media guru whose reputation preceded him, proved by Stone's respectful nod.

While Chad turned and spoke quietly with a few of our new contemporaries, I booted up my laptop and readied the presentation he'd scrambled together in the limo, based on our strategic conversation at the time. Since bandaging Trey Stone's reputation was directly linked to confidence in Stone Global Corporation as a whole, we'd have to use a multi-pronged approach that was likely to change by the second, though these notes gave us a decent place to start.

"Miss Montgomery, will you be taking part in the

presentation? I'm looking forward to hearing your ideas."

That voice again. His nearness again. The most excruciating example of *heaven and hell* life had ever thrown at me.

I carefully swiveled from my spot at the projector to make sure my ears weren't playing tricks on me. At first I thought he must've been joking—cruelly so—but Killian Stone had his midnight stare pinned directly onto me, as though he actually expected my answer to be yes.

No. Don't look forward to hearing my ideas. Don't look forward to anything from me. Please!

Right on time, Margaux barked out a laugh. The sound could've been charming, if someone enjoyed listening to injured seals. "Oh, Killian, you are such a funny one. Our Claire is sweet but inexperienced as of yet. She's great at crunching all the numbers and data, though."

"Mr. Stone will be fine, thank you. And I happen to like numbers and data." He maintained the pose like a wildcat in waiting, a clear dare for Margaux to refute him.

She didn't. Instead, she swallowed hard and shrank back. Though a few snickers peppered the air, I firmly decided to stay out of the fray. Preferably, out of Margaux's blast zone altogether. I lowered my head and busied myself with the menu screen on the computer, congratulating myself for the move when Andrea came to salvage her daughter's dignity.

"In the interest of time, I'll present our preliminary plan solo, Mr. Stone. I hope that will be acceptable?" She beamed her megawatt smile, the one matching the engagement ring my father had slipped onto her finger three months ago, with an extra glint in her light-green eyes. Her expression communicated *You're my number-one priority* and *Don't fuck with me* in five convenient seconds.

Stone returned the stare as if she'd tried to crack a joke that wasn't funny.

"Great," he declared. "Let's get started, then. I have other things to attend to before calling it a day."

The air in the room shifted as everyone complied with the request that really wasn't a request. Chairs squeaked and papers rustled as everyone took their seats. I clutched opposing elbows again, like the speechless idiot I'd become.

Clearly, this man did everything his way—the way he expected everyone else to do them too. It was a simple fact in his world. Disputing the point was useless, just as was denying I didn't instantly add it to my list of arousal factors about him. When I mixed in his physical pull, shifting from a carnal pulse to a breath-stealing force when he came nearer than fifteen feet, I came to a pair of harsh conclusions.

Resisting the urge to idolize him was going to be agonizing. But indulging it would be worse.

Time for a *fast* lesson in separating reality from fantasy.

The lights dimmed. I took the seat at the front end of the oval conference table, nearest the equipment in case technical problems arose during Andrea's presentation. The show wouldn't last long, considering we'd received the call from SGC's team less than eighteen hours ago.

My heart stuttered when Killian dropped into the seat beside me. *Fabulous.* Just when I'd reclaimed a scrap of concentration, along with the hope Margaux didn't have enough inspiration to order up a voodoo doll named Claire.

Sure enough, I looked up to confront Margaux's glare, practically forging daggers for me across the table. Damn it. She and I would need to talk, and soon. I'd done nothing to attract Killian Stone's weird attention laser beam.

Except enjoy it, girlfriend. A lot.

That didn't mean I was going to do anything about it.

Yes, he was breathtaking. His tall, proud physique looked hard enough to bounce coins off. He wore a suit better than any Versace model. His thick, shiny hair made my fingers twitch, wondering if it was soft as satin, rough as plywood, or both. I was certain he did bed head even better, especially with a jaw of stubble to go with it. So beautiful. So alluring. So commanding.

So off-limits.

The die had been cast years ago, during one semester that changed everything. Margaux and I were both seniors, and she'd gotten pissed off enough at Andrea to move out of their La Jolla palace and slum it in an off-campus house I shared with three girlfriends. Since she had a sex tape to extort my roomie Bonnie with and was willing to share her high-end hair products, we all agreed to tolerate her for a few months.

That was when things had gotten tough for Nick, the man—the *boy*—to whom I was all but engaged. So desperate to pay his pre-med tuition, Nick was ready to sell his body on the street until learning that selling prescription drugs would turn him a better profit. I'd listened, beyond in love, as he gave grand speeches about how the medications should be available to everyone anyway and the corrupt pharmaceutical companies were holding the patients hostage with huge bribes to the government. It was a crime, how some students had to carry horrific credit loads to succeed in their majors and couldn't survive the stress without some artificial help. It wasn't like the dispensaries at the rehab facilities where he worked would miss the pills, either. Like the infatuated idiot I was, Nick became my Lancelot, Saint George, and Robin Hood in one. He was a savior, not a criminal—a knight, not a drug dealer. Like the noble Maid Marian I refashioned myself into, I'd let him store his stash in my room. And like the shrewdest Sheriff John on the planet, Margaux had gathered plenty of photos, videos, and assorted paperwork to prove it.

Inevitably, the police unearthed Nick's scheme. But when they came and raided the house, Margaux pulled a shocker by covering completely for us. Nick repaid the favor to Margaux on a convenient installment plan, faithfully rendered on the first of every month. He repaid the favor to me by getting my best friend pregnant six months later. I was also stuck with the cleaning bill for the comforter he'd been screwing Darcie on, plus Margaux's oh-so-intact evidence against us both, backed up to the Cloud in all its well-inside-the-statute glory.

As a graduation-day present, Margaux had assured me that the evidence would never leave the darkness of her computer files. Continuing my pinhead streak, I'd believed her. I'd even felt safe enough to accept the position offered by her mother a year later.

But as I said...I'm a pinhead.

The situation wasn't worth dwelling on, even now. Forward, not backward. Plenty of hard work lay ahead as therapy *and* redemption, reminding me of all the perfect reasons why my personal life would always take a back seat to career. Some people simply weren't meant for happiness in love, and the Montgomerys were such a clan. I should have learned that from the loneliness I saw for so many years in Dad's eyes, but I didn't. I went ahead and jumped into the relationship fire as well. Gave my heart fully to a man. Nick had returned it burned to a crisp.

It wouldn't be happening again.

Happily Ever After was a phrase for little girls and movie stars. Grown women concentrated on their careers, maintained their dignity, and *never* let anyone inside their heart's walls. Peace and safety on the inside, pain and weakness on the outside. *Keep the line moving, folks. Nothing to see here.*

I blinked in horror when the lights flipped on. Andrea was done with her report, and I hadn't heard a word of it.

As the projector and screen retracted into the ceiling, Andrea folded her hands with the serenity of a nun and gazed to the man at my right. "As you can surmise, we all have a lot of hard work ahead of us, but I'm confident we can repair the damage." She turned her regard to Trey, sharpening it to an ice pick. "The key at this point, Mr. Stone, is to help us stop the bleeding. That means no more stabs of the indiscretion blade. I trust we're on the same page?"

Trey barely lifted his eyes from his phone. "Take it easy, blondie. Little bro with the big mouth has already taken care of the lecture duties." He snorted at Killian, who lifted his fingers to the bridge of his nose.

Chad straightened his glasses and glowered at Trey. "Mr. Stone, the mandate includes complete restraint from texting, Tweeting, posting, and pinning. And for God's sake, *no* sharing photos or videos with *anyone*. Think you can handle that for a week or so?"

Killian's fingers slid from his nose to his chin. Even that part of his face was carved and perfect. "Should he just shut down the accounts?"

"No," Chad replied. "That instantly implies guilt. Just don't respond to any of it." He stood, put both hands on the table, and pressed on the gleaming surface. "Including right now."

"Back off, Poindexter. Last time I looked, I wasn't in jail."

Without a word, Killian stood. With three brisk steps, he made it to the space behind Trey's chair. Inside of one swift yank, he snatched the device up and Frisbee'ed it across the table to Chad. Trey lunged for the intercept, but Chad bested him on reflexes. He pocketed the phone, grinning from ear to ear.

"Problem solved," Killian growled.

"Says the tightest sphincter on the globe," Trey snarled.

Chad twisted his lips to stifle a chortle. I could tell he enjoyed the way Killian got things done. I couldn't help a fast smile myself, feeling like my best friend approved of my latest crush. The moment also verified I was officially losing it. High school and I had parted ways a long time ago. I'd been without a new crush for nearly as long.

Killian straightened as if Trey hadn't spoken at all, immediately looking to Andrea again. "You'll use this room as your command center for however long you need it. My office is down the hall. I want to be regularly apprised of progress."

"Of course." Andrea dipped her head in a gesture of submission, something I'd never believe if my own eyes hadn't witnessed it. "Though our retainer is for six months, I suspect things will go faster than that, if Wooten backs off his vendetta—and when we're done with him, he *will* back off. Currently, we estimate two to three weeks for this news cycle to pass, a few more for revitalizing the family name, and four more for final cleanup. If we're lucky, some pop star or activist will pull a larger stunt, making the world forget the name Trey Stone. This means Trey Stone himself has to keep his clothes on and stay antics-free." Andrea bore a hole in the back of

Trey's head like a parent with an errant toddler. "Is the point clear, Mr. Stone?"

"Yes, Mother." He had the nerve to chuckle when he said it. No one at the table joined him.

Killian leaned down again, bracing a strong arm on each side of his brother's chair. "I suggest you start taking this very seriously, brother. If SGC's stock continues to slide because of your stupidity, you'll have enough party money for a blow-up pool in the backyard and some week-old cocktail weenies. Ms. Asher and her team aren't fucking around. Neither am I."

Trey's reaction was a strange mix of stunning and weird. He lifted his head, a smirk still on his face, though the discomfort vanished from his lips. In its place was a menacing confidence that actually scared me for a moment. He met Killian's stare directly before issuing three quiet words. "Back off, *Killy*."

The silence between the two of them was thicker than incense in a church.

"My goodness, where has the time gone?" Andrea turned on her charm a little strong, but nobody seemed to mind. "Tick-tock, everyone. Wooten's press conference is going live in fifteen minutes, so take your comfort breaks and grab your popcorn for the spectacle."

With eager swiftness, everyone shuffled into action.

Senator Wooten's briefing went live at the stroke of six, ensuring plenty of sound bites for news outlets across the nation before network shows took over. Between the reporter's salacious witch-hunt questions and Wooten's blustery protective papa act, everyone had a bounty of material to pick and choose from.

By the time we'd collated and cataloged the comments, the

clock inched past eight thirty. Margaux and Andrea departed for the hotel first. Michael and Chad hung back to wait for me, but I wanted to look over a few of the emails that had come through while we were giving the presentation, especially the missive from Talia. She'd hit some snags on her own project, a movie star who'd gotten turned on to voodoo during a filming in New Orleans, and since the star was headlining the studio's summer tentpole film, half of Hollywood was in a tizzy.

I waved Chad and Michael off with a promise to turn off the lights and close up shop and then opened the first of Talia's emails for a session of laughter and tears combined. My poor friend had a mess on her hands. Things had seemed under control until today, when her movie star had sneaked out to perform a sacrificial ceremony in the bayou—naked. Grateful for the silence that had descended over the SGC offices, I composed a detailed email to her. The thoughts flowed. I often did my best brainstorming alone, likely a result of spending so much time in solitude as a child.

After sending off Talia's message, I scrolled through the rest of my inbox, pausing at one message in particular—then wincing. Dad. I loved him with all my heart but dreaded having to respond. I had to pick and choose every piece of communication with him. What *did* you say to your father when he was bowled over by the seminarcissistic ice queen who'd given you the biggest break of your career, especially after she'd fallen for him in return and was planning for their wedding in two months?

I pansied out and decided to compose the email from my hotel room. After a bath. And with a glass of wine nearby.

Once I'd shut down my laptop and stored my things, only my phone charger remained to be packed. Michael had plugged the line in for me when we arrived, commandeering one of the outlets in the middle of the conference table since the easy-access wall outlets were snatched up. I'd let him, as my power situation was dire by that point due to saving myself from playing nice with rat girl during the flight. The upside? I'd never been more on top of my *Plants vs. Zombies* skills and had learned a hard lesson about packing my e-reader in my checked bag.

As I'd dreaded, Michael's gallantry returned to bite me in the ass. This was a big-ass conference table. The outlet was farther than I could reach without crawling under the table and coming up from the center or climbing and pulling it out from the top. Okay, tugging on the line would give me the cord but only with the USB connector at the end. I needed the whole set.

"Seriously?" I added a growl simply because I could.

For the sake of my dignity and Andrea's reputation, I stomped over to the open doorway and peered down the deserted hallway. The building was still and quiet. The few SGC employees with offices on this floor were gone for the evening. The last person I'd actually seen was the janitor, over twenty minutes ago. His vacuum roared in the distance, around several corners.

I turned back, glaring at the behemoth piece of furniture occupying most of the room. I *really* needed that charger. I'd packed for this trip faster than a soldier on emergency deployment and had only had time to grab the one unit.

"Damn it."

I circled the table, thinking things would look less impossible from another angle.

"Really, Claire." I slammed my hands on my hips. "How

does this shit always happen to you? You're just lucky, hmmm?" With a huff, I continued, "No. This isn't only about luck. It's a curse. And now you're talking to yourself about it, which is even worse."

While proving the sanity fairies had really skipped off with my brain, I stood at the side of the table, my back to the door and skirt hiked over my knees. There was no way around it. *Up and over, Montgomery.*

After halfheartedly crossing myself, I climbed up on one of the chairs and started making my way across the table. Damn, this thing was slippery. What did they use for polish? Maybe the janitor could tell me. The shit yielded a really good shine.

I was up on all fours and feeling fourteen kinds of ridiculous. But I took it slow. I had no choice. Rushing might result in a position more humiliating than this.

A soft chuckle resonated in my head. I figured, like so many occasions, Mom was involved. She always found a way to look after me, especially at night. It made sense that the universe had turned her soul into a star.

"You enjoying this, Mom?" I muttered. "Because I'm sticking with my original allegation. This vertically challenged shit is a— *Damn!*" Saltier words came to mind, but I bit them back as my knee slipped. "See? I'm right. It's a curse. And I'll gloat if I want to. Yeah, yeah. Dad says it's unattractive, but he isn't here, is he?"

The last of it got muttered past my locked teeth due to securing the cord in them. Moving carefully, I started scooting back. God only knew what kind of trouble a full U-turn would've gotten me.

"I'm not sure where your father's logic lies. Everything

from this vantage point is very attractive, if you ask me."

Killian Stone's voice, lush and confident and unmistakable, filled the room.

I froze. Hands and knees planted. Charging cord between my teeth. Skirt hiked above my knees. Ass jutted toward the doorway now dominated by the presence, so powerful and palpable, that turned my limbs numb and my bloodstream into a superhighway of heat.

This cannot be happening.

I shook my head and smiled. Of course it was. This was the story of my life, especially on a day like today.

A huge hand came into view. Unmistakably his. The action was accompanied by the voice that left no room for argument.

"Need some help?"

Despite yanking the cord from my mouth, I gritted my reply. "I'm fine."

"Indeed you are. But there's nothing wrong with accepting assistance."

"I'm. Fine."

His terse growl told me there'd be only one victor here and the name on that medal wasn't *Claire*. I raised my hand and slid it against his, thinking if the earth ever had a desire to open up and swallow me whole, now would be a perfect time.

CHAPTER THREE

Killian

Damn.

The woman wasn't just gorgeous. She was nervous. As in *truly* nervous.

The revelation struck me the instant her fingers touched my palm, trembling and a little chilly. For a moment, I didn't know how to react, either.

When was the last time I'd really put a woman on edge?

Out of necessity, my life was lived behind giant doors, at the top of lock-key elevators. The females who made it past those barricades were sure as storm troopers in every step they'd taken to arrive. If they developed nerves it was an act, usually in thin disguise, to appeal to my protective masculine side. Within seconds, their thighs would be brushing my crotch, their fingers would be trailing my chest, and any shred of interest deflated from my cock. After that, beneath my own veneer of chivalry, I'd walk them back to the town car, the elevator, the stairs, the lobby, or any other alternative to permanently sideline their game. I didn't have the time or patience to learn playbooks by anyone's rules but mine, especially if pretense was involved. Life had already dealt me a shit ton of overtime where *that* offense was concerned.

As for the need left behind by those females? Those

physical drives were easily handled with one or two phone calls. A number of the city's most stunning bachelorettes, all requiring discretion for varying reasons, were only too happy to make the service entrance of their building, followed by their naked and willing bodies, available for my breach.

In the end, it worked out for the best. Being crowned the Enigma of the Magnificent Mile was, after all, an honor of sorts. I'd managed to make the title work for me on a number of levels.

But I didn't want to make it work right now. There was a heavy ache in my chest, easily recognized as a physical plea to let go, to bask in how I *did* feel...just once.

With a woman you just met, dumbass? A woman who looks at public reputation in numbers and statistics instead of your hard work and life?

She stood upright again—in a manner of speaking. The stability lasted for two seconds before she tottered again, frantically seizing me for purchase. "Whoa there, San Diego." I reached and braced both hands around her waist in an equal knee-jerk reaction—but as soon as I damned myself for it and tried to yank away, she squeezed back, spreading her slender fingers above my elbows.

"Oh." Her touch stretched across the bottoms of my biceps. "Oh, my."

There had to be a slick comeback to that *somewhere* in my head. I was a well-educated sonofabitch. Why was my mind suddenly a wasteland?

Christ. I was losing it. I'd just capped my mental pen after writing her off as an employee—a temporary one, at that—yet I never wanted her touch to end. Her fingers were long and tentative, with nails filed into graceful ovals and groomed in a striking shade of navy blue that had a hint of sparkle to it.

As soon as she noticed me gawking at her fingernails, she curled them under. Not that I complained. The little torque she gave my shirt with the move was insanely arousing. My mind instantly filled with a fantasy in which I guided her fingers forward and commanded her to remove the shirt. I wondered what those little nails would feel like against my bare chest, scraping my nipples, following the trail of hair down the middle of my torso...

"I—errr—managed a dash to the salon on the way to the airport," she explained. "I can't do the French manicure thing but figured Andrea wouldn't fault me for matching my shade with the SGC logo. I'll change it if you insist."

"I insist that you don't. I'm impressed by your originality."

Not smooth.

Her fingernails? Seriously?

I should have just told her something nice about the stilts. Admiring a woman's shoes, if done right, was a more subtle way of commenting on how gorgeous her legs were. And fuck, Claire Montgomery had beautiful legs.

She reacted with a subtle blush and a tiny, captivating tilt of her lips. I was stupidly enraptured by the expression. While her combination of shy and saucy caught my dick's attention once more, my body wasn't done responding there. The weight on my chest suddenly lifted. My gut performed a back spring that I hadn't experienced since high school.

Christ.

I should've been scared. I needed to wish she'd do something to give up her jig, to show me her sham and let me return to my own, feigning the courtier, keeping everything distant, respectful, and safe. But God help me, I didn't want to be respectful right now. I wanted to flatten her on this conference table, spread her wide, and keep her that way until her thighs gripped my head, her sex trembled under my mouth, and her screams filled the air.

"Oh, yeah. That's me. The original one."

Her mumble pulled my attention back to her face. More specifically, the grimace putting creases into it. She—or someone—had assigned meaning to the words that added disturbed depths to her eyes. I scowled. Those shadows weren't acceptable. They didn't belong in the beauty of her features. Frankly, they pissed me off.

But her gaze still amazed me. Aside from the matchless color of her irises, like honey crossed with amber, she retained the same soft curiosity that had arrested me during this afternoon's meeting. Even now, despite distress, she maintained the open wonder that had driven me to shun the CEO's chair in order to sit next to her during Andrea's presentation. Those eyes made me think time had reverted instead of advanced, and soon I'd be simply a snail-wrangling boy in the garden once more, in those days before life took such a complicated swerve.

I wasn't indulging artlessness. Given what she did for a living, the woman wasn't an innocent. But for some reason, the garbage of PR didn't appear to stick to her. To get damn poetic about it, she seemed to float above it.

She fascinated the hell out of me.

I had to learn more about her.

That wasn't a crime, was it?

And learning more about her didn't mean she had to learn more about me. For at least the next couple of months, I was technically her boss.

"Well, they say originality is the purest form of sincerity." I attempted to tack on a charming smile. But real charm was definitely harder than the faked shit. Hell of a time for life to inflict *that* lesson.

"They say that, huh? They who?"

I shrugged. Christ. *Me*, shrugging like I had no more clues about life than Trey. "The 'theys' who matter."

"Aren't you a they who matters?"

That was my cue to strut like a rooster who'd fucked half the hens. Instead, discomfited spiders swarmed my chest. *Hell.* I wanted to just tell her the truth. What would it feel like to do that? To expose myself to just one person on this earth besides Trey and Lance, who didn't count because my secret was hidden in the same closet of disgrace as theirs?

No. Not now. Not ever.

"Mattering is all in the way you look at things, Miss Montgomery."

There was her cute lip-tilting thing again. She went for the other side of her mouth this time. "And how do *you* look at things, Mr. Stone?"

"I'm sure you know most of the answer to that already."

"Oh?"

"A search history on your laptop will return my name in a hundred ways, won't it?"

"We both know the Internet reveals only the tips of the icebergs." She took a deep breath, as if debating whether to let her next words have life. "And I have a feeling your iceberg is really fascinating."

Before I could stop myself, I grinned. Yes, she'd just compared me to an iceberg. She'd also called me fascinating and been genuinely apprehensive about the flirt. The comprehension shot adrenaline through me, along with a rush of attraction best crammed down and fast forgotten. Fuck. Masochism was *not* my thing.

"All right, tell me this." I deliberately squared my shoulders, a tactic I usually saved for meetings when I needed to appear taller than my six-foot-three. "If you were after the next inch of my iceberg, where would you look?"

My intention? To throw her off guard again. I never anticipated my plan ricocheting on me, that *she'd* topple *my* focus with her own determined stance, both hands on her hips. The pose was a perfect showcase for her high, taut breasts and the supple curves leading to those incredible legs...the imagination of what their juncture looked like, tasted like...

I clenched back a groan. Masochism was worse the second time around.

"The next inch, huh?" she returned. As if I needed *that* phraseology at the moment. "Hmm. From what I know of you right now...probably your office."

I arched both eyebrows. "The personality through osmosis approach?"

"More like simply taking a tour of someone's home. And since I already know you're here more than anyplace else..."

I chuckled. "Guilty as charged."

She returned a strange little frown to that, stepping back with a fresh flush. "Or maybe I'd better pack up and call it a night."

A strange surge of panic pounded me. Reacting at once, I grabbed her hand. "Without your full dose of osmosis from the inner sanctum?"

Hell. From masochist to idiot in less than a minute. While there was nothing to hide behind the doors to my CEO suite—

my secrets were buried in much better places—I simply had a firm rule about mixing business with pleasure. Taking Claire Montgomery's hand was a blur of those lines, a gray scale I pushed wider by the minute and seriously needed to correct.

What the fuck was she doing to me? Why did she tempt me to break so many rules? Good rules. Guidelines that existed for damn important reasons, like keystones in the archway of SGC's success. *She* was the one thinking straight around here, and what did I do to reward her?

Drag her farther down the hall to my office, of course.

But maybe a visit to the hub of Stone Global was the perfect solution for my ass-fool wanderlust. And to satisfy *her* curiosity, as well—so it would stop taunting me from her mesmerizing gold eyes.

"You prepared for the resplendence, San Diego?"

"As I'll ever be, Chicago."

She wasn't going to let me catch a break. The sarcastic slide to her words begged for a response—something like whirling on her, pinning her to the wall, and stripping the tone from her mouth with my tongue.

Gray scale. Corrected. Now.

I stopped at my door. The patter of her heels halted in a hurry, becoming another erotic taunt as I remembered what those shoes did for her legs.

"After you." I swept an arm out, palm up, while opening the door. She clattered by me with an inquisitive smile—

That dropped into a gape.

"Okay, wow."

I'd certainly gotten that reaction before. But none disappointed me as much. Her blurred lines had no doubt begun a refocus. From this point on, she'd see me through the filter of the technical wonderland office, the sparkling cityscape view, and the desk, once Dad's, that rivaled Odin's throne. I would be all these things to her, never again a simple guy to trade snarky lines with or to feel up through my shirt just because she liked my muscles.

Back to nothing but the tip of the iceberg.

"I hope that's a good wow and not a bad wow." I knew the answer already but threw it out as a comfortable conversation filler.

"A good one." She bypassed the wall full of video monitors, as well as the kitchenette and designer meeting table, in favor of the pictures mounted on the opposite wall. One photo in particular drew her in. "Is this you and Tippi Hedren?"

I walked over, letting her see my surprise at the observation. There were a number of photos on the wall, including a shot with the president himself, but she'd zeroed in on this one. "That was a special night for me," I admitted.

"No shit." The sarcasm was gone. In its place was genuine awe.

"You're a Hitchcock fan?"

"No." She blushed again. "Animal geek. My dad had a thing for the weird cable channels, like Discovery and National Geographic. Watching the specials with him..." A wistful expression took over her face. "Well, those are good memories. He indulged my fascination for everything adventurous, especially the wildcats. Lions, tigers, panthers...such beautiful creatures. What Hedren's done at her Shambala Reserve is so amazing."

I indulged a shit-eating smirk. "That picture was taken at Shambala."

"Son of a bitch!" She slammed my shoulder with a slap

before, regrettably, her reserve clicked in again. "Sorry. God, I just beat on the client."

A little furrow marred her brow. Once again, I fought a bizarre impulse to yank her close and kiss it away. This tiny woman, full of such huge life, pushed at every damn boundary I possessed—leaving me helpless for definable action on the matter. I should've been seething at the recognition. Instead, I went for mindless humor. "It didn't hurt. I promise."

"I don't imagine it did. You have—"

"I have what?"

The crimson flags in her cheeks widened. "Really great muscles."

Heat filled my own neck. And other places too. It felt fucking wonderful. How long had it been since a woman's *words* made me hard? Like the answer mattered. I thanked myself for dragging my ass out of bed to practice with the water polo team this morning despite the mess going down with Trey—but royally cursed myself for being so stressed about the crisis that I skipped the extra ten minutes to jack off in my private shower at the gym. "I'm willing to keep things a secret if you are."

She gave me an adorable sigh of relief. "Thank you."

"But my silence comes at a price."

"A price?"

I grabbed her hand. To my pleasure, extending deeper than it probably should, she issued no protest as I walked her across the office and into the anteroom. I'd added the space as a concession to Britta, who'd threatened to quit if she came to work and found me asleep at my desk one more time. It housed another kitchenette, a sofa that could convert into a bed, and full bathroom facilities. It also contained the sole cabinet in my suite that was always locked, especially when Trey was around.

Once I'd taken the key from its hiding place, I moved to an ottoman next to the sofa. One well-placed twist into a hidden lock, and the ottoman's lid swiveled back to reveal six bottles of wine inside. Each vintage was housed in its own temperature-controlled tube. Claire's little gasp of surprise provided another moment to feel like the goddamn king of the world.

"*This* is my price?" She chuckled a little. I echoed the sound.

"Do you enjoy wine?"

"I thought this was about *your* iceberg, Chicago."

"Humor me. I'll even let you pick the poison. Red or white?"

She let the giggle become a full laugh. The sound of it was close to music in its own right, and I reveled in listening to it. In the feeling of knowing I'd inspired it. *Damn.* After everything that had happened today, I should've had the disposition of a rabid grizzly, ready to eat small children and anything else that crossed my path. Instead, I popped the cork on the Barolo she'd picked and strutted my way toward the kitchenette for a couple of glasses. Yes. *Strutted.*

I poured a little of the wine into a glass and handed it to her for the first taste. She swished and tasted the liquid like an expert. I arched my eyebrows, almost teasing her with my approval.

"Okay, I've done this before," she admitted. "My dad's in landscape design. In Temecula."

"Ahhh. The Southern California version of Napa Valley."

"Points for the geographical trivia, Mr. Stone."

"Points for the polished sip and swish, Miss Montgomery."

She settled her glass on the counter with an expression I couldn't decipher. Shyness? Sadness? Another attack of discomfort? "It's really all I should have." Rubbing her forearm nervously, she stepped back. "I'm sorry. I know you just opened the bottle. It's very good—*and* expensive—"

"Which I don't give a shit about."

My glibness didn't ease her tension. "For all intents and purposes, you're now my boss."

"Who wants to buy a drink for his team after a hard day's work." I sneaked in a smirk while filling her glass all the way. "Can we help it if you're the sole definition of 'the team' right now?"

She laughed before taking a shy sip. "Rah rah."

"Their loss." I poured my own glass. "Everyone left before the fun began."

"And here I was, thinking that was Wooten's press conference."

A cloud skidded over my disposition. Wooten's three-ring circus of a press conference hit my memory with all its ugly force. "Hypocritical bastard," I snarled. "He's got Trey's balls in one hand, and with the other, he's likely groping some intern's ass."

"We can only hope." Humor crept back into her tone. "More than one intern would be even better. Preferably one of each gender."

I gave her a reaction I hadn't indulged in for a very long time.

I laughed.

Fully. Openly. Daring to enjoy the freedom of it, if only for a second. A risky move? Probably. But she was taking just as large a leap. Something told me Andrea Asher wasn't one for the minions enjoying themselves during an assignment, no matter how firmly the client insisted on it. I should be respecting that boundary too—but fuck, it felt nice to be laughing in the face of this shit day, my gaze filled with the warm beauty of this woman, my mind cleansed by her easy companionship. Selfishly, I insisted on hoarding her a little while longer.

Grabbing the bottle and my glass, I made my way out of the kitchen. "Come," I charged. "Bring your drink but leave the Wooten hashtags back there."

She turned but didn't follow me. After a moment of my questioning stare, she issued one word, purposely drawing it out. "Please?"

I cocked my head, confused. What the hell was she begging me for?

That was before I raised my scrutiny to her face. There was no sign of supplication on her features. The woman, from the top of her copper waves to her stilt-clad toes, wasn't pleading me for a damn thing. She was issuing a decree. If we were counting this as off-the-clock time, I should behave a little better than a gutter-raised thug in a well-cut suit. And goddamnit, she was right.

After setting my glass and the Barolo down on the coffee table, I returned to her with deliberate steps. In a smooth sweep, I pulled her hand into mine. Her fingers still shook a little. The quivers worsened when she lifted her head and our gazes locked. The result on my own system, the heady power of knowing I affected her as she did me, was a more potent buzz than the wine could ever impart.

"Miss Montgomery," I murmured, "will you *please* honor

me by sitting for a while—and discussing anything in the world besides Gerard Wooten?"

She surprised me with a giggle while letting me lower her to the couch. "All right, then. Name your non-Wooten subject."

Easy answer. "You."

She dropped the humor. Took a tentative sip of her wine. "Mmmm...no. I'm not that interesting."

A thousand rebuttals pelted my mind. Her face alone, with those surreal amber eyes, that naughty pixie nose, and those beguiling coral lips, was enough to keep me fascinated for hours. Focusing on the base of her throat did no good either. It only made me think about what her skin tasted like there. Would she be sweet as honey or tangy as lemon? Would she sigh in response, dig her hands into my hair, lean back so I could suck more of her?

She'd slap you and knee you in the balls, you dumb fuck.

The words were truth. Claire Montgomery, while equally stirred by the physical attraction between us, had clear boundaries for those feelings, proved by all her adorable and awkward efforts to scramble out of my path this afternoon. Hell, the woman had radiated so much tension when I'd sat next to her during the presentation I wouldn't have been shocked if she'd glowed when the lights went down. She clearly took great pride in being a member of Asher's team, so letting my lips wander in her direction would be like asking her to cuckold the company. I had no right to proselytize on the subject, either. I was the guy who commissioned artwork for my office instead of my home.

"You had that answer good and ready, didn't you?" I finally asked. "You have a lot of practice at it?"

She took another sip of the wine. It was damn good stuff,

a fact I was grateful for as she sneaked her tongue over her lips to catch every drop. "What? You hoping the Barolo's loosened me up more?"

"Has it?"

She sighed. "I'm an open book, Mr. Stone. My life consists of work and my dad. And maybe a few favorite pairs of shoes."

She lifted one of her legs and grinned at the navy platform pump at the end of it. All I saw was a high-fashion death trap for her, but her smile was worth swallowing my opinion. My fortitude doubled in light of the question I wanted to ask next. I waited for her to take another sip before taking the risk.

"I haven't heard you mention your mother."

She let her leg descend—along with her grin. "She's gone."

"I'm sorry."

"Don't be." Her voice deepened to a rasp. "Long time ago. I was six. Brain aneurysm. It was sudden, and she didn't suffer."

"Shit." My guttural reaction was the real deal. "That's still rough." I meant every syllable of that, as well. "Did your dad remarry?"

Her lips lifted again, but the expression seemed forced. "No. He hasn't even dated until the last year and a half."

"So he has somebody now."

"Yes. I guess you could say that."

"All right." I drew it out with a little humor. "I could say that...how?"

Tension claimed more of her posture. Her eyebrows drew together. "What the hell? It's not like I'm sharing state secrets." She could've convinced me otherwise with the next sip she took, belonging more in the gulp category. "In a couple of months, Andrea Asher will be my new stepmother."

"Damn."

"Nothing like a little weirdness to go along with the fourteen-hour work days, right?"

"It's quite a twist."

"Sorry for the bombshell. Pretend I didn't tell you, okay?"

A strange anxiety overcame her face. I bore my gaze into her, yearning for my reassurance to seep through. "The Enigma of the Magnificent Mile, remember? Poker face is an art form when I want it to be."

"Thanks." Though she didn't lose the tension, it took on sardonic edges.

"So how did it happen?"

"Fast," she supplied. "Dad came to pick me up for lunch one day, and by the next week, he was redesigning Andrea's new backyard. Two months after that, they sprang the news on me."

"Goal-driven man."

"Yep." She popped the final *p* with more of her impish sarcasm.

"Unless he knocked her up?" I ventured.

"Oh, God!" She grimaced. "You didn't just go there."

"Guess I did. But now I observe where *your* intensity comes from."

"Yes, you do." She pulled in a long breath. "His family, including my grandfather *and* grandmother, were caught in the paramilitary shit storm in Ireland during the eighties, so he took advantage of a cousin's sponsorship to escape and come here. He worked his ass off from the second he arrived. After a few years, he was able to start a small business of his own. He specialized in creating new gardens for people that were stunning but tolerant of our dry conditions in Southern California."

I smirked. "Unique choice for a guy from Ireland."

"Right?" A mix of humor and pride shone in her eyes. "But my dad's one of the best at drought-resistant beauty. Before long, a lot of celebrities started using him. The *au pair* for one of those stars was my mom. They met one day, declared their love two weeks later, and were married three months after that." She glanced back up and shrugged. "Crazy, huh?"

I shook my head and risked brushing my knuckles on the edge of her shoulder. "It sounds kind of...nice."

I could've sworn she trembled, though she covered for it with a delicate snort. "You going sentimental on me, Chicago?"

I let the jibe pass in favor of risking my touch at the outer curve of her shoulder. "Bet they didn't wait long to work on creating you."

"They waited three years," she insisted. "They wanted to get established, hopefully buy a home. They were finally able to, though it wasn't much, just a bedroom, a den, and a kitchen on the rough side of town, in an LA suburb." She smiled around the rim of her glass as she sipped more. I was tempted to join her, but watching her lips play over that lucky stemware had me forgetting to do anything except stare at her. Study her. Be more deeply enraptured by her. "Those were some of the best days of my life," she said wistfully.

"You were very young," I argued gently.

"Agreed. But to this day, I can remember those summer days on our tiny front lawn, running through the sprinklers with a homemade ice pop in my hand as Mom looked on. She always had a sketch pad around and enjoyed helping Dad with conceptual drawing of the gardens he was designing." Another soft laugh spilled from her. "She would always add a little image of me in the pictures too. She told me I was Dad's 'wee garden good luck fairy,' and sometimes she wouldn't tell me where she'd drawn me in. It became a grand game for me to peer at the drawing, trying to find myself." Her head bent, and she sniffed. Though she emitted such a quiet sound, her tears were heavy on the air. I turned my hand over in order to squeeze her shoulder. "I'm sorry." She swiped at her face. "What a morose mess. It must be the wine."

"Then have some more."

"No. Really, I—" She huffed as I tipped the bottle over her glass once more. "You don't like the word no, do you?"

"Astute woman." To make her feel better, I poured some more into my own glass. "So. Summers in the sun. Ice pops and sprinklers. Magical garden fairies. Sounds pretty good." *Better* than good. For a brief, vicarious moment, I was able to experience a childhood I'd never really had. "What about your siblings? Did they enjoy the front lawn as well?"

Her answer startled me. "No brothers or sisters. Wasn't for lack of trying—or so Dad tells me, much to my horror." She chuckled again, turning to settle an elbow on a throw pillow. "I imagine it's a blast to grow up with siblings, though. There *was* a time when you, Trey, and Lance liked each other, right?"

"Of course." I forced myself to return her stare, to avoid giving up the lie. The feat was sheer hell, and I had no idea why. By now, the deception had become part of me, like a whore using tender talk on a client she barely knew. A job requirement.

"So what happened?" she pressed. "How did the three of you sail on such separate tides?"

There was another lie prepared for that too. I couldn't bring myself to use it. Maybe borrowing the truth for an ambiguity would feel better. "We grew up," I hedged. "It happens fast when one is answering to the Stone empire."

I took another drag on my wine, disguising the torture of holding back the bitterness from those last three words—another anomaly to this conversation. Normally I evoked the Stone name with reverence. Tonight, it felt like a lead chain around my neck.

"Okay," she replied softly. "So what about *your* parents? You're close to your father, right? And tell me about your mother."

I kept my stare fixed on the burgundy depths inside my glass. "That's an easy one." *Liar.* "I...owe her a great deal." In truth, the boundaries of words couldn't contain my gratitude to Willa Stone.

"What do you mean?"

I pulled in a deep breath. Answering that wasn't a luxury I could afford. Not now, not ever. "The subject of this conversation is you, Miss Montgomery, not me." As soon as I asserted it, she crossed her legs. Though she remained angled toward me, the new pose was a clear intention to shut me out. Nevertheless, I charged. "Tell me what happened to bring you here. Between the ice pops...and these."

I pulled on one of her shoes, bringing her foot with it. With my thumb against the top and my other fingers around her ankle, the gesture was meant more as demonstration, not flirtation.

It was a nice attempt at logic.

It was also a complete failure.

Once more, her skin trembled beneath my touch. But this time, she wasn't only nervous. The fast intake of her breath, the hitch of the pulse at the base of her throat, the heated parting of her lips, all told me otherwise. My breath seized. My cock, hot but obedient until now, pounded in rebellion.

God*damn*, I wanted her.

"Sacrifice."

The word tumbled from her on half a whisper. I shook my head a little to banish its aroused fog. "What?"

With a wince, she tugged her leg from my hold. "You want to know what happened to get me here, Mr. Stone? A lot of sacrifice. It was my dad doing without so many things so I could go to college. It was him not taking a single day off during my freshman year. He also sold our family home and lived in an apartment so we'd make my tuition payments. You're amazed at my focus skills? Well, I learned them from an amazing man. Colin Montgomery."

I didn't reply to that. The renewed set of her shoulders conveyed how much she didn't want one. She gave me further confirmation by putting down her glass and scooping up her purse.

I nodded. It would accomplish nothing to tell her that having a glass of wine with me didn't constitute an insult to her father. After the way we'd just damn near shorted out the electricity in the room with one touch, I understood her anxiety.

I also had to respect it.

"Thank you for the honor of your time tonight, Miss Montgomery."

Hell. How had my attempt to keep it professional ended up sounding like a line of innuendo?

"The honor was mine, Mr. Stone."

She didn't help matters, damn it. Every syllable she spoke, soft and polite, sprouted vines of heat through my blood, winding their way right around my cock. *Of course.*

"I'll have the town car brought up to take you back to the hotel."

"It's all right. I can call a cab."

"It's *not* all right." I beelined toward the en suite phone on the kitchenette counter. "It's late. Freaks are still lingering in front of the building—"

"And I'm a grown woman, capable of taking care of myself."

"Where? In San Diego, where the worst thing to fear is a sunburn?"

She shot up too. Her nostrils flared a little. Her lips bunched a lot. Just my luck, she was sexy as hell even when pissed. "That's pretty naïve."

I snorted. "I assure you, baby girl, I am *not* naïve."

Stunned silence weighted the air—hers because of the endearment I'd flung, mine from wondering if I'd ever known a day of naïve in my life. Our gazes wrestled as proxy for our wills. Our bodies tightened as sacrifices for our desires. I allowed a trio of harsh breaths to break free, hoping they'd assuage the craving to stalk over there, yank her into my arms, and kiss her into submission. And yes, the kiss would only be the start. Of so much more...

Fortunately, she was an observant woman. Her eyes widened, reading the heat beneath my stare. Between shaky breaths, she declared, "I—I'd better go."

I nodded again. Firmly. "In the town car."

"No."

"Yes."

I expected her escalated wrath. In a warped way, I looked forward to it. This woman, in the throes of rage...damn, it was exciting. I knew what that made me. *First-class asshole coming through, kids.* She'd been through a flight from California, a meeting ending in my pissing contest with Trey, Wooten's press conference, and retrieving her phone charger on all fours. Yet selfishly, I still reveled in how gorgeous she was, marching back toward me with a stabbing finger. How *alive* she was. When was the last time I'd felt anything close to alive?

"Okay, *look.* During business hours, you can play dictator as much as you want with me. I even went along with your game tonight, trying to be nice." She stopped in place and straightened her shoulders. "I'm not going to be nice anymore."

"And I wasn't playing." Fascination gave way to irritation. I imitated her defiant stance. "I'm still not. Your safety isn't a goddamn game, Claire."

She jerked up her chin. "I'm calling a cab."

That did it. Chafing against my arrogance? Alluring as hell. But shoving aside her wellbeing to make a point? Unacceptable.

I approached her with firm but slow steps. Luckily she didn't know me well enough yet to decipher my intent—or the level of my ire. When I was a foot away from her, I stopped. Slid my hands into my pockets. Touching her wasn't going to happen this time. Spearing her with the force of my glare was another matter. From the sizable gulp vibrating down her throat, I was certain she'd gotten the point.

"Go ahead. Call your cab," I murmured, serene as a Tibetan monk. "Only, when you hop in, tell the driver to take you all the way to the airport."

Her mouth formed an *O.*

"You'd throw me off the project for this?"

"I don't tolerate stupidity in the name of pride, Miss Montgomery. My patience for that game has been tapped dry by my brother."

She snorted again. "Maybe all the rumors about you are true, Mr. Stone."

Touché. She'd landed a good stab beneath my armor. But like hell would I let her see that. "There are many rumors spread about me. Can you be more specific?"

She gave a false smile. "My pleasure. All the ones involving the words *overbearing bastard.*"

I rocked back on my heels. "Hmm. Sounds about right."

She blinked as if that surprised her. Before she stepped completely away from me, I could have sworn another look crumpled her features behind it. A grimace of sadness?

"I'll go get my things from the conference room. Tell your driver I'll be down in ten minutes. Good night, Mr. Stone."

"Goodbye, Miss Montgomery."

My gut had nagged me to use the more permanent words. Giving her closure on this—whatever this had been—would assure her I had no intentions of inviting her down the hall for wine sampling every night. Restoring boundaries was my expression of respect.

Though I doubt the woman presently agreed with me.

Want to punch me that bad, San Diego? Get in line behind the two dozen people who were there before you.

In this case, I'd gladly pay the penalty of her fury. At least she'd be safe to wield it.

So why did those parting words still taste like shit in my mouth?

CHAPTER FOUR

Claire

My phone alarm went off at five thirty a.m. I shut it off in a morose haze, wondering if there was any chance at all that yesterday had been a dream. If so, I wouldn't be a speck sorry.

My head throbbed. Strangely, so did my heart. I'd never had any trouble disengaging from a project before, especially just one day in. Margaux's ultimatum on Killian should've made this one a no-brainer, though Andrea discouraged serious client mingling as a large unwritten rule. The woman set a daunting example for us all too. She could eat, drink, joke, flirt and do coy with a source for hours, all the while sharpening a knife for their evisceration. Dad even knew this. He thought it was "savvy and sexy." When he'd confessed it to me, I'd been left wondering if the woman's blowjobs were *that* good.

"Ew," I whispered.

The thoughts waiting for me on the other side of the exclamation weren't much better. How had this happened? I'd only spent seven hours at Stone Global yesterday—time that included the train wreck of last night.

Damn it.

What the hell had I been thinking? And doing? Letting him haul me down from the conference table. Clinging to him like a newborn colt. The gut spill in his private sitting room.

And the clincher, the brat act I'd given him about a stupid issue like my ride home, sparked by feeling so out of control around him.

Because I *was* out of control around him.

If the day were a fish, I'd throw it back.

Remarkably, a smile bloomed on my face. Dad had the expression hand-painted on a little plaque in the potting shed in his backyard. I always looked at it and groaned, calling him a maudlin Irishman. Yesterday had sure proved me wrong, hadn't it?

I sat up, switched on the light, and peered around the room as a distraction for my aching chest. Already, I was way off my game. Normally I would have all my suitcases unpacked, my toiletries lined up on the vanity, and relaxation candles out—in short, moved in and ready to start my day as if I were in my little house back home, on the hill overlooking Old Town. Instead, I got up and had to paw through my luggage, searching for the least-wrinkled blouse and skirt I could find.

In the shower, yesterday's events came barreling back again. Humming Maroon 5 didn't help, either. *Nothing* had moved like Jagger from the second Stone paralyzed me with my ass in the air on that table before dragging me into his private hidey hole, the perfect setting for spewing my life story after three sips of wine...

I groaned.

Was I that much of a lightweight?

No. My stupidity had nothing to do with the wine and everything to do with the strange fog that slammed me in that man's presence. I never opened up like that, not even to Dad, especially not to a client. And, damn it, not to a client like him. He graced magazine covers. Did consulting gigs for CNN.

Dined at restaurants with unpronounceable names. Could probably see to Canada from his home, at the top of one of those buildings that disappeared into the clouds...

I shivered with mortification and cranked up the hot water. As the spray pelted my face, one question taunted. How would I face him this morning? By now, he'd likely formed a few definitive thoughts about me. Weak-willed. Imprudent. Immature. A woman—a *girl*—who babbled like a tipsy sorority sister to every man who poured her some wine, never mind how expensive and fabulous the vintage.

The worst thing of all?

I'd reveled in every minute of it.

God help me, I couldn't deny my attraction to Killian. Maybe I could've if he hadn't touched me, but it was too late for that. The damage was done. My stomach flipped over on itself when I recalled him helping my balance after pulling me from the conference table...and then reliving the current that passed between us like lightning arcing between storm clouds. Every time we'd brushed, that connection had flared all over again, brilliant and searing, so that when he leaned close, I'd let him. Inwardly, I'd damn near begged for his nearness.

I smiled, remembering every one of those heart-halting moments. Why not? For a few special minutes, I'd been treated to a glimpse of the man beneath the bespoke suit. He was funny and engaging when he let his guard down, though I quickly comprehended how difficult the exposure was for him. That was only the beginning of his labyrinth—a psychological maze I simply didn't have time for. Trying to decipher a man like Killian Stone was undoubtedly a full-time job, best left for some bored upper crust woman with nothing more complicated to ponder than matching her shoes and handbag for the city's next society event.

Scoffs the woman who matched her nail polish to the company's damn logo.

"There's a difference," I seethed. Coordinating a manicure was miles from dropping panties for the man. *That* distance was *not* going to be breached—even if he caused my body to tingle in places that I'd long forgotten. Illicit places. Wet, pulsing places...

I brutally turned the knob toward the *C* setting and finished my shower with chattering teeth.

When I climbed out, coffee was in order. I brewed the java while my straight iron heated, thanking God for the SGC travel department, wise enough to set us up in a hotel with single-cup brewers. Final decision on the look for the day? A sleek top knot formed a classic match for my no-nonsense gray pinstriped skirt suit, paired with practical pumps. Since it had been so cold in the conference room yesterday, a long-sleeved blouse and the suit jacket would do fine. I always received compliments when I wore pale pink, and luckily, that was the blouse most ready to go.

As I slipped into my shoes, I stopped for a long second. *Hell.* I was actually putting extra care into my appearance, though realizing it a few minutes too late.

"Okay, Montgomery," I muttered, perusing myself one more time in the full-length mirror on the door. "This behavior needs to stop. You're here to do a job. Only that. End of story. Nod your head. You understand this. Now nod again."

I complied and then realized one affirmation was still missing. No matter what happened between Stone and me yesterday, it was back to business, *only* business, today. Those minutes together, that feeling when he focused those midnight eyes solely on me...that kind of shit could become addictive. I didn't have time in my life for addictive. I didn't have room in my heart for the disappointment and betrayal that would follow. I'd had enough of both to last a lifetime.

I stuffed my laptop into my briefcase, grabbed my cell, and headed for the elevator. The team usually met in the lobby and then took a shuttle to the business we were working with. I hadn't heard different plans, so I hit the button for the lobby while taking advantage of the elevator's mirrored wall to get my lip gloss on evenly.

The doors slid open, and I caught sight of the team—as they exited through the hotel's revolving door. Fortunately, Chad turned to make one last scan of the lobby, his face creased with worry. Relief took over as he spotted me.

"Shit, Claire. I thought we were going to leave you behind."

"What the hell? We always leave at eight forty-five. I'm ten minutes early." I tried and failed not to fume as he hustled me across the lobby. Obviously the plan had been changed and I hadn't been clued in. The switch-up wasn't a big deal, but being kept in the dark about it? *Not nice.* Secrets, big or small, were a major pet peeve, thanks to the significant baggage Nick had left behind in my psyche. The sordid side of our work often provided stunning justification for the mindset too. The truth, however messy, ultimately did set a person free.

"I've been texting you," Chad snapped. "Is your phone dead? The rich guy sent his car, and the queen and her spawn said it would look bad if we made them wait, so you could find your own way to SGC. I offered to come up to your room, but Andrea gave me *talk to the hand* faster than Margaux could summon her laser-lizard stare."

Since we neared the limo, I flung back my *what-the-fuck?*

glare at him. I received his fast shrug in reply, another silent code between us, generally meant as *at least I tried*. I couldn't argue.

While climbing into the town car after him, my gaze locked with the driver's. Oblivious to the political tangle that awaited me inside, he gave a friendly nod and murmured, "Nice to see you again so soon, Miss Montgomery."

I plastered on my best pageant smile in return, hoping to God nobody else had heard him, before settling next to Chad. "Good morning, everyone. I hope you all slept as well as I did. Damn, the mattresses here are fantastic. How are you this morning, Andrea? I'm so glad I came down when I did. Please let me know if there are any other changes in our usual routine so I can go ahead and make a note of it now." I stared at her with dewy expectancy. I wouldn't be caught off guard again.

Margaux had already primed the princess-zilla glare. "The change was made several hours ago, Claire. Were you really working *that* hard, got in *that* late, and weren't on top of your emails this morning? I mean, where were you? Mother and I enjoyed some wine in the hotel bar for an hour and a half and still didn't see you come in. What kept you so long?"

'Zilla had clearly added bitch-flavored creamer to her coffee. "A lot of my emails couldn't wait until this morning," I supplied, "so I hopped right on them last night." It wasn't a lie. I had nothing to hide. Not really. It simply wasn't the whole truth. Technically, there was nothing wrong with that.

"And then...?" Margaux prompted.

I grabbed my forearm and started rubbing. "And then what?"

Her face, made up as flawlessly as a Lancôme ad, took on a suspicious air that turned my nerves to icicles. "It took over an hour to answer a few emails?"

"I'm sure Claire just got caught up with some of the other SGC staff." What Chad lacked in physical height, he made up for in commanding presence. His stiffened posture made Margaux back off a little. He tossed a wink back at me. "So did you pick up on any office gossip about our boy Trey?"

Poor guy. He had no idea that his query threw me on the defensive as equally as Margaux's. "They...errr...all seem pretty tight-lipped. I tried to appear friendly and open, hoping to convey that we're available if any of them wish to share ideas with us."

Michael smiled. "Sounds like a great approach. Wooten's press conference was on every channel I flipped to last night. This story is media catnip. Damn. We really could use a natural disaster right about now."

He joked, but we all recognized it as truth. A diversion in the news would give us a huge break. Instead, every news broadcast in the country led with the Wooten event, his accusations dissected by a thousand media "specialists" who arrived at the same conclusion. The senator was out for blood. He swore he'd bring charges against Trey, mentioning every nightmare accusation from statutory rape to the corruption of a minor. By tonight, Trey would be the punch line for Jimmy Fallon, Jimmy Kimmel, Jon Stewart, and every stand-up comedian from New York to California.

It was going to get uglier before it got prettier. With that shared knowledge, we greeted the car's stop with grim stares.

Chicago had rolled out one of its finest blustery mornings for us. Looking every inch the wimpy Californians that we were, we grabbed our bags and briefcases with frantic haste.

Five minutes later, we stepped off the elevator at the sixty-seventh floor. Our first sight was a frazzled version of Killian's assistant, Britta. Her hair, a polished blonde Scandinavian waterfall yesterday, was shoved atop her head and secured with a pencil. Her earrings were yanked off and thrown to the side, her coffee hardly touched. She waved us toward the conference room without a greeting. We weren't hurt. Her phones played dueling ring tones, and by the number of times she repeated, "No comment," we all jumped to the same conclusion. The press was so hungry for answers, they were finding ruthless ways to get through SGC's first-level switchboards. Not good. We had to wrangle this narrative back from Wooten—about five minutes ago.

I discreetly pulled Andrea to the side, requesting a moment. Margaux followed us. Not a surprise. I attempted a dismissive glance but, when it didn't work, simply focused on Andrea. There was no time to waste on turf wars.

"This is just a suggestion, so hear me out," I began. "We all know why Britta looks cornered. Every one of those callers is a reporter. They're not letting up. The poor woman looks like she's already put in an eight-hour day, and it's barely nine. I think someone from our team should give her a hand." Like clockwork, Margaux tensed at my suggestion. She was the press wrangler on our team, logically the best person for the job, but she looked at the vacant seat next to Britta like it was a steerage berth on the *Titanic*. "At the same time, we can coach Britta on how to route and handle press calls." Hurriedly, I added, "So we don't walk in on this every morning."

Andrea took a long moment to ponder what I said. "I think you have a very valid point, Claire," she confirmed.

I smiled with pride, even managing a diplomatic glance at Margaux. "Thank you for listening. I appreciate it."

"Well, we are a team, and we all have input on how we handle crises. That's how I like to do things." The response doubled my appreciation—until Andrea smiled in return. Her transparent veneer was back in full force. "So, darling, why don't you grab yourself a cup of coffee first, perhaps freshen up Britta's while you're at it? I know you'll be wonderful with her. I'm sure she will benefit from whatever you can teach her. And don't worry—we'll bring you up to speed in the conference room when you join us later."

She walked away with Margaux on her heels. The only thing missing from the moment was Margaux turning to stick her tongue out in triumph—though her sashay accomplished the same teardown on my confidence.

Another sigh from Britta made me push aside my selfishness. I quickly put down my case and bag and then let her in on the plan. She looked so relieved I almost expected her to tackle me with a hug. Margaux and her gloat were officially forgotten.

I ordered Britta to put the phones on hold while I got us both some fresh coffee. In the warmly decorated lounge, I ran into Chad and gave him the synopsis of what just happened. His reaction was as predictable as Margaux's, meaning I had to shove him into a chair and tell him to breathe through his instant temper blow.

"That little bitch," he muttered. "She's going to get hers one day."

"Stand down, Lerner. She didn't call this one. Andrea did. Even if she had, she's not worth the powder and we both know it. Can we just chill about her for one day?"

He cocked a curious glance. "Well, hel-lo, happy surfer girl. I wasn't about to ask if you secretly got laid last night, but there *is* something different about you today. And you haven't been answering your cell." His eyes widened. "Woman, do you have a secret Chi-town fuck buddy you haven't told us about?"

I headed to the coffeemaker, not about to let him detect my lie. "You say crap like that every time I wear my hair like this."

"No, I don't."

"Chad, I *really* don't have time."

"Fine, fine. But now *I* get to play surfer-brah on *your* ass. The only reason Margaux didn't step up for the phones is because she wants to be free for rubbing her wet spot all over Killian Stone. That red silk number she's wearing today? Before you came down, she told Michael that she packed it especially for attracting the man. Apparently, he likes curvy blondes in red."

"Thanks for the trivia." I made my sarcasm win over my jealousy. Was Killian as huge a skirt chaser as Trey? If that was the case, then it was best I found out—and could be grateful for—having the knowledge now. I could be at peace leaving him for Margaux's clutches, as well as knowing my judgment about men was just as shitty as ever.

"Whether it's true or not, I observed the guy during the briefing yesterday, and I can tell you this—Stone's about as into the 'zilla as a vegan is a slab of bacon. Karma makes one hell of a center ring, Claire, and I hope today's the day it dings the full count for Margaux. When it does, I'm going to be in the front row with popcorn."

I forced a laugh to my lips, despite what his comment about Margaux and her wet spot did to my stomach. "It's time to get to work," I told him. *Thank God,* I added inwardly.

While it had been ages since I'd manned a phone, I actually

enjoyed the pace of the job. Spending a few hours with Britta was a bonus. The woman was smart, funny, and very open about her experience working for *the* Killian Stone. I listened to every word—for the good of the team's effort, of course.

Through everything Britta said, one message was blindingly clear. The man was exceedingly generous to those he allowed past his shell of self-control. Britta told me about the time he'd waited in the ER with her after her son had fallen off his bike and broken his arm. And the night he'd summoned the corporate jet at midnight so she'd been able to fly to Florida to see her dying father. And the Christmas season they'd both missed due to working day and night on a new merger— for which she'd found a brand-new car in her driveway on Christmas morning, courtesy of her thankful boss.

Inadvertently, she also opened a window on some of Killian's personal quirks. He was an avid water polo player, practicing three mornings a week with his team in the pool at his gym up the street. He had a weakness for everything fried but hated ice cream and pizza. And he was an avid geek about his stamp collection. I nearly spewed coffee on my laptop when she imparted that fact, wondering if he'd ever stop astonishing me. And if I really *was* attracted to a halfway-decent guy.

No. *Attracted*, along with any descriptor connected to it, could not be part of my vocabulary for the man again. Once he got an eyeful of Margaux in her red silk man-catcher dress, things would change anyway. She'd have Killian Stone between her thighs, and I'd be able to sleep without stressing about the DEA pounding on my door.

We slowly wrestled the phones under control once the reporters realized we really meant *no comment*, no matter how often they got through. Britta was on the phone with an actual client when another line lit up, so I punched the button to handle the call.

"Stone Global Corporation. Killian Stone's office. How may I direct your call?"

"This isn't Britta." The man sounded distracted, harried, and a little annoyed. His voice was half-drowned in street noise. Gusting wind, blaring horns, and a passing police siren made it hard to hear him. Still, my pulse raced and my insides lurched—in ways they hadn't since last night. But Stone was here already. His office door had been closed all morning.

"No, I'm sorry. She's on another line. Would you like to hold, or can I direct your call?" I breathed deeply, forcing decorum to my voice.

"Who the hell is this?" The siren screamed a block closer to my caller. It didn't constitute an excuse to become a jackass.

"My name is Claire. To whom am *I* speaking?" *Two can play this game, buddy.*

"This is Killian Stone."

Oh, hell.

That didn't explain his closed door, though it justified the heartbeat sprint and the flipping stomach. Too bad it couldn't excuse my attack of haughty and snotty, which he apparently found amusing. The snicker beneath his reply had been unmistakable.

"I—I apologize, Mr. Stone."

Another flash from last night blazed through my mind. The image of him, anger creasing his face as he said goodbye, telling me I could do what he said or go straight to O'Hare. God, how he'd enraged me. Then, damn him, aroused the hell out of me. But now I plunged into dread, remembering what the man could accomplish when he was pushed.

Thankfully, he preferred chuckling at the moment. "Apologize? For what? Answering the phone? But out of curiosity, where is the woman I pay to do that job?"

"Ummm..." My hand still shook like a teenager on the phone with the boy she liked from science class. "She's still on another line. The phones were really busy this morning, so I suggested we help her with some strategies on how to handle the press. The bastards have been relentless and somehow found a way to breach the front switchboard. Hopefully they won't bother Britta too much longer..."

I was rambling. Worse yet, I knew it. I wanted to crawl into a hole for at least a week of hiding. What was it about this man that made me act half my age? It was ridiculous. Unprofessional. It had to stop.

Britta had finished her own call. She stared at me with open alarm, clearly reading my gawk and sensing I had Killian on the line. "I can take that now," she prompted.

"Uh, yeah," I mumbled. "Sure."

"What?" Killian asked.

"Done," I blurted. "I mean—errr—Britta's done. With her call, I mean. I'll hold you now. I mean I'll *put* you on hold. Then you can talk to her—"

"No." One syllable. Solid steel. "Don't."

"Sorry?"

"I'd rather talk to you." His pause was formidable. "About last night."

"Not happening." Pointedly, I amended, "Please. Okay?"

"Why?"

"Because now's not the time. And here's not the place."

"Why?"

"Because it's *not*."

"Are you always so bossy, Miss Montgomery?" His undercurrent of humor had returned. The traffic noise faded.

"Said the pot to the kettle?"

I swallowed hard and turned from Britta, not wanting the woman to hear the way I was talking—make that sparring—with her boss on the phone. *Great.* That put my vision in line with the door to his office. Like I needed any more reminders of the forbidden territory. The sanctum I should've never entered to begin with. No matter how magical those minutes had been...

"Listen, I need to get back to work." I forced myself to say it. "I—uhhh—assume you're out at meetings, Mr. Stone?"

He grunted. "Yes. Couldn't be helped. Some stockholders need to have their hands held after the last few days. Fortunately, I haven't been assaulted by any of your reporter friends." A long moment went by. "But damn, if I were in their shoes, I'd pick pursuing you on the phone instead of me in the rain any day."

"I'm sure you're very interesting in the rain."

He let another long moment pass. Thank God. I had a moment to recover from my horror. What the hell was I doing, snipping at him one minute and flirting the next, after I'd ordered myself off from *both*?

I was a huge damn mess. An awful, terrible tease. And confused. So freaking confused by what he did to me.

I listened to his longer breaths...enduring shivers down to my toes because of them. When he spoke again, the words were tight and intimate. "And I like the way you think I'm interesting."

"You could be standing next to the president and I'd think you were interesting."

I had *not* just said that.

"What if I were standing next to Melinda Gates?"

On the other hand, who cared what I'd just said? His bombshell, making me openly gasp, erased half the thoughts from my head. Few people knew about my fascination with Gates, who used her wealth for some of the most far-reaching humanitarian efforts in the world.

"How— How did you know—?"

"You're not the only one who likes to tap at icebergs, Miss Montgomery."

His tone dipped into lower registers. He spoke of ice, but searing smoke wove seductive tendrils through every nerve ending in my body. Killian Stone had Googled me.

I gulped before stammering, "I—I have to go. Will you be here later for the strategy meeting?"

"Yes. I'll be in around four for the update from your team."

"It's not my team, Mr. Stone. Regardless, I'll see you there."

He responded at first with another thick pause. On the other side of it, every note of power and confidence had returned to his voice. "Miss Montgomery?"

"Yes?"

"I'd like to think you'll be seeing more of me than that."

Click.

I hung up the phone and put my face in my hands. And tried to calm my heart. And fought to string two thoughts together.

What the hell was going on with that man? What was he trying to do to me?

I didn't have answers for either but knew two things for certain. First, I needed to get my shit together. Technically, I was on the clock. *His* clock. Secondly, Killian—*Mr.* Stone— and I needed to get a few things cleared up or this was going to be the longest, hardest project of my career.

The rest of the morning and early afternoon dragged on. The conversation with Killian had dunked my thoughts into fog. I continued to assist Britta but couldn't recount what went on around me.

At two, Andrea sent Chad to round me up. We would meet as a team before the Stone brothers and their people arrived. Andrea, Michael, and Margaux tossed around strategies about our counterattack to Wooten's slur campaign. The details were gory. Andrea ordered that the Wootens, along with their friends and staff, be gashed open and dissected from every angle. No ex-lover, bank record, immigration document, or medical file was off-limits.

I typed notes as fast as I could. Thank God, because I would have to review it all later back in my room. My senses were still a blur, all caused by my conversation with the model-gorgeous flirt who wasn't even in the building. A man I barely knew. Who had a cute thing for french fries and a sigh-worthy loyalty to his employees. But so do mob bosses. And boyfriends who deal drugs and then knock up your best friend before skipping town.

But denying my feelings would be like stopping my breath. Heated attraction. Giddy arousal. Mounting frustration. Dizzying desire.

Oh, yeah. *That.*

This was crazy. Didn't I just need to be grateful? How many women my age could seriously complain about a problem like this?

I laughed aloud as my thoughts tumbled atop one another,

which made the conversation stop. Everyone turned and stared. I froze in place, mind scrambling for a fast save. "You— uhhh—mentioned Wooten's affinity for waffles," I stammered. "It made me think of this YouTube video...waffles and cats... maybe we could hire some college kid to do a Wooten-style riff on it? Stranger things have gone viral." When they all kept staring, I tried to smile. "Anyone need coffee?"

I'd almost made my escape when the conference-room door opened. I felt him before I even stared up at him. Killian's presence ruled the air from the moment he entered, weaving through my senses in three seconds flat.

I dropped back into my chair before he could notice me swaying like a doll. Besides, Andrea would start the presentation right away. The client was never kept waiting.

Trey followed his brother, now looking like a puppy being brought to heel, complete with an impeccable suit and a fresh shave. He sat next to Killian, of course—meaning I *had* to look at the man now.

My memory had short-changed me. He was more gorgeous than any image in my mind. Heat crept across my cheeks as he caught my glance—directly across the stretch of table he'd helped me down from. His muscles were tight under his shirt, exactly as they'd been when he'd lowered me and then steadied me. My body filled with the same electricity as then, the same exquisite awareness of him. His looming height. His expensive cologne. The heat radiating from him, alluring as a self-contained furnace. The way he'd felt under my hands. The way he'd held me with so much strength yet so much care...

I shook my head. *Head back in the game. Now!*

Andrea commanded the room by moving to the head of the table, launching her synopsis of the action items tackled by the team today. I fought to listen, hoping to catch the ideas I'd already daydreamed through. God, this was so unlike me. I was hideously out of place not being to-the-minute on with a project, especially one of this magnitude.

The conversation progressed around the table, with each team member adding their ideas about how we'd move forward in combating the damage inflicted by Wooten's press conference. The secondary layer, dealing with the senator's threat of legal charges, was addressed by Michael, who hoped to be sitting for the Bar next year. I wasn't surprised when he dazzled the hell out of SGC's legal team, though every moment that went by without an official court summons gave us all hope that Wooten would pull a one-eighty on the threats.

As the rotation neared me, I was still pathetically off my mark. Though I was supposed to have preliminary details about the best course for the project based on the overnight ratings for the news outlets, compiling it into sensible form was an obstacle course my mind couldn't seem to navigate. I dashed a private message to Chad on his laptop, telling him to pass me over. The rest of the team tensed. Andrea wouldn't care that I'd spent half the day on the phones and had had no time to compile data. She only knew we had a glaring hole in the information stream to Killian.

At least one person was happy about my downfall. Margaux preened like a forewarned guest to the Red Wedding, finger sliding around her touchpad as she waited for the bodies to fall.

Andrea shot to her feet after Chad's bullet points of tomorrow's plan, smiling with overbright zeal. "Mr. Stone?" She nodded toward Trey. "And...Mr. Stone? Are you comfortable with the approach thus far? Any questions at this point?" Her plastic smile gave away the rhetorical slant of the questions—which added to her obvious surprise when Killian rose.

"It's all excellent information, Ms. Asher." He glanced my way. Also a stunner. An unwanted one. "I want to particularly thank Miss Montgomery for assisting Britta this morning in dealing with the phones." He nodded at me. "You have my sincere appreciation for the help."

"My pleasure." I tried to smile, but the knives Margaux inserted to her gaze turned my expression to one of desperation. *Enough, damn it!*

He went on without flinching. "But I'm not glutted with gratitude as to overlook that *you* haven't had the chance to speak yet. I've been truly looking forward to your input, Miss Montgomery." He angled more fully toward me, slamming me with the full force of his tall, polished grandeur.

"My input?" I barely avoided squeaking it. "Why?"

His dark eyebrows drew together as if I'd just questioned whether two plus two got someone to four. "Because nobody else in this room has touched more of the media today than you." He dipped his head, looking deferential, beautiful—and determined. "That makes your feedback the *most* valuable to me right now. So...your thoughts, if you please."

If I pleased?

Hell, no. I *didn't* please.

As the shriek raced through my head, everyone shifted in their chairs to stare at me.

Crap, crap, crap.

Anyone have a free hand to save the deer in the headlights?

CHAPTER FIVE

Killian

If a person could really turn a glare into a dagger, I was positive hers had me diced a hundred ways. I returned to my chair, bracing my elbows on the rests and returning her glower like an indolent king. Clearly the woman had no idea how much practice I had at being vilified. More importantly, at my capability for ignoring it.

Most importantly, how much she'd thank me for this. She had no idea how tightly she'd been crammed into Asher's tidy little box, did she? Oh, it was all right to step out for a bit, perhaps do something more than run presentation slides, answer phones, or fetch coffee, but to be stretched and challenged, be told she could run and push herself? That expressing herself was okay?

I couldn't wait to see her embrace that freedom.

And damn it, I couldn't wait to be the one giving it to her.

The thought was a dance with fire. But I was already halfway to hell with the subtle-as-a-grenade line during our phone encounter this morning. I still couldn't explain the slip, only that once I heard her voice, I realized how everything had felt...*off*...since our parting last night. The sensation terrified me. Trey had already taken care of all the unbalance my life could afford right now, meaning I needed to make things right with Claire—which should've led to a sincere apology and a promise to keep things professional from now on.

Instead, I'd let my dick do the talking. Every word. I did want to see more of her. Lusted for it. Craved the idea of claiming her. Taming her. And, hell yes...fucking her.

Factors that had nothing to do with my demand of her now.

Climb out of the damn box, Claire. Show me—and everyone here—the spitfire I found on this table last night. The innovator with blue nails. Colin Montgomery's fighter of a daughter.

"I—uhhh—" She flung a nervous glance around the table. "I requested to be skipped. I knew how pressed we'd be for time, and the others undoubtedly have more insight at this point than I do, so..."

As she trailed off, she looked up to her boss. Andrea waited with a stare like a corporate Mother Superior, ready to rap a student's knuckles for screwing up a Bible verse. Witnessing the exchange made me lower my hands to the armrests, clawing at the leather.

"Mr. Stone." Andrea pivoted back toward me. Mother Superior was still in place, hands joined, smart phone in place of a rosary between them. "With all due respect, Miss Montgomery is correct. Our job is just beginning. Her specialty is data and media analysis. She's our ace for watching trend graphs, demographic skews, and how the public perceives our efforts. At this stage, her input to the plan is—"

"Just as vital as everyone else's."

Andrea's nostrils flared. "I beg your pardon?"

Trey, who'd been obedient and quiet to my right, snickered. "You like poking bears, brother?"

I ignored him, maintaining my scrutiny on Andrea. "I

think you heard me perfectly well, Ms. Asher, but I'm happy to repeat it. My assistant informs me that Miss Montgomery spent five straight hours at the desk with her this morning, helping with funneling hundreds of media calls to you, as well as five photocopier vendors, seven misdirected job applicants, and three reality-television producers wanting to get their hands on my brother."

Trey grinned. "Seriously?"

"Don't even think it."

My decree withered him into a slump. Andrea Asher's posture was another story. The woman, clearly undecided whether to glare or hiss at me, stiffened her stance. "Miss Montgomery volunteered for the duty, Mr. Stone."

"I'm aware of that, Ms. Asher. The attitude further justifies her input to this conversation." I steepled my fingers. "*This* conversation, where I need thinking just like that. Where we'll *all* benefit from ideas outside our normal parameters, right?"

When I angled to Claire again, I was glad to see she'd stashed the daggers. The amber depths of her eyes carried a new glow now, matching the anticipation across her face.

"Very well," Andrea murmured. "Claire, do you have anything you'd like to contribute?"

"Well—" She stopped herself after looking again into Andrea's firm stare. By now, I was certain the woman knew how to communicate whole sentences with her eyes. The slogan on this glance to Claire? *Screw this up and you'll pay big time.* "I'm— I'm sorry," Claire finally stammered. "I really don't. I didn't have time to prepare anything, Mr. Stone."

"Bullshit."

The room thickened with tension at my interjection. I didn't give a rat's ass.

"Excuse me?" she blurted.

"Of course you're ready. You've been ready since nine this morning, when you gained firsthand access to those reporters. After listening to the mob, *before* they've had a chance to compose themselves for Andrea or Margaux, what's your take?" I leaned forward, elbows on the table, abandoning indolent king in favor of a man who had more at stake than a castle. If Stone Global suffered permanent damage because of Trey's stunt, thousands of unemployed people would be on my conscience. "I don't want what you've 'prepared,' Miss Montgomery, or what Ms. Asher's told you to prepare. Push outside that damn envelope and give me the truth of what your gut's telling you. *That's* what I want. Don't give me your numbers and statistics. Just tell me what you *feel*."

Claire blinked. Afterward, the expression on her face made my tough-guy act worth it. She actually met my gaze this time. She even smiled a little.

Like a woman climbing out of a box.

Still, she queried, "What I...feel? Really?"

"Go ahead, Claire." Lerner gave her an encouraging nod. "Just don't go into a Celine Dion wail-fest on his ass. It's not pretty, Mr. Stone. Take my word for it."

That cracked some of the ice in the room. Everyone chuckled, even Andrea. After the laughter dissipated, she spoke again. "My teammate, in his demented way, has helped to prove my sole point." She pulled in a breath as I leaned forward a little more. "People enjoy feeling good more than they enjoy feeling bad." She peered around the room. "We all just proved it. We enjoyed that laugh, right?"

Margaux Asher, who'd been quiet since I singled Claire out, folded her arms. "Very fascinating, Claire. But what's your point?"

I resisted glaring at the woman for her thinly masked sneer. Claire simply boosted my respect for her by giving Margaux a patient smile. When she faced me again, she went on, "I'm not discounting any of the ideas we've flown so far, Mr. Stone. But people like a comeback story more if it's told with a smile—especially the press. If you want to really turn this around, perhaps a campaign focused on boosting Trey rather than tearing down Wooten will serve your family's name better."

Trey set down his handheld blackjack game. The man had more nervous energy than a recovering smoker, especially because I still had his phone locked away. "I like the sound of *that* plan."

"Well, it won't happen without your help, Trey," Claire asserted. "And I'm not saying it will be easy. You'll have to make a public apology. That'll only be the start."

Trey shrugged. "Cool. Okay. Like go talk with Jimmy Fallon?"

"No. Like go talk with Oprah Winfrey."

"She's not as much fun as Jimmy."

"Exactly."

Trey squirmed. "I don't know how to talk to somebody like Oprah Winfrey."

Claire rose. "That's okay. It's what we're here for. Margaux and Michael really know their stuff. They're here to coach you. I'm here to make sure you appeal to the right demographics— the people who are going to listen to *your* side of this."

"Yeah." There was warmth in my brother's voice. And enthusiasm. And for the first time in the last two days, hope. "Okay. That's good. My side."

"Whoa." She held up a hand. "I said that'll only be the start." She paced a little, her confidence clearly growing. "After that, we build a campaign of targeted exposure. First, you're seen around town at places like the spirituality book store, the health-food store, the gym."

"Oh yeah. The gym. I'm into that."

"For working out your *body*, Mr. Stone." Margaux rolled her eyes. "Not your contacts list."

"We work our way up to public events next." Clearly already reading Trey's mind, Claire emphasized, "*No* dates! Social events and charity affairs, got it? You arrive alone, you depart alone. You have *one* drink and then switch to water. You'll tolerate every bad joke thrown at you about senators' daughters. You'll be jovial to the men, charming to their women, and you'll pretend their daughters don't exist. It will help if the charities involve kids or animals. If we can get your name as one of the main sponsors for one of these things—"

"Done."

The conviction in my voice made her jump a little. I was glad. I wanted her to see how fucking proud I was of her, how great she made me feel by trusting my lead and stepping outside her comfort zone. Her ideas had galvanized everyone in the room, especially Trey. But if they wanted to embrace her in support, they could march their asses into line behind me. On second thought, they could all drop her an email. Thanking her for this new direction was going to be my sole, pleasurable responsibility.

"Done?" The lilt of confusion made her voice five times sexier. Or maybe it was the impish curl to her lips. Or the way her blouse hugged her breasts as she braced one hand to her hip. Screw it, I'd take them all.

"I'm on the board at the Lincoln Park Zoo," I explained. "And we always do a gala fundraiser in the spring. This year, it's May eighth."

Andrea nodded, though the move was tense. Wisely, the woman observed that Claire's ideas resonated with the whole room. Her own vote of support was clearly not cast as easily. "We can work with that," she stated, "*if* that's the direction you're set on following, Mr. Stone."

"It's gutsy." The taller man from their team met my gaze across the table. "And it'll be a steeper battle to win. But once you win it—and with us on board, you *will* win it—you'll be miles higher, PR-wise, than Wooten and his shit-stirrers."

Trey nudged me a little. "I feel better about this plan too."

I turned to lock gazes with my brother. Conflict roared in. I knew how I *should* have responded. After everything he'd cost the company and family name with this stunt, his "feelings" carried no fucking weight here.

But I didn't listen to that voice.

Instead, I indulged the Killian of nineteen years ago, a desperate eight-year-old who dreamed he'd do something cool enough to earn the respect of his big brother. Maybe he'd accomplish something even better, gaining something bigger. Not just Trey's respect. His love.

I leaned closer toward him. "You really do?" After Trey nodded and smiled, I did too. "Okay, man. We'll make it happen."

Trey raised his hand in a sideways fist. "Rock and roll, Kill Shot."

I lifted my hand and met his bump. I couldn't remember the last time he'd called me that. No, I could. He'd been eight and I'd been five. We were in the formal garden with Lance, our own little commando force, stalking the groundskeepers. We didn't care about the world we were growing up into. Birth order didn't matter. Stockholders didn't matter. Josiah Stone's whims didn't matter. Getting the bad guys was the only thing that mattered. Trey, Lance, and Killian were simply *Torch Burn*, *Land Mine*, and *Kill Shot*.

Andrea and her team, earning every cent we paid them by immediately aligning the campaign with Claire's compass, outlined an action plan for the next twenty-four hours. It felt good to watch Trey engaging with the suggestions.

Correction. It felt fucking great.

After the meeting concluded, I walked back to my office feeling higher than the clouds outside the window.

Ten minutes later, the day took an even better turn. When Claire Montgomery appeared in the portal, I didn't care that the contract in my hand represented fifty million dollars' worth of business.

A smile easily broadened my lips. Goddamn, she was stunning. The stormy afternoon light flowed across her classic features. Her eyes gleamed like magic lamps, burnished and brilliant despite the gloomy twilight. Tendrils of hair fell loose out of her Marian Librarian hairstyle, leading me to fantasies of slamming her into a case full of encyclopedias and researching every inch of her body. I'd make sure she maintained a library whisper by capturing all her moans with my mouth...

Which was going to be fucking hard if she kept up that tight glower. Or shoved my door shut with any more vehemence, making the pictures rattle on the wall.

I frowned, officially confused. "Good evening, Miss Montgomery—I think."

She took two steps before squaring off at me again. "You

actually do that, Mr. Stone? That *thinking* thing? Because I'm not convinced right now."

"What the—"

"No, sir. That's my line, and I plan on using it." She pointed a finger the general direction of the conference room. "What the *hell* was that?"

I set the contract slide to the desk. "You mean the opportunity I handed you on a golden plate?"

"Opportunity?" She spat the word like I'd dunked it in acid. "That wasn't an opportunity. That was an ambush."

I rarely had problems finding a reaction for a situation. But at this moment, I admitted to the exception. I was stunned into silence.

By now, most women with her ambition—make that *all* women with her ambition—would've had the door locked, my ass in a chair, their knees on the floor, and my fly down, eager to show their gratitude for the break I'd just delivered with everything but a big red bow on my dick. I didn't expect or want that from her. A goddamn smile would've sealed the day with perfection.

"Pardon me?" I bit out every syllable—making her retort more astounding.

"Nope. Not ready to do that yet."

I folded my arms. "Really? So fucking sorry for the bother, then. Guess I was too busy wondering if I should call Britta to put out a tracking number on your sanity. Clearly it's not in the building anymore."

She growled—*growled*—before sweeping her arms out, fingers splayed. "I wasn't prepared! Don't you get that? I wasn't throwing out some bullshit line. I *really* wasn't ready."

I arched both eyebrows. "Could've fooled me, San Diego."

"Are you seriously pulling flippant right now? Thank God I did have a few ideas to pull out of my ass—"

"Brilliant ones, I might add."

"No," she spat. "You may *not* add a damn thing. The integrity of Andrea's reputation might have been compromised by your curve ball—also meaning my ass would be on its way to the unemployment line right now." A humorless laugh spilled from her. "Wouldn't that be a peachy wedding gift for my dad, telling him I'm moving back in because I was just canned by his sweet little bride?"

"Not a possibility." I growled too—though mine was issued in deep conviction. Andrea Asher didn't strike me as a woman reckless enough to ax a team member for stepping outside their comfort zone in a private meeting purposed for the free exchange of ideas. Even if that were the case, I knew at least three companies here in town who'd snap up a jewel like Claire Montgomery. I had a feeling she'd like it here. Chicago was passionate, creative, and vital...like her.

Hell. Could I deal with this woman working and living up the street? Permanently? Maybe that would be a good thing. Perhaps I wouldn't be so transfixed by her. Right now, she was a shiny but transitory indulgence, captivating me to dangerous levels with her fleeting stop across my life's path.

"You might as well have stripped me naked."

She didn't help my cause with the thoughts her line evoked. I used the act of circling out from the desk to help beat my brain into obedience. "All right, calm down. I'm sure you've dealt with curve balls before, Claire. And hell, you hit this one out of the ballpark." I forced myself to stop several feet from her. Letting the warmth back into my face was an easier feat. "And you were amazing."

For a second, her features softened. But just a second. "That's not the damn point."

I cocked my head. "Then what *is* the damn point?"

She averted her eyes. "It was a curve ball from *you*."

"And?"

I hadn't moved. She scooted back as if I had, shaking her head. "It was a curve ball *because* of you."

The room dimmed a little. Night was encroaching, and I'd only turned on the desk lamp. Even in the dissipated light, I watched her fingers tremble as she rubbed her forearm. Her soft words threaded my chest with a sensation I'd never known before. The confession had been petrifying for her. I could see that. But now I felt it too. In the stillness of this room, in the tension of this moment, I couldn't write off our connection to any more excuses. Neither could she. No wonder we were both terrified.

"Sit down." I quietly pulled out a chair.

She backed off again. Started rubbing her other arm. "I have to get back to work."

"*Sit down*, Claire."

I deliberately snarled it, going for the edges of her frazzled composure. Was the tactic a hundred percent fair? Technically, *no*. But when she flashed me that hot Irish glare before hurling herself into the chair, I almost pumped a fist in triumph.

Now we could get somewhere.

"How may I help you, Mr. Stone?"

Or maybe not.

Her voice was sweet—and false—as a barista asking if I wanted extra foam on my latte. It was a good thing she really wasn't. If I had the drink in hand right now, I'd be hurling it at the walls. Britta would have beheld my new artwork, clucked something colorful under her breath, and then asked if I'd lost my damn mind. At this point, I nearly wondered the same thing.

What *did* I want?

I wanted a simple thank-you.

I wanted a little smile.

I wanted her goddamn truth.

I lowered into the chair next to hers. Every muscle in my body, especially the one between my legs, screamed to pull her closer. It was hell to rein the effort back, bracing one elbow on the table. She smelled so good. A Chanel something, probably Chance. Light. Luminous. Alluring. *Fuck*.

"You know, San Diego, it'd be damn easy to box you back up as a precocious priss right now."

She let the chair swivel a little. "Sure. Why not?"

"Why not?" I slid a finger along my lower lip. "Because I've never been one for easy, that's why not."

Her eyes sparked with challenge. "Maybe it's time to discover a new horizon."

I dropped my finger. "Too late." Let it descend to her knee. "I already have."

A heavy gulp vibrated down her throat. She dropped her gaze. I let mine follow. Together, we stared at my finger on her skin. Burnished against pale. Rough against soft.

I dared a trail higher. And didn't try to hide my coarser breath as I headed for the shadows beneath her skirt.

"Stone." Her protest was a sparse rasp. "I don't think—"

"Why are you still thinking?"

"Because one of us has to!"

I paused my finger's journey. We both lifted gazes again, letting them tangle in silent questions...wordless need.

"Tell me you want me to stop. Tell me and mean it, Claire, and I will. But I don't think you can. I don't think you want to."

"It's not a matter of what I want, damn it." She swallowed and huffed. "It's a matter of what I've fought for."

"You don't think I understand that?" Of course she didn't. She had no clue what I'd done to be sitting in this office today, guiding Stone Global from the office with the door that once bore the name *Josiah Stone*. No one in the world knew. And they never would.

She stiffened and jerked her knee away. "You're kidding, right? How the hell can you understand anything about me? About what's at stake for me here?"

I pulled away as well—and hated that the action came easily. "Wow. You're absolutely right. I'm Killian fucking Stone, which means I was born at the end of the most beautiful rainbow on earth and then spoon-fed milk and honey by angels in see-through gowns who rode on unicorns that barfed thousand-dollar bills. I haven't had a moment of strife in my entire sun-kissed life. Being raised in a constant spotlight was the easiest damn thing in the world. Then growing up to assume responsibility for the livelihood of thousands? Hmmm. Hasn't exposed me to a second of pressure in my existence, either."

She swallowed again. Her chin trembled a little. *Damn it.* I'd made her chin shake. As if the broadside I'd dealt her in the meeting wasn't enough, I had to add a heaping scoop of asshole on top of her shit sundae. *Real smooth, Kil.*

"That— That's not what I meant, and you know it."

Her rasp, soft and brave, tore deeper at me. My psyche came to a crossroads of reactions. One of those paths led to kissing her. Hard.

I picked the easier road. Raw rage.

"Then what the hell *do* you mean?"

She gasped as I reared up, yanking on both arms of her chair to position her directly under me. Her blouse was stretched tight by her pumping lungs, its pink shade matching the most vulnerable part of her inner lips. She was fucking breathtaking. One small click over from my fury laid my lust, pounding at my inner thighs, more than ready to take over my better judgment. Just one tick of permission from my mind and I could lift her, trapping her lips and her body and her will beneath mine...

Back off. I let my anger whip my body into compliance.

"We both know the answer to that." She jabbed her chin up. "This is bigger, *much* bigger, than your kinky angels and puking unicorns, Mr. Stone."

Her sneering emphasis on the last two syllables was a good thing and a bad thing, feeding my rage even more. "Not an answer to the damn question."

"The hell it isn't. Or was I right when I first walked in here? Are you really that inept at putting two sensible thoughts together?"

"And are you that inept at addressing a direct inquiry?" I gripped the chair tighter. Loomed closer over her. Plunged my glare into her face.

"I'm adept enough to tell you to back off, Stone. Now."

I didn't move. She didn't either. Her sable lashes flashed wider, unleashing the twin flames of her gaze back at me. I almost relented my stance. I didn't expect how fury could change her gaze so quickly and then skewer my gut with equal speed. The brilliance in her amber irises intensified by a thousand, screaming at my senses to get lost in them—and my cock to be possessed by them. For one amazing second, I let myself feel all of it. The feeling was euphoric. Catastrophic. And agonizing. Clothes—mine *and* hers—had never seemed like straitjackets before.

"That's really what you want?"

"Yes." Though it was a small whisper, she maintained the regal hold of her head. "Yes, it's what I want."

Though I already hovered less than a foot over her, I lowered a few more inches. Her face consumed my view. Her scent filled my head. In just twenty-four hours, her essence had sneaked beneath my constant, careful armor. I adored her for it. I hated her for it.

"For the record, I don't tolerate dishonesty from my employees, Claire." Against every screaming protest from my mind, I dipped my scrutiny to her lips. "In any form."

She tried to press deeper into the chair. "Are you calling me a liar?"

I let one side of my mouth twitch. "That's an answer only you can provide."

She sucked in a ragged breath. "Mr. Stone..."

"Yes."

"Leave me the hell alone."

She clutched her thighs, her hands still nowhere near *my* body. I pushed away as if she'd sucker-punched me.

She might as well have.

I wheeled away, surprised I didn't drip blood in the doing. A brutal voice resonated through me about how this was for the best. If she'd gotten this far under my skin in a day, what kind of destruction could she bring in the months ahead?

My fury told the voice to go fuck itself.

I backed away as she rose from the chair, looking wobbly yet beautiful as a newborn fawn. Satisfaction merged with frustration in my chest. Even if she denied it a million more times, the woman's body all but proclaimed its awareness of our attraction.

"Miss Montgomery?"

She came to a stiff stop in her retreat from the room. Without turning, she snapped, "What?"

"Be careful what you wish for."

★ ★ ★ ★

Hours later, ensconced in my condo office with my fourth glass of Scotch in one hand and my second contract in the other, I fought to remember that moment with the same fervor I used to forget it.

Officially, I'd won the skirmish. Had the last word. Sent *her* fleeing from *my* office, looking flustered as hell about it on the way. *Down she goes. Kill Shot lands the point.*

Some goddamn victory.

Why the mope, Kil? Wait. I remember. She came to you expressing frustration and concern, and you returned the favor by coming on so strong she bolted from the room. Considering you were ten seconds away from plunging your tongue down her throat and your hand into her blouse, she did you a massive favor, shithead.

Which blew apart my justification for the alcohol stupor. *Fuck.*

Hope flared. There was a flaw in that logic, something circling back to the fact that I remembered this afternoon at all. Right. That was it. I wasn't plowed enough.

Another long swig of the Glenlivet slid down with a harsh burn. The contract's words swam in my vision.

"What the fuck are you doing?"

I blurted it aloud. Well, thought I did. At least my tongue was hopping on board the train to oblivion. As for my gut? It still listened to my mind, which answered the question with vicious clarity.

What the fuck *was* I doing? Nothing. Not a goddamn thing because it had already been done. The damage was complete. I'd cauterized Claire Montgomery, relegating her to the bin she should've remained in from the start. She was a vendor. Brilliant, beautiful, and focused about her work, yes— but anything more than that, no.

It's better this way. You're safer. Stronger.

Why did I sense she said the same thing to herself tonight?

Why had I stared into her eyes this afternoon, detecting the fires there that concealed their own secrets?

Why did I feel her fear of me, of *us*, as something that extended beyond trepidation about sleeping with the boss?

"Claire." I etched her name on the air in a croak. Even in my trashed state, her name sounded like a poem from magical realms. "What are you keeping from me, fairy queen?"

The invocation was all it took to conjure her in my mind's eye. *So stunning...she still wore that cute gray suit but had taken her hair down, letting it tumble in deep-copper waves around her heart-shaped face. A Mona Lisa smile played on her lips.*

You'll never know, Killian Stone. You'll never know.

With a groan, I slammed my empty glass to the desk. Before I turned my chair to face the window, I shut off the desk lamp. The darkness consuming the room, along with the wind howling past the windows, should've eased the heat in my body. Fat fucking chance. I tore off my T-shirt, letting it fall to the floor as I watched the strands of car lights, white and red, along both sides of Lakeshore Drive. They turned into wet splotches as rain began to mix with the gusts.

In my mind, the two of us were in one of those cars.

We were wearing trenches against the rain. Beneath our coats, we were naked.

My head fell back as the fantasy took over.

"Tell me your secrets, Claire...and I'll tell you mine."

"Never, Killian. Ever."

I kissed her to silence her. Slid my hand inside her cloak to thumb one of her nipples and then the other. As she mewled against my lips, her flesh puckered beneath my fingers. Her skin was silken and soft, except for the stiff nubs that turned harder for me by the second...

My groan sliced the stillness of the office. I chopped it short by clenching my teeth—and reaching beneath my sweats. As my fingers reached the moisture at the head of my cock, I laid my dream Claire back on the car seat. *My free hand slid between her thighs. She gasped, arching into my touch.* My dick swelled against my fingers. "Yesssss," I hissed. *Her body was hot and wet and ready, slicking my skin, enticing me to delve deeper...*

"Killian!"

"Sssshhh, my queen. This is just the beginning."

"Of— Of what?"

"Your pleasure. At the mercy of my hands...and my mouth."

"Ohhhh...God..."

"Spread yourself for me. Let me into your pussy, sweet Claire."

Her sigh filled my head as my grunt mixed with the howls of the storm. With a feverish jerk, I pulled my erection out of my sweats. My cock throbbed against my hand, veins distended, skin taut, blood pounding. I stroked myself with a mix of relief and anger, thankful to give in to my lust, furious it had to be like this.

I slid my tongue through her slick pink folds, lowering my head to reach deeper. I could almost taste her now, tangy and rich and perfect...

"Ohhh, Killian..."

She grabbed my hair. I pushed on her thighs, spreading her wider. She hooked one ankle over the top of the car seat. The other, she wrapped around my back. I ran my hands along her inner thighs until I got to her ankles, shoving off her heels so I could explore the contours of her feet. Moving back to the middle of her body, I tugged at the tie on her overcoat, fully exposing her.

In the dark office, I pumped harder at my cock. My precome was distributed everywhere now, even trickling along my balls. They throbbed an encouraging refrain in return. *Soon. Soon. Soon.*

In the back seat of my dream car, the city lights flowed across Claire's perfect body. She was aqua then pink then orange, my carnal queen, my private fairy to be fucked. Alfred buzzed on the intercom, asking if there was anywhere we wanted to go before returning to the condo. I slammed on the Return button, issuing two terse words in response. "Yes. Canada."

The wind whipped harder. The rain began pelting the office window. I pumped harder at my erection, all the while clenching my thighs. *Not yet.* I didn't want to let it go. Not before the best part of the fantasy.

"Killian. I need you inside me. Please...please!"

Thank fuck the best part wasn't far off.

"Take the condom, Claire. I want to watch you roll it on me."

The perfect smile on her lips as she took the rubber. The perfect pressure of her fingers with every inch she sheathed me. The perfect angle of her hips, offered so sweetly to me.

The pure, perfect paradise of her body.

"Claire." I rasped it aloud, needing at least a part of the dream to be real. "Dear God, Claire. Your pussy is pure heaven."

"Can you fuck me deeper? Please. Oh, please..."

I thrust my hips, ramming my flesh ruthlessly through my fingers. I rocked my head back as I imagined hers doing the same thing in the car, her breasts jutting up, her bare body a brazen offering to me.

"Killian! I'm...it's..."

"I know. I know."

And I did. With blinding, blazing heat that rocketed up my shaft and burst from me in a thick torrent, saving me and damning me in the same cataclysm of sensation.

Because now my fantasy fairy smiled up at me with idyllic acceptance, cupping my face, pulling me close for a soft kiss, lulling me into the spell of her adoration.

"It's all right, Killian. You can tell me anything. You know I'll keep it all safe for you."

"No." I knew my lips had formed the sound, but it seemed a part of the dream now too. "No," I repeated, "you won't keep it safe. In the end, nobody will."

None of that felt real either. But I'd said it, hadn't I? I'd felt it, right?

I dragged my head up but then laughed. Did I expect the blackness beyond the windows to render answers? Or the shadows in *here*? Between the Scotch dulling my mind and the orgasm draining my body, the answer to that was a blur. Which turned this darkness into my new best friend.

Who the fuck was I kidding? The shadows had been my closest companions for years. Nearly twenty-three of them, to be exact—since the day Josiah and Willa Stone had signed the papers, including my damn birth certificate, to falsify me as their son. The week after that, they'd bought out half the Navy Pier for my fifth birthday party.

And my life of lies had begun.

But tonight, just this once, I'd speak the truth to my friends...and to my dream lover. They'd hear my secret, and when they vanished in the morning, my lie would be safe again.

I inhaled. Exhaled.

Then spoke.

"My name is Killian Aidan James Klarke. I'm the son of Nolan and Damrys Klarke, and I swear that I'll never forget it—as long as I live."

CHAPTER SIX

Claire

"Hi, Daddy."

I waited for his tender greeting to wrap me in its embrace. The day had been impossibly long, and I really wanted to hear the familiar cadence of his voice.

No. Not wanted. Needed.

"There's my li'l Claire bear." I sensed his smile through the phone line. Remnants of his Irish brogue slipped through when he spoke with affection. Picturing the laugh lines around his mouth along with the twinkles in his dark-green eyes made me tear up as I leaned back in the conference-room chair. As usual, the rest of the team had left for the day.

"Yeah," I replied softly. "Here I am. Still in the Windy City. Yay, me."

"Hmmm."

Uh-oh.

His response had *that* ring to it. The I'm-looking-into-your-soul-and-reading-it-like-a-book ring. But his tone was still as comforting as hot cocoa as he went on. "Why don't you just get it out, honey?"

I sighed, the verbal version of rolling my eyes. "Get what out?"

"Come, now. Tell me what's going on, and don't toss me

off with *it's fine*, because I see right through you. Besides, my big-shot daughter never just calls to say hi to her boring old dad anymore."

Ouch.

The arrow to my heart couldn't have taken a more direct path. Or carried more painful debris in its path in the process.

We'd been in Chicago for three weeks—that felt like three months. My nerves were frazzled, my sleep patterns shot, and even my fingernails, once the object of Killian's admiration for their sleek creativity, had half the color picked off. I gave them a forlorn stare while attempting *another* self-therapy session, hoping the outcome would be different this time. That my pretense would prove true, and my stress really could be written off to all the pressure on the team.

Riiiggght.

The retort belonged to the mocking little voice inside my head. Even she was fed up with my crap.

It was time to come clean. To admit that my anxiety had nothing to do with Trey Stone and everything to do with his brother.

Who sure as hell was a man of his word. To excruciating detail.

Be careful what you wish for.

My mandate in his office on that stormy afternoon? The one about backing the hell off? In twenty-one days, he'd honored it to the letter—while also finding every way possible to violate it. I was plunged into a crazy science-fiction universe where nothing was as it seemed, especially him. He was SGC's personal Loki, shape-shifting at will, controlling my emotions with the whims that accompanied each new face.

Would I encounter the CEO who matched his last name,

hard and cold, seeing me as nothing but another subcontracted employee? Or would I be inexplicably drawn to stop in the middle of a task, turning to discover his shadowed stare waiting for me? Or perhaps he was in the mood to toy with me asshole-style, demanding a news release be rewritten for the fiftieth time—before disappearing from the office for fifteen inexplicable minutes, only to return and set my favorite coffee drink in front of me. There were more examples than that, a growing pile of memories of the man who'd decided to make himself my bad cop and good cop, my shark and my dolphin—and yes, my Loki and my Thor.

Except he was a hundred times more sinful than Loki and a thousand times better than Thor in the god-come-to-Earth department. As if my dread about Margaux and her blackmail ax, aimed at my neck in constant little reminders from the woman herself, didn't fit the bill for my anxiety quotient on their own.

What the hell *had* I wished for?

I offered a dismissive laugh. "Nothing's wrong, Dad. I'm just tired. We've really got a mess on our hands this time. The strategy we're using for the project is unconventional too. Exciting but unconventional."

"Yes," he replied, "Andrea told me a little about it. I know her new approach means you're all working harder, but I also told her that I support the idea. A positive campaign will make your boy a winner, not just a survivor. Remember, honey, in the end, the rainbow wins over the gloom."

"*Her* approach, huh?" Gritting my teeth around a smile, I forced out, "Sure. Winners. Rainbows. You're right, Dad."

"Of course I am." He added a self-deprecating chuckle. I didn't echo the sound.

"Dad, I don't want to talk about...all this." I waved my hand in the air as if he could see me. "I called to see how *you're* doing. Distract me." I didn't hide the desperation from my final word. "Please."

I kicked off my heels and put my feet up on the neighboring chair while he launched into a narrative about his latest bid, a terrace in the garden at one of my favorite wineries back home. His tender brogue was a natural balm on my nerves, exactly what I needed. With a grateful sigh, I worked the bobby pins loose from my updo, welcoming the smell of lavender shampoo from my unfurling hair. I closed my eyes and smiled. This was exactly what I needed, listening to Dad go on about climbing roses, coastal sage, salvias, grasses...

As I injected coos of interest in the right places, I ran my fingers through my hair again, letting my mind drift. And my fantasies.

How different would it feel if Killian tousled my hair instead? Then let his touch travel to other places...

Chills ran through my whole body, followed by a wave of intense heat...pooling between my thighs. In my mind, his fingers coasted down my neck. Along my collarbones. Then lower, sliding beneath my blouse and then my bra as his ink-dark gaze penetrated mine...

Oh, God.

I shivered again. And forced myself to a hateful admission. These feelings had become much too synonymous with Stone. They needed to stop, period. Right now would be a good time. I was on the phone with my *father*.

I forced my attention back to Dad—though all too fast, my mind wandered back to the one man who truly held me prisoner. His force field of presence. His intensity of attention.

His fusion of strength, beauty, grace, and power—of never touching me once while invading every free thought in my head.

Who—*what*—the hell was Killian Stone that he kept me shackled in this needy cage?

"Claire?"

"Hmm? What?" I shook my head, fighting to rid it of images of Killian with shackles in hand, approaching me with the devil's glint in his eyes. "Sorry, Dad. I zoned out."

"It's fine, honey. I'll let you go. I know you have work to do. It was so good to hear your voice, though. Call me again soon, okay?"

"I will. I promise." I hated how the words cracked with emotion. I was ashamed to feel this unsteady, though I recognized it as another clear sign of how my common-sense radar was blown to hell.

"Claire?"

"Yeah, Dad?"

"You're still my lucky little garden fairy. You know that, right?"

I spewed a watery giggle before telling Dad how much I loved him, at least *one* feeling I could completely trust. But after ending the call, a golf ball still stuck in my throat. Was it from Dad bringing up Andrea, the Ice Queen of the Western World? Or the special memories he'd evoked of Mom? Or was it option number three...that every time I had a spare moment of sanity to call my own, a dark-eyed god in a custom-fitted suit strode in to override it?

My breath spilled out, shaking on a sob. "Damn it!" I choked. "Stop!"

Great. Now I spouted orders as if the thin air would

manifest Killian. Like that would do any good. He'd just glower and tell me to hold still while he pinned me in a chair and rendered me motionless or whipped up his shiny town car for my next ride.

I swept my printouts into a heap and shoved them into my briefcase. My coffee—from the cafeteria this time, since Stone had been in a meeting with SGC Asia all afternoon—was untouched. I ditched it and my uneaten protein bar in the trash, packing up the rest of my crap in record time.

I had to get out of here. Now. I needed fresh air. A lot of it. Confusion stormed my mind. I struggled for breath, certain I was suffocating. My cheeks burned, yet my palms were cold and clammy. I'd grabbed a bottle of water on my way out and cracked it open in the elevator during the descent to the lobby but quickly changed my mind. I wasn't thirsty at all.

What the hell?

I wasn't sure what a panic attack felt like, but this had to come close. I didn't have the time or desire to sit and run a Google pass at the subject, either.

Only one path made sense. *Outside.* I needed to be free from this building, where everything I saw, everything I touched, reminded me of Killian. The onyx marble floor was the exact shade of his eyes. It was newly polished, gleaming like his irises when he plunged into deep thought. All the architecture educed his body, sculpted into graceful, towering lines. The paneled walls were like his skin, hard and dark and smooth, begging me to touch...so I did. I skimmed the perfect surface with one hand, tracing the grooves in the wood, imagining they were the contours of his skin instead...

I dropped my hand while emerging into the well-lit lobby. My face flamed again, embarrassment now the cause. I dipped my head and hunched my shoulders, shoving at the large, brass-encased pane rather than waiting for the doorman.

Have to get away.

I didn't look back. If I did, there'd even be something about that damn door that evoked Killian, ready to mock me.

Have to get away.

I was in uncharted emotional territory but certain this was the approach to a meltdown. I had to escape. The floors, the walls, the pillars, the building. *His* building. Watching me. Caging me. Taunting me.

Have to get away!

"Good evening, Miss Montgomery."

I jumped as a hand descended to my shoulder. All of SGC's doormen had come to know us all from our daily comings and goings. "H-Hi, Walter."

"Hang tight just a moment. I'll have the car brought up."

"*No.*" I battled to summon a smile. "Thanks, but not tonight."

"You trying to get me fired? You know what Mr. Stone says about you going home unescorted."

Shit. He had to go and do it. Speak the man's name aloud. Call to life every reason, from Margaux's blackmail to my own churning heart, why I could hardly call any breath my own anymore.

The golf ball in my throat gave way to a hunk of glass-covered granite. Tears pushed at the backs of my eyes.

"I'm all right." The waterworks broke through as I yelled it over my shoulder, racing down the stairs to the sidewalk. "Good night, Walter!"

Out on the street, I quickly blended in with the crowd, grateful as hell for every drop in the human ocean. I fell in step with the late commuters and started walking toward our hotel, setting my mind on recovering my clarity and self-control, hoping lucidity wouldn't be too far behind. In, out. In, out. I filled my lungs with each breath, inserting a mental *chill, brah* after each cycle. Chad would've been proud.

I resolved to have a balanced dinner at the hotel and then focus on sleeping well tonight. I was worn down, and this unnatural thing for Killian had made it worse. I'd just stared into a horrible darkness and never wanted to revisit that place again.

I was done with Killian Jamison Stone.

Officially, completely, agonizingly done.

The bustle of the city boosted my confidence. Lively music played from street-level shops. Savory food aromas, representing cultures from across the globe, wafted out from eateries. People around me laughed and swore and yelled. Car horns blasted as traffic rules were bent and broken.

I kept walking, determined to keep my promise. I smiled at a little boy holding an Elmo plush in one hand, his mom's hand in the other. Took a deep breath of curry-infused air, deciding Indian might be good for dinner.

This was good. Two minutes in. I was doing all right. I could do this. He-who-wouldn't-be-thought-of remained that way.

I kept walking. Even as a sleek town car swooped to the curb.

A pair of sharp honks cut the air. The town car's driver had cut off two cars. Their drivers followed with a couple of impressive flip-offs. The town car remained still and impervious, now flashing its hazards, a high-class version of the flip-off. Making nice was definitely not part of that driver's mission.

I would've laughed at the whole scenario, except for the panic that rushed back in the space of three seconds.

The moments it took for me to focus on the vehicle's damn license plate.

"No," I snarled beneath my breath.

Had my blissful bubble been too thick to notice it? Clearly, the answer was yes. Clearly, it didn't have to matter. I could just keep walking. *Yes.* I'd already vowed not to be this man's puppet. I couldn't return to that alarm, that suffocation, that aching, awful need that I'd felt three blocks before, in the heart of the Stone empire's castle. Forget it. This time, if the man wanted to threaten sending me back to San Diego, he could do just that.

The town car's back door flung open. Sure enough, Killian Stone unfolded onto the sidewalk. Charcoal suit. Crimson tie. Endless limbs. Proud stance. Penetrating gaze.

Glorious.

Damn it.

I stopped walking. So did over half the women on the sidewalk. Heat curled through me all over again, this time with a not-so-nice possessive streak. What the *hell?*

He gave me one stare. One. Then simply stood with the car door open.

I rigidly stood my ground. *I was not going to do this.* My vow was only ten minutes old, and now fate wanted me to climb into a confined space with that man?

That mind-blowing, thought-stealing, logic-altering man...

Who tilted his head to one side, silently ordering me in.

Chicago whirled and bustled around us. Couldn't they

see the ground tilting beneath me, the sky careening, my world shifting?

He walked toward me. Correction—prowled toward me. My eyes widened. With what? Fear?

No.

Arousal?

Nailed it.

He was sexual prowess on two legs. It was both rapture and torture to watch him. As he strode closer, I found myself hypnotized by the flexes of his thighs alone. I tried stepping back, but the crowd trapped me now. A couple of pedestrians bumped me, swearing as they passed. That didn't ease Killian's tension level.

"Claire." His voice was a harsh warning.

I battled to ignore him, whipping my head side to side, but my pounding heart led my gaze back to him. Marvelous. Our cat-and-mouse act had me so jacked up I didn't know whether to stay or run—a perfect summation of the last three weeks.

Men on the street stopped with their women now, mere feet from where I'd obviously grown roots. Many pointed and whispered as they recognized Killian.

"*Claire.*" He used a stricter tone.

"What?" So did I.

A pulse throbbed in his jaw. He took a long breath before walking over and gently pulling on my elbow. When he spoke again, his voice was only loud enough for my ears. "Beautiful fairy...come get in the car."

Wisely, he followed it with a nervous glance. In the end, I didn't care. I jerked away and slammed my glare to his face. "You do *not* get to call me that. *Ever.* Are we clear, Mr. Stone?"

His features hardened to the texture of the sidewalk

again. The effect wasn't softened by the single chunk of black hair that the wind pushed across his forehead. "Get in the car, and we'll discuss—"

"No. We won't discuss. There's nothing to debate except for the fact that I'd rather walk five miles in these"—I stabbed a finger at my four-inch Manolo Blahnik peep-toes—"than get in that car with you."

"*Claire.*" His eyes turned the color of hurricanes. "Damn it!"

"What the hell are you doing, anyway? Stalking me?"

"I arrived at the lobby right after you," he growled. "Walter mentioned that you were crying, so—"

"I wasn't crying."

"The hell you weren't."

"I *wasn't* crying."

He brought a finger beneath my chin. Given the brutality of his tone, his tender tug was a surprise.

Once my face was high, his dark stare awaited mine. Hell. His eyes pulled me apart from the inside out. I swallowed as he shifted closer, consuming the last space between us. A sizeable crowd had collected, and thankfully one of us had the sense to squash the dramatics. He leaned in so his lips brushed against my ear.

"Get in the car, Claire, or you'll be cleaning up your own mess by morning. I'm not here to hurt. I'm here to help. What part am *I* not making clear?"

He backed away by a steady step and then another. God, he was gorgeous.

He was also right.

More stupefied than ever, I finally relented. Before I climbed in with my purse, I let him stow my briefcase in the trunk.

Silence stretched as the car moved into traffic again. That was just fabulous by me. I never communicated well when I was furious, and despite his attempt at playing gentleman on the street, anger percolated in my blood. I crossed my arms and looked out of the window, unable to fully pick apart the feeling. Was I more pissed at his high-handed move or that it had instantly turned me on?

"You never should've—"

"What the hell were you—?"

We fired our attacks at the same time. Killian swept out a hand, palm up. "Ladies first."

Self-righteous bastard.

"By all means," I crooned, "after you. That's what you're used to, right?"

He blew out a harsh breath. The gravel beneath his reply was just as stark. "Miss Montgomery, I'm so far out of familiar territory with you it scares the hell out of me."

I forced myself to peer out of the window again. His words were as beautiful and riveting as his face.

I couldn't fall prey to either.

It had been less than an hour since my phone conversation with my dad. The pride in his voice still warmed my soul. How proud would he still be of a daughter he had to visit in jail once a month? And what would Killian do if he found out? Player or not—and the more I researched him, the more I was convinced of the latter—the man wouldn't think twice about cutting ties to another potential scandal for his family.

About cutting me.

I twisted my arms again, battling the tightness in my throat, the exhaustion in my body, and the turmoil in my mind.

I lost the skirmish. Everything piled up in one awful moment. Tears welled, traitorous and hot, threatening to spill down my cheeks. I gritted my teeth against the attack.

I felt the padded leather dip as he slid closer, making me plaster myself to the wall of the car. His starched handkerchief came into my vision. I wordlessly accepted it.

Embarrassment surged. If anyone on the street had caught my behavior on a cell phone, he and I would be all over the internet in fifteen minutes. Had I thought about that at all? Of course not. Because when this man zeroed all his attention on me, I couldn't function beyond the depth of a *Barney the Dinosaur* special. "I'm— I'm sorry," I stammered, "for the drama-queen antics. The ambush? *Still* not okay. But neither was my stab at Sarah Bernhardt'ing the reaction." It killed me to finish. "If— if you want to release me from the team, it's okay."

He took my hand in his. "No."

I dared a glance at him. "No?"

"No, I'm not letting you go." His grip tightened a little. If it was possible, his gaze darkened. "Because I'm just as sorry."

"Huh?"

I raised my face to study him more intently. A smile tugged his lips. I stared harder. I'd never seen such a change in him before. It was as if a soft-focus filter had gotten thrown over our interaction. The whole effect made me woozy, without the pleasure of the wine beforehand. I would've felt cheated, except the new look transformed him, Mr. Darcy-style, from brooding and stunning into approachable...and remarkable.

"Finally," he murmured, "you'll look at me."

My mouth remained open. "I'm trying to figure out why you're apologizing."

He brought his other hand up so he could flatten mine, engulfing my fingers between his long, strong ones. Despite his confident hold, his smile descended into a subtle grimace. "You were right. About the nickname. Using it on you was out of line. You weren't the only one working through a little tension out on the sidewalk." He took a deep breath through my stunned silence. *He'd* been stressed back there too? "When Walter told me you'd been crying, all I could think about were those tears blurring your vision while you tried tromping down the street in those heels, and—"

"I don't *tromp*."

"But you did share that story about your mother with me. I treasured that night, Claire. Every moment of it. You trusted me with that information, with your secrets. I don't take that kind of trust lightly." His head dipped a little. "I sure as hell never meant to abuse it."

I had no idea what to say. How to react. My mystification became utter shock as he opened his grip, exposing my hand before lifting it to his mouth. As he touched his lips to my knuckles, I shivered beneath waves of both hot and cold. He lingered over my flesh, his plea for forgiveness turning into an urgent appeal for more.

I yanked my hand back into my lap.

Who was this guy, and what had he done with the controlling son of a bitch who normally occupied Killian Stone's skin? My brow bunched. Black, white. On again, off again. Loki and then Thor. This game was worse than any I'd ever had to play with the media, the most capricious gang of double-talkers in the universe. I couldn't do it anymore. Not with him. Not when my heart was the damn playing field.

I was throwing in the towel. In this case, the handkerchief.

I flung the white square while crawling forward to knock on the divider between us and the driver.

"Please pull over and let me out," I called.

"Damn it, Claire. Stop!"

"No, Killian. *You* stop." My temper, in all its blazing Irish glory, was ready for this shit now. "What part of *stop* do you just *not* get?"

His fist wadded into the handkerchief. He glared back with eyes that actually flashed at me, onyx ignited. "What the fuck are you—"

"Exactly. You have no damn idea what I'm talking about, do you?" I crumpled to the floor of the car, my knees beneath me. "I want off your crazy ride, Stone." My voice broke, and I didn't care. "Please, *please* don't tell me you're lost about this, because you're not. For the last three weeks, you've taken me to the strangest carnival of my life. Every day, sometimes every *hour*, is a different damn experience. Every time I turn a corner, I never know what to prepare for—and whether I'll be racing to get in line for another spin or dashing to the trash barrel to barf my guts out."

His jaw tensed. The glints in his eyes got sharper. "And it's all my fault?"

"No," I admitted. "It's not all your fault. I'm the one tied into the big, screwy knot, after all."

"Why?"

"You don't see?" I answered his silent scowl by throwing up my hands. "You really *don't* see how I have to bust my ass to prove myself on this team? That even though I was hired for my talent and *not* my dad, everyone now assumes I'll free-skate because he's engaged to the boss? And gee, get this—I'm this weirdo who thinks my dad should have happiness now, after sacrificing so much for his only daughter. I think that if he wants to be in love with Andrea Asher, Lord help him, that he should have that gift, even if it means I've got to work three times harder than everyone else."

"I do see that," he stated.

"All right, then *listen* to this. What I *haven't* needed in this house of mirrors is the extra sugar high. Do you get that? I'm having enough trouble keeping my balance without the extra temptation of lust and fantasies, courtesy of the man at the top of the food chain. Thanks to you, I don't know whether I'm coming or going, backward or forward—"

I interrupted myself with a huff as a wolfish smile spread across his face. What was the man up to now?

"Lust?" he drawled. "And fantasies?"

I dropped my head into my hands. "Why is this car still *moving*? Goddamnit, Killian, let me out, or I'll call nine-one-one and tell them I'm being held against my will."

I yanked out my phone and swiped the screen.

Killian pulled it from my grip and slipped it to the ledge behind his head.

In its place, he gave me a perfectly chilled glass of chardonnay.

I fought against the temptation by fuming harder. "This is *not* letting me out."

"Traffic is heavy. We can't just pull over. Calm down and take a sip. Being this upset isn't good for you—or me."

I hated waving goodbye to the kinder, gentler Killian, but at least I knew *this* arrogant bastard. "Thanks for the advice, Daddy."

He barely flinched. "You have a father, Claire. I'm not him."

Ahhh. No flinch because he saved all the bark for his voice. I'd earned the wrath this time, so I took a sip of wine as an olive branch. I recognized the flavor the moment it crossed my lips, but I didn't want to let on. It was one of my favorite vintages from one of the wineries in Temecula. Did the man normally have the car stocked with Temecula wine, or was this a recent thing...as in the last three weeks?

It was best I didn't know that answer. It was *really* best I didn't drink any more or let the vintage's buttery warmth slide deeper through my veins. I wanted—needed—to stay pissed at him. Damn. Why did he do this to me? Press all my buttons at once?

I reverted to habit. Closed my eyes and began counting backward from ten.

"What are you doing?" Killian's voice was soft.

"Trying to calm down."

I kept counting. *Four. Three. Two. One.* When I opened my eyes, it was to see him shucking his Armani jacket before settling back in front of me.

"Did it work?"

"Did what work?" I snapped.

"Are you calmed down?" A smile spread across his lips. *Crap.* It was *that* smile, the one Lucifer himself had taught the man. He loosened his tie, another move that screamed *player*, but my libido refused to see or hear all the warning signs. She was too busy harmonizing with the devil behind his smirk. Traitorous bitch.

I set my wine back in the car's holder and slammed my hands against both my thighs, trying to ignore that I was on my knees, on the floor of the Stone Global town car, at the feet of the company's chiseled demigod of a CEO—and fighting to ignore the obsidian depths of his stare, alive with every sinful possibility for the situation.

I clashed with myself, as well. Because my mind flared with all the same scenarios.

"Damn it." I balled my fists. "What the hell is going on here, Stone?"

He stroked his chin with one graceful, beautiful finger. "That question's only as complicated as you make it, Miss Montgomery."

His diplomacy smoothed me out a little more. I welcomed the chance to take a deep breath. "Okay. I think we need to put all our cards on the table."

"About what?"

"You *know* what. This. Us. Whatever this all is or isn't. I just want the truth so I can get off this Tilt-A-Whirl and stop making an ass out of myself on a daily basis."

He slipped that mesmerizing finger to his lips. "I agree."

I took another long breath. "Okay, good."

"Yes. Let's get you off that Tilt-A-Whirl." He didn't move only his finger this time. He shifted his whole body, forward and down, until I found myself surrounded by him, bracketed by his arms, thighs pressed by his, breath mingling with his. Killian Stone was on his knees now, crouching over me like a panther who'd found prey. "Or perhaps," he murmured, "I'll just jump on with you."

So much for smoothing out. "Is that so?" I managed. "You may not like this ride, Stone. It's rough. The safety belts break. You could fall. *We* could fall."

"We won't fall." His lips firmed and his jaw tautened, telling me he comprehended the allegory as deeply as I did. "I won't let that happen." I opened my mouth, hoping words of protest would come to it, only to be silenced by his fervent, perfect whisper. "Claire...sweet Claire." He lifted a hand to my face, using that same long finger along my cheekbone. "You utterly fascinate me. You're genuine and pure, funny and honest...and your layers intrigue me. *All* of them."

Through some miracle, I found enough breath for a reply. "A-All of them?"

While nodding, he pressed his forehead to mine. "Fuck, yes."

"Wh-What do you mean?" Oh, his whispers. His strength. His scent. His desire. He flooded me in all of them, and I gladly gave into the drowning.

"I want you. I've fantasized about having you. I've touched myself with the force of it. Is that what you want to hear? I've wrapped my fingers around my cock and pretended to be inside you instead. And when I came, it was your name on my lips."

"Oh." It was nothing but a breath. It was all I could manage.

"I want you in my bed, sweet Claire. I want to make love to you for hours on end, to feel your body wrapped around mine. I want to watch your face as you shatter beneath me, with *my* name on *your* lips too."

The car lurched forward again. Our heartbeats throbbed against each other. Our heavy breaths mingled.

"Is that enough cards on the table for you?" No kiss came after it, despite how every cell in my body longed for the contact. I sensed Killian waiting for the right words from me, perhaps the right *word*, period.

A simple *yes*.

I couldn't muster it. I was stunned silent. My senses whirled, processing what he'd said. My mind short circuited as

I pushed up and grabbed for my wine again, battling the urge to toss it back like a tequila shot instead.

The car slowed. I looked out of the window at the circular driveway of my hotel. Killian shifted away from me, also quiet. Within ten seconds, the air had transformed from thick and lusty to awkward and unsteady. I felt around for my phone, grateful when he reached back and then handed it over to me. Finally, I screwed together the courage to look up at him again, directly meeting his unblinking onyx gaze.

"Aren't you going to say something?" He could melt me with those eyes.

"I—I don't know what to say. I'm not sure I expected what you said. I think I'm a little overwhelmed."

He laughed. The sound was deep and oddly comforting. "Can I accept that as a good thing?"

I tried to join him on the chuckle but couldn't. He made everything sound so easy. So worldly. Sure, I'd traveled a lot of the world, but *being* a worldly person was really different. "I just don't see how it all fits."

"And I'm not standing here with a glass slipper, Claire."

The driver stopped at the main lobby door, but Killian directed him to proceed to the hotel's side entrance, where guests were dropped for formal events in the large ballroom beyond a pretty gold staircase. Fortunately, the entrance wasn't being heavily used tonight. After what had just happened on the sidewalk, the last thing we needed was more lookie-loos with high-resolution camera phones—or Margaux and Andrea during their all-too-regular visit to the lobby bar. When the vehicle stopped, Killian gave me another soft smile. "Maybe sleep will help us both. Perhaps it's simply time for good night."

When he exited the car with his trademark grace, I was

plummeted into silence again. He was really going to take the chivalrous route. Killian extended his hand into the open door as proof, open-palmed and ready to help me out. His grip was strong and sure, pulling me into a night that had obtained a biting wind. I was suddenly glad I hadn't walked all the way back—for a number of reasons.

"I'll see you tomorrow." He released my hand to brush a wild strand of hair behind my ear, though he burrowed his hand against my scalp for a few moments after that, locking it there. His stare pulled me in, dark and bottomless, black pools that entranced with a thousand textures at once. My heart lurched with the certainty that I was the substance of at least a few of them.

"Okay," I finally whispered. "Tomorrow."

Though I said it, I deliberately lingered until I visibly trembled.

Killian bracketed my shoulders with his big hands and gently turned me. "Go," he urged into my ear. "You're shivering. I'll wait until you've made it in."

"Who's bossy now?"

His chuckle followed me up to the door. Once there, I pivoted to see him leaning against the side of the town car, hands in his pockets, wind lifting his hair and plastering his shirt to his perfect V of a torso.

He was the most breathtaking man I had ever seen. And he was standing there, waiting and watching—me. Then lifting a little wave at me, almost dorky and sweetly sincere...

I returned the gesture, resisting the longing to run back and tackle him for that kiss my lips ached for. But it wasn't going to happen. I wasn't sure I'd be able to stop at the kiss. The rest of my body already thrummed at a higher frequency of need. My chest warmed, my heart danced, and my pulse sprinted from all the words we'd just exchanged.

He was right. He wasn't offering a glass slipper, a bed in the castle, or a happily-ever-after. At best, this would be a clandestine carriage ride, filled with stunning vistas, new adventures, and thrilling speeds. But it was getting harder and harder to say no to the invitation.

No one had to know. No one *could* know, especially Margaux and Andrea.

It would have to be enough. It *was* enough.

Because, God help me, I was falling hard for Killian Stone.

CHAPTER SEVEN

Killian

So this was what a kid felt like on Christmas morning.

After kicking everyone's ass at polo practice this morning, I quickly showered, shaved, slid some goop into my hair, and finger-combed it in the car on the way to the office, bypassing both the gym's salon and shoeshine station. For the first time in a long time, I grinned as the SGC building came into view. The place no longer seemed my prison. It was a portal to possibilities.

And the walls in which I'd see Claire again.

Going after her last night had been a knee-jerk action, driven solely by visions of her being blown down the street and into the lake by the wind that had been predicted for last night. Silly California girl. Her idea of a weather front was a drop of three degrees and a balmy breeze from the desert. But who was I to call her shit on being silly? I'd chased after her like a desperate boy before slapping my cards on her table in a gamble that had nearly ended with us horizontal and naked on the town car floor. The move had been pure impulse, total idiocy.

And sometimes, fortune favored the idiots. *Thank fuck.*

Despite the aches I'd felt in my cock afterward, I was glad we'd put the brakes on our bodies when the car had. Though horizontal and naked were still very much parts of my plan for Claire Montgomery today, it felt important to make things right. Had I forgotten she'd be returning to the other side of the country in less than ten weeks? Not for a second. Maybe that was the core of my reasoning. This wasn't going to be forever. So damn it, it had to be perfect.

I smiled at the conclusion, lips curling higher when remembering Alfred's knowing smirk as I instructed him to direct the housekeeping staff on making the changes to my bedroom. Egyptian cotton on the bed. White roses in the vases. Temecula Valley wine in the cooler. And yes, a few candles too. Pillars, not tapers. I wasn't the goddamn Phantom of the Opera.

My next instructions had gleaned Alfred's biggest smirk. After they finished with the bedroom, everyone could take the night off. He was included in the directive, though I doubted he'd collect. The only full day the man ever took off was Christmas, forced by my threats to look up his real name if he didn't. There was a time that I think he really expected me to believe his name was Alfred. I'd explained how I grew up in a North Shore mansion, not under a rock. We had a mutually sarcastic understanding about it all, unless it was Christmas Day. On the other three hundred and sixty-four days of the year, the man took great delight in mother-henning me to the point of reading my damn mind, a fact that irked the shit out of me on most occasions.

Today wasn't one of those times.

Today, the banks of the river could turn into a tsunami down Michigan Avenue and irked wouldn't enter my vocabulary.

It was Christmas. And my special present was just a few

steps away.

"Good morning, Britta." I slapped a palm to her desk after stepping off the elevator. "Fine day, hmm?"

The woman scrutinized me over the top of her sleek reading glasses, now dipped to the bridge of her aquiline nose. "It's twenty and looks like Mother Nature belted 'Let It Go' on the way to the L."

I glanced out of the window with a chuckle. "It's brisk. Refreshing."

She peered harder at me. "Is your hair still wet?"

I pawed my damp nape. "Maybe. A little."

She uttered something in Swedish and shook her head. "Somebody had a good evening. Maybe even a good morning."

I ignored her innuendo in favor of a glance toward the conference room. Just a glance. I'd thought about Claire's actions from last night on my way home—then in the shower, and again in bed—concluding that the discretion part of this thing was just as key for her as me. Of course, I didn't know the reasons why yet. That would change. I wanted to know all her secrets. And keep them all safe. Keep *her* safe.

"Who's in from Asher's team so far?"

I observed shadows through the conference room's frosted glass but couldn't discern their owners. The team usually arrived together in the company's service town car, so shadows were a good sign, though Claire was known to escape to the cafeteria for chats with our own media team. It felt good to think of my people rendering their stamp of approval on her. While the asshole in me decreed that their feedback shouldn't matter, the man in me took precedence for a moment. I'd hired those people because I valued their viewpoints. Observing their camaraderie with her imparted a fantastic high.

"They're not here yet," Britta supplied. "That's just the catering team. Ms. Asher told me they'd be working through the day spinning Trey's appearances from yesterday, so I took the liberty of ordering them some snacks."

I smiled through my disappointment. "Perfect. Good work."

After heading to my office, I closed the door and booted up my computer. An audible groan escaped when my email loaded, seeing the demand from SGC's Beijing office that I make an appearance to personally triage Trey's damage. Before I could even hit Send on my acquiescing reply, the door opened. Margaux Asher damn near flew into the room, leaving a fuming Britta behind in the hallway. She looked like a game show contestant who'd just won the big package with the car and the boat.

"Mr. Stone! I arrived to find brilliant-ness in my inbox this morning! I had to tell you personally, before anyone else!"

"Of course," I grumbled.

If I had an explanation, which I didn't, Margaux cut it short anyway—by trying a move that was half hug, half long jump. As she plastered onto me, she gushed, "Oprah's agreed to the interview—and *People* wants to do a four-page spread during the same week! Isn't it exc—" Her hold slackened a little.

Somebody cleared their throat in the doorway. I raised my head, readying a pleading stare for Britta.

"Shit," I blurted.

It wasn't Britta.

The shock in Claire's eyes stabbed me like a hundred shards of glass. But it was the pain she added after that, when recognizing Margaux as the human barnacle on me, that hurt worse. *Fuck*. Much worse.

"I—I have the demographic feedback from yesterday." She rasped it while throwing her gaze to the floor.

My chest imploded on top of my ribs. "*Claire*."

During the two seconds it took for her to throw the report on the table, she didn't look at me. Ditto for the two seconds it took for her to whirl and start to leave the room.

Margaux wrapped her arms around my neck and stared up into my face. "Leave her be. She's a little...socially awkward. I, on the other hand, am not." She added a grind of her hips.

"Oh, for Christ's sake." Although Claire mumbled the words, her reaction stunned Margaux enough to loosen her hold. I didn't need another moment to seize the opportunity. After grabbing her wrists and shoving her away, I left the office at a run.

"*Claire!*"

I easily caught her in the hallway. The verb was appropriate. I had to snatch her elbow to halt her frantic retreat from my door.

"Let go." She issued the order from tight teeth.

"Sure thing. I'd be happy to keep you here through other means."

The way I smashed the emphasis on *other* made her stop, whirl, and slam her arms over her chest. "I'm not your anything, Killian. I think that's been made clear enough now."

"Why are you whispering?" I guided her over so the wall cushioned us on one side. "There was nothing going on in there to whisper about."

Her gaze swirled over my face before she spurted a laugh. "Okay. If that's what you believe."

An unfamiliar sensation tugged at my gut. It hurt.

Recollections came to mind of Trey and Lance pulling pranks during our lunch breaks at Triton. Every time, they found a way to make it look like my fault. Mr. Nayed, a fan of medieval torture methods, was Triton Academy's detention master.

I *was not* taking the fall for this.

"Okay, I know what it looked like—"

"What it looked like was none of my business." She followed it with a tired sigh. I looked down into her face, noticing she *looked* exhausted too. It was eight in the morning, and those shadows under her eyes were my fault. Now the tightness around her lips was as well.

"But now you feel like you're on the Tilt-A-Whirl again."

She rolled back until both shoulders hit the wall, lifting her face as if asking for divine guidance. "Why are you bringing that back up?"

"*Back* up?" I leaned closer. "I never dropped it."

"Killian—*Mr. Stone*—" She averted her eyes. "Please, can we just—"

"No. We can't. Listen to me. *Look* at me." I had to pause when Brett from the mail room strode by. I abhorred doing this here, exposed in the hallway. "Everything I said last night? I meant it."

"I'm sure you did. At the time." One side of her mouth kicked up, another clear battle for self-composure. "We were both jacked on adrenaline and wine, and—"

"Damn it." I flattened a palm to the wall next to her head. Coming from any other woman, I would have felt played by her words, strung out in a game. But this was Claire Montgomery, who couldn't hide anything from her delicate face, especially her fear and insecurity—and the cavalier act she tried to cover both with. "Yes, I meant it then," I said, locking her stare back into mine. "But only half as much as I do now."

Holy God, did I mean it. With her perfume tickling my nose and her stature damn near pinned by mine, my blood spiked with new awareness and my body stirred with fresh need. And this morning, I *had* jacked off in the gym shower. I'd wanted to last for her tonight.

Tonight—when I'd be on a plane to Beijing.

Fuck.

My human reminder note, a sickeningly cheerful Britta, appeared in the hallway as if the power of my frustration had summoned her there. "Asia on the horn, boss."

"Tell them I'll call them right back."

The five seconds of our exchange were all Claire needed to duck beneath my arm. When I tried to claim her shoulder again, she didn't try to shrug me away. She hauled out heavier ammunition.

Her tears.

Her eyes pooled with liquid as she gazed back up to me. "Please. Just let it go, Killian. It's all right. *I'm* all right. Let's get off the roller coaster...before we both puke."

I watched her walk down the hall behind Britta. She'd worn an ivory pantsuit today, a contrast to Britta's professional black silhouette. Clashing against them both was the figure waiting for me in the doorway of my office in a figure-hugging crimson sweater dress—Margaux Asher, who bared everything to me except her claws and her breasts.

Perfect. All I needed was a stock-market crash or a report of Trey hopping in the sack with another virgin to top off my Christmas stocking with coal. Ho fucking ho.

★ ★ ★ ★

"Miss Montgomery has arrived, sir."

Five simple words hadn't shaken my nerves this much since *Congratulations, MIT has accepted you.*

I took a full breath as clouds swirled past the window of my condo and pushed my steepled fingers harder against my chin. "Thank you, Alfred. Show her—"

She burst into the room before I finished. Eyes blazing gold. Hair falling in fiery torrents. Cheeks and nose smudged in beautiful bursts of pink from the cold. In short, more gorgeous than she'd ever been.

"Forget it, Fred," she snapped. "Mr. Stone summoned me so Mr. Stone can show me in."

Alfred's gaze met mine. His salt-and-pepper brows kicked up, but amusement glimmered in his eyes. "Very well." He backed out of my home office and closed the door.

As I expected, she didn't let a second of downtime expire. "I'm here." Her voice was ice, her posture frostier. "You happy now, Your Highness? Show me your 'issue' with the press release *this* time—which could have been handled via email, by the way."

I stepped forward, leaving the desk behind. I'd removed my coat and tie too. The moment was balanced on a damn precarious precipice. After six hours, I'd resorted to issuing a *professional* command for her presence, without a single professional thought in my body. Blurred lines...one of my biggest anathemas. Steps were missed when you fogged up the path. Mistakes sneaked through open doors. Secrets got exposed.

At the moment, I didn't give a fuck.

Finally, *finally*, she was here. Alone. Mine.

We just had to clear the damn air.

"I'm having trouble with my emails today." It wasn't wholly a lie. Between pre-adjusting my brain to Beijing time and forcing my body to wait for her, focusing on correspondence had been impossible for the last six hours.

She answered my assertion with a thin laugh. I ignored her derision. "Let me take your coat."

She tightened the cream-colored trench. "I'm fine."

Not acceptable. I moved forward again, taking steady steps until I braced both feet in front of her. When I spoke, the growl was regulated solely for the air between us. "Take off your coat, Claire."

She swallowed, pulled the tie free, and began to shrug out of the coat. I stepped behind her to help.

She shivered as I peeled the whole thing from her body. And forced myself to stop there. God help me, I didn't want to.

With the coat still in my hands, I pressed closer to her. I hovered above her hair and took a deep breath of her rich lavender shampoo. "Why didn't you answer my texts?"

She snickered. "Right. Those. Emails weren't working for you but texts were, huh?"

"That's not an answer."

She moved away until the desk stopped her. "Couldn't pick the one I liked best. You gave me a choice of five hundred, after all."

"At least one of us had choices. You didn't leave me with much of one this morning, after jumping to every conclusion in the book."

She whirled back at me, eyes blazing. "Margaux was climbing you like a tree frog."

"Yes, she was." I draped her coat over a chair, moving in on her again. "*She* was climbing *me*. Funny thing about trees and frogs, Claire. The tree doesn't get much of a say, does it? She was excited about Oprah agreeing to interview Trey and broke in, uninvited, to my private office—"

"Of course." She snorted.

"What the hell is going on here, Claire? Drama isn't your style. What's *really* happening?"

She averted her eyes. "You have no clue about my style, Mr. Stone."

"Like hell I don't." I'd studied every thread of her style for nearly twenty-one days. I knew it well enough to detect that despite her tight jaw and pursed lips, she liked my nearness. A lot. I took another step closer.

She squirmed and closed her eyes. "I—I don't know what—"

"Nice try." I went for it. Dared to tug on her a little, drawing her trembling body closer to mine. To my shock, she didn't resist. Fuck, she smelled good. And felt even better. "But you're also pretty shitty at lying. So let's start over. All this bluster about the scene in my office...it's absurd. You know that, don't you?"

A long swallow moved down her throat. "Killian. *Mr. Stone*. Please—"

"A pretty word for table manners and sex requests. But not effective at the moment, Miss Montgomery."

Her gaze flew wide. "I beg your pardon?"

"You can certainly have my pardon. But I'm still calling your bullshit." I trailed the words down her face—while backing her against my desk again. "This has nothing to do with Margaux. It has everything to do with your insecurity again, doesn't it?"

Beautiful little huffs came out of her nose. "I'm *not* insecure."

"The fuck you aren't. I know fear when I see it, Claire. I've experienced enough of the shit to be an expert, especially now." I returned her stunned stare with a jerking nod. "Yeah. It all terrifies me too. But to make up roadblocks just because you're scared, to keep protesting that we don't fit..."

I interrupted myself with a tight moan as I pressed my lower body to hers. Christ, she was perfect. Even through the layers of our clothes, the heat of her sex welcomed me. The tight juncture of her thighs tempted me.

In a feverish sweep, I shoved all the shit off the desk. And flattened her to it. My head fell against her neck. I scraped at her carotid with my teeth. She tasted so fucking good.

"Oh..."

Her desperate cry filled my ears, spiked my blood, engorged my cock to painful intensity. I drove a hand against her scalp, meshing her hair between my fingers in furious satisfaction. I'd waited so long for this. So goddamn long.

"Ohhhh," she sighed again.

"You want to tell me again how we don't fit?" I growled into her ear.

"Killian," she gasped. "I'm— I'm here to— to work on the press rel—"

I stole the rest of the words from her lips by smashing mine against them.

CHAPTER EIGHT

Claire

I'd heard kisses described as crashes before but always laughed at the metaphor. Fate knew how to teach me a hell of a lesson, didn't it?

I was midsentence when he rammed me at full force, inundating me with his taste, surrounding me with his strength, a deluge of one hundred percent Killian Stone. Was there any other way with this man? He stopped my breath with the force of a storm wind, taking what he wanted, when he wanted. And heaven help me, he wanted me.

Or maybe it was better if heaven took the night off.

His smooth lips covered mine with skill I'd never experienced. He knew every curve to explore, every crevice to lick, every moment to press in until I opened for him, letting him sweep inside with confidence that was both thrilling and infuriating. A moan escaped me, flowing into his open mouth. He pushed the kiss deeper, stroking his tongue to mine, blatantly testing my resistance.

Oh, damn...

He stole my breath and my sanity in one swift move, laying me out on his desk until his lithe, hard body hovered inches over mine. I didn't dare gaze up. I couldn't help myself. He was everywhere, his body hot and strong, eyes alluring as sin. Everything about him beckoned me over to the dark side. *His* dark side.

I attempted a feeble protest. "K-Killian. W-We can't..."

"We can." He lowered himself, flattening his broad chest against mine. If I'd been capable of breathing—and that was a big *if*—his weight obliterated the option. I didn't care. If I had any dilemma at all, it was how to keep my hands from roaming over every inch of his long, muscled body.

"Claire." He cupped a hand to my cheek. "My beautiful fairy queen." The words I'd blasted him for yesterday became an honor he'd earned now, an ambrosia that tumbled from his lips into my thirsty senses. "I've been waiting for this...for you."

I laughed softly while pressing my cheek into his palm. "I get that one."

"You do?" His eyes closed for a moment. "I'm so fucking glad." When he reopened them, I met his fathomless stare and tried to speak.

"But we still both know this is crazy. We need to stop—"

"Fighting it." He moved closer, tightening his hold. "That's all we have to do. I already have." He pried deeper into my soul with that gaze, layer by ruthless layer, taking what he desired from me there, too. I shuddered from the exposure but was unable to move, completely in his thrall. "You have me on the ropes, Claire Montgomery. I'm done resisting."

Without another warning, he swept low to kiss me again. *God, the way he kissed.* His lips, though barely touching down, sent shivery sensations up and down my limbs as he brushed my mouth with velvet-soft strokes. This time, I forced my eyes open, bewitched by the jet-black fronds of his eyelashes resting on his high cheekbones. He smiled a little when gazing at me again before he pressed in harder for a long, delicious moment.

"What are you thinking?" He took advantage of my slightly parted lips to tease the inside of my mouth with the tip of his tongue. His voice held an equal hint of seduction. "And why are you staring?"

"I'm afraid to close my eyes," I finally admitted. "What if I open them to learn I've just been dreaming?"

"Hmm." His lips lifted with sensual slowness. "I get *that* one."

Even his deliberate tribute to my words didn't assuage my anxiety. "Killian," I persisted, "this is wrong on so many levels." But my body didn't want to hear anything about that. The fluttering in my stomach, a nonissue in my life before shaking this man's hand three weeks ago, was undeniable and unquenchable. Still, I tried. "It's not wise for you, and it's outright—"

Dangerous for me.

They were to be the next words I spoke, if not for his next kiss, so searing and demanding. His renewed fire wasn't surprising. The man had undoubtedly logged fewer celibate days than me, but every muscle in his body thrummed with an undercurrent of desire, flicked on by switches of no-nonsense lust. His passion punched every button in my own body's control panel, eliciting a high whimper from deep in my throat.

Dear God, he rendered me helpless. His hot tongue, his bold taste, his urgent desire... He intoxicated me, and I never wanted sobriety. He enslaved me, and I never wanted freedom.

He leaned up on his forearms, fitting more of his weight against me. Arousal, lust, and need built between us. While tangling tongues in another hot kiss, we knocked the remaining items from the desktop. I moaned and parted my legs so he could settle between them, a place where he fit perfectly.

Killian brushed the hair from my forehead and then bent closer, trailing kisses along my jaw, scraping a path with his rough stubble that made my skin tingle.

With a long sigh, I finally gave in to the temptation of touching him in return. I gripped his straining shoulders, kneading the contours of his muscles as I went. With his mouth now at my ear, he let out an approving groan. Shivers shot down my spine...and lower. I arched my back, sliding my body even closer to his.

"Claire," he said with reverence. "Damn...Claire."

If I had words to give in return, his eyes swallowed them up. They seemed made of boundless velvet onyx, able to make grown men quiver and grown women simper. I saw the reasons for both yet so much more than that too. *He* was so much more than that. Were his layers what he chose to show me or simply what I was able to see? The answer to that was like wondering what caused the beauty of a sunrise. Why worry about a triviality when the creator gave such an incredible view to savor?

Killian returned to my lips with thorough nips and nibbles, finally pushing inside my mouth again. I held him tighter as another sigh floated up my throat. He matched it with a rough rumble of sound that gained intensity as it reverberated through our bodies. There was no denying our attraction anymore. On a visceral level, it was potent, but once the quakes of my mind and soul were factored in, the force was like nothing I'd ever experienced in my life.

I was terrified.

I was electrified.

I was in a lot of damn trouble.

Killian possessed my mouth deeper, pulling my senses

even higher. He moaned, clearly telling himself to be patient and coercing, but as soon as I sighed again, he plunged down with intensity. Each kiss after that grew, spiraling with passion and heat until we both panted hard, seeking deliverance from the flames even as we ignited more.

"Come to my bed," he growled. "Now. Please." He suckled impatiently down my neck to the hollow at its base while tugging my blouse from where it was tucked into my slacks. "I want you naked under me...taking my body and squeezing me tight...screaming my name..."

World War III had commenced in my head. He had no idea that when he spoke of me screaming, I didn't think only of pillows, sheets, passion, and sweat. My mind filled with arrest warrants, handcuffs, prison jumpsuits, and...sweat.

The images fought each other while my stare tangled with his. There were so many layers to his eyes, so much beauty in his face. It was official. I'd met the most glorious man of my life. His body was pure heat as he rubbed mine in sinuous thrusts, a blatant promise of possibilities to come. But Margaux's threats, while delivered with the social finesse of a seventh grader, weren't empty. The woman had done worse to adversaries simply in the name of the company's projects. Delivering on behalf of her personal spite would be even less of a screw to turn. She'd destroy me—and in the process, Dad too.

And what about her mother's joy as possible collateral damage in the hit? My blood chilled from the answer. *The apple never falls far from the tree.* Margaux had learned her technique from the best of the bitchy best. Something told me Andrea would be just fine, with or without Dad at her side. The same instinct didn't hold true when I thought about Dad having to deal with his child in prison and his engagement broken.

Which meant this recklessness needed to end here and now.

I clutched my blouse with one hand and pushed at Killian with the other. He reared back, bringing a blast of chilled air across my body. I hated this. I didn't want him to stop. But I had to—before it was too late.

"We— We have to stop." My voice was thick with desperation, clinging to a last vestige of common sense. He didn't hear it. More likely, chose not to.

"No," he whispered, scraping back my hair again. "It's all right this time. It's perfect this time."

To my shock, I laughed. "This is your idea of perfect?"

He tugged on my hair, compelling my eyes to meet his while heat sluiced through my whole body in reaction. "*This* is my idea of perfect." He stroked a thumb across my cheek in emphasis.

"Killian—"

"We're safe here, Claire." He pressed back down, lowering his forehead to mine. "Everything. All of it. All our desires...all our secrets..."

With the single word, he turned my body into an ice floe. "Secrets are exactly why we have to stop."

He fought me with a harsh breath. "Then give yours to me. All of them. I'll keep them safe. I promise."

My laughter dissolved into a sob. "You can't keep that promise, Killian. Nobody can."

His fingers, so long and warm, bracketed my head. "Then leave them behind and stay with me anyway."

It was a plea as deep as his coal-dark eyes. A promise of the sweetest pleasure I'd likely ever know, the most incredible sex I'd probably ever have, the kisses and embraces of the most breathtaking man I'd ever met.

I squeezed my eyes shut again. I'd regret this moment forever, that much was clear already. But staying would equate to the biggest mistake of my life. Margaux and her threats, while the easy reach for explaining my strife, were really only the start of my conflict. The bigger peril came from the heart ramming at my ribs with agonizing force—the acknowledgment that my secrets weren't the most dangerous thing Killian could now wrest from me—another rash risk I'd resolved never to take again.

"Y-You're leaving for Beijing tonight," I finally stammered. Though the words were shaky, they lent enough strength to roll free and regain my footing. "Even if you weren't, this isn't going to work." I peered around for my trench. "There are *so* many reasons why this isn't going to work."

How could I trust the man with my secrets when I'd abandoned trust in my own heart and soul from the night I'd found Nick with Darcie? When the choice of trusting a man with my secrets had become a mistake to haunt me for years?

Finally spotting the coat, I grabbed it and headed for the door as if the room had caught on fire. I wasn't sure it hadn't.

"Claire... Damn it!" Killian's tone was full of more tension than his shoulders, still hunched over the desk. In an unwanted moment of transcendence, I saw my body in the space below him once more. Hot for him. Spread for him. Wanting him.

I grimaced and turned. "If there is really an issue with the press release, email me, okay? And Killian? Please—"

Don't do this again.

I fell into silence, unable to speak it. Unable to *think* it.

I bolted before he could say another word, stumbling

through the living room with its sleek cream-on-black décor and its panoramic view of the lake, wondering if I'd pass out on his butter-soft rug before getting to the door. Once again, being in his presence had the power to suck every breath from my body. What the *hell* was his power over me? I'd never known such intense feelings for another person. Was this what the experts meant by animal attraction? Was this some pheromone thing, a crazy concoction brought on by his cologne meeting mine? Was it even more basic than that? Had my moon ascended into his karma at just the right time, some cosmic bullshit Chad could explain?

Whatever the hell it was, I had to make it stop. Otherwise, I might not survive this damn assignment.

I flung myself out into the hallway and stabbed the elevator call button while battling to pull myself together and assess the answer to one question.

What the hell had just happened?

★ ★ ★ ★

I must see you again.

I turned the card over again before setting it down on the small table in my hotel room. Nearby, my room-service order sat nearly demolished. Something about pizza, macaroni and cheese, and apple pie was a perfect beginning for a night when a girl wanted to stay inside and wallow. My favorite flannel pajamas and fuzzy socks helped the effort, along with the in-room movie channel cued up with *Sixteen Candles*.

Yep. Wallowing. Big time.

I'd ordered the dinner with a whole bottle of wine and poured myself a third glass. It was a really good cabernet, and I tried to focus on all the oaky overtones that the label bragged about instead of the man I'd left behind in that condo overlooking the lake. "Don't do it," I seethed at myself. "Don't you dare."

It didn't matter how gorgeous he was, how great he kissed, how good he smelled, or how fantastic I knew he would be in bed—I had to purge Killian Stone from my system. After a long bath, a ton of carbs, and all the wine, I thought I'd be well on my way to that goal by now.

Instead, I sat on the bed and stared at that damn card.

I'd pitched it into the trash twice, only to fish it out again and set it somewhere safe. I dialed my dad once and hung up, deciding he didn't need his half-plastered daughter crying on his shoulder—or giving him a reason to have a "chat" with Andrea about my mental stability. Chad and Michael had called and damn near dictated I'd be going for some good sushi and bad karaoke with them, but I'd declined, needing a chunk of self-pity time. The makeup was officially scrubbed, my hair pulled back in an old scrunchie, and I was set to finish my food coma with some John Hughes therapy.

If only the note would stop taunting me.

"Small steps," I muttered, taking an encouraging sip and forcing my sights on the TV. "At least you're not crying."

I'd just hit the Play button for the movie when there was a knock at the door. I huffed and slammed my glass down, glaring across the room. Couldn't a girl be miserable in peace?

Trudging over, I started my rant at Chad during the last two steps to the portal. "Listen, you little bitch, you'll just have to find another *Freebird* partner tonight, so—"

My mouth dropped in an open gawk.

Alfred stared back, surprise in his kind eyes.

"Fred?"

"Good evening, Miss Montgomery." He lifted a polite smile.

"I'm sorry. I thought you were someone from my team, and—" I frowned again. "Wait. Why are you here?" Guess I wasn't done being rude, after all.

"I'm delivering a message for you."

"A message? From who?"

He only had to arch one eyebrow before I blushed, recognizing the silliness of the query. Fortunately, he didn't waste any more time before pulling a small envelope from his breast pocket—a perfect match to the missive he'd given me earlier.

"Thanks." Feeling like the card would bite if I weren't careful, I accepted it and then gawked at it. My mouth turned into the Sahara again. My pulse throbbed in the base of my throat. Though I told myself to stop being silly, I watched the envelope tremble in my fingers.

After a huge breath, I realized poor Fred was still standing there. I attempted a smile and murmured, "Thanks again, Fred. Have a good night."

The man shifted and cleared his throat. "Respectfully speaking, Miss Montgomery—"

"Claire. Please, just Claire." As if I'd ever be seeing him again after this.

"Well then...Claire. I'm to wait while you read it."

"No offense, Fred, but do you always do everything he tells you?"

The man lifted both eyebrows at me, just like Dad did when I had an attack of snark or drank too much. In this case, it was likely both. Guilt washed in. "Sorry," I repeated. "It's been a tense night."

"Indeed." While his response was neutral on the surface, it came with a second jump of brows, speaking volumes. Apparently, Killian was being more irascible than me.

"Why don't you come in?" I offered while opening the envelope. The ivory note card inside was exactly the same as the first one Killian had sent—however, this message was comprised of a single word. My hand fluttered to my throat as I read his handwriting.

Please.

Tears clouded my vision. I swiped at my eyes. The action was no use. New tears replaced the old ones. One word, a multitude of meanings. Entreaties weren't easy for a man like Killian Stone. Confessions were even harder. But in many senses, I held both in the palm of my hand. From him. Penned by his hand.

Why?

It spilled from me in verbal form too. I stared up at Fred as if he could crack his boss's mysterious code for me. "What does this mean?" I choked out. "Please *what*? What does he want from me?"

Forget trying to stop the tears now. I sped right past stunned and into the valley of confused. The simple answer to that? Killian had given me the answer himself, in his office. He wanted nothing from me except *me*. The attraction between us turned into a more alluring path every day, beckoning to be explored and enjoyed. As we inched nearer to it, I saw more pieces of this man, parts that he showed few besides me. I gave him safe ground for that, and in return, the cocky guy promised my own safety, completely blind to the enormity of his promise...

Fred shifted his stance, not hiding his nervousness about being in an enclosed space with a crying female. "He's, uhhh, asked me to bring you to him—if you'll agree, Miss Montgomery. The car is double-parked, so we should go soon."

For a long moment, I didn't say anything. I looked down at what I was wearing and panicked. I was in flannel pajamas, for Christ's sake. And fuzzy socks. And a faded purple scrunchie in my nonexistent hairstyle. And what *wasn't* I wearing? Earrings. Makeup. Panties.

Hell.

"Do I have time to get ready, at least?" I added an imploring stare.

"I'm sorry, miss. He'll be on his way to Beijing in just a bit. If you delay, you'll miss him. If I may make a suggestion, your trench coat will cover most of your clothes." Fred offered a guilty little smile. "If I may be even bolder, you look splendid as you are. I am sure Jamie—err, Mr. Stone—will agree."

I hung my head, still flustered. Wasn't this stepping into the damn time machine, hitting the button marked This Afternoon, and repeating the same fiasco from his penthouse? He'd beckoned. I was dropping everything and running. But we'd have the same maddening result. There were more reasons we couldn't be together than reasons we should.

But even as I thought it, every cell in my body was pulled by the force of his vortex...the promise of *him*. Hot on the heels of that sensation was the panic that had hit me in the office yesterday. I leaned on the wall from the dizzying force of it. Could I resist Killian, even if I wanted to? This pull toward him was primal, biological, a connection I cherished and hated at the same time. Maybe this was how it felt to have a twin—only without the visions of ripping his clothes off and roaming my hands over every inch of his hard, naked flesh.

I was supposed to feel guilty about that, right? And the fear...where was that, too?

Gone. Both had been usurped by an exhilarated defiance. Damn it, I needed this moment of bliss, if only as a reminder that sometimes, for a few magical hours, the glass slipper *did* fit and there was nothing else in the world except joy and fulfillment. And for some strange and magical reason perhaps known only to the universe, Killian Stone yearned to give it to me.

And yes...I longed to give him the same in return.

A stolen moment. A secret time. That was all it ever could be, before Margaux leapt back at him, perhaps literally, with wiles turned up, claws sharpened, and ploys aimed in his direction again. I felt a little better now, knowing she'd never succeed. Though Killian had subjected me to a thrill ride of attitude over the last three weeks, he'd astounded my mind in equal measure with his acumen and intuition. He'd seen through Margaux's games before she could bat her eyelashes twice.

Only one question remained.

Could I maintain this clinical distance even when I stood in front of the man again? Could I be okay with having him in my arms and inside my body, naked and intimate, without baring my soul just as openly...and dangerously?

My senses answered with maddening silence.

I looked up to Fred, hoping he'd have another piece of bold advice. No help this time. Instead, the man walked to the door again and reopened it, standing with a patient but expectant light in his compassionate eyes. "Miss Montgomery? What is your decision?"

CHAPTER NINE

Killian

My tension spiraled with every jostle, bump, and shout from the ground crew as they readied the plane for takeoff. I watched the men move efficiently across the tarmac, tapping off their checkpoints on handheld devices. Frosty rain pelted from above, dripping off their beards and gloves.

I wished to God I could join them.

If I were active and freezing, at least I wouldn't be counting every thrum of apprehension in my pulse, every needle of frustration through my temples. I wouldn't be feeling like a goddamn prisoner in my own private jet.

I wouldn't feel like climbing the hell out of this thing and telling Beijing they needed to suck up their nerves and honor the contracts they had with SGC, just like the other big kids at the table.

I woke my computer for the fiftieth time, struggling to concentrate on my email inbox. For every hour I ignored the fucker, a hundred more messages made it past Britta's screening process, landing in the column for my response.

The words meshed into each other. My thoughts were worse puddles. I peered out into the rain once more, waiting— damn it, hoping—for a pair of headlights to pierce the night.

The rain fell harder.

I bit out the F-word and clicked open my first email. It was time stamped from four hours ago.

"Mr. Stone?"

The voice was deep, matching the tall figure in the pilot's uniform who stepped into the plane. The man's lantern-shaped face crunched into a frown.

"Vaughn." I forced a cordial smile at the guy. "Good afternoon. Thanks for rearranging your schedule for this flight. A trip to Beijing isn't exactly a hop to New York."

"That's what I'm here for, Mr. Stone." His face didn't relax. "But...did I write down our takeoff incorrectly? We're not due to leave for over an hour."

I lifted a hand in reassurance. "You're good. Don't sweat it. I got on early to get some work done."

He answered with a commiserating snort. "Things are chaotic at the office these days, eh?"

"That's a nice way of putting it."

"I take it they won't leave you alone at the home office, either."

"Things are a little messy there too."

If this conversation were a *Jeopardy!* category, it would've been *Ironic Understatements*. The answer involving my home desk would be an ideal Daily Double. After Claire bolted from the condo, I'd gawked at the aftermath with just as much remorse. And felt like just as much of a jerk.

Which thoroughly explained why I'd sent those goddamn notes out with Alfred.

I hadn't used the word *please* with someone—and meant it—in over ten years. It was always a convenience of my life, of my masquerade. And now, like the pathetic fuck I was, I couldn't even call her to say it. I sent it in a note, delivered by my damn butler.

No wonder she wasn't coming.

As Vaughn made his way into the cockpit and turned on the saxophone-heavy preflight music, I slammed my laptop shut.

Just as headlights cut through the rain, glaring through the window.

I jolted to my feet. Raced to the open doorway. Doubled back, pacing like an idiot, stabbing fingers through my hair. What if it was only Alfred arriving with bad news instead of Claire? I whooshed nervous air out, jamming my tie back into place like some stupid shit getting ready to pick up a girl for prom. As if I knew what that felt like. The closest thing I'd gotten to prom was the Haversham Girls Academy's annual cotillion, where the upperclassmen from Triton were forced to escort girls in dresses resembling wedding cakes. That never made me nervous so much as scared.

Guess I'd had ideal preparation for this, after all.

As I stood there trying to comprehend that the sheen on my palms was really sweat, Alfred's calm voice broke through the rain pinging on the air stairs outside.

"Careful, Miss Montgomery. In this weather, the steps are slick."

In an instant, I forgot about my palms. And my dread. Irritation took its place. Had the damn woman worn a pair of her stilt heels in this weather? She was going to slip and smash her head open before I could—

Stand and gawk at her like I did through the next moment. And the next. And the next.

She'd pulled her hair up into a ponytail, which emphasized the angles of her face and the little tilts at the corners of her eyes. Burnished strands trailed down against her cheeks, some dotted with rain drops. Her skin was scrubbed clean of makeup, deepening her beauty a thousand more levels for me. Her eyes seemed darker, her lips softer, her skin creamy and clean, begging for my touch...my kisses. In a violent slam of thought, I realized this was probably how she looked first thing in the morning. I immediately imagined her in my arms, yawning as she awakened...only with a lot less clothing. Certainly not with that overcoat, and with—

What the hell *was* she wearing underneath?

My lips quirked. I was guessing, but her ensemble looked like a matched flannel pajama set. The soft-pink fabric was dotted with little purple flowers that matched the tie in her hair. To finish off the ensemble, she'd put on a pair of running shoes, which she now jabbed at the carpet as she took in the plane's cabin, gaze wide, hands grabbing at opposing elbows.

She looked so small. So unsure. So confused.

So perfect.

Air throttled my lungs at full force. I tried to combat the effect by forming dual fists, realizing too late that appearing like a fire-breathing asswipe wasn't the best welcome for a woman I'd dragged into the night with a couple of ridiculous notes.

"You came."

Nice going, slick. That's so *much better than the fire-breathing dragon.*

Claire swallowed and wrapped her arms tighter. "I shouldn't have."

My chest constricted. Regret was another feeling I didn't like to visit very often. I sucked it up and faced the shit anyway. "Probably not."

She scooted forward by a hesitant step. "This is a bad idea."

I took one too. "Probably is."

She lifted her head. I willed her gaze to lock with mine. When it did, I returned to the land of stupid and silent again, not ready to limit this moment to words. Her face was full of torment. I should have said something—done something—to alleviate her conflict. All I could manage was the awe of having her back. Seeing her here. Surrendering the miracle to time's selfish grip simply wasn't an option.

"God." She half moaned it before breaking our connection, shaking her head. "Look at you!"

"Why?"

"Seriously? Now look at me!"

A wry laugh escaped me. "I haven't been able to do much else for weeks, baby."

She shot back a glare like I'd grown a damn horn. "This isn't the royal dance at the palace, Killian."

"Thank fuck."

She ignored my sarcasm. "That means you can't turn my rags into finery and then waltz me out of the door, thinking we're going to leave the world behind." A sound escaped her, perilously close to a sob, before she added, "It means I can't consider it either—and it was a *really* dumb idea to come—"

I cut her off with a vicious growl. Before I talked myself out of the feeling, I crossed to her, shoved my hands to the sides of her face, and cradled her there, subjecting her to the full force of my glare. I didn't plan on fucking this up again. Nor would I allow her to. "Your rags are the hottest things you've ever worn." I pushed my body closer to hers, purposely sliding my cock against her cleft, grinding against her even harder than I had in the office a few hours ago. "And, God help me, dancing's only the beginning of what I want to do with you."

With a brutal sweep, I dipped her whole body back, forcing her to grip my shoulders for balance. A mixture between a moan and a sigh fell out of her while she did, reverberating through my lips as I let them fall to the column of her neck. When I raised her back up, the movement was merely a formality. With my hand, I quickly found her thigh, swinging it over so she rode on mine while I ground our bodies tighter, moving in time to the sultry rhythm streaming through the speakers. I never thought I'd be so damn grateful for jazz muzak in my life.

"Killian?" She raised a hand while rasping my name, scraping her fingernails up the back of my head.

"Yeah?" I worked to press volume into the reply. She felt incredible in my arms, her arms wrapped around me, her floral scent surrounding me. My blood raced. My nerves zinged. My cock swelled. Every sense in my body opened for her—to her.

"This...this isn't waltzing."

Her coat finally fell open. I lowered my head to the top button on her pajama top. "And I'm not the goddamn prince."

She let out a little mewl, responding to my undulations by rocking her hips in return. And fuck if it wasn't the sexiest thing with her body encased in those damn pajamas. "So...I don't have to worry about the clock striking midnight? About having to run back to the pumpkin?"

I dragged my head up in order to meet her eyes. Hers were heavy-lidded, the irises clouded beneath a golden haze of longing...and lust. Dear fuck, I wanted to kiss her again. And I did. Though the contact was brief, I lingered on, biting at her sweet coral lips with open offerings of my teeth, now bared in a joyous grin.

"No waltzing," I finally murmured. "And no clocks. And no pumpkins. And *no* running."

Both her dimples appeared in her cheeks. "Good," she whispered. "Because God help me, I don't think I can."

CHAPTER TEN

Claire

As Killian groaned in approval and pulled me tighter to him, my nerves and adrenaline battled with disbelief and wonder. Was this really me, bantering with him about pumpkins and waltzes? Was this really him, breathing harder as I ran my fingers up his nape and through his thick, beautiful hair? Was this my body, tingling low in my belly, moistening for him, craving more of his commanding touch? All the answers led to one word, shrouded in my haze of lust.

Yes.

"Let's get you out of this wet jacket." He ordered it with his devil's grin—and a panty-melting glint in his eyes. "I'd like to show you the rest of the plane." While scooting behind me to help with the coat, he added in my ear, "As soon as possible."

"There's more?" My awe was genuine.

"Oh, yeah. The best part." He walked back around, taking my hand with a playful wink, dissolving me deeper. I wondered how many people in the corporate world, if any, had seen the playful side of Killian Stone.

He continued walking me toward the back of the plane. I let my jaw fall, admitting I'd never seen anything like it in my life. I'd only had glimpses of first class, let alone been in a private jet. Rich wood panels replaced the normal white plastic cabinets. Sleek metal trim outlined compartments for storage, accented by matching knobs and inlaid handles.

But the most glorious sight of all was the man in front of me, dark and tall and perfect in his tailored-to-the-millimeter suit, his steps confident as a king, his warmth alluring as a panther. His elegance reminded me of my own ridiculous state. Despite the command of his handclasp, I winced and hesitated. He stopped too. I dropped my head to avoid his scrutiny. And, if I was honest, to indulge my anxiety.

He pressed close again, surrounding me with heat. I swore God had replaced one of the man's vital organs with a furnace.

"What is it?" He bypassed a questioning tone in favor of an outright demand. "No more stop signs, Claire, remember?"

"I'm not running," I protested.

"No?"

"No. I'm—I'm embarrassed."

A long index finger lifted my chin. "Open up," he directed softly. When I obeyed, opening my eyes only to be consumed by the midnight depths of his, he pressed, "Why embarrassed?"

"Earth to Killian Stone?" My attempt at sarcasm backfired into a trembling mess. "I'm standing here in my pajamas, mister. Not even my good ones."

His lips twitched. "You have more than one pair of these?"

"If I hadn't promised not to bolt on your ass—"

He stopped me with another kiss that had my toes curling inside my shoes. After he let me breathe again—at least I *thought* I could—he drenched me with a stare full of pure seduction before murmuring, "I have the perfect solution to your dilemma, sweet damsel."

After a few more steps, we arrived at the back end of the plane and stopped in front of another door. Killian turned and looked down at me again, beaming even more of his wicked, secretive smile. I gazed back, watching a million thoughts flash through his eyes, including a frisson of uncertainty. For a second, I knew the heady feeling of having power over Killian Stone. It was...bizarre.

He opened the small door and stood back, letting me enter the private room. My whole body trembled as I stepped forward. A queen-size bed took up most of the space. It was decorated with luxurious pillows and a downy comforter, all in rich hues of mahogany and chocolate. The space also contained a small dresser and another door, apparently leading to a bathroom and dressing area.

Everything knotted and pulsed in my stomach...and then trailed lower. I kept my composure by taking a deep breath before turning toward Killian. He'd followed me and now stood inches away, hovering as if assuring himself I wouldn't change my mind. He wrapped an arm around my waist, stabbing his intense gaze down at me before hauling me close. With his other hand, he pulled the tie free from my hair and then buried his face in my loosened tresses. I rested my cheek to his chest, letting the pound of his heartbeat resonate through my senses.

We sighed together. Then moaned. Damn. *Damn.* He was so hard, so strong, so close, so warm. So *here.* I rolled my head against him, practically a pleading kitten in my need for more. I didn't care. Judging from the deep resonance of Killian's answering groan, he didn't, either.

He squeezed me tighter. Tunneled his hand deeper into my hair, tugging gently so my scalp ignited tiny bites of tantalizing pain.

"I love the way you smell," he grated.

In an equally rough surge, he twirled me around then

yanked me back against him, fitting our bodies into each other. I gasped as my backside pressed on the long, hard evidence of his desire.

"I love the way you feel." He rocked me along his erection, breathing hard in my ear. Heat exploded through my body and roared through my head, an effect that intensified as he reached back and shut the door with a distinct *click*. My pulse spiked as he returned both hands to my body, trailing warm kisses down my neck while spreading his grasp across my waist.

"You're so tiny." He punctuated the whisper by sinking his teeth into my shoulder, making me cry out in stunned arousal.

The way he handled me, targeting every bite to render the most carnal reactions from my flesh, plunged my senses deeper into their most primitive state.

"I could eat you up in one bite, baby." His tone became rougher. His touch did too. "But I'm not going to. I'm going to savor every lick, every taste, and every sip of you. You're my special little dessert." At last he cupped my mound through my clothes, enforcing how much he'd soaked me already. "Goddamn. I've never tasted a fairy before...and now I can't wait to know what every drop of you is like."

I leaned my head back on his chest and moaned. "I want you so much..." I ended it with a mortified gasp. My hands flew up to cover my mouth as he chuckled once more. That damn wine. It loosened every ounce of foolish boldness in me. I couldn't believe the words had spilled out like that.

He didn't help my nerves at all by sneaking around to face me again, his steps smooth, his face intent. With a commanding rumble, he pulled my hands from my mouth and then held them in front of me, as if preparing me for prayer. Not a bad idea. Maybe divine intervention would keep me from jamming my entire foot into my mouth.

With both my hands gathered into one of his, he flashed me that Hades-born grin again. My pulse kicked up. It pounded in my throat as I tried to swallow.

"Now." He drew the word out, turning the sole syllable into a sensual work of art. I gulped again. If he was going for intense effect, it was working. Brilliantly. "I think it's time we take care of these pajamas."

"Oh," I squeaked. "Can we...errr...turn out the lights first?"

He shook his head with slow deliberation before I finished. One of his black eyebrows arched up. Without releasing my hands, he used his free fingers to slip my top button open. He let one finger loiter in the space, tugging back the fabric to reveal the first flesh of my breasts.

"Beautiful," he murmured.

I, on the other hand, was engaged in some speed math. The pajama top only possessed four buttons, though the bottom one had gone missing six months ago. I couldn't bring myself to put it in the Goodwill basket yet. That meant he only had two more buttons to go.

Correction. One more.

Killian bent and used his lips on the opening as he freed the next button. I shuddered from the reverent contact of his mouth. When he exposed more skin with the last, he moved his magical lips into that space too.

He released my hands so the shirt could slide off my shoulders and then down to the floor. I instantly blushed, dunked in embarrassment. Everything I knew about foreplay wasn't like this. I was used to groping and rushing *in the dark*. This was so strange and new and—

Mesmerizing.

It was the only word to describe the look on his face. His eyes held complete adoration. Their corners showed crinkles of admiration. He even sneaked his tongue out, moistening his lips as he emitted a low growl.

Once more, just for a moment, *I* had power over *him*. I closed my eyes, hoping to process the enormity of the feeling. In the end, I settled for simply savoring it.

"Open your eyes." His voice was a rough abrasion on the air. "Look at me, Claire."

I willingly obeyed. My stare locked with his. My senses celebrated how he drank me in like a parched man stumbling on an oasis. "Wow," he stammered.

"Good wow or bad wow?"

We both laughed softly. My reference to that first night in his office was an assurance of shared memory. As the chuckle faded from his lips, he reached out to stroke my nude flesh with both hands. "Good wow," he grated, thumbing my nipples to attention. While I sucked in a breath at the electrifying contact, he went on, "You're more beautiful than I ever imagined. How that's possible, I'll never know."

He lifted both my breasts and then tugged at their taut points. I moaned and pressed into his hold, needing more contact. I'd dreamed about this so much, but the reality was far better than my fantasies.

"Killian," I blurted. "Ohhh..."

"Tell me." Thank God he didn't command me to look at him again. That possibility had been flung to the land of the impossible. I was drunk on the sensations he surged through me, swaying from them as if I'd downed a dozen bottles of wine.

"Your hands on me...my God..."

"*Tell me.*"

"It feels so good," I confessed. "Tingles...and heat...and pressure...*damn*. Don't stop. Please don't stop."

"Greedy girl." He chuckled as I nodded fast in agreement. "Mmmm. *Beautiful* girl."

He pinched harder on my erect tips before rolling them between his fingers, extending my pleasure with the slight pain. He didn't let up, even while lowering himself to the edge of the bed. Once there, he shifted his hold to my thighs, caging them as he applied his mouth to the same tasks, kissing and licking my nipples until they pouted and throbbed for more. When I writhed against him, certain I couldn't take more, he added little bites. I gasped as he captured each hard nub between his teeth and pulled gently at the flesh. Then not so gently.

"Killian! *God!*" I dug my fingers through his raven hair, holding on for balance. His lips, so talented and hot, zapped jolts of desire from my breasts, down my torso, straight to the core between my legs. A storm raged over my body's landscape, and its glorious name was Killian.

"Oh yes, baby..." He kissed his way into the valley between my breasts, officially turning the majority of my body into mush.

"Please," I begged. "My knees are buckling."

He looked up and grinned, clearly pleased with himself. Smug, stunning bastard. Nevertheless, his happiness was contagious. Overwhelmed with the feeling, I leaned down and kissed his luscious mouth with all I had. He groaned as I plunged my tongue in, reveling in his spicy, masculine taste.

Within seconds, I started thrusting in and out, emulating what I yearned for him to do with other parts of his body. In this position, filled with lust and need, I was finally able to forget Killian the CEO, Killian the public figure, even Killian the half jerk who'd flung my senses on the weirdest emotional roller coaster of my life. He was simply Killian the man, entwined with every cell that made me a woman. Awakening that woman in so many miraculous ways.

A satisfied snarl prowled up Killian's throat, as if the universe had ratted out my thoughts. I didn't care, especially when he grabbed both sides of my face in return, reclaiming control of the kiss. As our mouths and tongues mated, he dropped his grip to my shoulders. I gasped when his hold tightened, pitching the sound into a squeal as he leveraged it to flip me over onto the bed. The Taj Mahal mound of pillows cushioned my fall, billowing as he laid me back and kissed me deeply again.

When he pulled up, his jaw went tight and his eyes darkened to midnight. The starch in his cuffs turned his caresses down my arms into sizzling teases, making me shiver all over again.

"I want the rest of my dessert," he declared while sitting up. I emulated the move, but he sent me back into the pillows with a determined push. His long fingers became commanding wands. "Ohhh, no. You stay right there. No more running, fairy, remember? This bird is outfitted with a lot of perks, but the last time I checked, there were no little cages or leashes to be found."

That caused me to hitch up on my elbows, a glower in place. "*Cages* or *leashes?*"

"You heard me." He sent the admonishment with a sly smile. "You run for the damn hills every time I turn my back. Hell, even when I *don't* turn it."

My gut twisted a little. Despite the grin, I detected his words had come from a hurt place inside. I said nothing, knowing I deserved the jibe.

The decision turned out to be for the best. The next moment, I wasn't sure I'd be capable of words anyway. I watched with parted lips and a hungry stare as Killian unbuttoned his dress shirt, pulled it free, and then laid it on the stool at the foot of the bed. *Damn.* He had to be the most beautiful man ever created, his torso a collection of chiseled bronze muscles, tapered into gorgeous rows of abs. Breathtaking, meet thy new spokesmodel.

I was pretty certain my mouth watered. I *know* my palms itched from the yearning to touch him. The sight of him kept me riveted, despite the unnerving stare he fixed in return. He didn't avert his gaze an inch while unbuckling his belt, unfastening his slacks, and letting them slide down his beautifully carved legs. All I could do was lie there like a fool in my pajama bottoms, wondering what the hell I'd done to deserve these moments with this incredible man.

Still moving with deliberation, he reached into his pants before draping them atop his shirt, pulling his wallet from the pocket and producing several condoms from within. Like a dork, I stared at those too—all the way to where he placed them on the table by the bed. My gaze didn't have far to travel from there to the sight of his boxer briefs, tented from the erection that strained to be freed.

I quickly wet my lips. That tent was impressive.

Killian, clearly pleased with my perusal, slanted a cocky smirk. "Now, where was I? Hmmm. Ohhh, yes."

Without further warning, he leaned over, reached for the waistband of my pajamas, hooked his index fingers in, and dragged the fabric off my hips. His heated stare made me forget I had no panties to pull off with the clothes. He made quick work of tossing the pants away before climbing back on the bed and pulling me up into a groaning, open-mouthed kiss.

It was heaven, albeit an unbelievable one. I was naked in a huge bed in the back of Killian Stone's private jet, making out with the man like we'd become air to each other. The realization sent bubbles of giddiness through me and a giggle up my throat.

Killian lifted his head, bewilderment on his breathtaking features. "Do I amuse you, Miss Montgomery?"

"I— I just—" I shook my head. How did I begin to explain my ridiculous stream of consciousness? "I'm having a little trouble believing this is real."

"I know the feeling."

"You do?" I shrugged and bit my lip, hoping for a dash of impish levity. "Maybe you'd better kiss me again, just so we're both convinced."

Glints of sensual intent flashed through his gaze. "Sweet Claire, I'm going to do more than kiss you...I absolutely promise." His hands drifted down, cupping my ass as he suckled my neck. "I don't want an inch of your body untouched by my mouth, a shred of your memory not filled by my touch." He trailed his lips around to cover mine, kissing me, commanding me. His fingers threaded through my hair, locking my head in place while he laid a trail of carnal kisses over my chin and down the column of my throat. As he worked his way back up to my neck, each nibble grew more intense until I whined and whimpered beneath him. "Every time you look in the mirror tomorrow, you'll remember who's been all over your delectable body. You'll feel my touch on you, my body twined with yours...inside and out. Repeat it to me, Claire. Tell me you understand."

It took his words a few seconds to pierce the haze of my senses. Several more before I comprehended his crazy demand. My thoughts whirled at least a thousand miles outside my body, and he wanted me to lasso enough of them to form words? "Y-Yes," I finally stammered. "Oh yes, Killian. Your touch in my memory..."

He reached up to twist my left nipple, deliberately rough. The jolt of pain surged yet more moisture between my legs. "And my name in your thoughts," he growled.

"Yes. Your name in every thought."

"And on your lips." He administered the same sexual torment to my right breast.

I moaned in unabashed pleasure.

"Yes. *Yes*. On my lips."

"And screaming from your throat...every night when you pleasure yourself."

With his final filthy thought, his hand slipped between my legs. He glided his strong, sure fingers through the soaked layers there. Some distant instinct yelled that I should have been embarrassed by my condition, but only one need consumed my brain, and it fell from my pleading lips.

"More. Please, Killian. I need more."

"Oh, there's more, sweet girl. Trust me. This is only the beginning...for both of us."

"Wh-What do you— O*hhhh!*"

One moment, he used his fingers to slick arousal deeper into my pussy. The next, his tongue was there, blazing heat into my folds as his hands pressed my thighs apart.

"Lie back, my fairy queen. Let me make you feel good. Let me drink you up before I fuck you hard."

My body sank against the sumptuous pillows again,

melted by the erotic power of his words. "Killian..." It spilled from me on a moan as his tongue explored me more, sending pressure and heat through my sex, my thighs, my ass.

"Spread your legs for me. Farther, baby. That's it. Damn, you have no idea how many times I've dreamed about tasting you here, about how sweet you must be. Now I know...your pussy's as delicious as it looks."

I couldn't speak. I simply watched him, fixated on his face as he refocused his decadent mouth between my thighs. His dirty talk spiked my need so high I already drifted on a plane somewhere between ecstasy and explosion.

"You're ruining me," I finally rasped.

"Oh, I hope so." He flashed his Lucifer grin in response to my mocking glare. Damn it, the man knew exactly how to use that foul, beautiful mouth, and I couldn't do anything about it but wait, trembling and needy, for his special touch of sin on my swollen flesh.

He pulled my thighs even wider, propping my feet up on the bed and spreading my trembling tissues with his strong, sure thumbs. I'd never had a lover make such a production over me before...or made me wait longer, taut and edgy and breathless, for his tongue to find me—

There.

"Ohhhh!"

I gripped the bedding, trying not to writhe as a matter of pride, accepting my failure a moment later. After the anticipation he'd built, I'd been afraid of hitting orgasm as soon as he touched the tenderest part of me. That didn't happen, thank God, but as he toyed with my clit, swiping it with expert motion, my pleasure soared to mind-bending proportions.

"Claire." He worshiped me with the word. "You're so

perfect. So pink and soft and wet. My sweet Claire."

"Oh, my God." The words burst from between my frantic breaths, manifestations of pure instinct. I didn't have a thought to call my own or a sensation that wasn't commanded completely by his magical mouth.

He pressed in again, flattening his tongue along one side of my engorged ridge and then down the other. He repeated the motion again—then again and *again*—warping my senses into erotic madness. When I adjusted to the sensation, he added a new move, circling the delicate nub at the top. After that, it was a small nibble before sucking my entire clit into his mouth. I was on edge for what felt like hours, my lower abdomen tight and so damn ready, my throat vibrating with a constant mewl, begging for something to send me over the top.

"Claire?"

"What? *What?*"

"Are you ready to come for me?"

I almost laughed. Confident bastard. Did he think he knew exactly what he was doing, that my body was that easy to control?

He slid two fingers up inside me, proving that he did. And could. And would.

"Holy shit," I gasped. "Oh, Killian. It's— It's never been so—"

"Let it go, babe. I don't need the thesis. I just want your surrender. That's it..."

"Please." I had no idea how I didn't tear the stuffing out of at least three pillows as I thrust my soaked body deeper onto his long, masterful fingers. "Please, Killian, *please.*"

"That's it, beautiful Claire. Release it for me. Come for me."

A few more circles of his clever tongue, along with the steady pumping of his fingers, and my body burst into a thousand points of light. With my mouth parted on a silent scream, I let the explosion crash through my limbs and then shimmer through my whole body. It was, without a doubt, the most fantastic orgasm I'd ever experienced. Wave after wave of heat pulsed through me until I finally dissolved, limp and amazed.

As Killian sprawled himself beside me, I lay back with eyes closed and what had to be the dumbest grin on my lips. I felt the weight of his eyes on me but couldn't bring myself to look back yet. He started dropping little kisses to my shoulder, and I let out a long, high sigh.

He finally whispered, "Hey, you okay?"

"Of course I'm okay." I still smirked like a fool. "That was... fantastic. Thank you."

He seemed to consider that for a long moment—before rolling right on top of me. "Just fantastic?"

For a second, I forgot to answer. His erection, still hard and trapped in his boxers, pressed incessantly against my belly. But even in that condition, the man's size and heat were breath-stealing. Remarkably, my heartbeat revved into the red all over again. I'd never had a lover keep me in such a state of constant desire.

He's not your lover. He's not anything except the center of one of the best hours of your life—so enjoy him while you can, Montgomery.

"All right," I responded on a little giggle. "Maybe better than fantastic. *Much* better..."

My words trailed off into the thorough kiss he lowered to my lips. As he pushed inside my mouth with hungry intent, I reached between us to stroke him through his boxers.

"Claire," he grated, circling his hips against my fingers. "Fuck, that's nice."

I relished his groan as I squeezed his hard, hot crown, now moistening his underwear with evidence of his need. "Hey, Chicago?"

"Hmmm...yes, San Diego?"

"It would appear you're overdressed."

He groaned softly. "I will *not* contest that point."

With a smile, I took advantage of the moment to curl *my* fingers into *his* waistband, tugging his shorts down his lean hips and over his firm ass. Finally, I hooked them with my toes and dragged them the rest of the way, setting his cock free. Harsh breaths sawed from his nose as I roamed my fingers up his body, exploring his sleek physique with their tips.

Wow. Every inch of him was magnificent, but his backside was a work of art. I couldn't keep from kneading the muscles there as he prodded my legs apart and fit his body into the apex. The position flooded me with memories of being on his desk in his penthouse. Had it been only a handful of hours ago? And had I really been that scared of him—and then that snotty to him?

I buried my face in his shoulder, drowning out the negative thoughts. I swore every one of them off, vowing to bask in this moment. Perhaps tasting *him* would help banish the demons. Without wasting a moment on hesitation, I sank my teeth into the tempting meat of his shoulder. His skin was hard, a little salty, a lot delicious—but as I went in for another sample, he speared me with a mocking glower.

"Naughty girl. No biting for you. That's my job."

A shiver skittered through my body. "Is that so?"

He nodded while reaching for the condoms. His attention to the foil in his hand wasn't so suave. With a fast rip, he pulled the latex out and then leaned back on his knees to roll the protection on.

"Killian...wait. I should..." I hoped the way I looked at his shaft, licking my lips, conveyed that I'd be more than willing to return the favor he'd just done for me.

"No way." His retort was damn near a drill instructor's bark. "No shoulds for you right now, fairy. And no regrets. And no fears. No other orders to heed—but one."

He punctuated it by looming back over me, his full erection in hand. I couldn't help slicking my lips again, watching him poised at my weeping entrance. "Wh-What's that?" I managed as he braced above me, re-securing my stare with his. My fingers dug into his forearms as I waited, breathless with anticipation for the first flood of ecstasy as his body filled mine.

"My name." He guided his head through my wetness and pushed his way in. "On"—he was achingly slow—"your"—exquisitely hot—"lips."

He was still only halfway in. Until that moment. With a thrilling thrust, he slammed all the way in—stealing my breath, my thoughts, and any hope I had of thinking this was a night I might, in thirty or forty years, forget. Dear God...*this man*...

We moved together now, thrust for thrust, my hips meeting his lunges with perfect timing. He never looked away. His stare was hypnotizing, drenched in countless layers of dark intensity. I couldn't clear my head or catch my breath. I was captivated. Annihilated. I dug my hands into his thick black hair and pulled at his scalp. An aroused growl curled deep in his throat, so I repeated the move, crying out my own pleasure as he buried his face in my neck and sank ravenous teeth into my skin. Once again, he was right. *He'd* do the biting. And I'd be the one reveling in it.

After the hurricane of carnality he'd wrought, I was stunned to feel a second orgasm building low in my abdomen. It was a rare event in my sexual history, one never achieved like this. But oh yes, the pleasure mounted as Killian readjusted his angle, pulling away to achieve the full distance between our bodies. My eyes widened as I waited, almost nervous about the next marvel he'd unleash on my body.

His carved face, still concentrated so fully on mine, broke into a smile as he slowly glided his cock into me. Every clench of his jaw and press of his lips told me how thoroughly he enjoyed every inch of our union. I closed my eyes for a long moment, doing the same.

When he was seated fully, he began grinding his pelvis into mine, directly rubbing my labia and clit, winding my arousal to excruciating tension, before withdrawing and doing it all over again. The mastery of my body and the ink-dark adoration in his eyes became my anchor *and* my freedom, melding our souls as one.

Over and over, out and back in, he plunged and teased and thrust until my channel dripped with need, my orgasm achingly close to the surface. Killian clenched his jaw so tight I watched his thundering pulse through its steely skin. It was a small consolation to see how the strain taxed him too.

"Please, Killian," I finally sobbed. "I can't take any more. Please...make me come again."

Unbelievable. I'd never begged a man for release in my life. I had no idea how it had happened this time, but Killian Stone held the keys to my body's kingdom. Insanity would be my new best friend if he didn't release me soon.

"I, too, want you to explode, little fairy." He stroked into me again with solid purpose. "But remember our rule, baby."

"Wh-What? R-Rule?" I could barely breathe, let alone recall rules. What the hell was he talking about?

"My name on your lips, Claire. Mine." A bead of sweat dripped off his forehead and onto my lips. Without thinking, I skirted my tongue out to lick it off. A dark growl escaped from his chest.

"Yes," I returned. "Oh Killian, *yes*." I was seriously about to lose my mind. "Killian. Killian. *Killian*. Oh, hell!"

As soon as I spilled the words, he braced his elbows on either side of my head and slammed into a high-octane pace with his cock. His eyes were brilliant onyx, his skin burnished with sweat. He pumped into me like a madman, fucking me deep and hard and rough. I slicked my hands down his back and gripped his straining ass, certain I'd never been more thoroughly consumed by pleasure in my life.

When I thought it couldn't get any better, it did. He reached between our bodies, stroking his magical, long fingers over my abused clitoris. With that action, he finally unhinged the locks. My release burst over me in a white-hot ball of sensation, though a thousand colors sparkled behind my closed lids. My head jerked back into the pillow as I screamed Killian's name over and over, just as he'd commanded me.

But the word was more than just obeisance to him. It was praise and plea and adoration, erupting from the deepest reaches of my heart. I didn't bother to question why—as if I were capable of advanced thought right now anyway.

Only one thought dominated my mind. One word. His name. I could've shouted it a hundred more times. And, God, how I tried—not caring if the entire damn airport heard me

CHAPTER ELEVEN

Killian

I was a fucking god.

I grinned like an idiot at the thought, confident I might as well have just scaled Mount Olympus. Budget goals? Profit targets? Personal aspirations? What the hell were those, compared to the triumph of bringing the ecstasy to this woman's face? Of feeling the walls of her body convulse around me as she splintered in passion? Of hearing the sob in her voice as she chanted my name like a lusty prayer?

Oh, yeah. I was the man. I sucked droplets right off my little fairy's skin, savoring her salty perspiration as I locked my mouth to her neck once more. The new positioning angled my cock deeper inside her, enabling me to feel every new drop of her arousal around my length, every squeeze of her flesh against my own.

My smirk faded. My lungs got stingy with my breath as my heart pumped more blood to the juncture between my thighs. She gripped my ass, worsening my torment from abstinence yet making it a hundred times better. Every cell in my balls roared with the entreaty for a green light on my orgasm.

I clenched my fists and held back. Drove into her harder. Deeper. Slanting myself back a little so my shaft slid along the front wall of her tunnel, until—

"Holy shit!"

She screamed like that.

I dragged myself in and out at exactly the right angle. Claire's hands plummeted to the pillows. I grabbed them and meshed our fingers, watching the new arousal take over her face. Her mouth dropped in a wordless scream. Her nipples jutted at me, pink and tight and perfect. She wrapped her legs around my waist, clenching me hard. Her sex started shuddering in beautiful waves of fulfillment.

I stared down at her, aware of nothing else but her breaths, her cries, her sighs. Rain pounded the roof above us. I didn't care. On a nearby runway, a jet touched down. I didn't care. Here, now, there was nothing but her glistening beauty, her golden passion, her body's perfect union with mine.

"Claire," I whispered. Now I was the one praying. "Sweet Claire."

"Killian. Oh, Killian..."

I pulled in a quivering breath and let it out on one word to her. "Now?"

"Yes," she gasped. "I need you. Come inside me. Now."

I climaxed with my gaze twined to hers, a tight groan escaping with the release that rushed up my flesh and burst deep within her core. At the same time, her pussy clamped me with rigid force, coinciding with the new ferocity on her face. Witnessing her completion a third time spiraled mine even higher, making me wonder if the come would ever stop. In so many ways, I wished it wouldn't. I thrust again and again, shuddering as waves of release poured from me.

Even as the heat subsided, I couldn't let go of the moment. I bent my head and kissed her with long, lingering plunges, exultant when she returned every pass with equal fervor. Even after I pulled out and tossed the condom, I didn't let her go. As we lay on our sides, I explored every curve and crevice of her body that I could. My search yielded a heart-shaped freckle on her left shoulder. A tiny childhood scar below her right knee. Even a couple of ticklish spots behind her elbows.

She watched my every move as if I fascinated her as much as she did me. The idea was preposterous, but I reveled in her attention—until her face noticeably tightened. A frown automatically claimed mine in return. I threaded my fingers across her forehead, into her hair. "You still okay?"

She gave a bashful shrug and dipped her head a little before scooting closer, burrowing against my chest. "Hell yes. Definitely. As in...definitely to the power of wow." She waited a couple of seconds before adding, "Go ahead. Start preening, Mr. Stone. You have my clearance. Those were officially the three best orgasms of my life, okay?"

I laughed, though the reaction felt forced. "Just...the orgasms?"

I sounded like a goddamn girl. She was right. My chest should've been puffed like a rooster who'd claimed the golden hen, but there I was, fishing for performance clarification. Needing to know I wasn't alone in feeling like the axis of my world had just been tipped.

"No," she chided, "not *just* the orgasm." She raised her head in order to scoot her hands beneath her chin. She grew silent again, making me study the darker lights in her eyes and tuck a strand of hair behind her ear. "I'm just..."

With my hand still in her hair, I pressed, "Just what?"

She gave a tentative smile. "Trying to memorize everything," she murmured. "That's all."

I hitched an elbow beneath my head, trying to appear

casual—feeling everything but that. "You make that sound like it's the last day of camp."

She giggled. "What?"

I didn't return the mirth. "Sad," I explained. "You sound sad but resigned to it."

She lifted her head a little, to get a better angle for our mingled gazes. The glints in her eyes darkened even more. "I guess I am."

Thunderheads stretched across my mind. And the squeeze of anger in my heart? Better it went ignored. *Much* better. I finally muttered, "Why?"

"You know why." Her tone landed somewhere between reproving and terse. My tension rose in proportion, getting thicker as the crew began fueling the plane and loading the galley.

"Maybe you'd better humor a guy during his last few minutes on American soil."

"Don't get morose." She sighed against my chest, fidgeting a finger against my right pectoral. As she neared my nipple, I had to fight the craving for her all over again. And the realization that her assertion was right. I was being morose. And resentful. And frustrated that though we'd finally ridden the Colossus roller coaster to its giddy, amazing end, I loathed the thought of climbing off. "Okay, I'm not saying that it wasn't good or that it wasn't an amazing experience—"

"An amazing fuck, you mean."

She jerked away, face twisting and shoulders stiffening. I glared back, steeping in self-righteousness that bordered on asshole, but I couldn't stop myself—couldn't hold back the angry sarcasm from seeping in. But if she wanted cavalier here, then damn it, she'd get it.

"Excuse me?"

"Have I misspoken, Miss Montgomery? Forgive me. You can't blame me for jumping to the conclusion. You've been pretty damn clear about what would be possible between the two of us, so—"

"And *you've* been pretty damn clear that *possible* was acceptable." She pushed from the bed, swinging her legs out and tempting me all over again with their silken curves. I reached for her hip, but she yanked away, heaving to her feet. "You told me you weren't the prince, Killian. You never promised me a glass slipper or doves in my window, and I was fine with that." After stepping back into her pajamas, she sat at the foot of the bed with a softer expression. "You also talked about secrets," she murmured. "Mine *and* yours. You told me they'd be safe."

I readjusted the sheets with a sharp jerk. She didn't need to know what the sight of her bare chest still did to me. "What's your point?"

She curled her fingers around my calf while lifting her gaze to my face. "Will our secrets be safe if we continue this?"

My frown deepened. The answer to her question was plainer than the arrow of arousal that her touch shot up my leg. The contact was a continuation of our connection, its filaments more tenacious with every minute we spent together. The woman had me spellbound. Humbled. Opened. I looked inside and saw parts of my soul that I'd considered vaulted so long ago. With her, they were unshackled.

Which made me her complete captive.

I almost let out a laugh. God, what a tangle. My brother's recklessness had brought Claire into my life, but my own could be the fatal tug at the whole house of cards. And the most hilarious catch of it all? I wasn't sure I cared.

No. I *had* to care. The woman, damn her brilliant soul, saw to the essence of that. Insisted on it. Was stronger than I in accepting it, evidenced even now by her determined movements as she buttoned her top back up. I watched her with heated reluctance. Flannel pajamas would forever have a new meaning for me.

When she was finished, I finally rose, used the facilities, and shoved back into my dress pants. I found a clean black T-shirt in one of the dresser drawers. It was over twelve hours to Beijing, so the dress shirt and tie could wait until later.

As I expected, the crew was busy preparing the interior of the plane for our departure. When I emerged from the bedroom with Claire, a sly smirk spread between the two flight attendants. I responded with a don't-go-there glare, already guessing the intent of their grins. To my relief, they toned down the snark and plastered on affable smiles instead.

Claire shifted and rubbed at one of her forearms. Though she slanted her head back toward me, her gaze never reached mine. If it had, she would've witnessed my visual warnings.

"On *that* note"—I pressed a hand into the small of Claire's back—"I'm walking you out."

She squirmed a little more. "That won't be necessary, Mr. Stone."

Mr. Stone?

"The hell it won't." I didn't try to temper my growl.

The rain had stopped, but the wind had kicked up, whipping her coat tightly around her as I grabbed her hand during our walk to the town car. Alfred stood waiting next to the vehicle, as impervious to the cold as a Buckingham Palace guard. He opened the back door as we approached, and Claire moved toward it with an urgent energy.

I jerked her back forcefully. *Not so fast, little fairy.*

My chest tightened in all the good ways when she moved back into my embrace without resistance. I pulled her face up, inundated with protective fervor when my hands encountered her chilled cheeks. Without thought, I locked my lips to hers— needing to taste her one more time. Needing another long drink of her warm, sweet essence. Longer. *Longer...*

Our bodies quivered against each other when we finally pulled apart, our breaths thick clouds in the night air. Behind me, Vaughn ignited the plane. "Fuck," I gritted.

"It's okay." Claire lifted a brave smile. The corners of her mouth quivered. "Go."

"I'll call." I hammered my intent into both syllables. My longing. My need for hope.

Her smile descended. "Don't," she rasped.

So much for hope.

But she was right about that too. Didn't mean I had to be happy about it. And I wasn't. But wrapping myself back up in my wrath gave me the strength to let her step free. Then, the determination to turn and stomp back to the plane. As I climbed the steps, my soul dove in the opposite direction— deep and low—back into the shell of Killian Jamison Stone, a stranger I'd never hated more than in this moment.

CHAPTER TWELVE

Claire

"Mmm?" Nothing answered my sleepy mumble. I opened one eye and tried to see the clock on my phone, only to realize I'd spoken into the wrong end. "Uhhh...he-hello?"

My other eye popped open, pried by shock. It was one in the morning.

"Hey, fairy queen."

Heart, meet throat.

Okay, not a total shocker—except that Killian had used *that* nickname. The precious words that now tumbled all my nerves into my stomach and tripled the pace of my pulse. In ten seconds flat. In the middle of the night. When I wasn't prepared. Or clothed.

I bolted up bed and started fumbling with my hair, as if he could see me. "Is something wrong? Why are you calling now? Are you all right? Damn it, did Trey—"

"He's fine. I'm fine. I'm sorry I woke you, babe."

His voice dipped into husky registers that gave me the impression *he'd* just woken up. Even after a week and from nearly seven thousand miles away, the sound gave me wonderful chills. I scraped the hair off my face, firmed my chin, and snapped, "Please don't call me things like that. We've been down this road. So...Trey's fine. You're fine. Why *are* you calling? It's the middle of the night."

"I know. I've tried to keep my calls to business hours for you, but...this isn't business." His thick exhalation filled the line. "I had a small break, and—"

When he fell into silence, I huffed again. "And what?"

"I miss you."

My heart didn't make it to my throat this time. It stayed in my chest to entertain my rib cage with a dozen backflips. "Oh."

There was a discernible rustle from his end. When he spoke again, a more intimate murmur took over his tone. "I miss you. I can't stop thinking about you. I keep wondering what you're doing. Who you're doing it with. What you're wearing."

He edged toward humor, making me smile and settle against the pillows. Through the crack in my room's drapes, the lights of the city beamed, but the glow was meaningless and cold. The only warmth in my world came from a tiny hole in the device in my hand. The awkwardness of our parting at Midway, though only a week ago, seemed a distant memory. The man was so damn hard to stay mad at. Yes, I missed him too. But letting him in on that tidbit? *Not* a good idea.

"So." His voice was even lower this time. Rougher. "What *are* you wearing?"

I groaned and then laughed. He stuck with determined silence. "Pajamas, Killian," I finally stated. "I was sleeping, remember?"

He cleared his throat. "Your flannel ones?"

Hell. The seduction in his voice was unmistakable. And irresistible. But I wouldn't let him get the upper hand this time. "This pair is satin, actually." I underlined the announcement with flippancy. "Black satin with white piping around the edges. Boring, boring, boring."

"Nothing about you is boring, Claire Montgomery."

Upper hand, Claire. "Oh, yeah? Well, I'm wearing thick white knee socks under them. How's that for glamorous?"

He snorted. "Socks? Why?"

"Because it's damn cold here tonight, and—"

"And what?"

And you're not here to turn on that heater you call your body. "I'm a wimpy California girl. There. You got me to say it. Satisfied?"

"No."

"No?"

"Satisfied would mean being there with you, stripping off those socks along with the shit that's covering them up." I listened to the rugged sough of his breath, picking out a tinge of melancholy in his tone. My empathy for him was the key to my undoing. Within seconds, my mind punched the Rewind tab, taking me to memories that I'd worked so hard to block.

"You do...strip me...quite well," I whispered.

"You inspire me to greatness." His voice was a whisper too. "Fuck. Claire—"

"We should say goodbye." I nodded to reinforce myself. Like *that* would be effective. "Aren't you on your way to something? A meeting? An appointment? A tea ceremony?"

"Not for hours. I'm in my suite, all alone. *Claire*—"

"Yes, Mr. Stone?" I offered it smoothly this time. Urgently. It was easy, given the sinful demand in his tone. Even so, my voice was odd in my ears. I sounded breathless. Needy. I was going to hate myself in the morning for caving like this. I didn't care.

"Take your pajamas off. And tell me about it."

His graveled tone thrilled me. His commanding words moistened every delicate tissue between my thighs. Nevertheless, I retaliated, "I'll do no such thing."

Or...would I? There were a lot of things I'd never done before Killian came into my life.

"Do it, sweet girl. For me. No one will know."

"More secrets? Isn't that the last thing we need between us?" I said it as I began unbuttoning my top, though I wasn't about to tell him that—yet.

"Please, Claire. Are you sure you don't want to?"

"Are *you* sure your middle name isn't Persistent?"

He sent over a growling sigh. "Does it excite you to hear me beg?" I could picture his eyes, dark and determined and anything *but* begging, as he asked it.

"You could stand on the corner selling hot dogs and I'd be turned on."

His rich, full laugh warmed my heart.

Brakes. Brakes. *Who said anything about bringing your heart into this, girlfriend?*

"So what are you doing now?" he inquired.

"Just finished unbuttoning my top," I said it with a little gasp as his lusty grunt filled the line. As usual, I couldn't resist him for long. "Now I've let it drop open. Your turn, Stone. What's your next move?"

"Fuck."

"Not exactly possible."

"Oh no?" He chuckled again, but the sound was guttural with lust. "Mentally, I'm preparing to fuck you right now, fairy. I'm remembering how it felt to prepare you. How your tight, erect nipples felt in my fingers and in my mouth." His heavy breaths vibrated across the miles. "Do you remember how responsive your tits were for me, Claire? How your nipples turned hard as stones as I licked and sucked them?"

"Mmmm." The sound careened up my throat, high with desperation. "Yes, Killian. I remember."

"Touch yourself now and pretend it's my hands on you."

"Ohhhh..."

"Are you doing it?"

"Yes," I rasped. "Oh yes, Killian." I closed my eyes and slid a hand across my chest, seeking out the nipples that ached for attention. The nubs greeted my touch with rock-hard arousal, poking between my fingers. I tightened my grip, rolling the peaks brutally, reliving the pleasure I felt when Killian pulled at them, stunning me to deeper arousal with the tiny jabs of pain. I sucked in my next breath and forced myself to squeeze harder.

"You're pinching your nipples, aren't you?" he charged.

"M-Maybe. A little."

"Or a lot?" He sounded amused, in all the sexiest ways. "It's all right, fairy. I remember that sound well. It's stamped in my memory. When I close my eyes, I can see the look on your face too. Do it again, baby."

I obeyed at once. Arousal sparked through me, brighter than all the neon in the city beyond the windows. "Killian... yessss..."

"I know, baby. I know." He groaned low once more, capping it off with a sharp hiss of his own.

"What about you?" Though my room was dark and no one could hear me, I whispered the words. The moment felt exquisitely intimate. "Are you touching yourself too?"

"The whole fucking army of this country couldn't stop me," he returned. "Claire...you have no idea...every morning

I wake up with a hard-on so painful even the shower doesn't settle me. It's because I wake up thinking of you."

My hand stilled. I dipped my head, rubbing it against my phone like a damn star-struck teenager. "Killian..."

You have to stop saying things like that.

Don't ever stop saying things like that.

"I don't know what you're doing to me. I don't even know if I *want* to know. It's some crazy Claire spell..."

I punched out a little laugh. "Some crazy *what*?"

"I just know I never want to wake up from it," he went on. "I think about you constantly. I hardly think of anything else. I'm stroking myself now, insane from this shit. I'm rock hard... insane to be inside you again. When I finally get there, I'm going to spend hours on you, baby. I'm going to pleasure you in so many ways—"

"And you too," I interjected. "*You* get fulfillment too?"

"Hell yes. I want to take you hard, from behind. I picture your pussy riding my shaft while I explore your beautiful asshole with my finger. After I've come inside you like that, I can't wait to watch you wrap your pouty mouth around my cock before taking me deep in your throat."

My lungs gave me air in ragged spurts. Dear God, the havoc this man wreaked on my body with a few growled words. "You've— You've been putting a lot of thought into this, haven't you?"

"Mild understatement." As he paused, I heard the sound of flesh sliding on flesh. The strokes corresponded to his heavy huffs on the line. "What are you doing now?"

"Kicking off my pants."

"And those sexy tube socks?"

"Those too."

"*Goddamn.*"

"I'm naked now, Killian. I'm lying on my bed, hot and achy. My pussy is bare and open and waiting for you."

"Taunting temptress."

"I'm sorry..."

"No, you're not."

"You're right." I sighed into the line. "I'm not sorry. Just warm and wet, with a quivering, needy clit. Tell me what to do, Mr. Stone."

"Don't be coy, Miss Montgomery. You know exactly what to do. Rub that gorgeous pussy of yours. Pretend your finger is my tongue, sucking at every bit of you there. Do you remember how it felt when I tasted your flesh for the first time?"

"I don't think I'll ever forget." My voice was breathy and shameless as I slipped my hand between my thighs. The moist folds of my sex waited, pulsing in readiness when my fingers made contact. I keened softly, answered by the increased tempo of Killian's breathing. I could tell he was pumping his cock ruthlessly now. With increasing speed, I circled my swollen bud before pressing in, spiking the thrill at my core.

"Killian..."

"Yeah?"

"It feels so good. Touch me some more." I released my imagination to our fantasy. In my mind, his hands were all over my skin, his mouth covering mine, pulling the air from my lungs and the thoughts from my head.

How the hell had this happened? For ten days, I'd been so careful to keep these memories locked away, but in less than fifteen minutes, he'd hauled all of them out of my mind, beyond my control.

"Talk to me," he ordered. "Tell me everything, Claire. Tell

me exactly how you want me." He panted like he'd just sprinted through the Beijing pollution.

"Inside me." Stressing about the dream wasn't going to erase it now. I bucked my hips, surrendering to the power our words created. "Please, Killian. I'm spreading my legs farther for you. Fill me with your cock." I slipped my middle finger into my channel, thick cream coating me right away. "Ohhhh, God."

His answer gave life to the panther I always likened him to. "Slide a finger into your cunt, sweet girl."

My breath clutched. I tried to laugh. His nasty words turned my senses upside down and my sex to pure butter. "One step ahead of you," I replied.

"Then add another."

As I followed his dictate, my breathing sped up to match his. I slowly worked both digits in, gasping as pressure and lust pulsed through me. This had to be one of the dirtiest things I'd ever done—and because of the strength in Killian's presence, even from the other side of the world, I reveled in every illicit moment of it.

"I'm so wet for you," I whispered to him. "My pussy walls are so tight. They're clamping down on me, just like they'd squeeze your cock while you fuck me..."

"Damn. *Damn*, girl, I love your naughty mouth. Keep talking. I'm so close, Claire."

"Me too. Don't leave me like this, so hot and needy. I need more of you, Killian. More of your body filling mine, more of your cock fucking me hard." As the words left my lips, my mind lived out the fantasy. I imagined his thighs encased by mine, his shoulders straining with each fierce thrust, the rugged plateaus of his face etched with passion. "Take me with you," I begged between heavy gasps. "Let's come together."

"Oh baby, it's good. So...fucking...good."

"Mmmm...hmmm."

We groaned, moaned, gasped, and grunted together. Miles apart...breaths apart.

"Come for me, Claire."

"Yes..."

"Say my name again. Scream it as you explode for me."

"Oh yes, Killian. Yessss..." My lungs held the rest of it, too selfish to free my breath, afraid to acknowledge the cataclysm about to strike my body and carry me away.

"*Now*, Claire!" It was a grinding growl.

"Oh...Killian..."

Then I was mute. Lost to the pleasure traveling through my torso and out of my limbs. The orgasm rocked me for what felt like forever yet ended all too soon. I floated back to my bed in the dark, sucking air through my nose, trying to settle my breathing—when I remembered the phone in my hand.

Shit.

Embarrassment flattened my pleasure. I slammed a hand to my forehead. What the hell had I just done? My thrumming body and vibrating pussy provided the glaring answer to that. Once again, *that man* had smashed past my barriers and made me fly in skies I'd never imagined in my life.

Phone sex. With my boss.

It had been fucking fantastic.

And completely inappropriate.

It's a little late to be concerned about appropriate behavior here, Claire.

There was telling silence from Killian's end of the call. Seven thousand miles stretched farther with every second that passed...and every minute of wordless silence that we allowed.

God. I could practically see his uncomfortable scowl, even in the gloom of my room. I could sure as hell feel his uneasiness—as well as my own mortification and self-doubt.

One of us *had* to say *something.* "Well, ahhh...I need to be up in four hours, so...I hope the rest of your day goes well, and... umm..." I picked at the sheets, stumbling for something droll but instead blurting, "Thanks?"

He grunted hard. "Thanks?"

I prayed for a freak interruption in our connection. No such luck. "Sorry. I forgot to read Miss Manners the day she addressed correct follow-up for phone fornication."

"Why are you being so odd?"

"What's your point? This whole thing is odd, Killian."

"It doesn't have to be." His voice was quiet.

"Of course it does." The words *and* tone were pure bitch, but the man had me tied up in enough knots to justify it. "Everything with you just...is."

"That's not fair." Now he sounded wounded, and I wished I could take my words back. The "odd" in this equation wasn't solely his fault. That meant the knots weren't, either.

"You're right," I mumbled. "I apologize. I'm just really tired."

"Are you sure that's it?"

Great. He had to pick *now* to convert his take-no-prisoners Attila into a cable-sweatered sweetheart.

"Yeah, I'm sure. I'm going to hang up. I'll—I'll talk to you soon."

"Have sweet dreams, baby."

"Have a good day, Mr. Stone."

I pressed the End button before an electron of his hurt could invade the line—or an ounce more of my remorse could crush my chest. Could I have concluded our conversation with more callousness? But what alternatives did I have, aside from spilling the tears that slid down my cheeks now, spurred by the confusion that crushed me all over again?

I'd violated my own mandate. Let myself give in to the man again. The tryst on his plane was supposed to be the dessert I sampled just once, a sin never to be repeated, a secret never to be discovered. Staying out of jail was damn good motivation for the resolve. Keeping my heart intact was a better reason. Maintaining my sanity was the best of all.

Because this person I became around Killian...she was *not* logical. Or sensible. Or safe. She wasn't the Claire I knew, who damn well knew the difference between sex and attachment, who kept her heart and soul away from a man's pretty words and whispered seductions. A Claire who was missing so blatantly now I contemplated slapping her face on a milk carton.

Trouble was...I liked the new Claire.

The bigger trouble? She wasn't new at all. I'd seen her before. She'd trusted a man named Nick McCoy and had ended up with a torched heart and a blackmail threat because of it.

This was a mess.

But moping in bed wasn't going to make it any better, despite the temptation to order everything from the room-service menu with chocolate on it, along with a box of tissues and the newest Nicholas Sparks release on my e-reader. I forced myself out of bed and slunk down the hall for some ice to jam over my puffy eyes, not even looking forward to my normal work-until-I-dropped therapy. Every minute of every task would only remind me of Killian.

The sun wasn't up yet, and my day was already screwed.

★ ★ ★ ★

It was almost time to let out a breath of relief.

The gala was in full swing, and Trey was the epitome of a reformed rake, thank God. We'd spent the last three days coaching him on behavior, attitude, and etiquette, especially with the media. Now, the press all but swarmed him, eating from the palm of his manicured hand.

I looked on with pride, a tiny part of me even wishing Killian were here to see his brother's transformation. Since I'd severed every communication with the man except the bare minimum required to give him project updates, I didn't know the details behind his delay returning from Beijing, only that he'd told Andrea some suppliers needed extra attention and he didn't feel optimistic about making it to the gala in time.

I snorted softly to myself. "Suppliers." *My ass.*

As soon as I indulged in the doubt, I mentally kicked myself. *You walked off that plane swearing you'd both gotten what you wanted and were done. But then you got naked for him again, those seven thousand miles be damned, before flipping the tables on him again and damn near hanging up in his ear.*

So who's the rightful winner of the mixed-signals trophy, Claire?

Michael couldn't have picked a better moment to appear, ready for me to hand off the "Trey Watch" duties. After giving a glowing report, I excused myself to get another drink from the bar, admiring how the gala committee had transformed the Peninsula Hotel's ground floor in keeping with their theme, *A Wild Night at the Ball.* In a nutshell, it was Cinderella goes to the jungle, complete with palace walls draped in tropical vines and a midnight-countdown clock fashioned out of stacked tribal drums and palm fronds.

Despite the opulence of the surroundings, I was relieved the night would be over soon, allowing me to cab-it back to our hotel—and my private misery. The last few days had been hell. The press had glommed on to Killian's trip to China like moss, meaning I'd seen more pictures of the Stone brothers in the past two weeks than I had in my entire life. The realization made me shoot a morose grin at the floor. Hell. If I could move better in the bodice of this gown, a clingy one-shouldered Grecian in light blue, I'd give myself a pat on the back. We'd come to do a job, and everything couldn't be going better. Killian was a media darling, with his brother as the next obvious contender for the position. Almost. Wooten still hadn't made a move with legal proceedings, so we all continued to hold our breath. Tonight's success would help our efforts along for days.

I leaned against the bar to accept a fresh glass of chardonnay, attempting to relax a little while watching an older couple glide by on the dance floor, lost in each other's eyes. Now all I had to do was ignore the pang in my heart that followed.

"You're getting ridiculous." I fired the reprimand at myself from locked teeth. What was next? Bursting into tears if the band started a sappy tune? Returning to my room and crying over the life-insurance commercials?

More couples danced by. I focused on the women's beautiful gowns—and the gorgeous shoes beneath—as the minutes seemed to drag by. When the band brought the song to a melodic ending, the crowd submitted a round of well-deserved applause.

Only then did I notice a strange stillness in the room. While the band prepared for their next song, nobody left the dance floor. Couples at the tables leaned and whispered to each other.

Panic fluttered in my stomach. The night had been going so well. If Trey blew things now, I envisioned Andrea ordering an emergency castration for the guy. Surreptitiously, I peered around. The cognizance wasn't just mine. More members of the crowd, mostly the women, traded eager murmurs as their stares turned the same direction. I pushed from the bar and turned to follow suit.

And instantly gave up the air in my lungs.

The ballroom's grandly decorated entrance framed a late arrival to the party, straightening the cuffs on his tailored tuxedo without surrendering an inch of his towering, proud stance. Without a doubt, he was the most perfect man I'd ever laid eyes on.

Killian.

He didn't linger in the doorway very long—especially after he spotted me. Those endless legs burst into powerful motion, carrying him closer by the second.

I tried to swallow but couldn't. He consumed every second of my attention. I yearned to—needed to—run, but my feet suddenly felt formed of lead.

I can't do this. Not in public. Not with you here, Killian—please.

Though I tried to plead to him with my eyes, he didn't falter in his approach. His steps were broad and determined, his smile a grim curve, his gaze zeroed right in on me. It felt like the entire room was gawping at us now. With every step he closed in, heat crept deeper into my chest and cheeks. My heartbeat cranked to Mach ten.

How did he do this to me? After all the events of the last

two weeks, how *could* he do this to me? It wasn't fair. He was magnificent and flawless. I was speechless and dizzy. The condition worsened as he stopped, mere feet away.

Had an angel manifested in the middle of the room and flown to me, I would've been less dazzled. Every detail about him seared my senses. The shine of his hair, slicked back from his face in formal fashion. The scent of his cologne, Mediterranean and musky. The way every thread of his tux seemed fashioned just for him. Even the buttons on his crisp white shirt had black onyx covers, perfectly matching his eyes.

Divine intervention was with me at least a little. The band began their next song, restarting the movement and volume through the room. Regrettably, my heartbeat joined the trend, with no surcease in sight if Killian had any say in the matter. Without a single word, he pulled the wineglass free from my hand and set it on the bar. I said nothing, trapped in his spell.

He took my hand and pulled me out to the dance floor. His eyes never left mine.

I still couldn't say a thing. He still wrapped me in his thrall.

I opened my mouth, hoping the protest in my head would translate to my lips. The last thing I wanted to do was dance with him, unsure my legs would even carry me. As usual, all my options vanished as soon as he pulled me close. Warm. Strong. Unfightable. Magical.

We swept seamlessly into the midst of the other dancers, though I barely noticed them. The room faded in the shadows of him. The world fell away beyond the force of him. Nothing seemed safe except his embrace, though my mind screamed that the perception was a sham. Strike that. It was a mistake— Biblically proportioned. I couldn't let him literally waltz in here, toppling me off my game with the surprise appearance, before sweeping me off my feet with some fancy dance moves and romantic music. And, damn it, I was going to tell him just that—as soon as I could form a coherent sentence again.

CHAPTER THIRTEEN

Killian

Though sitting on the board for the zoo was a passion rather than an obligation, the annual gala wasn't an event I looked forward to. Evening gowns, monkey suits, drunken smiles, political games... No fucking thank you. I almost chuckled every time a society-page editor hunted me down at one of these fancy things to request a quote. If this was a picture of what society really was, I feared for the world.

But, tonight, fear wasn't in my vocabulary. Nor was hesitation. I'd phoned Alfred the moment the plane crossed into domestic airspace, stating I'd need my tuxedo as soon as we touched down. Though Alfred had agreed and had been on the tarmac with the new Tom Ford suit, the undertone in all his actions betrayed his belief that I was insane. I'd be nearly two hours late to the party.

Clearly, the man didn't grasp my intent. I didn't give a shit about attending the party. I only wanted the perks. One in particular.

Now, I swiftly scanned the room for her.

Frustration set in when my first pass didn't yield any results. Damn it, had Claire left already? I couldn't just show up at her hotel room door, not after the fumble of an ending to our phone exchange last week, but I damn well would if that had to be part of the plan.

And what the hell plan would that be, Kil?

I scowled deeper, tempted to tell my psyche to fuck the hell off. No, I didn't have a plan. No, this wasn't like me. Yes, I was aware of both facts, neither of them huge enough to surmount the motivation that had brought me here tonight. This cavern in my chest was so deep I was surprised there weren't miniature tour groups tromping through it, shining flashlights into the new fathoms that were carved by the day. More accurately, with every conversation I'd managed to secure with Claire.

That wasn't right, either. A conversation was defined by the active participation of both parties. The woman's one-word replies and business-only brevity were the equivalent of leaving a wad of cash on my nightstand and slipping out of bed before dawn. I'd never *initiated* such a scenario, let alone endured one from the receiving end. My questions about her behavior, whether subtle or direct, had yielded nothing but a tight, polite change of subject from the woman.

That stopped. Tonight. Even if she was already in bed— holy God, I could only hope—I would hunt the woman down and drill to the heart of why she'd persisted at widening the emotional distance between us. Didn't I warrant dialogue that consisted of more than "Mr. Stone" and statistics sheets? Hadn't we come further than that?

If she still wanted to keep her pajamas on after we talked, fine. But treating me like a complete stranger was *not* acceptable anymore.

My second scan of the crowd delivered a direct hit. Instantly, I was glad the pajamas promise had only been made to myself. Seeing her again led to an immediate renege on the oath.

Damn.

She'd truly turned into my living, breathing queen.

Her hair, swept off her face into a regal twist, shone like spun candlelight. The sparks in her eyes were just as brilliant, intensifying as they reacted to the strange hush befalling the room as the band ended one song and prepared for the next. She twisted around, wine in hand, threatening to drag my tongue out of my mouth with her beauty. The slender cut of her shoulders. The graceful grip of her hands on the glass. The creamy glow of her skin, encased so perfectly in that dress. Dear *fuck*, that dress. Its ice-blue fabric artfully draped into a one-shouldered bodice that nipped against her waist and then flowed around her hips, swirling down in layers that moved like water with every subtle shift she made.

I couldn't stop staring at her in that dress.

I couldn't stop wondering how it would come off her the quickest.

Without deviating my gaze, I began my march across the ballroom to her. I'd achieved three steps of that goal when the diversions started coming. Bunny Persipine had a seat saved for me at the board of directors' table, "just in case." Harry Treacle happened to be sitting with Richard Branson, who had a new merger idea to discuss. Harry's daughter, a sophomore at Vassar, home for a spring break she clearly wanted to remember, flashed a winking wave from behind her father. As soon as I looked at all three of them, they backed off. It was a small consolation to know my bother-me-now-and-you're-dead attitude was still in good working order.

Unfortunately, Claire Montgomery had as much game in that department as I did. Her posture stiffened and her features tightened as I closed the last ten steps to the bar. But she didn't run. Aside from the ramrod now jamming its way up her spine, she didn't even move. I pulled encouragement from that and breathed deeply. An incredible bouquet hit my senses. Her perfume, a richer choice tonight than her usual, filled with notes of exotic spices. The wine in her hand, a vanilla-influenced white. The ever-present lavender in her hair, made more luxurious by the product slicked into it.

Like an imbecile, I became the one who couldn't move.

As soon as I breathed her in, all her energy wound tighter through me. The air between us arced and zapped with unseen voltage and heated to the same tangible pressure as the first time we met. In many ways, it felt as rickety as that moment again too. After our time together on the plane, we'd parted so quickly and the ending of last week's phone call had doubled down on that awkwardness. Now all those carnal memories danced in the air between us, satyrs we had no idea what to do with. We were back to square one with nothing but left feet and a lot of unresolved issues.

The difference? I was no longer seven thousand miles away. I was in a position to pry that wine out of her hand, set it on the bar, and replace it with my grip instead.

And I did.

I was in a position to use that hold to yank her toward the dance floor, giving me a socially acceptable excuse to get her close to me again. Really close.

And I sure as hell did.

Her backlash wasn't unexpected. I dug fingers into her rigid back, ramming her hips against mine while pushing at her feet, taking the lead in our steps. She huffed and resisted. I grabbed her left hand, twisted her fingers into compliance and shoved at her feet again. Though the song was a contemporary tune that required only the most basic moves, I had a message to convey with unmistakable authority. Only one of us was in charge right now.

"Mr. Stone." It was less a greeting than a snarl.

I lowered my eyes and lifted my lips. "Miss Montgomery."

"You're really late."

"And you're fucking beautiful. But I'm sure every single man in the room has told you that already. Probably a few of the married ones too. Bastards."

She was too tense to surrender a giggle, but I hoped she'd at least relax the posture. No joy on the goal—though, for a tiny moment, the shards in her eyes turned to molten honey. The artful blush on her cheekbones was joined by a pair of natural flushes.

"This is a bad idea," she muttered.

"The last time you said that to my face, the results were goddamn awesome."

Her adorable nostrils flared. "That's *not* happening again." When I purposely replied with nothing but silence, she persisted, "All right, how's this one? I'm in five-inch heels, damn it."

"Then perhaps it's best you hang on so we don't cause a spectacle."

She huffed. "Perhaps it's best that you let me go back to work."

"Michael's on Trey Watch now. I watched your pass-off. My brother's nearly won his gold star for the night, anyhow."

She tugged up her chin. "Good. Then that means I can..."

"Stay right here with me." I took advantage of the chance to directly meet her gaze. "Where we can have a little chat."

Her features twisted as if my words were needles in her neck. "I don't know if I want to chat with you, Killian."

If her words hadn't cracked from such pain, I would have rejoiced in them. At least we were back to Killian instead of the name on my goddamn office door.

"That's exactly why we're going to stay right here—all night if necessary."

Her brows shot up. Then her eyes narrowed. "You're completely serious."

"And you're still completely beautiful." I tilted my head a little. "You're also completely right. I'm pretty fucking serious."

She fumed through at least four bars of the song before gritting, "What the hell do you want, Killian?"

Wasn't that the sixty-million-dollar question of the night? As such, the answer deserved a pause for careful thought. Trouble was, I already had the words prepared. I'd been able to focus on little else during the entire flight back from Beijing. "We've climbed off the Tilt-A-Whirl, right?"

She slanted a glower up at me. "What's that supposed to mean?"

"Hey, just checking. Because I swear I'm still stuck at the carnival—and now I'm lost in the goddamn Haunted Maze."

She tossed back a huffing laugh. "Aww, is that so?" As she flopped her head in the other direction, accusation sliced from her gaze. "Demons around every corner, huh?"

I blinked, confused more than ever—and doubly determined not to relent to her now. "Demons don't scare me," I stated. "Darkness does." Did she hear the deliberate solemnity I gave the words? The message I wove into them? "Why have you tossed me into the dark, Claire?"

She brought her head level, though her gaze descended

to the center of my tie. "I'm not sure that's a question for me, Killian."

"The hell it isn't." I punched the words through my teeth, the verbal equivalent of grabbing her chin. When she jerked her stare up to my face, I was waiting with a hard glower. "I'm not about to leave on a plane, and you sure as hell can't hang up on me now."

Her lips flattened. "I didn't hang up on you."

I snorted. "Yeah. Sorry. My bad. You *did* give that a parting line, right? 'Thanks for the orgasm. Have a good day, Mr. Stone.'"

She winced, giving me a shred of hope. Some part of her recognized the absurdity of our detachment as well. The disconnect *she'd* pulled the trigger on. "Killian. Please—"

"Please what?" I snapped. "'Have a good day, Mr. Stone.' It was officially the warmest thing you said to me in the last fourteen days." I was on a roll with the wounded sarcasm, so I went for one more. "I wonder what kind of kiss-off your vibrator got every night."

She whipped her head around, panicking that I'd been overheard. "Can you at least try to remember where we are?"

I arched both brows. "Start shedding some light on things for me, and I might consider it."

"*Killian.*"

"A little goddamn light, Claire." I yanked her closer as the song ended. I'd dance with her through twenty more if I had to. Thirty. Forty. "I'm not asking for skywriting or a floodlight. Just a sentence or two to help me understand why you sterilized what we've shared into nothing more than a business exchange."

Her laugh, though laced with bitterness, came as a

surprise. "That's funny, coming from the man who seems to like his business exchanges."

"What's that supposed to mean?"

"I'm leaving. Good night, Killian."

Her retort was more a seethe, retightening my tension level. Was I *ever* going to solve the Rubik's Cube of this woman again? Though I inhaled deeply to temper my own tone, it was impossible to wean all my frustration from it. I followed her retreating figure into the lobby as she waited in front to the elevator bank. Just as I caught up to her the door to an available car opened, and I stepped in with her, capturing her once again. The air was heavy with our breaths, the anxiety between us higher than ever before.

I bit the bullet. Kissed her into silence. It wasn't a move of passion—it was a smack of anger, and she all but spat at me in the seconds after. I answered her with a small, one-sided smirk. "Claire, my sweet, you taste like Häagen-Dazs."

She glared. "What?"

"Yep. At least a few quarts. Probably an exotic flavor to remind you of home, like piña colada. You'd never go for chocolate if you wanted to wallow in a really good mope."

She shoved against my chest and then spun to the button panel and punched the number for a random floor, escape the only thing on her mind. "What are you even talking about? This conversation is over. *This*, Killian, is over."

I moved up behind her, even more calm and confident in my steps—yet never more invigorated in my life. "So you're acknowledging there's a 'this'?"

"No!" she shot. Relief sagged her shoulders when the doors slid open. "I don't know what I'm—" She jolted to a stop, her gown swishing around her legs, her head dropping into her hands. "Damn it, don't you understand?" She laughed bitterly before muttering, "Of course you don't. How could someone like you possibly comprehend the terror I feel every time—"

"What?"

I whipped around to stand in front of her again. So much for feeling in control. She stripped that shit from me the moment tears encroached on her voice. All of them sparkled in her eyes when she raised her face toward me again and confessed in a little rasp, "Every time I look at you and feel all the things that I do."

I was really going for the idiot punch card tonight. Ten paralyzed silences and you got a free smoothie with your next visit to Moron-land. But I had no idea how to process what she'd just confessed with such precious, honest simplicity. I hadn't shaken it, kissed it, or aroused it out of her—so now it turned around and smacked *my* ass with pure shock. And when I should've been taking elated advantage of it, I stood there like a dumbfuck while she burst with an anguished sob, sidestepped me, and ran out to the terrace.

The Shanghai Terrace was one of the city's most popular open-air restaurants, with its trendy Asian vibe, but had closed early tonight, likely because of the brisk spring wind now whipping at the red drapes on the four-poster couches positioned across the patio. I barely noticed the gusts as I followed her—fuck it, chased her—and caught her by the elbow, slamming her against me once more.

"Tell me," I demanded, lowering my face inches above hers. I didn't elaborate. I didn't need to. She knew what I demanded—and that I wouldn't let go until she'd surrendered the words. The certainty of that knowledge glistened in her eyes. And the dread.

"I can't," she whispered. "I *can't*, Killian. Please—"

"Why?" I heard the vicious bite in my growl and didn't care. She'd talked about secrets during the hour that had changed everything, back on the tarmac at Midway. I followed instinct in chasing that subject now. "Is it Andrea?" I charged. "Margaux? Do they have something on you? I can protect you, Claire. You just have to—"

"No." She struggled again, but I had her by the waist now, resolute against making the mistake of letting her go again. "No. That's only the start of it, okay?" She squeezed her eyes shut, releasing tears down her cheeks. "God! If that were all there was to this now. If only—"

"What?" I demanded when she didn't fill that telling pause. "If only *what*, Claire?"

She drew in a shaky breath. "If only I hadn't gone to you in the plane. Or answered the phone when you called last week..." Wind rushed across the terrace, pulling thick strands of her hair out of its twist, tangling with the tear tracks across her high cheeks. "And stopped myself from getting lost in you. Giving too much of myself away to you."

I caressed a hand up her face. Dropped my forehead to hers. She felt so damn good in my grasp—her body tiny and sheltered by mine. So perfect. So right. "Why is that a bad thing?"

She reached up too, trying to push my hand away. But after a second of hesitation, she meshed her grip into mine instead. "When is being lost a *good* thing?"

The wind blew stronger. I didn't need a second sign. If the elements themselves were letting go of doubt and inhibition, then I was ready too. "If I've got to walk away from you, then I never want to be found again."

Her face turned up. So did her lips. Her stare, glowing like illuminated amber, seeped warmth and completion through me. "Oh, Killian…" She murmured it like a chastisement but rose up on tiptoe in a gesture of entreaty. "Be careful what you wish for."

I had no idea who kissed who first, nor did I care. With the fusion of our mouths, I finally had fulfillment for my soul. I clutched her body tightly, letting my fingers press into the flesh exposed by her gown's scooped back, rejoicing as her arms slipped beneath my jacket and found my nape and scalp.

I needed more.

So much more.

Now.

Barely breaking the contact of our lips, I swooped an arm around her knees and lifted. Though I braced myself for at least a squeal of protest, Claire only mewled her encouragement, sending adrenaline to my legs to cover the half-dozen steps to the nearest deck couch. After laying her on it, I pounced in a circuit around the thing, hauling the drapes shut in four clean sweeps.

When I returned to her, my heart thundered and my body pounded, drawn to her like a ship finally finding its harbor. I stretched my body beside hers, but in the space of one consuming kiss, I stroked a hand beneath her dress and up her thigh to find the lacy scrap covering the treasure I sought most. As I yanked impatiently at the fabric, I rolled to position myself between her legs. My body muffled the distinct tear of the lace giving way to my force.

"Oh, my God." Her stunned stare beamed up into mine. "Oh, my *God*!" she repeated as I pushed away the panties, sliding my touch inward and lower. Then lower…

"Perfect," I murmured in return. "Holy shit, Claire, your pussy is so perfect. And so hot for me. And oh...feel *this*...so very wet for me..."

It sounded like pillow talk, but every fucking syllable was the truth. Her flesh, so pliant yet tight, so quivering yet sure, was the gateway to bliss I'd been dreaming about for two interminable weeks. Her little moans were just icing on the erotic cake. She emphasized each by gripping my shoulders harder, finally shoving my jacket off in order to grab at me through my shirt.

"I swear, if you keep doing that...oh, and *that*...dear hell, Killian, I'm going to scream..."

I couldn't help emitting a wolfish chuckle. "That'd be a fun twist to the evening."

"You're evil."

"I'm yours."

"Stop saying things like that." She said it wistfully, adding a long gaze full of equal yearning. In return, I leaned low and sank my mouth against hers. When I pulled up, our stares still locked, I rocked my cock against her cleft, wondering how much longer I could take the torture of my pants and briefs.

"What should I focus on instead?" Another feral smirk— that disappeared as soon as she issued her reply.

"Getting lost," she whispered. "With me. Inside me. Please..."

CHAPTER FOURTEEN

Claire

As soon as the words spilled from me, his expression tightened and intensified, turning his face into the definition of shadowed beauty. Oh, God. My plea had affected him on a deeper level than I intended.

You really going with that, girlfriend?

All right, it may have been exactly what I intended. Being here with him, cocooned in this crimson hideaway with the silken wind around us, liberated something inside me. Killian's nearness set more of my spirit free, his strong body and fervent embrace giving me the security I'd longed for, the bravery I craved to finally admit things—to him *and* myself.

I fumbled at his waist while we continued kissing, consumed by our passion. His dark carnality dragged me like an undertow after a summer storm, and I never wanted to be saved. Surrender was the only choice. I gave it with a long, willing moan.

Killian finally leaned back and unbuckled his belt, working his tuxedo pants and briefs down around his trim hips. He returned to me quickly, settling eagerly between my thighs, where we were finally able to slide flesh against flesh. I gripped his shoulders and sighed from the nirvana of his rigid cock against my pulsing pussy, teasing my stiff, needy clit. As he pushed a little harder, I abandoned my effort for silence. My cry of pleasure tumbled free, flying with my spirit now.

"I'll never get my fill of you." The faint stubble on his jaw was an erotic caress as he growled the words into my ear. "It's only fair to warn you now, Claire. You're a fever in my blood. A torment in my dreams."

I stared into his dark eyes. "Is that why you won't leave mine, either?"

He pulled back a little. I couldn't define the look on his face anymore. It had surpassed intense, shifting to a force that clutched at my throat, even stung at my eyes. His lips parted as if he had words for me in return, but nothing came out. I was glad. Sometimes, consonants and vowels were crimes against the splendor of the universe, especially when its gifts were something like *our* something. My chest tightened, but the rest of my body trembled, terrified and electrified in the same crazy moment.

I finally blurted the only thing that made sense.

"Make love to me." I yanked at his hair, pulling his face to mine in a long entreaty of a kiss. "Please, Killian. I need to feel you...everywhere."

A gorgeous smile spread across his lips. "Hold on, baby. Let me suit up." He already had a condom yanked from his pocket and ripped the packet with his teeth to free the latex.

"Oh," I squeaked. It was the only possibility, given the new hardness in his jaw and seduction across his features. Both turned more intense as he wrapped my fingers around the rubber.

"Roll it onto me." His voice was gritty. "I want you to feel how much my cock's missed you. How deeply I've longed to be part of you again."

The wind gusted, coinciding with his fierce hiss as I fitted the condom around his shaft. His flesh swelled, steely and hot, against my touch. I gasped as he pushed into my fingers, his pulsing veins and searing crown filling my grip.

"Killian. You're beautiful."

He buried his face in my neck while realigning his sex with mine. "And you're my obsession. Dear God, Claire..."

The curtains billowed as he stroked his erection through my soaked folds, all the while kissing a trail from my ear to my gown's neckline, his growl holding thick, sinful promise. He teased my clit until I moaned like a wanton fool.

"What— What if someone comes out here?" The line wouldn't be earning me an acting award. Desire spiked my words more than fear, adding to my shivery excitement. I'd never done anything like this before in my life. Another first on my list, courtesy of Killian Stone.

"What if they do?" His drawl was filled with molten surety. As always, he'd somehow peered in my mind and spooled straight to the source of my lust. "Maybe they'd see our shadows through the curtains...maybe they wouldn't."

"So maybe we should hurry." I ran my fingers through his hair, scraping my nails on his scalp. He hummed with pleasure like he usually did, and my heart glowed. I was starting to memorize his hot buttons too.

"I think you'll say anything right now just to have my dick inside you, baby." While we shared a chuckle, his eyes conveyed how much of the truth it really was.

"Would you rather I beg, Mr. Stone?"

"I would rather you never call me Mr. Stone again. Ever."

On the last word, he rocked his hips and entered me, eliciting my immediate cry of ecstasy. When I was able to open my eyes again, I found him staring down at me, inches from my face. His warm breath feathered across my skin. His stunning black eyes danced with desire.

"You take my breath away." He withdrew a fraction and pushed in fully, circling his hips while I clung to his ass, digging my nails into his burnished flesh. "You took it away the day we met."

Thank God I was on my back. The man, with his eyes and his body and his heated confessions, would have knocked me there anyway. As my soul flooded with emotion, I wrapped my arms around his neck, interlocking my fingers so I could pull myself up to kiss him. I licked his lips, moaning from the spicy taste that was uniquely him, now mixed with the salt of his sweat from the sexual pace he was setting in his wool tuxedo.

Until voices drifted across the terrace.

So much for pace.

We both froze. My eyes shot to his, resulting in the instant urge to smack him. Mirth played in his stare and a smirk tapped at his lips, deliberate pokes at my abject horror. Before I could think again, he leaned down and whispered in my ear as he started pumping at my pussy again.

"All you have to do is stay quiet, fairy. Think you can do that for me?" With deliberate timing, he changed up his pace to include those enticing hip twists again.

"Bastard," I hissed—and then sank my teeth into his shoulder to muffle my heated moan.

The man didn't alter his pace. "Your cunt feels so good," he growled into my ear. "I can feel every inch of you, clamping down on me."

"Ahhhh." I let it out on a breath. The wind picked up again. The drapes smacked the support poles, threatening to give us up.

"You're getting wetter, Claire. Hotter. You like this, don't you? The danger. The idea of getting caught..." I felt his mischievous grin against my neck. He'd discovered something new about me and started using it to his full advantage. "What if you came while they were out here? Could you keep quiet as you shattered for me? Could you be still while I came with you, my cock spilling hot come inside you? Or would you scream from the rapture, so everyone in the hotel knew what we were doing in our secret spot? Would you love it if everyone knew I was out here, fucking you into ecstasy, watching every moment of it on your face?"

"Killian," I rasped. "Oh, *hell*—"

He drowned my lips in a kiss that spiraled me higher, sucking on my tongue to the point of pain, reaching inside my bodice to pinch a pouting nipple. As I began to moan, the voices drifted away. A woman whined that it was too cold and she wanted to go back to the party. A man answered, complaining she had no sense of adventure anymore.

Killian finally released my lips but played along my jaw with hot kisses. "Oh, fairy, that was close. Maybe next time we won't get so lucky. But maybe next time you'll be coming for me."

"Okay," I blurted. When he only chuckled, I really did start begging. "Killian, *please.*"

"Please what? Tell me, baby. Let me hear it."

"It— It feels so good. *You* feel so good, fucking me. Faster...*please.* Harder...*please.* Do it until you come, Killian. Get lost with me..." I gripped his ass again and pulled him into me. His deep groan spurred me to hold tighter, wrapping my legs around his waist. My gown pooled down around me on the sofa, making me appear to be drowning in an ice-blue lake. The comparison was so damn accurate. I was submerged in heat, desire, and need, clinging to the only life raft that made sense. Killian.

"Hell, yeah." His face swayed above mine with the force of his thrusts, his features drenched in an expression of reverence, intensity, and joy. "Let it go, baby. All of it. I've waited too damn long to watch you come again. Do it for me, Claire."

I gasped and grabbed at his hair. "You— You too."

"I'm right here. I'm going under too. I'm ready. So fucking ready."

I was speechless again. The purity of his confession, the honesty of his passion...they turned me inside out. I adored him. I needed him.

I came for him.

The explosion slammed like a lightning strike, jolting me with a million sensations from head to toe, covering me in delicious tingles and prickles. Lights of a million colors sparkled behind my closed lids as I heaved in air, desperate to catch what I could. Killian's groan added more resplendence to the moment, his body seizing as his cock pulsed against my walls, an orgasm that surely tested the limits of the latex around him.

After a couple of long minutes, he fell on top of me. We traded smiles that resembled kids in a candy store.

"Holy fuck, woman."

"Don't you blame me!" I couldn't stifle my giggle.

"No blame," he stated. "Only gratitude." His face turned solemn. "You amaze me."

After he tossed the condom into a covered ash tray, we lay in silence for a few minutes, enjoying our afterglow and the play of the wind through the drapes. I started to get chilly since we weren't humping like bunnies anymore, so I snuggled closer to the furnace of his chest. He circled his arms around me, tucking my whole body close to his. I pulled in a breath. When I let it out, all the lead weights in my body seemed to float out with it.

"This is nice." My voice sounded almost like I'd sucked in helium. I nearly giggled again until Killian tightened his hold. While he still radiated warmth, it was joined by a sober stillness.

"What the hell are you doing to me, Claire?"

"What am *I* doing to—" I attempted a sarcastic huff while smoothing a hand over his shirt. "Sorry, sir. I'm afraid you have that one backward too."

"I'm serious."

"So am I." My tone wasn't so flippant now.

"I think we have to talk. To figure this out. And yes, there is a *this*."

He swung a finger back and forth between us in emphasis. I rose a little in order to see his face. As I expected, his focus didn't waver. As I *hadn't* expected, a clear truth nailed me between the proverbial eyes.

The man had feelings for me. This shit had knocked him just as sideways as me—and quite possibly scared him as much too.

I'll never get my fill of you.

You're a fever in my blood.

You're my obsession.

Holy shit. I'd written all of it off as pretty, empty words. After all, men said the stupidest lines when their little head ran the show.

Had his *big* head been in on his show too? Had he meant all of that?

"This is so complicated."

He tucked some of my stray hair behind my ear. God only knew what my elegant style looked like now. "Then let's simplify it."

I was almost thankful for the strong gust that whooshed across the terrace at that moment. It was a perfect excuse not to speak—not that I had any words to give him anyway.

Then Michael Jackson saved my ass.

"Billie Jean" suddenly blasted from my handbag, still sitting where I'd tossed it when we climbed onto the sofa. "Shit," I muttered. "That's Chad. I'd better—"

"Go ahead," Killian kissed my forehead in encouragement.

I picked up right before the King of Pop hit his chorus. "Hey," I said breathlessly. "What's—"

"Where are you?" It wasn't Chad. It was Michael. And he sounded like the horrified guy from those old radio recordings of the Hindenburg disaster.

"I'm...errr...at the Terrace."

"That's here, right? In *this* hotel? You're still at the Peninsula?"

"What are you doing on Chad's phone?" I glanced at Killian, who'd straightened in connection to the tension in my voice. "Michael, what the hell is—?"

"Are you still at the Peninsula or not?"

"I'm *here*, all right? What's happening?" I wouldn't have been shocked to see flames licking up the side of the building any minute.

What Michael revealed was worse.

"Trey's flawless manners?" he shot back. "Turns out

they've been helped along—by God knows how much tequila."

"What?" I realigned my dress. "But how the hell—"

"Remember the cute little blonde reporter? The freelancer?"

"How could I forget? She's been eyeing Trey's crotch more than his face."

"And apparently trading drinks with him while she does. We also found a flask at the edge of the reflecting pool. Chad's pretty sure he heard Trey sneaking gulps from it in the john earlier."

"Wait. The reflecting pool? You mean the big tank thing with the fountains that the decorators brought in?"

"That would be the one."

"Why did Chad find the flask there?" My imagination answered that for me. "No. Ohhhh *no*."

"Oh, yes. The guy's giving liquid courage a whole new meaning."

I traded another stressed stare with Killian. No sense in hiding the truth from him. "Dear God."

"I'm not sure He's listening."

I tried to jam my hairstyle back into place. "How bad is it?"

"You'd better just get down here."

When I hung up, rolling my eyes in misery, Killian's expectant stare awaited. "Let me guess. It involves Trey, some booze, and at least one woman."

I grimaced. "Michael didn't mention any women."

At that moment, a giddy female squeal resounded from the bottom floor. In its wake were three words, issued in loud enough shouts to echo up the street. "Go, Trey, go!"

"Mother. Fucker." With his pants already righted, Killian

braced an elbow on his knee in order to pinch the bridge of his nose. "How did this happen? I thought he was being watched like a toddler."

"He was. I guess next time a strip search won't be off the table."

"There can't *be* a next time," he growled. "Damn it, I thought we were done with his crap. I thought the Wooten incident was his rock bottom."

"I'm not sure he *has* a rock bottom." I shoved back into my shoes despite trembling knees. "I'm sorry. This is unbelievable. We worked so hard at putting all this together."

I felt like crying as we rushed toward the elevators, but that was *so* not happening right now. The car arrived and I stepped toward it, but Killian halted me, taking both my hands.

I averted my eyes, unwilling to meet his scrutiny. The second the call from Michael concluded, I should have expected this. The promises of *we have to talk* and *simplifying this*? Yeah, they weren't happening, either. At least I'd had the bliss of the dream for a minute.

But once again, he shocked the hell out of me. After tenderly kissing my knuckles, he lifted my chin for his reassuring gaze. "We'll figure this out, baby. *All* of it. Okay?"

If I'd found it hard to choke back my tears before, the feat was pure torture now. "Okay," I murmured before re-girding my psyche as we rode to the ground floor.

With one of my hands still locked in his, Killian pushed through the crowd toward the reflecting pool. Our journey wasn't easy. The mob was thick and rowdy, everyone whispering and laughing. Most had cell phone cameras in their hands, eagerly setting the devices to capture the antics of—

"Oh God," I sputtered.

The actual was worse than the imagined.

Trey looked like a bigger imbecile than I'd assumed, skipping across the faux pond with a highball glass in one hand and a leash in the other. At the end of that leash was Adara, the Lincoln Zoo's precious white tiger, one of several creatures on loan for special appearances during the party. I didn't know a thing about tigers, but the wildcat looked like it was debating whether to enjoy the bath or have Trey for a midnight snack.

I forced myself to look at the bright side. Though we'd heard a girl shrieking from the terrace, at least she wasn't in there with him.

My conclusion was Penny Treacle's ideal cue. At that moment, the girl burst from under the water, lacy thong in hand, shouting, "Spring break rocks! Woo-hoo!" She continued following Trey, shrieking in delight as he splashed her, still dragging the damn tiger.

"Oh, God." It bore repeating. "Killian, that tiger could turn on them any second!"

"Good," he snarled.

"You have to stop him." I forced myself to meet the dark fire in his glower, urgently grabbing his shoulder. "Please. I'll try to disperse the crowd, okay?" I turned, spreading my arms, attempting to redirect the throng. "Show's over, folks. Time to go home. Thank you for supporting the Zoo. Thank you. Please drive safely."

I might as well have been herding kittens. Everyone's eyes were fixed on Penny, Trey, and the giant white cat in the fountain.

Shit.

Where was the animal's handler?

I hurried through the room, finally finding the middle-aged man as he exited the restroom. Without preamble, I grabbed him and pulled him back toward the fountain—

Where there were now *three* people in the water.

Killian had waded in after his brother.

Everyone watched as the zookeeper grabbed the leash from Trey and guided the tiger away. At the same time, Harry Treacle showed up to collect his inebriated daughter, yanking her out and covering her with his jacket. Mary Treacle was right behind them, screeching at her daughter about the season being ruined, ignoring Penny's crocodile-sized sobs. Most of the onlookers stowed their phones and started toward the valet stand. The party was pretty much over, and other than some really bad film footage, at least no one was hurt.

Scratch that.

As soon as Trey and Killian stumbled out of the pool, Killian seized his brother by the back of his shirt, whirled him around—and drove his fist into the middle of Trey's face.

"Killian!" I shrieked.

Trey stumbled for a second, glaring at Killian and coiling a fist.

Smack.

After Killian clocked him this time, Trey crumpled to the ground like a sack of potatoes. Killian walked forward to stand over his brother, shaking out his bruised hand.

"Damn it!" I couldn't help rushing forward, standing on Trey's other side. "Why the *hell* did you do that?"

Killian grimaced like I was the village idiot. "Are you serious?"

"Are *you*?"

He lowered to the ledge of the fountain, sweeping a hand at Trey. "The fucker just undid everything you worked so hard for!"

I leaned over him like a mother to an errant child. "And you're doing everything in your power to make it worse!"

"Would you look at him for a second? Just one?"

"No. I'm too damn busy gawking at you. Your idea of helping was to wade in there after him and then go for the *roshambo* the second you got out? Next time, *don't* help, okay?"

The man sat there in silence, still looking utterly glorious despite his mussed hair and half-drenched tux. He worked his knuckles over both knees, letting my words sink in—or at least that was the impression he led me to. As I watched a couple of banquet servers try to revive Trey, I barely noticed the slow smile spreading across Killian's face again, even as he stood and walked to me. It was only when he let out a chuckle that I turned to him, exercising my turn to unfurl a you're-the-village-idiot glare.

"Perhaps you're right," he said, his grin turning even more cryptic.

"Killian." My frown deepened as he curled both arms around my waist and tugged me close. "What the hell are you talking about?"

"Maybe I should be thanking the bastard."

"Huh? Why?"

"Because now that we're back at square one, that means you'll have to stay longer, right?"

He buried his face in my hair and tickled my neck with his warm lips. I couldn't resist a wry laugh myself, and was tempted to nuzzle him in return, when we were interrupted by the sound of someone clearing their throat. A female someone.

We turned to endure the impact of Margaux's accusing stare.

She slid both hands to her hips, emphasizing the daring cleavage of her blood-red production of a gown. I still couldn't figure out if her matching, miniature top hat was supposed to look lopsided or had tilted that way by accident. There was no time to ponder the answer. The woman was determined that we wouldn't ignore her silent demand for an explanation.

"Shit." I shoved from Killian, swallowing hard though instantly grateful for the low growl he used for his answering command.

"Claire? What the hell?"

"Not now, Stone," I spat.

"What. The. Hell?"

Thank God for Trey.

I never would've admitted to the words crossing my mind, but the guy regained consciousness with flawless timing. As he sputtered and moaned, Margaux was forced to give in to confusion instead of accusation.

"What *exactly* is going on here?" she bit out. "Killian... dear?"

I glanced to Killian, hopeful he'd smooth Margaux out with one flawlessly worded sentence.

Regrettably, the Stone men were not ones for perfect words tonight. Or, for that matter, actions.

Without hesitation, Killian grabbed my hand. He swung back to my future stepsister in blatant declaration—and challenge. Though I tried to pry my hand free, he twisted his hold tighter. Margaux's eyes went wide with silent shock before narrowing in abject fury.

Ohhhh, hell.

Trey stumbled forward, rubbing at his swelling cheek and eye socket. "Killy! That's totally gonna leave a mark, ass brain!"

Thank God for Trey once again. Killian dropped my hand to spin on his brother, his don't-fuck-with-me glare now locked in place. "Shut the hell up before you draw a crowd again. And go *clean* up too. You look and smell like a drowned hobo."

"Psssshhh. So I can't have a little fun anymore?"

"Your fun is over, *assbrain*. Alfred will take you back to Keystone in the town car. You'll leave from the basement, where all the garbage departs the hotel."

Trey stared back at Killian with disdain but wisely stayed silent. Margaux huffed, shaking her head with a scowl that imparted disgust, disappointment, and determination all at once, before stomping off in the direction of the bar.

For one moment, I considered going after her, but what good would it have accomplished? No matter what I did now, it was clear she'd start prying into Killian's motivation for stealing a secret cuddle in the middle of the Lincoln Zoo's gala—as well as his aggressive stances with her afterward. Damn it. The man had poked the beast right between the eyes without even knowing it.

The best I could do now was pray that Margaux had already consumed half a vineyard of Cabernet and wouldn't remember this in the morning. Second on that supplication list was a fast resolution for Trey's exit, followed closely by the chance to get out of here and climb into bed, preferably alone. My libido—and my heart—had already gotten me in enough potential trouble for the night.

CHAPTER FIFTEEN

Killian

I'd had worse weeks at the office. It was simply impossible to remember any of them right now. Of course, nailing down a sane brain cell was also unthinkable at the moment. When Viola Exeter, party planner extraordinaire, wanted to screech about something, she scratched that itch until the damn thing bled, along with the ears of everyone else in the room.

Regrettably, "everyone else" was currently comprised of me.

"These expenses only cover the *human* damage from the stunt," the woman shrieked, brandishing the binder that held every detail pertaining to the zoo gala, "though at least your brother chose a legal-aged floozy to cavort with this time. We'd be ruined if Penny Treacle were a day under eighteen."

"Viola." It took every ounce of self-control to keep from growling it. "I assured you that Stone Global would provide restitution for all damages caused by Trey's...adventure. Submit the bills to Britta, and she'll take care of them for you." My mind snagged on a piece of what she'd said. "What do you mean, only the human damage?"

Viola winced. "Adara's handler insists that she's been traumatized by the event and needs to have professional help as soon as possible. The behavioral specialist they want to bring in is from Greece, and—"

"Wait." I flashed a confused frown. "Adara. You mean the tiger?"

"Why, yes. The poor thing hasn't been the same for three days. She hasn't been eating right, and her bowel movements have been completely—"

"So she needs therapy? From Greece?" One glance at Viola told me the argument wasn't to be won. "Make it happen," I muttered, waving a hand. "Whatever she needs." Just because I was miserable didn't mean *all* the caged animals in the city had to be.

Viola rose and smoothed her linen skirt. On a day like today, everybody had worn linen. And written sonnets about spring. And adopted lambs and puppies. And of course, journeyed to the Stone Global penthouse to make sure that the bill for the tiger's shrink was approved by the ogre fooling everyone in his nobleman's disguise.

Thoughts like that had attacked me more and more lately. The ticking clock on my time with Claire only made it worse. *All good things must come to an end.* And my reckoning was so fucking overdue.

"Oh, Killian!" Viola's embrace was my penalty for letting my mind wander. "You're an angel. Thank you so much, dear. I told them all that you'd understand."

I laughed. "We're all screwed up in one way or another, Vi. Why should Adara be denied the chance to reconcile her id and ego?"

She let out a genuine laugh and hugged me again. Though the woman was thin to the point of scary, she had the grip of an arm-wrestling champion, thanks to the energy she lavished on her brood of grandchildren. "You are an amazing man," she gushed before pulling away to let an appraising scowl take over her face. "At the risk of sounding scandalous, are you certain you're a card-carrying Stone boy?"

Ice clutched my gut. Her teasing tone didn't reveal that she was using the comment as a fishing expedition. But was my instinct about reckoning *that* accurate? "As long as I can remember," I jibed back. "Why do you ask?"

Her lips pinched. "Isn't it obvious? No offense intended against those older siblings of yours, but the good Lord saved the best genes for last, didn't he?"

Relief boosted my answering chuckle.

I escorted Viola back to the elevators, risking that another intrepid reporter would be waiting somewhere along the way, despite the fact that happy hour had started twenty minutes ago. Last week, one of the leeches had paid off a pizza delivery boy to let him make the run up here in his place. Yesterday, one of them had climbed all sixty-seven floors via the stairs, having learned the door code to enter from the stairwell. The asshole had dropped and crawled his way through the halls after that, caught only after Brett from the mail room had tripped over him in a spectacular crash.

The gamble was still worth it.

It always was when I had the chance of finding Claire nearby.

Luck smiled large at last. I would've thanked the beautiful lady, but she fucking owed me one by now. I grabbed the chance without taking time for formalities, striding directly to the open doorway of the conference room.

Andrea and her team were packing up, preparing to move on to Keystone, our family estate, for their evening fun— training Trey not to fuck up next week's segment with Oprah.

We'd all thought the timing on the interview couldn't be better, but now it couldn't be worse. The stunt at the gala had brought Gerard Wooten back out of the woodwork with a vengeance, along with some strange woman from Paris who claimed Trey had had sixty kinds of kinky sex with her, involving *him* in *her* lingerie and resulting in the birth of his love child last year. Nobody was amused, especially not the hardworking people in this room. They all appeared stressed, strung out, and tired—

Except the redhead my gaze was glued to now.

She was by far the most beautiful thing in this building. This city. My world.

"Mr. Stone."

Andrea's clipped greeting belied her exhaustion. Nevertheless, the woman crossed toward me with confidence on her platform pumps, which made strong thuds on the carpet as the rest of the team froze in their duties.

"Don't mind me," I said, addressing all of them. "I'm just checking on the troops. How goes the battle?"

Andrea smiled, but its brightness was as forced as her feet were into those shoes. "One day at a time," she assured me. "The days are simply a little longer right now."

"I understand." I rotated my stare around the room, able to keep my mien neutral—until I arrived at Claire. Once my gaze met the golden brilliance of her face, I was lost. Her pastel-pink sweater set, complete with the schoolmarm bun, didn't assuage the instant fantasy I developed.

"We're on our way to get some dinner before heading to Keystone." Margaux stepped forward as she supplied the information. "We've got a reservation at six, at Cicchetti. I'm sure they'll make room for one more if it's you."

I returned her all-innocent smile with a narrowed

scrutiny. Was this the same woman who'd all but tasered her glare into Claire and me three nights ago? Unlike her mother, who was simply an ambition-straight-up-with-a-chaser-of-bitch woman, figuring out Margaux Asher was like trying to balance an ice cube on one's nose. Her sexual designs on me had been plain from the day we met, but her tactics—a mix of coy, desperate, and undercutting—were unnerving at best and creepy at all other times.

This moment fell into the "all other times" column.

"Tempting," I answered with a cool smile, "but work presses. I've been delayed by an hour due to Ms. Exeter's visit, and I've yet to review the media demographics from last night." I flashed my gaze to Andrea. "I'll be at the manor on time to keep Trey in line for you, but I'll need to borrow Miss Montgomery to get me up to speed faster. I'll be happy to drive her to the estate when we're finished."

"Of course," Andrea replied while enduring her daughter's fuming glance. I almost didn't give a shit about the whole thing, but if I valued Claire, I had to care about Margaux's gloating acrimony toward her, as well as the subtle-as-a-heart-attack approach to me. I wondered if all this had anything to do with the secrets Claire kept alluding to. Was Margaux involved in the mysteries Claire still hadn't shared with me—the details of her own enigma? A link like that would logically explain why Claire continued to act like getting within an inch of me was akin to contracting an Ebola virus.

And why she grabbed at one of her forearms with the intensity of a kid who'd just been assigned detention. But *that* I could fix—just as soon as everyone got out of here.

She didn't move during the minute it took for them all to board the elevator and depart. Neither did I.

When silence descended, she still didn't shift.

I did.

"Mr. Stone." A tiny protest bled into her voice as she watched me close and lock the door and then turn back toward her. "Th-That's not necessary. The demo review won't take long, and then we can—"

I sliced her short by yanking her into my arms and taking her mouth with mine. Inside seconds, I meshed our tongues too. *Goddamn.* She felt perfect and tasted even better. Curves and softness against me. Coffee and cookies on her breath. And desire...everywhere. Fuck, yes. I soaked up the heated musk of it on her tongue. I groaned from the heady force of it as her ravenous hands pulled at my coat and tangled in my hair.

A sound edged in anguish burst from her lips when I ended the kiss and plunged my mouth to her neck. "We— We can't. If anyone forgot something and comes back to get it, or—"

"Ssshhh." I walked her to the edge of the table and laid her down over it. Hell. In this position, she was even more my wanton schoolmistress. My cock already wanted out of my pants. Badly.

"Killian—"

"It's all your fault," I interrupted, pulling her earlobe between my teeth and making her whole frame shiver. "After a day like this one, you think you can wear this outfit and *not* expect me to dream of fucking you like my naughty little school teacher?"

She giggled, spreading warmth along my neck. "Exactly what subject did we misbehave in?"

"All of them." I kissed her hard again, using her distraction to shove her skirt up over her waist. I scooped a finger in beneath her panties, joining my satisfied growl to her high, sweet gasp when I found her pussy soaked and engorged with arousal. "All of them, every day, through every minute. Thinking of this keeps me sane, baby. Thinking of *you* keeps me going."

Her face softened as she gazed up at me, bringing her hand along the plane of my jaw. "I'm glad I had to climb up here for my charging cord."

"The second I saw you that night, I dreamed of doing this with you." I twisted my hand in order to join a second finger to my first. Together, I slid both of them deep inside her. Instantly, her channel pulled me in, squeezing me hard. "I've been hot for teacher since day one."

She ran her tongue in a provocative path between her lips. "And she's been crazy about you." She joined her moan with mine as we kissed again. When we parted, her lips were curled more seductively. "I think I need some detention, Killian. Some hard disciplinary time."

I chuckled, leaning down again. I didn't just kiss her this time. The two of us sucked major face, biting and licking and pawing at each other like teenagers with hormones to spare. No, worse. I had never let myself get this crazy at sixteen. Claire Montgomery had given me permission to make up for lost time, and I adored her for every crazy, frenzied, lusting moment of it, especially as I succeeded in unclasping her bra and pushing it away enough to feel her erect nipples through that deceptively innocent sweater.

"Good Christ. You're so damn hot, and I'm so damn hard." I gritted it against her lips, dry humping her with heavy demand. "Claire, if I don't— *Fuck!*"

The loud groan fell out of me as she somehow found her way to my fly, wrenching open the fabric and then yanking down my briefs. My cock and balls spilled into her needy grasp, swelling instantly against her hold. I repeated the oath as she guided me to her core, not flinching when I reached down and broke her panties away with the resolve of Conan on a rampage.

Without another word, I plunged into her. With a beautiful scream, she welcomed me. Bracing my thighs against the table's edge, I sheathed my cock over and over again in the hot grip of her beautiful sex, locking her stare to mine by framing her head in my hands. The sighs on her lips became songs in my heart. The need on her face was a prayer in my soul. At the same time, my mind couldn't piece together what the hell was happening. Though I took her with primal violence, my senses couldn't cherish her with enough reverence. I never wanted this moment to end, while every logical thought I still had rendered me a ball of bellowing terror.

It wasn't too long before her lips parted on a needy croak. "Oh, God. Teacher needs to come."

I smiled and tenderly kissed her. "Then let's make sure I score an A plus."

She swallowed as I began rolling my hips, hitting her clit with the pressure she liked. At the same time, I drove my shaft in at a new angle, estimating that if I was lucky, that special spot in her core would be stimulated as well.

"Killian!" she cried. "Ohhhh, *Killian*."

I bit at her chin, her jaw, her lips. "You're such a good student too, Miss Montgomery. You know what that does to me...hearing you call for me like that."

"Yes," she rasped. "Ohhhh, yes."

"Say it again."

"Killian." She sighed.

"Now beg me with it."

"*Please*, Killian." She shuddered.

"Now tell me you're coming with it."

"I am. Oh, hell. I'm coming, Killian. I'm coming for you!" She shattered.

In the next moment, I splintered apart with her. My ass squeezed, my sac constricted, and my cock filled with a thousand shards of perfect, blinding release. I pumped her body full of my essence, wishing we could do it again before all my seed was gone...already hating myself for having to leave her sweet body. Loathing the pretense of a life that awaited my return.

After waiting for both our pulses to approach normal again, I dragged myself out of her, reaching for a nearby box of tissues to help us both clean up. Though Claire let out an adorable whine with my departure, she righted herself faster than I could get myself back together, scooting off the table with brisk efficiency.

Her demeanor was unnerving.

I scowled. It felt fucking criminal to shove aside our intimacy that fast. "Come here." I pulled her back into my arms, cradling her head with a hand. "I don't want to let you go yet."

She softened against me. But only for a moment. "Regrettably, letting go is our story."

I drew in a careful breath. "Maybe it doesn't have to be."

Claire slanted a wry smirk. "Yes, Killian. It has to be."

The limb of my instinct stretched larger and longer in front of me. I embraced the temptation and crawled out onto it. "What the hell are you so afraid of, baby?"

"And what the hell are *you* talking about?"

"It's Margaux, isn't it?" Though her averted gaze

confirmed the words, making my follow-up a moot point, I pressed, "What's she holding over you, Claire? Tell me so I can help, damn it."

She pushed away. "It doesn't have a thing to do with Margaux, okay?" She folded her arms, her fingers forming claws around her elbows. "Not anymore."

"What does *that* mean?"

"Nothing."

I glowered. "*Nothing?*"

"This isn't the time to be talking about this. I still have to brief you on the demographics, and everyone's waiting for us—"

I made her stop by confiscating the computer cord from her hand. In another decisive move, I pulled up her chin with my free hand. "All right. Now's not the time. But it *will* be time soon, fairy. I'll make it happen if you don't. Are we clear?"

She exhaled hard through her nose. "Fine. Yes. We're clear. Can we go now?"

I called down to Walter with instructions to have my car brought to the private valet in the building's basement. I hated subjecting Claire to my roundabout departure, but until the next wayward starlet or reality star became the media's newest distraction, this was my life.

I reluctantly released her hand as soon as we entered the elevator. Though the building's security camera feeds had been safe so far, any minute could bring a breach, as we'd warned all the SGC employees of, even before Treygate. Thank fuck the conference room was one of the camera-free sanctums in the building.

As we left the lift, a familiar engine purr made me smile a little. Until this moment, I'd never known the paradise of a great orgasm followed by the anticipation of a luxury car drive. Thanks to the sated woman by my side and the high-performance lady in the driveway, I hoped this wouldn't be the first checkmark on my experience list for this one.

"Ho-ly shit." Claire wrenched at my hand, pulling the syllables apart from each other in apparent shock.

"What?" I queried. "You all right? Did you leave something upstairs?"

She shook her head and stared harder at the car. "That's not the town car."

I didn't restrain the cockiness from my grin. Twenty-three hours and fifty-five minutes of nearly every day, the money in my bank account was often more a burden than a celebration. Right now, I selfishly seized every moment from my daily allotment of fun. "Hmmm. You're right. It's not."

"That's a twenty-twelve Aston Martin Vantage with custom rims."

I stopped to let her see my wider grin. "You're exactly right."

"And you're surprised."

"Yeah. But mostly turned on." I lifted wolfish eyebrows at her. "You can show me your Hot Wheels side anytime, San Diego."

She flushed and laughed. Goddamn, I loved doing that to her. "Well...she's beautiful."

"Not nearly as beautiful as you."

She narrowed her eyes. "You clearly haven't seen me in the morning."

"Then maybe I should." Our gazes met over the door I'd just pulled open for her. In the dancing amber depths of her irises was all the same curious passion that had drawn me in from the day we met—only now that magic was focused on me. "Maybe just for comparison purposes," I drawled. "So that I can roll over, pull you close, and again tell you that Damrys has nothing on you."

After I climbed behind the wheel and gunned Damrys from the garage, I expected the requisite eye roll and inquisition as to the sanity of naming my car. As always, Claire stunned me by simply stating, "So...Damrys. That's an interesting name."

I focused on the highway as we sped out to Highland Park. "You're right. It is."

"Do I get to know who she was?"

My mother.

The woman who couldn't bear watching me being raised by another and chose to leave my life instead.

I clenched my jaw along with the steering wheel to hold back from uttering it.

"She's dead now, baby. It doesn't matter."

Traffic was good to us, so we pulled up to the Italianate gates of Keystone in no time. Fate was in a generous mood—I received a bonus five minutes of fun watching Claire unroll her window to stare at the grounds as we passed the tennis courts, waterfalls, duck pond, jogging trail, pool, amphitheater, and the miniature forest that had been my childhood playground. When I finally drove beneath the lighted archway and parked in the tiled inner courtyard, I ended up having to lean over and push her mouth closed with two fingers. Surprisingly, she didn't retaliate with a single glare, good-natured or not.

"Are we in Rome?" she finally asked in an awed rasp.

I darted a fast glance around. The only eyes watching us belonged to Trixie, one of the kitchen cats, who lolled atop a decorative copper pumpkin outside the door to her home, currently cracked open a bit and bursting with the smell of fresh-baked soda bread.

With decisive speed, I pulled on Claire's nape and planted a hard, thorough kiss on her lips. "Welcome to Keystone. I'm glad you like it so far."

She gave me a soft smile. "You grew up here, Killian. Of course I like it."

With a goofball grin on my face now, I fought back the temptation to lead her toward the kitchen instead of the front door. I waved her up the graceful stone steps ahead of me, thankful that chivalry earned me an ideal ass and hips view. If I couldn't touch, I could sure as hell ogle.

"Mr. Killian. A very good evening to you."

"Hey there, William." As usual, I had to grab the butler's hand from behind his back to shake it. I couldn't stand the bow-and-scrape shit, even if I wasn't a resident here anymore. "How are you doing? How's the tennis elbow?"

"It's much better this week, Mr. Killian. My thanks for your concern."

Claire finally tilted a questioning smirk. "Mr. Killian?"

I shrugged. "Counting Grandfather Lawrence, there can be as many as five Mr. Stones in this place at one time. It's a necessity. For a few years, I tried for a simple Killian, but no dice."

"Mr. Stone values tradition." William's chiding subtext wasn't lost on Claire, who let the dimples deepen in her cheeks.

I sent a mock glower at the man. "That works for Scotch selection, Will, but not a world where people are known by their hashtags."

William's eyebrows rose to give me his silent censure once more. I grinned back, relishing our usual banter. "So what, may

I ask, is the hashtag for your friend?" he queried, smiling down at Claire. When he angled his gaze back at me, I watched one edge of his mouth lift, already reading the thoughts I had to sequester to silence.

How about hashtag-goddess? Hashtag-fairy-fantasy-queen? Hashtag-my obsession?

"This is Miss Claire Montgomery. She's a member of the team helping Trey out of his mire, though she stayed a little longer at the office at my request. I needed some data from the day explained."

Though William's nod was as urbane as always, his gray eyes studied Claire with all-seeing interest. "It's truly a pleasure, Miss Montgomery. If only Mr. Josiah and Mrs. Willa were here to make your acquaintance as well. Alas, they're in Paris for another ten days, at least. Perhaps another time?" His pointed tone told me the question wasn't intended for Claire at all.

"Another time, indeed," I answered, overcome by an odd nervousness. The idea of bringing Claire here for the express purpose of passing my parents' inspection... It struck me as all wrong and fucking disgusting. I should have known fate would find a way to get even for the bonus feel-good minutes. "Will, I've made Cla— Miss Montgomery late for her duties with the team. Are they in the upstairs or downstairs study?"

"Upstairs, Mr. Killian. I'd be most happy to show her there, since I believe a certain someone in the kitchen has been preparing for your visit."

"Yesssss."

After ensuring a plate of dinner would be prepared and taken to Claire, I hurried toward the kitchen. Though my stomach growled, my heart was just as overjoyed to behold the woman at the chopping block, humming her favorite Prince tune while slicing up the fresh soda bread. I slipped up behind her, lifted the gray-tinged mahogany hair off her face, and snaked a kiss onto her lightly lined cheek. She squealed and jumped.

"Lord love a duck! Killian Stone, you scared all nine lives out of your Kitty!"

My answering grin actually hurt my face. "Awww, come on. You baked that sin on a slab knowing I'd be slinking in here eventually."

"Slinking? *Pssshhh.* I expected you to come in asking for some with some manners to ya, not sneaking in like some pervert down the back stairs."

"You like perverts on your back stairs." I leaned over and grabbed a whole slab of the bread, taking a huge bite before she could prevent the swipe.

"I've got a knife in my hand, boy."

"I've noticed."

Her blue eyes spread wide. "My word. *You're* in quite a state tonight."

I took advantage of her shock to sneak another piece of bread. "Nah. Last time I checked, I was still in Illinois."

The door across the kitchen opened. My chest filled with more happiness when another familiar face filled the opening. The man's rugged jaw was ruddy from the chilly night, his eyes a little tired. Like Kitty, gray had started to edge his hair but was more noticeable due to the fact that he simply had more of it. "Well, well," he murmured with a smile. "Look what the soda bread dragged through the door." He grunted as I hauled him into a hard hug. Returning the ferocity of the embrace, he added, "Good to see you, Kil."

"That's our Banyan." Kitty added a snort to her deliberate use of the man's nickname, a direct reference to the man's lanky limbs and thick ponytail. "King of downplay, as usual."

The man sighed. "Now, Kit—"

"He's been concerned, Killian. Not that I blame him. Good Lord and all the saints, what you've had to deal with since February..."

"I haven't been battling the dragons alone," I interjected.

"Hmmpphh," Kit countered. "You mean that team from California? The land of the fruits and nuts?"

"Kit. God's toes!"

"Don't be bringing the holy pedicure into this, Ban. How much good are those people really doing if Trey got free long enough to take a bath with a Bengal tiger?"

"And Trey, a thirty-one-year-old man, wasn't one bit responsible for the foolishness?"

I waited, expecting Kit to rattle off another memorable one-liner. When she didn't, I decided to jump off a damn cliff and fill the air with something *really* interesting.

"They're doing more good than you may think, Kit."

Both of them straightened. They weren't stupid people, nor were they strangers to me. Hell, they were both the opposite. And since they both knew me better than I knew myself, their ensuing stares didn't surprise me. I just didn't count on the experience being so unnerving. I was used to dishing out this kind of scrutiny, not taking it.

"Kil?" asked Ban. "What're you saying, boy?"

Kit slammed her knife down with a loud *whump*. "Oh, are you that addled?" She swung her head toward me, a grin suddenly blooming across it. "What he means is, what's her name, boy? And while you're at it, just tell us everything else about her."

Ban shook his head. A contemplative smile twitched at his lips, too. "I don't think he has that much time, dear." He tilted his head and intensified his stare. "Do you, Kil?"

I couldn't help letting my lips lift as well. Fuck, it felt so good to simply confess this to someone. "No," I admitted, "I don't. But I can tell you that her name is Claire."

Kit's shoulders perked a little higher. "Ooohhh, that's a good start. What a beautiful...*Irish*...name."

I chuckled before adding, "How about adding Montgomery to it?"

"How about I thank the saints and faint dead away now?"

While I laughed, Ban scooted around the block, solemn intention on his angular face. "I don't care if she's half Swahili and half Martian." He stopped directly in front of me. "Do you care about her truly, Kil? In the depths of your heart?"

For a long moment, I remained immobile. I hadn't come in here planning to spill my damn guts about all this, especially since secrecy could damn near be the theme song for everything I had so far with Claire. Having to tamp down how I felt for her through so much of the day left me stuttering in the face of the question in its barefaced honesty.

What *did* I really feel for her? And now that I had permission to answer the question for the only two people in my life who didn't care if the name on my birth certificate read *Stone* or *Smith*, was I ready to admit the truth? Could I handle it?

With a twist of my own head, I looked back to Ban. "Right before we left the office to come here, Claire and I had a little tiff," I told him. "When I asked her to clarify a point for me, she answered me with 'nothing.'"

The wrinkles at the corners of his mouth twitched. "And what'd you do?"

"The same." I scowled. "Nothing."

"Excuse me?" Kit gawked like I'd confessed to having Claire's name tattooed on my penis.

"And the thing is, it's still bugging the shit out of me." I glanced up at Ban, feeling a hundred kinds of stupid and a thousand kinds of clueless. "What the hell does that mean, 'nothing'?"

The man scooped me into another warm embrace. "Congratulations, boy. That means you've got it bad."

I kept my eyes closed even when he pulled away, holding his scent in my senses just a couple of seconds longer. Soda bread. Smoke. Old Spice. Home. "I'm not sure I should thank you for that."

"Because it scares the hell out of you?"

"Yeah."

The man's face creased in a full laugh. "That's a good sign, Kil. A damn good sign."

CHAPTER SIXTEEN

Claire

As my computer booted up on the conference table, I checked my watch and smirked. If Killian was on his normal morning schedule, he'd be finding what I'd left on his desk right about now. I'd sneaked into his office this morning under the guise of leaving reports needing his immediate attention. What I'd dropped off instead was a shiny red apple, a wooden ruler—and the hope that he'd see the humor in my gesture.

I opened my inbox and struggled to focus. And nearly jumped out of my skin when my cell phone vibrated. Though it was still in the confines of my purse, I sneaked a peek at it.

Glad teacher approves. Guess whose ass I'm using this on tonight?

Instantly, my mind swirled with a new fantasy. I saw him with dark intent in his eyes, approaching me with the ruler. Heard my answering gasp as he spun me around and then yanked off my panties. Could imagine the taunting strokes he'd give my ass with the ruler while he whispered dirty things about pleasure and pain in my ear...

I squirmed in my seat and made three typos in my first email. I had no one to blame but myself. Awakening new sides of the man was a daily adventure, but so far, Playful Killian was my favorite. Strike that. *Second* favorite—only to Stunning Sex

God Killian.

After the Lincoln Zoo gala, the media seemed to be everywhere. They'd even started following our team around, knowing we worked closely with Trey and Killian. Creativity became a new game for Killian and me, especially due to the necessity of keeping things strictly professional in front of Margaux. To compensate, he'd opened an email account under an alter ego, Long Duk Dong, who'd grown fond of sending me messages every morning that alternated between filthy and hilarious. By the time lunch break came, I couldn't wait to have him all to myself. Naturally, we'd discovered every broom and supply closet in the SGC building while we were at it.

During one of those breaks, he'd surprised me by shuttling me off to a private lab, where he let me watch a tech draw his blood and test it for all the common STDs. I'd been so moved that I'd instantly done the same. Since I was on birth control already for controlling cramps, I'd been begging him to stop scrambling for condoms. We'd celebrated our mutual clean reports by attacking each other in the town car, entering the building through the basement when we returned. The secrecy sucked, but keeping our "thing" off the press's radar was a vital necessity.

We split many of our days between SGC and Keystone, consumed with damage control after Trey's escapade. During our few free hours during the nights, I was obsessed with control of another kind—my libido—as Killian drove me to higher planes of pleasure while I was wrapped around him in his penthouse. Though we kept my room at the hotel to thwart suspicion from the media *and* Margaux, I now came and went from his building with such regularity that the door staff were on standing orders to see me in without calling for Killian's permission. I was officially on VIP status at Lincoln Park 2550.

Mental high five.

Finally, Killian was fed up with what he called our Post-it notes of time. He called early on a Tuesday, ordering me to pack a bag and clear most of the upcoming weekend. We'd be in condo hibernation mode from Friday night through Monday dawn.

As the next three days dragged by, I admitted to fantasizing about the time more than any other date in my life. I shook my head more than once during the process. Calling Killian Stone a date seemed blasphemous. This man was in a league of his own.

Friday night finally came. I rolled my overnight case into the entryway with me, fully prepared for the weekend.

As soon as I stepped into the living room, my stomach somersaulted in all the best ways. The lights in the room were dimmed. The fireplace crackled. Soft music played through the surround-sound speakers. Fantastic smells unfurled from the kitchen, the savory notes hinting at a menu of things tasty, cheesy, and French. I vowed to wave the white flag if Killian could cook on top of every other drive-me-crazy element about him.

A quick peek into the kitchen revealed it as empty, though I saw two glasses of wine poured and waiting on the counter. Quickly after that, I noticed the open balcony door. A chilly breeze kicked in, blowing across the zebra-wood floor, past my high-heeled boots, and beneath my long skirt to my bare legs. It had rained most of the day, but the showers were full of springtime balm, so I hadn't worn anything except panties beneath my work clothes. However, the night had a nip, and I was still a California girl wimp, so I allowed myself a quick shiver.

I grabbed the glasses from the counter and headed toward the slider to find my handsome host. He turned as I approached, making me tremble for completely different reasons. He was more breathtaking than the city skyline view, dressed in a cream-colored sweater that enhanced his swimmer's torso to perfection, along with soft wool trousers.

"Penny for your thoughts?" I asked, extending a glass.

He smiled as he accepted the wine before stretching to wrap his other hand around my nape, pulling me to where he stood. Simply continuing the motion, he greeted me with a warm, thorough kiss that banished my chill, sizzled through my veins, and had me whimpering by the time he pulled away.

I couldn't help swaying toward him, prying my eyes half open to glimpse if I affected him nearly as much as he did me. My vision was filled with his thick lashes, still closed against his cheeks as he pressed his forehead to mine, appearing as though he was praying to some deity with a mixture of penitence and praise. His shoulders were tense around his ears, and I wasn't sure how to react. The man's intensity, both daunting and beautiful since the first moment we'd shaken hands, now seemed to climb exponentially with each passing day.

After a long moment, he exhaled and let his shoulders drop. He kissed me again, this time with a different purpose. Desperation? Need? Passion? All three? The latter seemed the most likely as he set his glass on the sheltered ledge and then lifted his other hand to my head, twisting fingers through my hair and plundering my mouth anew. I felt anchored to him, accepting the fervid strokes of his tongue with open mewls, letting him suck and bite at my lips and jaw while traveling his mouth to my ear.

"Sweet Claire. My fairy queen." He let out a harsh breath. I did the same. My stomach had taken up a full acrobatic act now, and my heart joined it. But gymnastics were *not* my thing.

Something was going on. I pulled my head back to gaze up at him.

"Tell me," I charged. "What is it?" I let my psyche dive into the black seas of his eyes, rejecting the life vest. The emotions in his inky depths extended for countless fathoms, made even scarier by the realization that most involved me. But a larger epiphany struck. This weekend wasn't just about hibernation. It was about revelation. There were still secrets between us, a fact I suddenly hated with a vengeance. His gaze confirmed that he felt the same.

I reached up, stroking his strong, proud jaw. "Tell me, Kil. You're safe with me, remember? No more running. Isn't that our rule now?" I grinned as punctuation, trying to inject a little levity.

He tugged my hand from his face and gently moved it over his heart instead. More emotional gymnastics, especially as he extended his gaze, regarding me with such tenderness, uncertainty...and fear? Dear God, I could feel him trembling too.

"Are you cold?" I queried. It seemed the logical thing to say. He never shook like this. Never threw me into confusion like this. Never looked so vulnerable like this. "Should we go inside?"

He laughed, but the mirth barely passed his lips. It sure as hell didn't make it to his eyes. "I'm not cold, baby girl." He kept my hand close to his chest. "I'm scared. Scared to death, actually."

I started to panic. Had Margaux finally said something to

him? No. He'd already have downed half the wine, and a deep instinct told me his tension level would be different.

That narrowed things to one option. What could Trey possibly have done now? I tried to pull my hand away, but Killian yanked back, gripping me tighter. "What happened? What has he done?"

"Nothing. Nothing at all. He's doing everything completely right. The picture of a reformed rake, down to his appearance at the Children's Hospital Fun Run this afternoon."

I frowned a little. "And that's a problem?"

A laugh tugged the edges of his lips, though sadness formed its underpinnings. "Damn right it's a problem. Everything's going so well that you'll pack up your things and go back to San Diego. And you'll take this"—he pulled my hand away enough to tap it back against his chest—"along with you." His eyes began to shimmer with glints of intensity. "I'm not sure I'm equipped to survive without you now."

With my free hand, I raised my glass and took a huge gulp from it. I suddenly had the driest throat in Illinois. And the most overwhelmed mind. I drained the glass before daring to look up again.

"Do you mind if we go inside? Now I'm kind of cold." I was stalling, and he probably saw right through it. But returning to the living room freed me to turn distractions into conversation. "What smells so good? Please don't tell me you can cook too, Stone. If this gets out, we'll be worrying about your fan club instead of the press this weekend."

"Perhaps I can, Miss Montgomery." He wiggled his dark eyebrows, making me burst into giggles. "Maybe we'll forget teacher's ruler in favor of a wooden spoon on that fantastic ass."

I continued laughing—until he pulled a big wooden spoon from the canister on the countertop. "You wouldn't dare!" I'd just refilled my wine but set it down on the counter, backing away.

"I would." As he stalked toward me, he tapped the implement against his thigh.

"Killian, I'm serious." I deliberately cranked up my moan.

"So am I, baby. So. Am. I."

"That— That thing will hurt." Damn it, my stomach was in knots. The good, squishy kind.

"Hmm. Probably. But only for a little bit, I promise."

My insides melted a little more. His "promise" looked hot and horny and heavenly. "Okay, *wait*. I'll make a deal with you." Yep, stalling again—but if I made a run for it, he would catch me before I cleared three feet down the hall.

His Lucifer's smirk spread across his sinful lips. "Hmm. A deal. Well, I *am* a businessman." He arched an eyebrow. "But a shrewd one."

I nodded, my solemnity not entirely mocking. "And don't I know it."

"Let's hear your terms, then, fairy."

I firmed my stance and raised my chin. "Truth or dare."

His features widened on a laugh. "What?"

"Truth or dare," I repeated with more confidence. "If I pick dare, you can spank me with that giant oar you're calling a spoon. If I pick truth, you can ask me anything you want."

He played at the hem of my skirt with the spoon. "The idea has merit. Go on."

"The rules apply both ways." I fought to keep my gaze away from his face, lust now clouding his features as he roamed the spoon up my thigh and across one cheek of my backside.

"But I'll think of something better for your dare because I can't imagine you'd consent to a spanking—ever."

His grin grew wider, which I interpreted as agreement to the plan. For a second, I almost reneged. What on earth was I getting myself into? On the other hand, maybe this was a good thing. We'd both been withholding things from each other, and we both knew it. Maybe now Killian would pry back a few of his masks for me, even a little. Maybe it would be worth the price of lifting mine.

He swept a hand toward the sofa and then turned to pull a brick of brie from the oven. From the sideboard, he scooped up a basket of crusty artisan bread. I grabbed our glasses and the wine bottle before sitting down. As he lowered next to me, one arm sliding along the back of the sofa, he appeared a little skittish. I grinned, deciding Nervous Killian was pretty damn hot too.

"All right, my queen. Ladies first."

"Really?" After his nod and grin of confirmation, I bounced a little, grabbed his hand, and declared, "Okay then, Mr. Stone. Truth or dare?"

"Truth." He answered with smug speed. That was all right. I was ready. *You might think twice about that next time, Stone.*

"How old were you when you lost your virginity?" I blushed in the asking, but it was a legitimate curiosity. Besides, given my refusal to consent to a spanking in this lifetime, he certainly wasn't going to tread lightly on his question for me. I had to take the opportunity now.

"Seventeen." He followed it with a simple stare. No details, despite the grin I gave him as a spur. Aha. *Now* I followed his strategy. I would have to word my questions more carefully.

Satisfaction gleamed from the handsome bastard's gaze

of my teeth, I nipped at the pad of his thumb, which didn't have a trace of cheese on it. It was time for this silly game to be over.

He pulled his hand back and took a sip of wine without breaking our eye contact. The charge in the air between us was tangible. When he spoke, his voice was a husky grate. "Your turn, fairy."

"But I *really* liked the new game we were playing." I said it with my best pout, making him laugh. I had to admit, getting him to open up was exhilarating. He was as movable as a mountain when an action plan wasn't his idea.

"Fine. Truth or dare?" I added a nice eye roll for good measure—though this time, he stunned me with his answer.

"Dare."

I snapped wide eyes at him. Sucked in a hard breath.

"Ohhhh, the possibilities, Mr. Stone."

He pressed close again, his burnished features a mesmerizing portrait of rigid and soft, command yet need. "Indeed, Miss Montgomery."

Screw the possibilities. There was only one thing I wanted right now. Needed. Screwed up my courage to demand from him.

"I dare you to make love to me, right here, on your living room floor, in front of the fireplace."

By this point, my stomach was a damn trapeze act of anxiety—but another part of me cheered. Phrasing anything to this man in the form of an ultimatum, even in the parameters of a game, felt like telling the president to strip naked in front of Congress. It just wasn't done. Killian's authority was like his skin. He wore it, wielded it, and protected it with a ferocity I couldn't explain.

Which meant I succumbed to a dozen kinds of insecurity

as he rose and walked out of the room. Despite my dread, I couldn't peel my stare from him as he turned toward the bedroom. I heard movement but had no idea what was going on. In a motionless mix of apprehension and excitement, I waited for him to return—hopefully.

He prowled back into the room carrying a large throw that was some type of faux fur in silver and black. I pushed the ottoman out of the way, taking care not to jostle the wineglasses, as he spread the blanket on the floor in its place. Still not uttering a word, he tossed the large pillows from the sofa on top of the throw. The result was a scene from some divine romance movie—as well as my wildest fantasies.

Killian toed off his loafers and kicked them to the side of the blanket. He guided my hands to his shoulders as he bent and unzipped my boots, tossing them in the same direction after I stepped from them.

For a long moment, we simply stood looking at each other. I tried to focus on getting enough air as I comprehended that, for this perfect bubble of time, this beautiful man was all mine.

The rain began again outside. Drops trickled down the huge window panes, but the fireplace kept everything warm inside—as if I needed those flames, with the radiance of the man who now slipped to his knees in front of me. When he tilted his head and gazed up at me, the coal of his eyes reached into all the corners of my heart, heating me from the inside out. The song on the radio flowed around us, sweet harmonies on top of beautiful words.

And if you fall, you'll always land right in these arms... these arms of mine...

"Claire." He uttered only that while resting his head against my stomach. I filtered my fingers though his hair as he wrapped his arms around my hips, worshipping me. Holding him tighter, I battled the feeling that if I didn't, I would be suddenly lost.

In that singular moment, our relationship shifted to strange new ground. We really did peel back masks, opening ourselves, being bare...being scared. Without words, professing our acceptance of each other's secrets and still wanting each other despite them. Because of them. A gift given mutually, freely, perfectly.

I'd never felt more beautiful in my life. More desired. *Forever.* I pleaded the word to heaven. Couldn't this simply go on forever? At the same time, I acknowledged my gratitude for it by refusing to rush anything. With slow care, I sank to my knees as well. We weren't one above the other anymore—and because of that, I resolved my mind and heart to a significant decision.

I wanted to tell him everything. I *would* tell him. After he made love to my body, I'd trust him with my truth. For the first time since Nick, I felt close enough to someone to take this chance. It had been nearly three years. I wanted to finally make this leap of faith because of this beautiful man. Killian would keep me safe. He filled my mind with his strength, my heart with his devotion, my spirit with all of *his* spirit. He gave me everything I needed to trust him.

Our lips met on a sigh at first. I kissed him tenderly, showing him what I wanted to give him—my heart. The intensity of his posture, his touch, and his face all showed how he saw and understood. He returned my kiss with reverence.

"Claire Montgomery, you are an amazing woman." He looked into my eyes, brushing hair away from my face while kissing his way down my jaw, neck, and collarbone. "Thank you, baby. I will never betray your trust. *Never.*"

His kisses were as earnest as his words. He tipped me down and covered my body with his, but he never ceased those caresses. While his lips still suckled and nuzzled my neck, he skated his fingers along my rib cage, taking the fabric of my sweater with them. I helped him pull the garment over my head, letting it fall behind me to the floor so I lay before him in my bra and skirt.

He pulled in an audible breath, releasing it with slow reverence while bending to kiss and lick my newly exposed skin. I sighed as his praising whispers rained over me, sending tingles through parts of my body that had likely never known arousal before. He covered every dip and swell, awakening torrents of pleasure through me, as I stroked the graceful muscles of his back and tunneled my hands through his thick hair.

My bra was an early casualty, as was the skirt. Soon I only wore a lacy white thong and was spread out for him like a virginal offering to a dark and glorious god. When Killian's gaze raked over me, I felt exactly that perfect too...that expectant and new. If that was really the case, the sacrifice would've been a willing one. I stared up at him with that thought in the forefront of my mind, hoping he knew how far I was in this with him. He hungrily wet his lips while running the tips of his fingers over my nudity, grazing his fingers from my shoulder to my hip bone and back again.

"So beautiful." The syllables spilled from him on fierce grunts. "So beautiful and so mine." His black gaze drilled into mine, daring me to say otherwise. As if that were an option anymore.

"Yes, Killian. Yours." I was done running. I didn't have an

ounce of fight left in me now. I didn't *want* to fight any longer.

In a passionate sweep, he tore off his sweater and tossed it atop my things. He stood to kick off his pants too. Good God, he'd already ditched the underwear. I sucked in a ragged breath when his arousal sprang free, stretched and stiff and proud. I would never tire of seeing the effect I had on this man. It made my ego stand and curtsy. *Yes, girlfriend. You did that to him.*

Before he could lower to me again, I was compelled to rush forward instead. He was as breathtaking as a bronze Greek statue with the firelight dancing across his defined nudity—especially the steely shaft between his thighs, glistening with the moisture that announced his body's readiness for me.

In a word, he looked...delicious.

I have to taste him.

Before Killian could protest, I knelt in front of him and took him in my hand. I savored every inch of his cock in my fist before looking up, beholding his face in the most beautiful combination of agony and ecstasy.

"You've slain me," he grated. "Because honest to fuck, I've died and gone to heaven."

I smiled up at him as I moved closer, sneaking a little lick of the drops on his tip before fully wrapping my mouth around his erection. His smell and flavor filled my senses, affecting me like an exotic drug, making me moan in appreciation. His head fell back as I slid my lips down his length, taking him into my throat as far as I could before having to stop.

"Claire!" he rasped. "Sweet God, that's so—"

His own groan served as his interruption, strangled as if begging me to stop, but I didn't heed. While tightening my lips, I flattened my tongue to the underside before sliding back up to his cock's dark-purple head, licking generously at the crest when I reached it.

Killian dug his hands into my hair. He squeezed harder when I took him to the back of my throat, this time pumping my hand around the base and skimming my fingers across his heated sac. A few repetitions had him groaning my name—and my heart leaping with joy. The thrill of serving him like this yet wielding such power over him... It was a giddy new sensation for me, and it intensified when he twisted his fingers into my hair, prickling my scalp with something close to pain. I sneaked another look up, finding his eyes screwed shut as he panted for air. His chest, hard and gleaming bronze in the firelight, was an even bigger turn-on to behold because of the erect pinpoints of his nipples.

"Stop!" He stilled my movement by holding my face.

I peered up at him with his cock still buried in my throat, feigning innocence in my wide eyes. "Hmm?"

His eyes narrowed as if contemplating reprisal, but he slid his flesh from my mouth instead. "Stay *right* where you are."

He circled around and then fell to his knees behind me. "I need to be in this sweet pussy when I come—at least *this* time." His tone was a devilish growl in my ear as he nudged his moist length against the entrance to my equally wet sex, prodding me, inciting more arousal along my trembling hole.

"Killian." It was my turn to gasp for air. He sucked at the sensitive skin of my nape while snaking a hand around to my front and pinched my breasts and nipples. With the other, he teased at my inner thighs and clit until I cried out in need. "Killian, dear *God*!"

"That sounds so perfect, sweet one." He bit the bottom of my ear to grind in his point. "My name *always* sounds wonderful on your lips but even more when you beg me with it."

"Th-Then I'm...officially...begging. *Please*, Killian. I need you inside me!"

"Mmmm. I could get really used to this."

"Killian! Damn it!" I was going insane. He'd started to pitch and roll his hips. It always felt like paradise when he did it from the front. Now, it felt like purgatory—a hot, sinful, decadent damnation that I longed to burn up in, cell by glorious cell.

"Are you wet for me, Claire?"

I managed to nod. I could barely think. And was embarrassingly ready to have him inside me.

"Say it, baby. Say the words."

"Yes, I'm wet for you, all right? God...Killian...my pussy is always so ready when you're around."

"That's my beautiful, dirty girl. Now bend forward and let me see."

I mewled a little, beyond self-conscious with the action. He'd already felt my readiness, so why did he have to observe it too? But when he pushed me forward to my hands and knees and prodded my legs apart, exposing my pussy to his gaze, I couldn't deny the hot sluices of new arousal that coursed from me.

"Shit," he muttered. "My sweet Claire. Look how juicy and ready you are."

With one hand on my hip, he used the other to swipe at my folds, gliding easily through my wetness. My head dropped. He knew how to make me feel like the trashiest slut and the most treasured lover in a single, amazing moment.

"Show me more," he ordered. "Spread wider for me."

I complied without thinking. I would do anything he wanted right now. Gripping my hips, he seated his cock again at my core, working his shaft into my wetness, pressing in with aching slowness. Inch by searing inch, he filled me deeper and deeper until his thighs butted against my ass.

"Finally." Though his voice was a whisper, his grip was a command. "Home. Right where I belong."

He slid out fully and then slammed back in. Again. Again. His thrusts rocked me forward, making me cry out from the agonizing pleasure.

"Killian!"

"I know. I *know*, baby."

"Please...don't stop."

"Never." He spoke it against the top of my spine before pressing a kiss there. "I never want to stop with you, my fairy. Ever."

"Oh," I whispered. His words wove as much magic into my soul as his sex pounded into my core. I became aware of every breath he took. Every groan he emitted. Every thrust he dealt. We were twined. Joined. One fire. One fever.

"Hold on, baby. Hold on tight."

He started moving. Really moving. If that wasn't enough, he braced a leg next to my waist, positioning his cock to drive deeper into me. I swore my eyes crossed. I could barely breathe as my orgasm mounted, fast and furious and blinding. I couldn't find my voice to warn him to slow down. I wasn't sure I wanted to.

"Killian," I finally panted. "I c-can't s-stop it."

"That's it," he growled back. "Let it go. Come with me, baby."

We both stilled as our releases tore through our bodies. I could feel his cock twitching in my sensitive channel as he exploded, spilling his hot fluid. I cried out and gripped the rug while my pussy clenched him tighter, my eyes rolling back in my head while my orgasm continued in wave after wave of shimmering, stunning bliss.

Holy hell, what this man could do to me.

Finally, I closed my eyes and collapsed to the floor. Killian fell with me, still inside me. We lay together, joined intimately for long minutes, enjoying the effortless combination of our bodies while rain pelted harder at the windows. After a while, Killian pulled the fur up around me, and we listened to the fire and the rain duel each other.

The world, with all its drama and threats and strife, was nonexistent. We were untouchable.

"I want to freeze this moment." I knew it was silly, but it was what I felt. Pure. Uncomplicated. Or, as he'd expressed in another context that still oddly applied, *home.*

"I know what you mean, baby girl." He played with my hair, his naked form spooned behind me.

I pulled in a deep breath. The time had come. There would be no moment more perfect than this for leaping into the hugest trust I could show this man.

"Killian?"

"Hmm?"

"Ask me now."

It *was* the ideal time. I had to keep telling myself that. I'd just shared the deepest parts of my body with him. Why shouldn't the darkest parts of my past follow?

"Hmmm?" Though confusion edged his voice, he continued stroking my hair and back in a languid flow. "Ask you what, fairy?"

"The game. Truth or dare." It felt easier to do it that way. If it was a game, the confession couldn't really hurt me, right?

"Ask me now." I rolled over and gazed at him, conveying my deeper meaning. "Ask me, and I'll tell you what you want to know."

His return stare held the solemnity of understanding. "Truth or dare, fairy."

I breathed in deeply. "Truth."

He did the same. *He knew*. I sensed it just by studying his face. Somehow, he already knew that this information might change everything for us. But he asked anyway. "What is Margaux holding over your head?"

I settled in his arms and told him the entire story. I didn't leave anything out, from the day she and I met in college until the day our parents became engaged. I cried—more than once. He wiped my tears every time and then held me closer. Not once did I feel his judgment or condemnation, only his listening ears and open mind. I was stunned yet wondered why. I should've given him the benefit of the doubt sooner.

When I finished with the last ugly detail, I finally had the nerve to look up into his eyes. For some weird reason, I still expected to see disgust and rejection hiding at the back of his gaze. Killian only wrapped his arms around me and pulled me closer.

"*That's* what you were afraid of all this time?" A grin sneaked across his lips.

I fired back an exasperated glare. "Would you be serious? I'm a criminal! I'm scared to trust anyone." I lowered my head, pushing it into his chest. "I was terrified to trust *you*."

"Because from the second we met, you felt the walls around your heart start to crumble."

I shot my gaze back up. "You could tell?"

"Don't worry. You covered it well. I only know it's what *I* felt."

Despite how his words made my pulse race, I ran a soft hand over his sculpted chest. "So now you get it. The last time I trusted someone with my heart, he shattered it—and turned me into a drug-fencing accomplice. When keeping someone's secrets has led a girl to a broken heart and a potential rap sheet, you can understand why she isn't so eager to try again."

He laughed—*laughed*—in answer to that.

"Being young, naïve, and in love doesn't make you a felon." He kissed the top of my head. "But it does add wicked appeal, which means I'm doomed."

I turned my caress into a little smack. "I was an accessory to a crime, Killian. And Margaux knows it. She won't stop holding it over my head until the statute of limitations runs out on this thing, and maybe even after that. If anyone finds out...if my *father* finds out..." I hadn't spoken the words in so long. Doing it now made my voice crack, unlocking the dam on a torrent of helpless tears too.

"Whoa," Killian murmured. "Fairy...come on. It's not horrible."

"No," I sobbed. "It's worse. It was stupid, and now it's hopeless. Futile."

He huffed, clearly perplexed. "I don't understand how this involves me. And us."

I sighed and gripped his neck. "Because Margaux wants you for herself, okay?"

Killian echoed my sigh, though his was angrier. "Oh. That."

"Yeah. *That*. From day one, she issued a warning to the rest of the team, right in front of her mother, laying dibs for herself."

His eyebrows shot up. *"Dibs?"*

"She's into you, Killian. If she finds out that we are... whatever we are...learning that I've knowingly outdibbed her—"

His growl was sharp and instant. "Neither of us planned this, damn it. It just...is."

"A woman like her doesn't understand that. She's been brought up to think of relationships like everything else in her life, as controllable commodities. She won't be above taking retribution, and she'll bring back all the dirt about Nick and the drugs to do so. And it doesn't just affect me now. It affects my dad—and now you too. Do you get it *now*?"

"Claire. Look at me." His words were firm yet warm. He pulled me closer. "I'm not afraid of bullies like Margaux Asher," he asserted. "Do you understand that?" The certainty in his beautiful eyes and the steadiness in his grip, now beneath my chin, restarted the sting behind my eyes. My chin wobbled all over again. "I eat pushy bitches like her for breakfast, lunch, and dinner every day. She's not going to stand in my way. In *our* way." He leaned and kissed the tears off my cheeks as he continued. "I will find a way to deal with her and keep you safe as well. I will not let her come between us. Now do *you* understand?"

I swallowed, struggling for the nod he demanded but unable to deliver. "She's worse than she looks, Killian. Under all that makeup and hair product is a woman who covers her issues with ruthlessness, power plays, and bartering other people's confidences."

"Pfffttt. Trust me, baby, she's an amateur in the secret-keeping world. A wobbling lamb." His voice was lethally soft on the declaration. I watched an odd darkness move through

his eyes, reflected by the storm clouds outside the windows. Unbelievably, the effect made me shiver, even in his embrace. The second I did, he blinked and moved away, offering to put more wood on the fire.

I observed him with adoring eyes—and, for the first time in three years, with hope in my heart. Maybe I'd met someone who really did have the power to stand up to Margaux, to deliver me from the dark cloud she held...and *would* hold, no matter where I went on the planet. The icing on that big, amazing cake? If that knight of salvation was also the man who'd captured my heart...the prince I'd fallen completely in love with. Killian Jamison Stone.

CHAPTER SEVENTEEN

Killian

"So in conclusion, Mr. Stone, we are—how do you say it in America?—kicking ass."

I leaned forward at my home-office desk, giving an obligatory chuckle in response to the Chinese man whose image filled one of the two other boxes on the video call. Cheng guffawed like he'd just performed the hottest stand-up comedy act in Vegas.

"I think we can all agree that my Beijing visit yielded optimal results," I stated. "We're glad to know your production orders are back up so soon, Mr. Cheng."

"Up, up, and away!" The man flashed a double thumbs-up.

I could practically see my own relief mirrored back from my monitor when Cheng turned solemn again. "Well said, Mr. Stone. And I apologize for the judgments we all made about your family's character. Clearly, your success has come at a price, including those who improperly attack you. How do you say it in America? 'Those in glass houses should not throw stones'?"

I didn't dare inform the guy that the expression originated from a source higher than all of us combined, though I gave another confident smile. "I appreciate the support, Mr. Cheng."

"You always have it. The character of your family has

prevailed through this crisis. It is clear to many of us that your enemies should focus less on flinging their sludge at you and more on cleaning their own pigsties."

As I exchanged pleasantries with one of our biggest allies in Asia, my cell phone detonated with vibrations. I rapidly wrapped up the call with Cheng, and as soon as he disconnected, I scrabbled for the phone, now at the edge of my desk.

What the fuck?

My nerves tightened and my gut clenched. A string of texts lit up my screen, and despite Cheng's effusive prelude, I braced for the worst.

What the hell have you done this time, Trey?

My stare narrowed in shock as I punched the incoming texts to life, giving first priority to Claire's note.

Sometimes, the stars simply align. Let's celebrate. I'm on my way over.

While her concluding sentence spiked my heartbeat, I still frowned with confusion. Maybe Trey's message would shed some light on the mystery.

This means I can get the fuck out of Keystone, right?

I promise I'll be good this time, boss.

"What the hell?" I mumbled it while bypassing messages from a few close business colleagues as well as some of the guys from the polo team, though I noticed that all of them contained phrases like *Congratulations* and *Thank God.*

With mounting curiosity, I skipped to Andrea Asher's message, which wasn't a message at all. She cut to the chase with a forwarded message straight off CNN's Breaking News feed. The time stamp was from thirty minutes ago.

Just in—The Beverly Hills Police Department now confirms that their raid of a house party at the mansion of Rayze McCloud, lead singer for the heavy metal band Bro-Hoof, led to the discovery of the singer in his bed with four females, among them Amanda Berne, daughter of Senator Edward Berne, and Emily Wooten, daughter of Senator Gerard Wooten. The two girls, aged seventeen and eighteen respectively, stated they'd been invited to the party as VIPs after McCloud made substantial campaign contributions to both Berne and Wooten and were "only watching" the activities in the bedroom. Claims of a hidden camera in the room, apparently on at the time of the party, may prove otherwise. Ms. Berne and Ms. Wooten were also allegedly involved in an incident with billionaire hunk Trey Stone in February, though the evidence in that case was declared inadmissible due to Ms. Wooten's age at the time.

I exhaled heavily while setting down my phone. No fewer than a thousand thoughts bombarded my mind. Liberation. Relief. Happiness.

Agony. Heaviness. Emptiness.

"It's over."

The world had finally found a hotter mess than the Stones' to ogle. I'd have staked my left nut that half the press were already booked on flights to California. And within a few days, after post-program reports were filed, Andrea and her team would be too.

Including Claire.

A sense of loss crashed over me like a sudden storm off the lake. I angrily fought the fucker. Fought myself.

Why was I suddenly so miserable? I'd endured shit like this before. I'd been six years old when it happened the first time. Unlike the moment Da told me Mam had left, I'd expected this moment. Prepared for its inevitability.

Hadn't I?

The answer struck like a second storm front—filled with lashing ice.

I thought there would be more time.

Damn it, we need more time!

Claire would be here in a few minutes, and I had no idea what to say to her. How to pull her into my arms and battle the yearning to never let go. How to give her some reason to leave her job, her father, and her life behind in California and stay here with me on the simple offering that she'd be my VIP. She'd sure as hell lack for nothing the title implied—a car, a credit card, the right to redecorate this whole place if she wanted—but how long would all that satisfy a woman like her? A creature I called fairy because she was as rare and amazing as one?

She'd never go for it. She needed so much more. She was worth so much better. A ring on her finger. A real home, even a family, with a man who wasn't living his life as someone else. A man who wasn't constantly staring at the walls, waiting for them to crumble in, exposing his fairy-tale life for the sham that it was.

That didn't mean I wasn't going to try.

I could make her happy, even if only for a little while. And god*damn*, would she make me happy.

I rested my chin on a thumb and slowly swiveled my chair

toward the window. The city skyline twinkled beyond the glass, shimmering in double time because of the night wind. To the left, on the vast darkness of the lake, distant lights beamed from a few ships. How many nights had I stared out at those dots on the water, relating so fully to those vessels? So close to home but bound by a course that had been preset for me by people who assumed they knew where all the rocks were—the biological parents who could do nothing for me and the masquerade parents who could do everything for me.

We'd all only been kids when everything changed. Trey had been eight when the doctors had leveled the news that the combination of syndromes he'd been born with would render him sterile for life. And Lance, though only seven, had shown his true colors even then about how likely *he'd* be to produce a Stone heir. While Willa would have loved both her sons had they been born albinos with three eyes, Josiah was from some of the oldest money on the globe. Producing an heir was still interpreted in the most traditional sense of the word, and his inability to produce one was like declaring he didn't have a dick, much less sons who respected it.

I'd respected Josiah. But oddly enough, unlike Trey and Lance, that respect was never accompanied by fear. Even as a boy of five, I'd looked at the big man as an anomaly, perhaps a challenge—a mountain to be conquered. I did that every chance I got, rushing him like Mowgli on crack, trying to scramble my wiry body up and over his. Trey and Lance would applaud and encourage my games. I'd had no idea they were laughing at me behind closed doors—until after the day Da and Josiah came to me asking if I wanted to be their brother in truth, not just a front we put on to the rest of the world. I had no idea I was just as much Josiah's savior as he was mine, a thread of hope for the Stone name carrying on "as it should." I'd moved into a bedroom at Keystone that instantly made me feel like Aladdin, the penniless urchin ushered to the palace. All my dreams had come true.

The reverie had lasted for about an hour.

Turned out Trey and Lance enjoyed me better as their entertainment, not their brother. Their scorn had been instant and transparent—and I'd vowed to one day overthrow it. To earn their love, one excruciating day at a time.

Took me a little longer to realize that fantasy wasn't coming true either.

And here I was, still the damn ship out to sea. Steadfast on my course...but sailing alone.

Wondering how I could convince my lighthouse to stay so I wouldn't have to do it in the dark.

My landline buzzed.

I punched the line to connect it after recognizing the caller ID as the doorman's desk downstairs. Alfred was gone, indulging his passion for the Bulls in the season seats I'd given him for Christmas, so I was greeter boy tonight. But I was only expecting one visitor, and the doormen already knew to let Claire come up without question. Maybe the guy on the desk tonight was new.

"Mr. Stone? It's Aaron from the door, sir."

Not new. One of the regulars but not sounding like himself. Confusion edged his smooth tenor voice.

"Hey, Aaron. What's up?"

"Young lady here to see you, sir. She says to tell you she's from the Asher team."

I lowered a hard frown. Harder than the one I'd already been wearing, at least. "All right." Both words were drawn out by my own puzzlement. When Aaron didn't respond, irritation took a bite of my patience. "Well, send her up."

The man cleared his throat. "Ermm, sir—"

"This isn't a multiple-choice test. Just let her up." Against my efforts at restraint, the order came out in gritted syllables.

"As you wish, sir."

I turned off my desk lamp and left the office, tugging on my loose shirt tails like a nervous teen waiting on his crush to emerge from pom-pom practice. Trouble was, I wasn't the football captain. Not really. Nothing like tearing open a few scabs from the past to remind me of that fact too.

I paced to the wine cooler in the kitchen and took out one of the new bottles I'd ordered from Temecula Valley. The Ruby Cuvee from South Coast Winery seemed a perfect choice for the occasion, despite my *un*celebratory mood. I popped the cork just as the front door opened and closed. "Your timing couldn't be more perfect," I called out.

"Is that so?"

The slow, sultry answer came from the woman who rounded the corner into the kitchen on her insanely high, really red, boots.

Margaux Asher.

I wore away a layer of tooth enamel as I gritted my jaw. Then sloshed the red bubbles down my hand from the force of slamming the bottle to the counter. "Remarkably, I'm going to greet you by thanking you, Miss Asher."

"Mmmm," Margaux purred. "How so?"

"Just learned a valuable lesson," I explained. "The next time one of my doormen sounds like he's seen a reject from *The Bachelor* auditions, I'll listen closer."

She actually giggled at that. "Oh, Killian. You admire

my pluck, and we both know it." As she advanced past the refrigerator in a form-fitting ivory sweater and matching wool leggings, she made weird circular steps in a pace she apparently thought enticing. The effect was more like a blind giraffe who'd already been nipping at the Cuvee, though a firm look at Margaux's face revealed she was still stone-cold sober. "You are, after all, the prince of ingenuity."

"I'm also expecting someone else." I fought the craving to shift backward as she approached, not from fear but repulsion. Memories from two nights ago bloomed like blood stains in my mind. I saw Claire curled against me, weeping from fear she'd be sent to jail because of the evidence this Lizzy Borden dangled over her like a sharpened ax. Her terror of shattering her father's heart, of towing me into the shadows of her secret. My sweet fairy queen. She had no idea how completely I knew of shadows or what people did in them.

Neither did Margaux.

A clueless smile slid over the woman's features as she continued her approach. "Of course you're expecting someone else. Why wouldn't you be?" She glanced at the Cuvee. "Some unique bubbly to go with your amazing view..." Her stare descended over my chest. "And oh yeah, that city skyline is pretty good as well."

When she followed the trajectory of her gaze with a seductive slide of two fingers, I pulled off the polite-boy gloves. Clutching her wrist with one hand, I squeezed with unmistakable force. "This is my nice way of asking you to leave, Miss Asher. Whatever you came here to discuss can wait until tomorrow. At the office."

She laughed as if I'd just spewed a great party joke. "The hell it can." Her twist from my grip continued into a sweep through her luggage-sized handbag, from which she pulled a bottle of cabernet. "Big victories deserve to be celebrated right away, and now that Treygate is over, we *will* toast."

"Tomorrow," I countered, sliding the bottle back into her purse.

"Tonight." She pulled two wide-bowled glasses down from the overhead rack. "Oh, don't be such a Debbie Downer. One glass, Killian, and I'll be on my way. We won't touch the stuff you have saved for your *special friend*, though you should know that some 'friends' are little redheaded lightweights and not a lot of fun as drinking buddies."

Wrath clawed through my senses as she made a move for the wine again, though I didn't stop her this time. I didn't trust myself with touching her. As angry as I was, I didn't want to hurt her. "And some 'friends' don't understand that real relationships aren't commodities to be controlled by information flow."

She tossed her head on another laugh, spilling her long blonde hair and showcasing her four inches of makeup beneath the kitchen's bright lights. Incredible. Every bit of the woman was an orchestration, a realization that actually made me pity her for a second. Margaux had told as many lies to the world as I had.

With one glaring difference. Hers had all been by choice.

"Do you believe that crap?" she retorted then, adding on a sneer. "Information flow just saved your family's ass, Killian."

I pivoted as if to square off with her. "There's a difference, Margaux. Manipulating the mass-media stream is one thing. Manipulating *people* for your own agenda, using mistakes they made out of loyalty and love, is another."

I'd officially outed her, and she knew it. Her gaze skittered to the floor, searching the polished wood in what looked like a mix of desperation and disbelief. Even the consideration that Claire had told me about their deal was clearly a mindblower for her. Poor misguided Margaux, dancing through life on the assumption that her own shit would never stink or be flung back at her. Yet, here she was, dangling over a river of it. I debated whether to drop her in or let her wiggle on the hook a while longer.

I had to give her points for aplomb. The woman recovered herself enough to uncork the wine and begin a couple of pours as she replied, "The truth is sometimes simply the truth, Mr. Stone, no matter how it's exposed." She extended a glass to me. "And wouldn't you agree that honesty is the best policy?"

I let the drink dangle untouched from her fingers. "Indeed. Especially when it's been decommissioned as a weapon."

The dark green of her eyes deepened to rainforest seduction. "I agree." She lifted her glass, slowly moistening her perfectly painted lips after finishing the sampling. "Let's use our...guns...for better purposes, Killian. And share our deepest truths." The last of it was a thick whisper, joining the full-court press she started with her body. After setting aside her glass, she molded her hips to mine, flowed her hands over my chest and abs and then around to my ass.

"Margaux." I stopped just short of growling it as I pushed her hand away. "I'm sorry. That may be your truth, but it isn't mine."

"And Claire Montgomery is?" Her gaze narrowed. "That was what the mooning over each other at the gala was about, right?" She moved back in with relentless drive, grabbing the front of my shirt. "Let me tell you something about our little Claire. She's on the prudish side, okay?" The woman studied me for a reaction. Wisely I gave none, despite the temptation to tell her how I'd been balls-deep inside "little Claire" atop the SGC conference table a few days ago. "She can't give you what you need, Killian. *I* can."

I hissed when her fingers tweaked my left nipple through my shirt. Margaux gave a seductive giggle and started moving to the other side. I grabbed her hard. "There's a damn good chance you're wrong about that."

She peered at our twined fingers with a delighted smile, not only oblivious to what I'd said but obviously making up a replacement statement in her head—something along the lines of *Gee, I want you, too, Margaux.* "Oh, Killian!" She leaned in, seized my shirt's top button in her teeth, and ripped hard enough to tear it away.

"What the hell?" I snarled it while she repeated the treatment with the second button. "Margaux, this is fucking—"

"Amazing." She licked along my jaw, down my neck, and to my sternum in one wild swoop. "Oh yes, Killian. You're as hard and perfect as I imagined. And you taste like a delicious mansicle."

Mansicle?

"Okay, we're done." I congratulated myself for not bellowing it as I pushed away—or at least tried to. Margaux had attached her lips to me like a damn barnacle. Despite the position, she found a way to use the force of my action to pop the third button free, as well. "Damn it, Margaux! We are—"

"Shut up." Her pitch from passion to rage didn't shock me. That was a good thing. Self-control, or my semblance of it, was easier to maintain as she went for the attitude with gusto. With a fiery glare and curling lips, she pushed toward me again. "We're done when I say we're done."

I didn't fuck around with niceties anymore. Circling both her wrists with my hands, I clamped down and then shoved her back. "We're done *now*."

She gave a bull-like grunt. Yeah, I'd just waved her red flag. "Drink. Your. Wine."

On the last word, she scooped up my discarded glass and thrust it at me. I took it with the intention of giving the thing a fast round trip back to the counter, but Margaux had other plans. She launched back at me, stare locked on my lips, once more a barnacle—demanding an upgrade. Since that wasn't happening, I fended her off with an instinctive push. But the wine was still in my hand. The glass didn't just tip. It spilled. All over Margaux's cream sweater.

"Shit." We blurted it together before she slammed her glass down. With the dish towel, she dabbed at the stains. The action only spread the mess.

"Fabulous," Margaux spat. "You treat all your house guests this well?"

"Not the ones who are actually invited."

She blew out another long breath. "Do you have any club soda?"

I ducked into the laundry room and came back out with a small spray bottle. "This is my valet's private concoction. It's potent enough to lift blood stains out of virgin lace, or so he tells me. Just take it and get the hell out of here."

She huffed. "The stain will set. I need to get it out *now*."

I clenched my teeth, fighting back the urge to bodily toss her out. The only factor stopping me was the cognizance that Claire's arrival ticked closer by the second. If she walked off the elevator to the sight of me leaving the condo with Margaux in my arms...*not an option*.

"Buy a new goddamn sweater and expense it to SGC."

"No." Her makeup caked into her frown lines. "This was a special gift from Mother. She got it for me in Italy."

"Margaux!"

I bellowed it into the bathroom door as she ducked inside, slammed the portal, and locked it on me.

Fuck.

I clicked at once into instinct-driven rage, sprinting for the stairs to the master bedroom. My fingers flew through the remaining buttons of my shirt, setting them free as I readied to shuck the thing in favor of a T-shirt. I'd clean up the wine in the kitchen if there was time.

Holy God, let there be time.

I'd only bounded two steps up when my dread came to life.

"Kil?" Claire's bell of a voice sounded in the foyer. She walked in on her own set of stilt heels, the boots I'd had so much fun peeling off her in front of the fireplace. Tonight, she wore them over a pair of blue jeans with a casual cowl-neck sweater in a shade of pink that had become my favorite. Her hair was pulled up into a messy ponytail, also one of my fetishes because of how it bared her beautiful neck for my mouth.

I froze.

Fifteen minutes ago, I would have been halfway across the room, on my way to hauling her close, kissing her senseless, and wondering how long I'd have to wait for the chance to slide my hands up her sweater. Clearly, she expected the same thing, explaining why she cocked her head at me, a curious smile quirking her lips.

Take a deep breath and think this through. You've been in crappier binds than this before.

Even if I couldn't think of a single one right now.

"Thanks for the great view," Claire quipped, setting down her purse and approaching me. "But why are you changing your clothes without my help, Mr. Stone?"

When she got close enough, I yanked both her hands into mine. "It's been...eventful around here tonight."

I tugged her knuckles up to my lips, hoping the action compelled her gaze to mine—and the adoration I had waiting for her there. But her perusal stopped at my chest level. "What happened to your shirt? And what's that red stuff on your neck...and your jaw? Shit, Kil. Did Adara develop a tigress-cougar thing for you and decide to pay a visit?"

I tightened my grip on her, forcing words past the goddamn cotton in my mouth. "Funny that you mentioned misbehaving wildlife."

"Huh?"

"I—" Was brain dead. Numb with fear. And couldn't simply spill that Margaux was here, without an explanation. This was where the nautical course hit a damn cyclone. I'd never had to worry about explanations before. Never had to worry because I'd never really cared. And never had to care because I'd purposely selected women who wouldn't care in return. It was easier that way. Safer. Cleaner.

This situation was *not* clean.

And turned into a shit bath of a mess when Margaux emerged from the bathroom, clad in nothing but her panties.

"Oh my *God*, Kil. We made such a mess that it got all over my pants too. Can you believe—" She stopped, folded her arms, and bit her lip like Bashful the Dwarf given a bitch makeover. "Oh...errr...hiiii, Claire. Great news about the bimbos and the rock band, yeah?"

"Bimbos." Claire rasped it from barely moving lips. "That's

clearly a subject I'll defer to you from now on, Margaux."

"Claire." I growled it as she yanked her hands from mine. "This isn't—"

"What it looks like?" She stepped back, shoulders hunching as she wrapped both arms around herself. "How stupid do you think I am, Killian?" A breath shook her whole body as she burst with a bitter laugh. "The answer to that one's on the wall, right? Or, more accurately, finishing up the mess you made on her in your bathroom."

"Damn it." The curse seethed from me as I wheeled toward Margaux and seized her elbow. Not a peep of protest came out as I dragged her over. "Tell her," I finally spat, jerking her to a stop. "Tell her exactly what happened, Margaux, and don't you dare try any lies!"

The woman slid a sideways smirk at me, as if we shared a daring secret. "Fine. We had a little celebratory wine. Some got spilled. I had to change."

The confession did nothing to change Claire's stance. She still huddled on herself, eyes down, quivering. "Did the spill happen before or after you let her run lipstick down your neck and rip apart your shirt?"

Her shivering gutted me. I released Margaux and reached for her, needing to be her warmth again. Her shelter. Her trust. "Claire—"

"*Don't.*" She skittered back. "Don't, Killian. Please."

The room literally tilted. Nausea rocked a nine-point Richter quake in my gut. My heart thudded so hard in my throat breathing became an optional choice on the survival menu. The only essential on that list was the woman who tugged her coat on and kept backing toward the door.

Fuck!

I released Margaux, now limiting my contact with her to nothing but my eyes, which burned with my rage. At the same time, I recognized the blinders that were yanked from them. I saw everything with sickening clarity. This had been Margaux's end game all along. She'd sneaked in tonight with the intent of nudity happening on one or both of our parts— and if Claire hadn't shown up to make the takedown easy, the little bitch would've found a way to capture the moments in photos or videos for later.

The schemer had gotten her way. Claire had warned me about how she operated, and I'd all but laughed off the threat. Now she'd taken down the tower she came to siege. And, goddamnit, the tower was me.

A thousand words rose to my throat, but I couldn't make sense of what to say first. Facts were always broken down for me, presented so I made the best decision possible. I always had an action plan. Now, confronted with one of the most important things I'd ever say, I was fucking rudderless. What could I say to save myself? What the hell could I do? There was no plan. And absolutely everything at stake.

My hesitation came at a price. Claire moved instead— toward the door. "Don't let me interrupt. Since you're both clearly so comfortable..." She stopped in the foyer but didn't turn. "Well, have fun."

The door shut behind her with a hideous sad click that echoed throughout the condo.

Or maybe I had the sound mixed up with the cavern in my heart...the pit my spirit tumbled into during the minutes I couldn't move. Or think. Or feel. Fuck, especially that.

With slow agony, I became aware of my body again, starting with the fists that coiled and uncoiled at my sides.

"It's...a misunderstanding," I stammered. "She'll have to see that. I'll make her see. I'll just find her and force her to listen. To understand—"

That the reason she held her heart back from you was because of a bastard who shattered her exactly like this? Only that time, she found the guy with her friend instead of a sad, manipulative shrew who's promised to ruin her life if she so much as sneezes the wrong way.

"Killian?"

Speak of the devil. Literally.

A haze of rage descended over my senses. I punched through it at a furious pace, sweeping Margaux's purse from where she'd dumped it on the counter after the spill and hurling it into the foyer. "Get out, Margaux. Now."

"But—"

"What part of *now* wasn't clear enough for you?"

Her huff was like razor blades on the air. "She's not worth this angst, okay? I know you don't believe me now, but you're going to be glad about this in a few days. Claire's a little...silly when it comes to handling relationships. You need a woman who knows more about your world and about—"

I severed her speech by whirling on her with a roar so feral, I wasn't sure it had come from me. But when the pain of it clung to the air afterward, I took full ownership. My voice, when I found it again, was a contrast of slithering fury. "You know nothing about my world, Margaux. Now get the *fuck* out."

Her eyes widened, indicating the bath of fear she clearly, finally took. I would have grinned in satisfaction, but feelings weren't luxuries I could afford right now. Claire had already endured so much stress because of the drug dealer she'd once fallen for, and I refused to add a murderer to her plate.

I kept fighting the emotions as Margaux retrieved her clothes from the bathroom. Clenched my jaw against the wave, huge and freezing and terrible, that pushed against my soul like a tsunami behind a glass wall. I maintained the barrier while I watched the witch leave without another word.

I made it through another minute after that. Another. This would get easier—I was sure of it. Besides, it was only temporary. I gritted the words to myself as I rammed open the slider to the balcony, trying to get air into lungs that still wouldn't cooperate, that listened too closely to the dread thundering in every goddamn beat of my heart. A din that shook harder and harder at the glass wall...

I closed my eyes and gripped the railing as the tidal wave broke through. It consumed me. Drowned me. Destroyed everything inside that finally, truly had *been* me.

★ ★ ★ ★

Nearly a month later, my mind and soul still floated like rotten jetsam in that goddamn storm. Making it worse was the scene in which I found myself, a springtime bower that looked like Martha Stewart had dropped acid and gone to town on Keystone's main pool deck. Giant urns overflowed with flowers in every shade of purple. Floating islands on the pool with the same blooms began to glow from the battery-operated twinkle lights hidden in the leaves. More mood lighting illuminated the miles of fluffy fabric adorning the gazebo where a jazz quintet played into the twilight, and the arbor, sheltering a buffet feast centered around an ice sculpture that read *65 Years Young—Happy Birthday, Willa.*

Laughter, music, and happiness sprinkled the air. As I walked to the edge of the lawn where tables for the party guests were scattered, people waved and smiled. I returned the greetings, barely remembering them the next second.

I'd never felt so disconnected from my life.

So dead inside.

Mother waved from where she held court like a humble, happy birthday queen. Her chestnut hair curled gracefully around her regal face, and her skin was as radiant as a woman twenty years younger. On her wrist was the bracelet I'd given her an hour ago, amethysts on a silver band with a message engraved inside. *You are my sunshine.* There'd been no need to personalize it. The song belonging to the words would always be our unique memory. She had separate tunes for Trey and Lance too, which gave the words of my song extra meaning from the day she'd first sung them to me. I always wondered if she knew that song was often the brightest part of my days— or if she realized that with a child's special telepathy, I felt the meaning she gave every syllable and the affection she strove to impart, as if to show how a falsified family could have love as well as a real one.

I'd accepted that love. Believed in it. Perhaps because *she* did with desperate fervency, clearly hoping I'd be the glue to seal the Stone family back together. For years, I'd fought to be that cement, craved to give that back to the woman who'd given me so much. And yes, I wanted it for me too. But over the years, chunks of that hope had tumbled away. All that remained were a few optimistic slivers, hoarded in my soul for occasions like this, when I sensed they might have the greatest chance of sticking to my brothers too.

Wasn't happening. Not today.

My soul was officially sitting this one out. On the disabled list until further notice. As a result, I became a brooding bastard of a party guest. A newly grateful Trey now doted on Mother, along with Lance, whose appearances here were so rare nowadays they were treated with the fuss of a papal visit.

It was all just fine by me.

I swirled my glass of Scotch and strolled farther away, taking refuge on a little ridge between the pool and tennis court. Beyond the court, Mother had started on a garden dedicated to purple blooms. From here, I could see Jacob's ladders, violas, pansies...and I could smell the fresh lavender.

Just how her hair smelled when I buried my nose in it. Nearly as perfect as the bouquet of her skin when I sucked her neck...and then the sweet tang of her arousal as I trailed my mouth lower...

I gulped more Scotch.

The liquid was sour in my throat. I put the half-finished drink down on a wall and jammed my hands into my pockets, redirecting my thoughts to their favorite pastime.

I had to figure out how to reach her.

She'd tripled the difficulty of the task by catching a flight to California three hours after leaving the condo on that fucked-up night. I'd started with texts and emails, but even the business-related notes were forwarded to one of her colleagues. The personal missives went unanswered. I called, of course—every day, five or six times a day—but my voicemails were ignored. I knew better than to send flowers, a charade she'd not only see through but be insulted by, so attempts were made at more meaningful gifts. A crystal fairy from Ireland. A pair of wineglasses from Italy. Even a donation to the Shambala Reserve in her name.

All the presents were returned unopened. For the donation, I received a computer-generated thank-you the website allowed her to create with one mouse click.

Even when I'd insisted on a video conference call with the Asher and Associates team to go through their wrap-up action plan, she'd begged out, pleading food poisoning from bad sushi at lunch.

Her silence was total, palpable.

And torture.

I'd run out of options. Translation—been cut off at the knees. Over a silly, stupid, goddamn misunderstanding.

Or was it?

Reflecting on that night, I realized why Claire had been so eager to go to the penthouse. She'd been hit by the same trepidation as me, that the end of Trey's mess also meant the end of her time in Chicago. She'd also seen the giant question mark of our relationship and had likely been hoping I'd had an answer for her. I'd had the reply ready but hadn't trusted it enough. I hadn't believed enough in the gift of *us*. My vacillation had been the ideal setup for Margaux, who'd sunk her fangs in faster than a viper, creating the scene Claire had walked in on. The situation played into so many of her nightmares, only one reaction made sense for her. She hadn't just yanked up her drawbridge. With the emotional C-4 laid, she'd slammed the trigger and demolished the fucker.

So here I stood, still tugging shrapnel out of my heart. And bleeding like a goddamn pig about it.

A presence on the path behind me drew my gaze around. Lance stood there, the picture of suntanned and suave in his cobalt-blue suit and black Arizona cowboy boots. A subtle smirk played at his lips, tugging at his close-trimmed beard by default. His dark-brown hair was equally tamed tonight, gelled into submission down his nape. As the party flowed on, parts of the mess started to rebel, tumbling across his forehead.

"Mother sent me to make sure you're not about to slash your wrists," he stated.

I chuffed. "Fuck you."

"Her words, not mine."

I slanted a questioning glance. "She really sent you?"

"Yeah."

"Shit." The woman had read me like a book since the day I'd lobbed a "grenade"—a leaf-covered rock—at Trey, only to hit the kitchen window and then try to lie my way out of the crime.

"That's a damn good way of saying it." He stepped a little closer. "But I think the only two people here who haven't noticed you moping are Trey and Father. T's celebrating his freedom from Keystone prison tomorrow, and Josiah still thinks you walk on water."

I sent over a glare this time. "Well, I don't."

"I know. What a shame." He looked out toward Mother's garden too. "Father will probably discover that someday too, which means all our lives will be fucked to hell again. Damn, Kil, can't you just find a nice girl, knock out a few kids, and keep everything at happy-happy status in Stone Land?"

I was tempted to hit Lance with a darker glower. Had the guy been sent on a deliberate information-fishing trip, or was he really just cracking a sarcastic line? And in the end, did it matter? "Sure, *brother*. Let me get right on that. The family stud horse is here to serve and please. What's one more person to push this lie on, even if she *is* my goddamn wife?"

"Whoa, whoa." Lance swirled his hand with an imaginary

lasso. "I was just fucking around."

"Right," I muttered. "Okay."

"But *you* weren't." He broadened his stance a little. "Were you?"

Hearing someone, *anyone*, recognize my pain...was worse than I expected. Much worse. I battled and failed to hold myself back from grimacing. "It doesn't matter," I snarled. "It's over." *Before it had a chance to begin.*

"Damn," Lance blurted. "I had no idea."

"Nobody did," I countered. "And I'd like it to stay that way."

Not surprisingly, the guy grinned a little. Where Trey had spent his childhood burning butterflies' wings off with a magnifying glass, Lance had spent the days drawing the insects in gory detail, starting at the pupa stage. In his own way, he was the optimist dreamer of the family. "Okay, so who is she?" he asked. "Does she live here? In the city, maybe?"

"No. She's from—" I growled and turned away. "I told you it doesn't matter."

"Wait. The firm you hired to straighten out Trey's PR... They were from San Diego, right?" He snapped his fingers. "A California girl, eh? Nice work, Kill Shot!"

I spun and bore down on him. "She's not a piece of 'nice work,' goddamnit." I backed off when confronted by the raw shock on his face. "Her name is Claire." The Scotch finally sank in, permitting some misery to crawl free from my stoic shell. "And she's beautiful. And funny. And smart...*so* damn smart. And stubborn...exasperating...infuriating. She sees through all my bullshit, and when she calls me on it, I want her twice as much as before..."

I let the rest of it die beneath a harsh choke. There was

still a small novel's worth of things to say, but even confessing this much made my whole body roil with impatient anger. Lance let me twist in the wind like that for a long moment before erupting with a meaningful chuckle.

"Well, I'll be damned," he murmured. "The Enigma has found his match."

Inside my pockets, my hands curled into fists. "The Enigma has nothing, brother. Remember the part where I told you it was over?"

I gave him the general details of the disastrous night in the condo. When I concluded, I braced for a typical Lance follow-up. The caustic laugh and biting commentary never materialized. Instead, I was stunned to see sympathy in the eyes that matched his trendy suit and a smile of comfort on his lips.

"Well, you're right." He rocked back on his slick boots. "That is a story full of big-time suck factor."

I nodded, resigned. "Thanks for listening, at least."

"Oh, I'm not done with your feedback."

Here it comes.

"Okay, *what*?"

His profile grew reflective. I was confused. If snarky commentary was forthcoming from a mien like that, Lance had spent some of that time in the Sedona sun perfecting the hell out of his technique. "The deal is, you've been through the suck factor before." He chuckled and shook his head. "Damn, brother. What Trey and I have put you through since your fifth birthday would've obliterated a lesser man."

I frowned. "What's your point?"

"What's *yours*?" He pivoted to face me fully. "You've all but told me that you found the woman of your dreams, but you've also told me that you let her leave the state and ignore the fuck out of you for nearly four weeks. This isn't behavior from the Killian Stone I know. Remember him? The unstoppable freight train? The same guy who let Trey and me dunk him repeatedly in Echo Lake every summer, only to grin like an idiot and beg for more the next day? That's one of a thousand examples, so let me know if you want more."

"Want an example, asshat? Meet me at the club pool tomorrow morning and I'll show you all about dunking."

"There!" he exclaimed. "That's what I'm talking about."

"What you're talking about *how*?"

"Why doesn't *that* Killian Stone have his ass on a plane for California? Why didn't he do it a goddamn month ago?"

While Lance's hoo-yah for my cause was awesome and unexpected, it didn't change a word of my answering argument. "Because I've had a chance to evaluate this shit—and conclude that Margaux Asher, in all her manipulative glory, likely did me a favor." I blew out a weary breath. "Because despite how my mother's so certain about my imminent suicide, maybe this was for the best." I inhaled deeply to prep my conclusion. "Claire Montgomery deserves better than what I can give her, Lance."

He narrowed his gaze. "Excuse me?"

"The truth." I loathed that even evoking the word made my head pound. "And yeah, I mean all of it. All the crap that went down in my penthouse that night... It wasn't the first time she'd been laid out by a man's betrayal. She saw what she saw and believed what she did about it because she's been lied to before, in huge and disgusting ways. Even if that weren't the case, integrity and truth are hardwired into her emotional needs. I've seen that circuitry at work hundreds of times over the last three months."

Lance gave a scoffing huff. "Kil, she makes a living from media spin and altering public perception."

"By taking the *truth* and letting it shine, not by fabricating attacks and lies." Even in the midst of my purgatory, a smile warmed my chest and burgeoned to my lips. "It's the most unique thing I've ever seen. She pulls out seeds from the shittiest situations and transforms them into the PR version of roses. She simply turns people into better versions of themselves." I couldn't help snorting out a laugh of self-deprecation. "Hell. She's turned *me* into a better person."

"I already like this woman."

We chuckled softly together. I rolled my shoulders, still nervous. On a day I hadn't even tried for the goodwill of my brothers, I stood here *laughing* with Lance. It was a smack of bizarre on top of the surreal my life had passed back in March. I didn't know what to do with it.

"I think she'd like you too. When Trey's behaving, she even enjoys him."

"Someone who inspires you to your best, though they've seen you at your worst..." His face mellowed into a faraway expression. "That's good stuff. I like it. I get it."

I studied him harder. "Yeah. You do, don't you?"

"It's what Zack has done for me." He turned his stare back to mine. "I'm in love with him, Kil. And God help the man, he feels the same way."

I returned his smile. "I'm glad for you, brother."

As fast as it had started, the man buried his lapse of sentimentality. The arcane cowboy artist returned. "I'm glad for me too—to the point that if Zack had the tiniest suspicion I'd been with someone else and then ran away and blocked my ass at every communication attempt, I'd be looking for the next transportation I could find, be it a two-thousand-dollar airline ticket or the back of a goat farmer's truck, to get my face back in front of his. Once I was there, I'd make him take a bath in my gaze until he couldn't breathe from the love I drowned him in and *then* dare him to walk away again."

"Even though you two have to hide what you feel?" I nodded toward the pool, where Father settled beside Mother once more. "From them, at least."

"Not for much longer." He returned my startled glance with a serene nod. "Yeah, I know *they* probably know already, but I'm going to tell them, Kil—out loud. Oh, *not* today. Ruining Mother's bash wasn't what I came here for." Resolve firmed the jaw beneath his beard. "But life is too short and precious to hoard secrets, brother, especially those that shackle you from grabbing at the big brass rings...the shit that really matters."

"You mean killing the enemy ninjas and taking back the base?"

He cracked a grin at my mention of our favorite boyhood adventure. It mellowed to an expression that stunned me. For the first time in our lives, it seemed Lance was at peace in his own skin—and, because of it, more confident than I'd ever seen him. "Joy and love, Killian," he answered. "Joy and love...and the right person to share them with."

Our stares locked for a second. I was fascinated by this person I'd known my whole life but didn't feel I'd truly seen before today. Some of that change was traceable to the changes in my own outlook, but most of it was Lance's power. He'd girded his balls, sucked back his fear, and yes, had fought ninjas—those in his soul—in order to face his truth instead of run from it. Now he stood here offering to lend me the same strength, a beacon of direction from the last place I ever would have imagined.

And I paid him back by clinging to my hesitation. Without apology. "I'm fucking proud of you, brother. I mean it. But slipping on my devil's advocate horns for a second, my coming out would spread much bigger ripples in the Stone Global pond than yours."

Lance returned a measured nod. "We all have levels of truth. Admittedly, yours are more complicated than most people's. I can't tell you which layers to peel off, Kil—but I *can* tell you that the one tangling your gut, strangling your heart, stealing your sleep, and dragging your psyche is the one you *must* fight for. *She's* the one you must fight for."

His words galvanized me. And terrified me. In a guttural mutter, I told him, "I'm scared shitless."

"Then you're headed in the exact right direction." There was a chuckle in his voice, making me want to hug him and deck him at the same time.

"This isn't a dunk in the damn lake, Lance. And I'm not the steel-sided freight train, either. This is bigger. Things could get...broken."

"No shit." He laughed again. Bastard. "Like your heart."

I dug a savage toe at the grass. "Yeah, goddamnit. Like my heart."

"Which means you have to dig deep for the courage this time, deeper than ever before. But if anyone can do this, it's you, Killian Aidan James Jamison Klarke Stone." He returned my sudden gawk with an assuring smile. "You want me to add on a few more names? It still wouldn't matter. The labels aren't you. Embrace the truth of *you*, Killian—the warrior who's always been my dauntless brother, no matter what anyone chooses to call you. Get your ass out of these castle walls, and go find the woman who cherishes that truth in you. Don't waste another second. Do it. Now."

CHAPTER EIGHTEEN

Claire

Early June in San Diego was one of the most beautiful times of the year. Southern California wasn't big on seasons, but the transition from spring to summer always brought a palpable change to the air, a livelier kick to everyone's step. The flowers seemed brighter. The bay seemed bluer. The sun was warm, and the breeze was balmy.

It was a perfect time for brides and weddings and fairy tales.

And heartache and headaches and desperate attempts at faking happy.

Yes, I was miserable. And saw reminders of Killian nearly everywhere I went, in almost everything I did. But if an Olympic event existed for faking happiness, I was training for the gold during my efforts at being the best second-string maid of honor in wedding history. What better reason to push myself than Dad and Andrea's big day, right?

While dunking my pain in miles of tulle and organza, I did everything humanly possible to steer clear of Margaux. That included making myself available to Andrea and Colette, her psychotic wedding planner, for each and every task they dreamed up. I forced myself to say yes no matter how trivial or mind-numbing the project.

In fact, the more mind-numbing, the better.

I spent an entire weekend hand-addressing envelopes for thank-you notes corresponding to gifts that hadn't actually arrived yet. Another weekend was spent hand-wrapping each of the wedding favors, cut-crystal flower vases in the art deco theme of the wedding. The seating chart took another weekend, and for three days after, I referred to myself in the third person, as was Colette's habit.

It didn't matter, though. As long as I stayed busy, I didn't think. Which meant I didn't think...

About...him.

No matter how many times his phone number showed in the window of my cell. Or a package arrived from him at my condo door. Or a memory of his touch panged me as I undressed. Or the beauty of his name spilled from my lips when I pleasured myself. Or the darkness of his eyes, haunting my sobs afterward.

It would get better. It had to. One foot in front of the other. Somehow.

Today, I had no other option. The big day had come, and the stage was set. The Crystal Ballroom at the US Grant in the historic district of downtown San Diego had been reserved almost the moment my father had proposed to Andrea two years ago. They were lucky to secure the hotel for a Saturday night in June, but the Grant was well aware of the publicity potential of having the Asher-Montgomery wedding in-house. The showpiece of the city's Gaslamp District specialized in weddings, and today's event was like no other. Andrea had hand-selected every element of the occasion to coincide with the ballroom's opulence, which transported guests to the hotel's heyday during the 1920s and '30s, when celebrities from all over came to enjoy the building's splendor.

Andrea was stunning in her custom gown, looking like a modern-day Jean Harlow as she walked down the aisle to Dad, who got misty the second he saw her. By the time she arrived at the rose-covered altar, his handsome face was streaked with tears. His emotion sent me over the edge too. I sniffled through the ceremony, my heart bursting with jubilance for him. By the time the ceremony was finished, they both practically glowed, and I nourished a sliver of hope that Andrea cared for Dad beyond wanting a piece of movie star-hot man candy on her arm. Maybe I really did need to give her a second chance. Maybe she wasn't the zero-depth dragon I kept making her out to be.

"Claaaaiiirrreee. Claire, darling!"

Or maybe I'd had a moment of temporary delusion.

I was tempted to answer "Yes, Mommy Dearest" but bit my tongue, set down the first plate of food I'd seen all day, and slapped on the fake smile I'd perfected to an art while scurrying to the bride's side to see what she needed—this time. At least I was actually able to move. Andrea had been sympathetic in choosing our dresses, opting for simple but stunning navy silk sheaths with jewel-encrusted spaghetti straps, making it easy to be at her beck and call. Not that the main maid of honor would know about such things. Margaux had slunk off to the bar as soon as her receiving-line duties were finished, almost seeming afraid to be around her mother. I had to agree that in full bridal glory, Andrea packed more force-of-nature punch than usual. The urge to genuflect before the woman did occur as I approached her, now standing near the head table mooning over Dad, her French-manicured fingers caressing his classic gray cravat.

"Andrea, I'm here. What can I get for you?"

"Oh Claire, you're such a dear. I left my lip gloss in the bridal suite when we went back to freshen up. I must have left it on the vanity." She winced. "I should have left behind these shoes instead. They're *killing* me."

Dad gently kissed her cheek. "Ohhhh no, love. We can't have that. Just take them off, darling. Nobody will notice."

"*Everybody* will notice. The line of the gown will be ruined. It's all right, Colin. I'll be fine for a few more hours."

"At the price of your arches?"

She ignored Dad's mutter. "Margaux still has both the key cards to the room, Claire. Can you ask her for one and then hang on to it in case my silly brain forgets anything else?"

"Sure," I said, forcing the smile again. "No problem."

Dad stepped over and bussed my cheek. "You've been such a big help today, honey. I'm so proud of you...and thankful for how you've gotten close to Andrea."

"Okay, Mrs. Montgomery, let's move toward the dance floor to set up a few candids." The photography team ushered Andrea away, giving us some privacy.

I kissed him back and then hugged him tightly, sniffling again as the backs of my eyes stung once more. He brimmed with a radiance I hadn't seen since my graduation day, and even that paled in comparison. I would do everything in my power to keep that look on his face, for today and forever if I could.

"Daddy?"

"What, magical one?"

"Please...just make sure...she always treats you right, okay?"

"Awww." He pulled me in again. "I will, sweet Claire bear.

And someday soon, your prince will come too, and you will be as happy as we are."

As I tugged away, I rolled my eyes. "That's not a subject for today, Dad." *Or ever.* Too late on the hint to my heart, a memory churned to life with bone-melting vividness. *I'm not standing here with a glass slipper, Claire.* Killian had murmured it before climbing out of the town car to watch every step I took into the hotel before giving that bashful, beautiful little wave I'd remember my whole life.

Sure you will, girlfriend. Until you get a clue and consider how many others he's used that wave on before. Maybe even Margaux, who was dazzled by it as much as you—and then did something about it.

I allowed myself a glance toward the bar. For someone who'd finally gotten her hands—and God only knew what else—all over Killian Stone, Margaux appeared confusingly miserable.

"You need to stop working so much and get out a little bit, Claire."

I shook myself from my ruminations to nod indulgently at Dad. "Yeah, yeah."

After we hugged one more time, I swiped at my tears and made my way toward Margaux for the suite key. As I watched, she was approached by Michael, Chad, and Talia, our teammate who'd finally returned from her crazy assignment in New Orleans. Their smiles were full of forced politeness, though Michael actually dared a hug as well. To my shock, Margaux accepted the gesture with a little smile. I released a relieved breath. Michael and his kindness might have just eased my day somewhat.

"Sorry to break up the party, gang." I gritted a smile of my own at my new stepsister. "Can I grab the bridal suite key and ask you to keep an eye on things for a few minutes? The new Mrs. Montgomery has a cosmetics emergency," I explained. "I'll be back fast."

Margaux fished in her wristlet before extending the keycard with a heavy-lidded glare. So much for Michael and his magical hugs. Apparently they weren't as wonderful as Killian's.

On that morose thought, I turned to make my escape— grateful as hell that Chad grabbed a champagne flute from a passing waiter's tray and quickly fitted it into my free hand.

"You can probably use this more than me right now," he muttered.

"You're right. Thanks." I left out the part that I'd only had a granola bar and a banana since this morning. This would be my third glass of champagne, and I anxiously waited for the buzz to kick in so I could finally forget just *one* word in my head.

Like that was happening, after the flashback I'd just entertained.

Hair in the wind. Gentle smile. Dorky wave.

Killian.

I slammed the champagne back, wishing it was Patrón.

But I still had lip gloss to retrieve. I hastened my step toward the elevator after I shut the ballroom doors, hearing a sizable commotion in the room behind me. The lift opened just in time. I stepped in and mashed the button, deciding that whatever the crisis, Margaux could handle it this time.

The hallway was deserted as I arrived on the floor, made my way to the bridal suite, and slid the card through the reader. By the third unsuccessful try, I was pretty sure Margaux had given me the key to her room instead of the suite. "Shit," I whispered, settling my forehead against the door. I barely paid attention when the elevator dinged again, but that changed when the approaching footsteps on the carpet registered. Heels. Hard and angry.

Speak of the devil, in all her Louboutin-and-Tiffany glory.

Margaux stopped, shot out a hip, and whipped out another card. As she cocked her head, her soft blonde curls contradicted her defiant green glare. "I gave you the wrong key."

"I was just figuring that out."

"So...what, Claire? Do you expect an apology? Because you won't be getting one. Not from me, at least."

Her flare-up wasn't a stunner. Now that we were away from the guests and our parents, the woman was unleashed to let her true colors show. That was fine by me. I didn't feel like making nicey-nice anymore, either.

"Trust me, Margaux, that's the last thing I'd expect from you." I edged the retort in sarcasm, but the bravado was a complete act. She was the last person I wanted to be standing here with. Just glancing at her was a piercing reminder of what I'd believed in once again and lost. *Of* who *I'd lost.* "Thank you for bringing this up. Now get the hell out of my face before I decide to crack this key in half and use it to slice yours open."

Through the haze of my anger, I heard loud stomps in the central stairwell, back near the elevator shaft, but Margaux moved in, wedging me into the alcove in front of the door. My sights were filled only with her leering face now, though I sensed a new presence in the passage with us, getting stronger... distinctly masculine.

And smelling of Armani?

No.

Enough with the stupid mind games, Claire. Three glasses of champagne and no protein, and you expected yourself to keep thinking straight? My terrible sleep habits weren't helping the situation, either. Rousing at three a.m. for two-hour bawling jags had made me feeling like a certified loon by now.

That brought the subject perfectly back to Margaux—who still hadn't moved. She kept glowering as if I were something she scraped off her shoe. "Well, well, well. Claire bear has claws, after all. You surprise me, *sister.*"

Her glare took on a gloating glint, already certain of the damage she wreaked by evoking our new family ties. As of six o'clock this evening, princess-zilla wasn't just my blackmailer anymore. My head throbbed harder, trying and failing to downgrade the awful comprehension.

"Well, *you* don't surprise *me*, Margaux. You've set this all up perfectly. You hold the sheaths to the claws today, and we both know it." I let her have two seconds of a smirk before adding, "But enjoy that party while you can, okay? I'd tell you karma's a scary bitch, but you beat her to that dance floor."

A little laugh tinged her features. "Very cute, darling. So glad we got that straight, because I won't be apologizing to you for this—or anything else, for that matter."

"And as already stated, I'm not standing here waiting on you."

At that, our stares locked and held. The air grew heavy with our shared knowledge of everything she referred to, especially that pivotal night in Chicago. By now, I at least knew Killian felt like shit about whatever kind of accident or chemistry they'd shared, but a thorough study of Margaux still yielded me nothing in the slightest-bit-remorseful department.

Ridiculous as it was, the discovery weighed like an anvil on my chest. But I refused to show my weakness, keeping my chin aloft and my gaze steady, no matter how painful the tears burned behind it. That didn't stop Margaux. The witch blowtorched through my defenses, seeing straight to my soul—and going for its center with a giant knife of venom.

"Oh, God. Would you stop sulking like a wounded puppy, already? You got exactly what was coming to you, Claire. You didn't just sleep with the boss. You did it with a man completely out of your league—and now you're hurting about it? Oh, boo fucking hoo. Nobody cares that you're hurting, in case you haven't noticed."

I wasn't sure she expected a response. For a long moment, I didn't have one. Wait. I *did* have one, but once more out of respect for my father, I couldn't break his new stepdaughter's face.

I went for the next best thing. My standby. A lot of sarcasm. "Wow, Margaux. Just...wow. You're really something. You have the guy. You have...well...everything, really. So you want to even *think* about stopping, already?"

She licked her lips and let a berry-red smirk slide across them. "At last we're in agreement, then. I do have the guy. There are still a few technical details to work out, but Kil's beginning to see the light—as well as what a silly boy he was for taking up with you in the first place. You know that video conference you ducked out of? Yeah...couldn't keep his eyes off me the whole time. Oh, I *will* make him happy. Claire. So much happier than you could have. I realize that you're ignorant about the specifics of fine-tuning a relationship and keeping it exciting, which isn't really your fault, considering that creature who raised you by himself. God, the overhaul my mother's had to perform, training that blue-collar hunk of mindless beef, but it's all in the past now. Onward and upward, right? You *can* see that Killian will be better off this way, right?"

I dropped my arms. As I did, my hands balled into fists. Taking back the moratorium on breaking this bitch's face looked like a better option by the second. "*What* did you just call my father?"

She rolled her eyes. "At the risk of sounding trite, *please, bitch*. Mother says your dad is a good fuck, Claire, and not bad on the eyes for the geriatric crowd, but essentially she took pity on him. You should be grateful for that, really. As they say, the apple doesn't fall far, so if Mother didn't have his rock on her finger, I'd be making sure you were out of a job too, paying your price for whoring around with a client. And you can be damn sure that Mother knows *everything* you did with him in Chicago. She's as disgusted by all of it, *and* you, as Killian now is."

Her words impacted me like a punch to the stomach. I stumbled back, slamming against the wall with a sickening thud as her vitriol spiraled in my senses. *It's only words.* I fought to rally back on that slim, stupid hope. But she was relentless, tearing ceaselessly at my self-will, her torture aided by the constant use of his name.

It was too much. *So much agony.*

"Enough," I rasped. "*Enough*, okay?"

I wasted my breath. Margaux was on a huge roll. Victory glimmered in her eyes, feeding off the pain in mine. "Awww. Poor little Claire. Of course you've had enough, which is why you made everything so damn easy for me. Your pathetic self-esteem makes you predictable, conquerable"—she waved her hand up and down as if showing me off like a game show prize—"especially how it turned you into a panting fangirl after Killian. Ohhh, the look on your face was so priceless, sweetie. I laid the trap, and you stepped right into it, believing everything you saw that night, *exactly* as I intended. You were such an easy mark, playing perfectly into the scene with your sad lack of trust. *I* should almost thank *you* for the sheer perfection of it." She moved back a little, folding her arms like a goddess of destruction who'd just decimated a city. "Let you in on a little secret, stepsister. Nothing really happened before you arrived that night, nor did it happen afterward, but you really bought into every illusion like the idiot you are."

For two seconds, I feared bursting into tears again. Then fury rescued me, making it possible to shove past her while she giggled like a lunatic harpy. I crossed to the other side of the hall, knowing I should leave but weirdly riveted to my spot— and hating myself for it. "At least I'm an idiot who can look at myself in the mirror at night."

"Though you'll be alone, won't you?" She stalked me again, slow and slinking with each step, still the victorious, violent goddess. "And I'll be with Killian Stone. Now that you've satisfied his white-trash fascination, he can flush his guilt about you down the toilet. He's performed his charity work and can do what's he's wanted this entire time. Me."

She struck an exultant pose, spreading her arms wide and tossing her head back—until a voice, lethal and wrathful, scythed the air.

"Margaux."

Three steps thundered on the carpet with determined fury.

"*Enough.*"

The thunder made its way to my chest as I swung my gaze

in tandem with Margaux's, responding to that unmistakable voice. Silken yet mighty. A command wrapped in a murmur.

Killian.

He stood next to the stairwell door in dark jeans and a button-front shirt he'd surely slept in. His hair was windblown, some of it tumbling into his eyes. Oh God, *his eyes.* They were very dark and very angry. Clearly, he'd just heard every vile word that had come from Margaux's mouth—which now loomed as a large, shocked *O* in her newly pale face.

He stalked toward us. With every step, he tore my heart out—a heart I'd assumed had received its last goodbye from my head, forever forbidden to feel like this again. Bursting. Joyous. Tormented. Terrified. The throbbing thing swelled and surged into my throat, cutting off my air, making it impossible to meet his stare even as he moved up and planted himself a few inches from me. Instantly, I felt the familiar heat from his spicy-scented skin—but I knew anger generated that more than anything right now. The stuff rolled off him in palpable waves.

With shaky steps, I backed toward the elevators. "For the record, I can't do this right now. Not anymore. Not with either of you." I was tempted to pull the navy platforms off my feet and leave them there. I needed to bolt—faster than they could carry me.

"*No.* You aren't going anywhere, goddamnit."

That made my conclusion official. I'd never seen Killian so furious, even after all Trey's stunts. It didn't change my get-the-hell-out-of-here goal by one millimeter. I needed some distance and a lot of time to process the information Margaux had dumped in my lap. Where was my phone when I really needed the Record button, to keep and analyze every word?

Deducing I was insane but knowing he'd never set me free

without it, I raised my gaze. His own awaited, blacker than a moonless night. He rolled his shoulders and neck, clearly trying to find relief from the tension that had mounted.

"No running, Claire." He frantically searched my face for something. "Please. You promised." What the *hell* was he seeking with that scrutiny? Possibly the connection we shared, seemingly unbreakable just a few weeks ago? That connection wasn't lost, this entire moment proved that, but the links in our chain were so tangled and knotted right now.

"Well, promises get broken, don't they?" My voice was strangled and raw, exactly how I felt inside. I couldn't fathom what else to say and sure as hell refused to launch a heart-to-heart with him here in the hall, with Margaux as our greedy voyeur. "I—I really need to get back to the reception anyway. My new mother is waiting for me."

I stepped to the side, narrowly avoiding the hand he shot out, trying to hook my elbow. Why was he here, today of all days? Why was he making this so much harder on both of us? Every word I'd blurted was the truth. I really couldn't do this. My *heart* couldn't do it. If it made the wrong decision again— and the statistics clearly leaned that way—the damage would be much worse than a simple month's worth of grief. My soul would carry the scars too. Forever.

I had to get out of here.

With a tight choke, I started running down the hall. At the end, I opted for the stairs over the torment of waiting for the old elevators. Killian's scent lingered in the stairwell, a taunting smell that dared the tears to well back up my throat. I forced them down with a clenched jaw as I pushed into the ballroom again, though I felt like Alice through the looking glass when I arrived. Nothing felt familiar or right. I shook my head and let a bitter laugh escape. Hadn't this been the story of my life for a whole damn month?

I forced down a deep breath. Another. When I had the strength to look back up, gratitude filled me. Talia approached across the dance floor, darting in and out of couples who boogied to the band's bad rendition of an old Commodores tune. Since I bested the woman in height by an inch, she could officially be called little, but today, her pixie characteristics were really emphasized. She'd styled her near-black hair in a creative mix of curls and braids, which were combined with a stunning sea-foam-green dress and strappy silver heels, making her appear like a sprite among the dancers. Despite the demure appearance, her features were intense as she came close and grabbed my hands.

"Where have you been?" she demanded without preamble. "Wait. Stupid question. Andrea had you off on an errand, right?" She rambled on despite my gape at having failed the lip gloss run. "Never mind. It doesn't matter."

I frowned. "Why?"

"Because Killian more-gorgeous-than-a-god Stone was here about ten minutes ago, asking for you. No, amend that. Not asking. Demanding. Incessantly. Claire..." When I responded with nothing but an evasive glance toward the bar, she seized my hands tighter. "*Claire!*"

"What?"

"What do you mean, what? You have some explaining to do, woman. I've been back from New Orleans for a bloody week. When were you going to tell me—"

She cut herself short as I let my face surrender to a crush of grief and confusion. After guiding me to the wall and shielding me from the crowd, she yanked me close and crooned in my ear. "Ohhh no, girlfriend of mine. Do we need to get two quarts of ice cream after this and camp out for a talk?"

I wrenched my head from side to side, shaking from the effort of trying to keep it together. I could *not* lose it here, during Dad's happiest day in nearly twenty years. But I couldn't hold back the helpless anger anymore. Things were a mess, inside me as well as outside. The scene at Killian's penthouse had all been fabricated by her. I knew that now. But what about the next time something like that happened? In so many ways, Margaux was right. I had let my trust issues rule my reactions, instead of believing in the strength of what Killian and I had built together. Maybe I'd never wanted to trust it in the first place. Maybe I was too fucked up to believe in anyone because I didn't trust myself anymore.

Dad had believed in Mom, and she'd died. I'd believed in Nick, and he'd lied.

I clung to Talia and cried harder.

"Oh, dear. Ice cream isn't going to help this, huh?"

"N-No," I sobbed, feeling more obnoxious for running my makeup into the halter neck of her gorgeous dress.

"Oh, *Claire*," she blurted. "What the hell did that bastard do to you? I swear to God, I'm going to kill him now. Killian Stone's fine ass is complete grass."

"Simmer down, spitfire," I managed. "It's not what you think." I tried a watery smile. Massive fail. Talia gripped me again, rocking me back and forth so we almost looked like a lesbian couple about to swap spit. She was a great friend, just like Michael and Chad, always knowing how to make me smile when things were shitty—like now. I thanked God she was home.

My reprieve from hell lasted all of those three seconds.

On cue, Margaux appeared in the doorway of the ballroom, her stance in full battle mode but her face consumed in a pure case of shell-shocked. I could only imagine what had taken place in the hallway after I'd left her there with Killian. I knew, whatever it was, I was going to need another drink. She looked just as mad, *and* tormented, as a junkyard dog with fleas.

"To the bar?" Talia queried, seeming to read my thoughts.

"Absolutely." I gave her one last hug and then dried my eyes and took the lead toward our cocktail oasis.

Talia yanked me back, practically ripping my arm from its socket in the doing. I flung a gape back at her, only to find her eyes already wide, staring at something over my head. "Holy. Shit."

"What?" I patted my hair. "Is there something in my—"

"No, sweetie." As she said it, the energy in the room shifted. The air molecules themselves seemed to change, to shiver with awareness...just like every drop in my bloodstream. "You look beautiful." A brilliant smile overtook my friend's lips. "But don't take it from me."

Before I turned, I knew he was there. My pulse raced with the certainty of it. My nerves tingled, and Lord help me, the deepest tissues of my sex stirred, already alerted to him.

Sure enough, I spun to watch Killian stalking across the dance floor, eyes riveted on me, parting guests like Moses through the Red Sea. The dancers suddenly stopped, staring at the commanding man in fitted jeans and untucked shirttails, advancing toward me with unwavering purpose.

The floor became my damn anchor. I was immobile, helpless to do anything but watch as he neared, captive to the beauty of his face and the darkness in his eyes. When he stopped and braced his legs, chest vibrating with the force in his lungs, I was painfully conscious of the stillness in the room—a mockery of the chaos in my senses.

"I—I thought you'd left."

"I'm not leaving unless you're with me."

"I really need you to leave, Killian."

"I'm *not* leaving unless you're with me."

"Damn it." I hated the desperation of the whisper. "I'm confused. And—"

"And you don't want to be. I get that. I don't like being confused, either." He wrapped a hand up to my elbow. It felt like the first time he'd ever touched me. The action wasn't a command or even a caress. It was a pure entreaty of movement. An invitation. "But let's face it together. We can handle anything, Claire, as long as we do it together."

I let his stare penetrate me for another long moment before dipping my head, unable to confront what I saw in his face. The man was a walking lightning rod for commanding presence, but his power pinged off the charts right now. "Look, if this is a ploy to go somewhere and talk, then—"

"I love you."

My stare jolted back up. "Wh-What?"

"It's the truth. I mean every word of it. I'm done hiding. Here are my cards laid on *your* table, Claire Montgomery. I hope you're ready to hear it all—and I don't care who the hell hears. As a matter of fact, the whole damn world can listen in."

Tears scorched my eyes again. I was certain my heart now lived at the base of my throat. A dizzying mix of joy and desire formed a mini tornado in my heart, though darkness swirled at the storm's edges—and he knew why. More than anyone else on the planet, he *knew* why. He'd now been the target of Margaux's machinations himself, and had to know the woman wouldn't stop trying to rip us apart, especially after the way he'd called her out in the hallway.

"Stop," I begged. "Please. This isn't the place, or—"

"It'll never be the place, Claire. That's my point. There'll be risks and ramifications, lots of them, for both of us. I know that. And yeah, I know you do too. I know what I'm asking of you, baby...of the danger that you're risking—" That same strange cloud crossed his face before dissipating in a heavy swallow beneath the taut cords of his neck. "But we'll face it all together." He shifted closer, now leaning over me, cupping both sides of my face to compel my gaze toward the beautiful onyx depths of his. "*Together.*"

I greedily grasped my turn to gulp hard. He was so dark and beautiful, sincere and fervent...and he could be mine. This proud, passionate, smart, sexy, incredible man stood here, pleading to be my partner, my lover, my best friend...my prince.

Tears brimmed and trailed down my face. "Oh, Killian."

"I love you." He imposed the point now by pressing his lips to mine. "I. Love. You. I'll say it a thousand more times if I have to."

I attempted a little laugh. "Be careful what you offer, Mr. Stone."

He grinned back. "Only what I'm confident of delivering, Miss Montgomery."

"I'm beginning to think there's nothing you can't deliver."

"True. As long as you're by my side." His fingers tightened, gripping my scalp, tangling in my hair. "The last four weeks have been the worst of my fucking life. Without you, I really *am* an enigma...a gigantic tangle of secrets that I don't want to keep to myself anymore. I'm empty, lost...somebody I never want to be again."

I forced a deep breath to permeate my body. "I'm—I'm scared."

He lowered his hands into mine, meshing our fingers between our chests as he pressed even closer. His dark eyes widened, exposing a near-childlike vulnerability. "So am I. Like I've never been before. I want to share everything with you—*everything*—and I promise that I will. I just need some time."

I pressed my fingertips to his jaw, loving how his stubble scuffed my skin. "Take all you need."

"You already have the power to decimate me. You know that, right? But here's my heart, and I'm giving it to you with everything I have. You're my brass ring, my fairy queen, the one thing in my life I can't imagine losing again."

I gave up a tearful laugh. "If I look like half a person, it's because I've felt like one for nearly thirty days."

"Then let's work this out. I won't say things are going to be perfect. What happened in the penthouse with that little bitch was proof enough. But we can be stronger than that. We *are* stronger. Please tell me you get that. Tell me I don't have to be without you anymore. I don't want to spend another sunrise without you."

He bent over to kiss the knuckles on my left hand, then my right, before pressing both of my palms over his heart. "It's yours if you'll have it, Claire Montgomery."

Only then did I realize the entire room was still completely quiet, everyone seeming to wait on my response. I swallowed again, my throat tighter than before, tears coursing harder down my cheeks. The earth rocked beneath me. My head spun. My bloodstream felt like an early version of the fireworks show scheduled for the conclusion of the reception.

Because my every dream was coming true.

And I finally surrendered to the magic of it.

I lunged forward to kiss his perfect mouth with all the love welling in my heart. Killian met my assault with equal passion, tasting my tears, moaning from the force of my embrace. Might we have really found our way back to each other? As my heart acknowledged the affirmative answer, I wrapped my arms around his neck and held on, needing to savor his body next to mine, his heartbeat pounding against my own.

He kissed me again, so much deeper this time, dipping me back and nearly sweeping me off my feet. When we parted and I looked up at him, his eyes glittered like a hundred stars on a velvety night sky, perfectly reflecting the amazement in my spirit and the enchantment in my soul.

"Careful, Chicago." I couldn't help a huge grin as I evoked our old nicknames.

"What's that, San Diego?"

"Your inner Prince Charming is showing."

CHAPTER NINETEEN

Killian

If princes froze in the middle of ballrooms grinning at their women like damn idiots, I had this gig nailed. I couldn't have held back if I'd tried. Her smile took on an impish edge with her jibe, exposing dimples that I traced my thumbs over as I pulled her back to her feet. I kept her close, treasuring the feel of her, filling my senses with the smell and presence of her...

Loving her with every single part of me.

"Well, you're definitely the authority on that subject," I finally whispered.

She tilted her head, my inquisitive little fairy again. "Oh?"

"You fit the slipper, baby." I shifted my hold to her nape, lifting her face so she'd have to confront the conviction in my eyes—and my heart. "I'd resigned myself to that space being empty, that I would never find anybody who'd fill it as perfectly as you." I dipped my head until our foreheads touched. "I'm so fucking glad I was wrong."

Her breath hitched. Because we were so close, I felt it too. When I lifted my eyes to hers, it was to watch tears glisten in their magical golden depths.

"Killian," she whispered. "I love you too."

A man's polite cough broke into our reverie.

When we broke apart, I turned toward a sophisticated

fellow who shared Claire's easy smile, unique eyes, and proud chin. His hair was a few shades darker than Claire's but just as thick, gelled into a formal style.

"Mr. Montgomery, I assume." I clicked into efficient business mode but couldn't stop my goddamn palm from sweating as I extended my hand. "My regrets for breaking into your special day like this, sir. My name is Killian Stone"—I slipped my free hand into Claire's—"and I'm in love with your daughter."

To my relief, Montgomery broke into a huge smile. "Lad, if we're going to be broken into, I can think of no better reason." He turned toward his bride, an elegantly attired Andrea Asher. "I'm certain you agree, dear one?"

"Indeed." Andrea's lips curled up as she said it, but the sentiment didn't climb to her eyes. She'd likely had a look at Margaux, who huddled in one the ballroom's alcoves like a cat thrown into the rain. I had no sympathy for the younger Asher. Out of respect for her mother and Claire's father, I'd held back from hurling Margaux's sad, vindictive ass right over one of the hotel's balconies. Since she appeared genuinely bereft now, I supposed a spark of humanity still existed somewhere in her soul. The excavation team who went searching for it could count me out.

"Andrea." I stepped forward and pulled her fingers up to my lips. "You're breathtaking today. I'm not surprised why Claire never stops talking about you."

Though Claire dug a fingernail into my palm, she had no other leg of retaliation to stand on. It wasn't a lie. I simply didn't embellish the truth, either.

"Killian Stone," the woman chided, "you could flatter paint off a building."

"Andrea, you know what a busy man I am. Flattery is a waste of time." I straightened and delivered the next words with all the conviction in my heart. "But the truth is always worth the time and pursuit." Gazing at Claire again, I emphasized, "Always."

She blinked and shuffled from foot to foot. "I...uh...wasn't able to get your lip gloss. I had the wrong key, and—"

"Oh, dear." Andrea pouted.

A little woman appeared, reminding me of a Chihuahua crossed with an elf. Several photographers followed on her heels. "No worries, no worries! Colette has a key, darlings." She produced a keycard from a sequin-covered binder in her grasp.

Andrea smiled at the weird creature. "Colette, you're a goddess."

"Of course I am."

Andrea swept the card toward Claire. "Do you mind going back, Claire dear?"

"Of course not," Claire replied.

"I'll go with her," I cut in. "Just in case she gets lost or something."

Claire gave me a mocking huff. "I've been to the suite a hundred times tod—"

"*I'm going with you.*" I was still locked in enough business mode to make it a command she couldn't ignore.

"Then you're both complete dears. Thank you so much."

"Colette is thankful, as well," the Chihuahua crooned. "Annnn-drea must have luscious lips for the cake-cutting photos."

Andrea pressed a hand to her neck. "How right you are, darling."

Montgomery clipped an arm around his bride's waist.

"But my fairest, you are *always* luscious."

"Oh, *psshh*, Colin. You know what I mean. Those photographers are from *Us*, *People*, and the Associated Press. It's not like I'm going to actually eat any of that garbage, anyway."

The man's jaw tightened. "That 'garbage' is a two-thousand-dollar cake with imported chocolate filling and gold leaf flowers."

"It still doesn't get to spend a second of time on my hips, Colin. You know that."

I took that as my cue to shake the man's hand and offer one more line of congratulations before gripping Claire's hand harder. I gave polite waves to the magazine photographers during their pursuit of us out of the door. Claire didn't issue another word of protest as we passed the hotel's security guard into the wing that was off-limits to everyone but the wedding party. I could barely stand still as she slid the key and opened the door. I took care of slamming the thing as soon as we were both through. I also took care of pinning her to the wall as fast as I could and getting my mouth on hers as hard and possessively as I could.

My senses barely registered the sound of the key plunking to the tile as they drowned in her magic once again. The lavender and wind scent of her. The silken, passionate warmth of her fingers. The jolting, amazing vibrations of the moans in her throat and the sighs on her lips. The way she opened to me. Meshed with me.

Fit me.

I missed her so much. Needed her so completely.

Wanted her so badly.

With a ruthless growl, I yanked up the hem of her gown

and thrust my hands along her thighs, guiding them around my waist. "Hang on," I instructed between breaths, swinging her around and carrying her like that to the couch. Once I set her down and shoved the coffee table away so I could kneel between her legs, she loosened her grip on my neck and pushed me off by a few inches.

"We— We can't. Oh, *Killian!*"

I grinned. "I love hearing you cry out my name like that."

Though I repeated the teasing tug to her panties, a second scream didn't emerge. "You're a wicked, wicked man."

"Who loves you more than my own breath."

"And apparently mine too. Oh— Ohhh, God! That's... that's..."

"A pussy I've missed very much." Despite our jokes about breath control, neither of us held back our passion-filled gasps as we exchanged furious kisses, soon timed to the rhythmic thrusts I gave her tight, perfect tunnel. I pushed one finger into her. Two. Three. The throb in my cock picked up on our rhythm too, straining hard at the zipper of my jeans, proclaiming loud and clear how it didn't approve of its captivity.

"Killian— Oh shit, we can't. We— We— Ahhhh!" She gasped as I worked my thumb along her hard, moist pearl.

"Baby...your clit is telling me something else."

"I'm supposed to go back to Andrea."

"In a little while. Damn, you're so wet, Claire. So wet and erect for me."

"The— The— Cake cutting—"

I kissed her with brutal impatience. "If I can't be inside you soon, fairy, they'll be able to use my cock on all four of those layers."

Suddenly, she giggled. Coupled with the tangle of her

fingers in my hair, it was a moment I consciously savored—and thanked the Creator for.

"If that's the case, then I want a slice of each, please." Her lips drifted into a soft smile. I felt myself copying the expression, wrapped up in her beauty, basking in her love. Her gaze gentled to the shade of a summer sunset, just as she coasted a hand to the buttons still tethering in my dick. "Or maybe I'll go for the more pleasurable option."

"Thank fuck," I growled, sucking her neck while she quickly opened my jeans. I pulled around and turned my attack into a full kiss again when she freed my erection from my briefs, giving her a groan when she cupped my balls and steadily fondled me.

With a guttural grunt, I reached around, caught her panties, and ripped. Her gasp exploded against my lips, her skin quivered beneath my touch, and her head fell back, opening herself fully to me. I jerked her to the edge of the couch and then right off, forcing her to fall onto my waiting cock. In one passionate thrust, I impaled her.

Connection.

Consummation.

Completion.

As I let my body soar higher into hers, I sank my gaze deeper into hers. I prayed she saw straight into the heart, the soul, and the spirit she alone had pulled out of their isolated enigma of a tower, into the light and clarity and power of her love. My maddening, challenging Miss Montgomery. My fairy queen. My princess who'd never demanded a glass slipper but was the only one who fit my life so perfectly.

I loved her harder, watching ribbons of desire wrap thicker across her features. I'd never grow tired of the sight. I'd never stop adoring this amazing woman, sent for me alone to worship.

When we were done, cleaned up and ready to return to the reception, I pulled her close for another tender kiss. I took my time, longing to memorize the moment with her. Moments I'd never forget. I shook my head at her unspeakable beauty. At the bewilderment that I felt in being the bastard lucky enough to love her. I'd never again deny the depth of my feelings for her.

"I love you," I whispered.

"I love you too," she replied.

Like a very good fairy tale, we were on our way to a happy ending.

But like the best fairy tales, we were only just beginning.

EPILOGUE

Claire

October...

"Come on, sleepyhead. You'll miss your flight."

Killian's command wasn't getting a moment of support from me, much less obedience. Instead, I groaned and covered my head with the warm covers of his bed again. In retaliation, he pounced on the mattress and began a barrage of growls, kisses, and tickles. This was definitely my new favorite alarm clock. Okay, second favorite. The amazing Killian Stone morning-wood alarm still topped the list. Sadly, I wouldn't be getting that ringer this morning.

"You do that on purpose, don't you?" he drawled into my ear.

Busted.

"So what if I do? Are you going to stop kissing me, Mr. Stone?"

"Never, Miss Montgomery." He gracefully rolled to his side next to me. "I would, however, like to be doing it more than two weekends a month."

I sighed. "They need to change that silly nickname of yours. The Stubborn Mule of the Magnificent Mile fits you so much better than that enigma crap."

"Hmmm. You're probably right."

"Which means you're going to say it anyway, right?"

"Mmm-hmm."

I tucked a pillow beneath my head and rolled my eyes. "Fine. Go ahead."

His approach was different this time. He burrowed his lips against my neck, slowly working his way along all the spots he knew to be the most arousing. "When will you quit that silly job and come work for me at SGC?"

I gasped softly and arched, hoping to give him better access. "We've been through this before, Killian."

"And just like before, this long-distance commuting is killing me." Dear *God*, the man could do magical things with those full, sensual lips of his. "I want to wake up like this every morning with you, baby."

"I know." Sadness tinged my response, half because I really meant it and half because he'd ended the declaration by pulling away to add the dark beauty of his eyes to his effort. "And when the time is right—"

"Which will be...?"

"I just can't up and leave my Dad, Kil. Besides, I hate being cold. It's already ass-freezing outside, and—"

"It's *nice*," he protested. "It's fall! Do your palm trees look as awesome as the park outside?" His hair fell into his eyes in all the sexiest ways as he jerked his head toward the window. I resisted the urged to pull him down to me again, focusing instead on my best beach-girl pout.

"If I survived a winter as a resident here, I'd be a raving bitch by the end, and you'd be dying to toss me into the lake."

"Never."

"Are you sure about that?"

"I'll keep you warm. Promise." He leaned down once

more, sucking my jaw this time. "I know all the best tricks in the book, fairy queen...the good ones *and* the naughty ones."

"Aren't they the same thing with you, Stone?"

"Guilty." He rounded my chin, inching his way up to gently nip at my bottom lip.

I sighed as he kept the path of kisses traveling down my neck. "If you keep this up, I'm absolutely going to miss my flight."

"Okay by me," he mumbled while dipping down the front of my neck, making me squirm in all the best ways as he slid toward the valley between my breasts. "I happen to own an airplane, my love."

"Errrm, I vaguely remember that cute little pile of bolts," I teased back.

"That pile of bolts *is* perfectly prepared to fly you home at a moment's notice."

I skated my hands down the muscles of his back to distract myself from a resigned laugh. How the hell was it possible to keep resisting the man's persistence? Simply put, I just couldn't. Not anymore. We'd finally found a happy groove, and it had been working for a few months now. Could all of this go on forever? We both knew it couldn't—but that was a bridge we'd cross together in the future, knowing we'd find a solution that fit us both.

I wished things were different for Dad. He hadn't said anything directly to me, of course, but I saw signs that things weren't right in paradise for him and Andrea. I could do little but be supportive until Dad spoke up, though I had to admit that might not ever happen. He was an Irishman through and through, including the stubborn-pride thing. And maybe all of those signs were simply my overactive imagination at work *again*, melodramatic misperceptions of two people in the adjustment phase of a new marriage. The first year was supposed to be the toughest, and Dad had been a bachelor for a long time. Some of the changes had to be weird for him.

Or maybe Andrea was a cold control freak nobody could live with. Oh yeah, *that*. I still wasn't sure what Dad saw in her, which brought me back to my *stellar blowjob* theory—a speculation I quickly dismissed despite the contradicting evidence.

After Asher and Associates wrapped Trey's case, Killian convinced Andrea to retain me as SGC's permanent consultant. Andrea had already considered extending such an option for other clients, and Killian simply exploited the idea. He'd made my bi-monthly visits part of the final contract, a necessity that hadn't hit Margaux well at all. I was certain the smoke from her ears reached three-alarm status when Andrea issued the announcement at the monthly team luncheon, which Killian himself had made a point to attend. Despite the constant surveillance he now kept on Margaux in one form or another, I didn't share his confidence that we'd heard the last of her spiteful retribution.

A couple of hours later, we stood at the VIP security checkpoint in O'Hare Airport. I sighed back tears and swallowed hard. Then again. This was the part that sucked every time.

I stood on the tips of my toes and wrapped my arms around his neck. I felt—and saw—the appreciative stares of other women at him, also not a new aspect of our public goodbyes. Killian was just one of those men. It didn't matter what he wore, said, or did—he simply attracted attention. His own sigh, deep and heavy, reverberated through us both as he locked his arms around my waist and lifted me off the ground to meet his lips. Our height difference was ridiculous when I wasn't in heels, and I always dressed in flats when traveling in case of the need for an OJ-style sprint through the airport.

"Just two weeks," he whispered into my ear.

I reacted with a choked moan. "It always seems like longer."

His grip tightened. He nipped softly at my earlobe. "You know, in this position, you're a bit helpless. I could just steal you away...walk you right out of here before you could fight back..."

He pulled back enough to let me see his attempt at a sinister leer. Instead, he looked a little dorky...and a lot sexy. I giggled and rubbed a hand against the weekend scruff lining his jaw. "I wouldn't even try to fight, and you know it."

We smothered each other in a lip-mashing kiss. At the moment I felt his crotch start to lurch against the puddle at the crux of my thighs, he reared back. With a deprecating grin, he murmured, "Wow."

"You stole *that* thought right out of my head."

His gaze darkened, and his lips lifted. "We've come a long way, haven't we?"

"That's a good thing, right?"

"Damn straight. Just think...how I was so afraid of you running away..."

I pouted. "I never ran very far."

"Would've been a lot *less* far if you were naked in my bed more often."

I smacked his shoulder playfully as he set me back down, but the overhead speakers blared with the boarding call for my flight. Instantly, I leaped back at him, overwhelmed and teary.

He was right—it would only be two weeks before I saw him again. The reassurance did nothing this time. I didn't want to let go. *No...no.*

I looked up into his dark velvet eyes, struggling to blink the sting out of mine. Alarm tightened the corners of his lips.

"Hey hey...why the tears, fairy?" He brushed my hair back and kissed my forehead.

"I love you so much," I rasped. "In such a short amount of time, I've fallen so far. I'm in big trouble here."

"This isn't trouble, baby. It's love. And it's the best thing a person could hope to find in their lifetime. This is the real deal...and we've found it with each other...and I'm so fucking grateful. So unless those are tears of happiness, no more crying, okay?"

His words, so pure and strong, lent me the will to nod. "Okay."

"You're stuck with me, Claire Montgomery, for as long as you'll have me. The ride's just beginning."

"Not a Tilt-A-Whirl, right?"

He chuckled. "Nope. No more throwing up, I guarantee it. This distance thing...it's temporary."

I giggled again. "Watch out, everyone. Killian Stone has spoken."

"Fucking right," he drawled, kissing me again before assuring, "We'll work it out. Maybe there's a Southern California office in the future for SGC, or maybe we'll buy a little farm halfway for both of us..."

I smirked. "You realize that lands us somewhere in Colorado."

"Hmmm. Perhaps a ranch, then. Or a little trendy coffee shop. I could wear a beret and make designs out of cappuccino foam all day." When I could answer with nothing but a long laugh at imagining him as a hipster barista, he answered with a dazzling smile and went on. "We don't have to decide today. Until we do, it's one day at a time for you and me. Now get your sweet ass on that plane before I really do have to fly you home myself."

We had a long-standing deal. I never looked back after I cleared security, so we kissed one last time before I turned and headed home.

The summer sunset gleamed through the window of the plane as I buckled into seat 1A, the same place I occupied on every flight. The first-class location was another nonnegotiable item Killian had insisted on in my SGC contract. When I'd questioned the extravagance, he'd growled that if his fairy queen insisted on commercial flights, *he* insisted she fly in front, and there'd be no argument. I'd known better than to reply with anything more than a thankful kiss.

A private driver waited for me at Lindberg Field when I arrived in San Diego, loading me up in no time. During the drive through the city, I turned on my phone, not shocked to see three text messages waiting for me. I slowly smiled. No matter how many surprises the man wielded, in some ways, he was breathtakingly predictable. I knew what the texts would say before even reading the screen.

I.

Must.

See you again.

And we lived happily ever after.
For now.

Continue Secrets of Stone with Book Two

No More Masquerade

Available Now
Keep reading for an excerpt!

EXCERPT FROM
NO MORE MASQUERADE
BOOK TWO IN THE SECRETS OF STONE SERIES

CHAPTER ONE

Claire

The world was exploding.

It was my usual reaction when getting swarmed by the paparazzi and their flashbulbs. It probably wouldn't ever change. I wasn't sure I wanted it to. Did anyone ever get used to this?

Eight months after I'd publicly become Killian Stone's girlfriend, the shutterbugs still enjoyed tracking me down when photo ops were thin up north in LA. Their latest opportunity—and a Fellini-like horror straight from my nightmares—occurred on a Saturday morning when I got home with groceries in my arms, a sloppy ponytail on my head, and my rattiest beach shorts paired with a faded Queen T-shirt. The tee was a classic, Mercury not Lambert, so I could get away with the rip in the right sleeve.

"Good morning, Claire. You look great, girlfriend. Give us a smile? Just one?"

"Guys," I protested, "aren't the Oscars in a few weeks? There has to be someone in Hollywood being fitted or waxed or plucked—or whatever they do to get ready for that stuff. You have to know where all the salons are, right?"

"*Pffft*. They all hire private stylists now. We're not getting anything before the red carpet these days."

"It's a beautiful Saturday morning," I persisted, "and we're only going to have this Indian summer for a few more days. Take the day off. Go to the beach. I give you permission."

They chuckled. Then kept clicking away.

"Speaking of you and the permissions you grant... You've captivated Stone longer than any woman before. Will there be a ring on that left hand soon, Claire?"

My gut clenched. It wasn't as though I hadn't been asked the question before. I was sure Killian had been asked twice as many times. But he wasn't getting down on one knee until a lot more of mine were answered. Until he exposed those shadows I could still see in the depths of his gaze...

"Answer's the same, Hal." I shrugged. "No comment. Can you make yourself useful and shut my car door, please?"

"Need it locked?"

"It'll do that by itself."

Of course it did. The winter white Audi A8 did everything on its own except yell at idiot drivers and levitate over traffic jams. After Killian had given it to me, I'd told him my name wasn't Captain Picard and refused to drive the thing for a month. But then he'd driven me in it for a long weekend in Santa Barbara. And had shown me how it detected every Starbucks within a five-mile radius. And had given me a couple of hours in its back seat, parked in a eucalyptus grove overlooking Goleta Beach, that still made parts of me tremble with desire...

Now I needed a cold shower.

I settled for a glass of ice water, retrieved after putting away the groceries and enjoyed on my favorite chair in the house, an old leather recliner I'd had since college. The chair joined the Napa-style décor in my rented Mission Hills bungalow, where I'd lived since graduating. I didn't care that planes flew overhead at all hours of the day and night. The neighborhood was my favorite part of the city and the chair my favorite part of the house. It was like a friend who knew all my warts and still loved me. It was just what I needed right now. A reminder of closeness on its most basic level.

Exactly what I was missing with Killian now.

I sighed. This feeling sucked. He'd given me so much already, and I didn't mean the material things. While being his queen was sometimes like walking through a luxury-living magazine, all of it was simply background to the magnificence of him. His power, grace, sensuality, intensity...all of it enthralling me more with every minute we spent together, even if it was over the miles and especially if it was face-to-face. With every consuming kiss, every sinful look, and every tingling touch, I gave the man more of my heart.

It scared me.

Too good to be true.

How many times were those words more right than wrong?

The doorbell couldn't have butted in with better timing.

I gratefully left my insecurities behind in the chair, despite the discomfort of what I faced. I liked Hal and his buddies, but having to shoo them off like magazine salesmen wasn't fun.

My door didn't have a peephole, but I slid back the small peek-a-boo door set into the heavy wood, checking it really was Hal and not somebody selling money-saving solar panels.

I blinked in surprise. No Hal. A small woman stood on the porch, neatly groomed and shyly smiling. I tried to make out the logo on her T-shirt, but the sun blasted me in the eye, bouncing off the neighbor's clay-tile roof from across the street.

"Can I...help you?"

She nodded quickly. "Hi. I'm Christina. From Mystic Maids?"

"Well, *I'm* mystified." I laughed, unable to help myself. She'd pitched it over the plate, but I was still down in the count. I hadn't hired a cleaning service. She glanced at her paperwork, clearly certain she was at the right address.

We stood there trying to figure each other out...and then it hit me.

Killian.

"Dear Lord." I unlocked and then opened the door. "Please come in. Christina, right?" I looked back over my shoulder while the young woman followed me in.

"Do you mind if I put my lunch in your refrigerator?" She was so adorable. It was going to kill me to tell her she wouldn't be here long enough to eat the meal.

"Listen, Christina...I didn't actually hire you. While I'm sure you do a great job, and I appreciate you coming all the way over here..." I grimaced as her eyebrows met in confusion. "Please, if you can sit tight while I make a quick phone call to my over-the-top boyfriend, we'll get this straightened out."

On cue, Justin Timberlake's "Sexy Back" blasted from my phone. Heat crawled across my face. Christina giggled. Again, endearing to the power of ten. Damn it, she was growing on me by the minute.

"Speak of the devil." I gave her a commiserating wink.

"Excuse me for one sec."

I picked up the call after walking into the front sitting room.

"Good morning, fairy queen. How's my girl today?"

God, he was so perfect.

And frustrating.

"Good morning to you too. I was just about to call you." I caught Christina starting to move things in the kitchen, dusting into the corners. *Better talk fast, girlfriend.*

"Oh, yeah?" His voice descended to a growl that would tempt a nun. "Were you dreaming about me again? Wait while I close my office door and you can tell me all about it."

"Why are you in the office on a Saturday?"

"And you're not working today?"

"Not...right at the moment."

"The door's closed. Better idea. Let me video call you. Then you can act out your dream for me. Go to the bedroom. I'll wait."

I swore I could hear his eyebrows waggling across the line. It made my blood dance in delicious ways. A lot of things mesmerized me about the man, but his lighthearted side neared the top of the list. He showed it to so few, and it made me kind of swoony to think I was the leader of that privileged crowd. I liked that position. A lot.

Where the hell was I?

Frustrating. Him. Same sentence.

"We have to switch to serious for a minute."

"Okay, but only a minute."

"This girl showed up at my house this morning. From Mystic Maids?"

"Hmm. Good. She's right on time. They came

recommended for their thoroughness and punctuality."

"So you not only hired a service but researched the whole thing."

"Yes and yes."

"Damn it, Kil."

"What? The new acquisition has been a boatload of extra work for your team. And with the unexpected damage control from Father's episode, added to your propensity for perfection...you've been working too fucking hard."

"Said the pot to the kettle?"

"The last thing you need to be worrying about is keeping the house clean."

"How is Josiah doing, by the way?"

"They released him yesterday. Simple heartburn, as everyone knows thanks to you. Don't change the subject."

"It's my subject, buddy. You're in the hot seat here, not me."

"You're not Cinderella, for chrissake. In spite of the wicked stepsister and the questionable stepmother, the mice on your hearth don't get to gawk at your cleavage if I don't." There was a beat before he got the humor of his own line and started snickering.

"Stop it," I snapped. "You're violating our agreement, and I'm peeved."

"We didn't have an agreement. We had a talk. I'm not violating a damn—"

"I don't need you to keep doing stuff like this for me! I'm sending her home."

"Don't. You. Dare."

Shit. Now I'd pissed him off. Big-time. And damn...was it hot.

"Really? Or what? What are you going to do, Chicago? Hmmm. That's right. You're all the way in Chicago. Oh, boo."

Why the hell was I goading him? *You know damn well why. He soaks your panties when he's in prowling panther mode, that's why.*

"I could be there by this afternoon, Miss Montgomery. Then I doubt you'd have such a pert little attitude."

Miss Montgomery. Shit. When he called me that...using that dark, dangerous tone...

"I'm perfectly capable of cleaning my own house, Killian. This is ridiculous."

"But I don't want you to." The line rustled. I imagined him straightening in his Odin's throne chair at the office, leaning over his big desk, the long fingers of his free hand pushing at the wood as his face hardened with command. "That should be enough of a reason. Do you understand?"

More heat suffused my face. My eyes slid shut, letting the heat of his imperative tone wreak all kinds of chaos on my bloodstream. I had no idea what to do with him when he got like this. While it was infuriating as hell, he elevated caveman to a new level of sexy. If he commanded me to jam my hand down my shorts and touch myself while he spoke I would've complied, even with Christina in the next room.

"Claire?"

"What?" I retorted.

"If you send her away, I will be very disappointed."

"Tell me." Only half my breathy emphasis was feigned. "How disappointed?"

"Don't push me," he grunted without embellishment. "Goddamnit, why do you make this shit so hard? I like doing things for you. It's important to me. And I won't be questioned over every single decision I make."

I stared out of the window, feeling pulled by an undertow and then slammed by a ten-foot breaker. After eight months, he could still do this to me. I seethed at him. Burned for him. Hated him. Wanted him.

Loved him.

"Claire? Are we done here?"

I fumed for another long moment. "Fine. Yes. We're done here. Jerk."

"I love you, baby."

"I love you too, jerk."

His chuckle filled my ear before I disconnected.

I showed Christina where I kept my vacuum and whatever else she needed to clean the place but drew the line at her doing my laundry. I'd wash my own damn underwear, thank you very much.

After packing my laptop, some files, and a bottle of water into my beach bag, I headed out. Before leaving, I demonstrated the alarm-setting procedure for Christina. Apparently, she'd be stopping by on a weekly basis from now on.

The second I was settled in with my towel, chair, and laptop at the beach, my phone rang for the fifth time. I already knew who it was. Persistence should have been the man's middle name, not Jamison—especially when he knew I was unhappy with him.

"Yes, dearest?"

"Why are you letting my calls go to voicemail?"

"I was driving to the beach. Sorry, I almost waited for the shoulder carriage but figured you'd cancel the order when learning about the four studs that came with it."

"I was worried about you." He ignored my sarcasm in

favor of a gentle tone. It was likely the closest thing I'd get to an apology right now.

"It was less than ten miles."

"Most fatal accidents occur close to home. And your driving scares the hell out of me. You know that."

"So I'm supposed to make it worse—and break the law—by picking up your call?"

"I'll just get you a driver too. Two birds, one stone. You can get more work done instead of stressing about the commute, and I won't have to worry when you don't—"

"Kil!" I couldn't help laughing. The alternative reaction wasn't pretty. "I swear, you're going to drive me to drink."

"Fairy."

"What?"

"Don't be mad about the housekeeper."

"I'm not. Anymore."

"You deserve to be taken care of."

"I'm over it, okay?" I sighed, my own version of a not-apology. "You're actually very sweet, Mr. Stone—if overbearing and presumptuous."

He cleared his throat with purpose, making my pulse race—and the rest of my body prepare for the tone that came next. Silken seduction. "You fell in love with me this way."

"And I still love you."

"That's damn good." He let a long beat stretch by. Another. "Because there's a little more coming."

I could hear him breathing in measured lengths, likely bracing for my tirade. Just listening to the sound made me take pause, halting everything—yes, even the rant.

A wince grabbed my face. What was my problem? The man adored me. He was doing his best to spoil me, and I was acting like an ungrateful shrew, all because of my unfounded fears about the what-ifs. I needed to live more in the moment.

I needed to be a better girlfriend.

"Th-There's more?" I finally croaked.

As he laughed into the phone, I pictured him running his fingers through his gorgeous dark hair, which was probably a little too long at the moment. Translation—completely perfect. "Hold on," he finally stammered back. "Are you really not going to yell?"

"I guess not. Do you want me to?"

"No!" He chuckled again. "That's completely fine. Shit, San Diego. You certainly keep me on my toes."

And what amazing toes he had. Yes, I'd treated myself to a full inspection one night at his place while we'd binged on *Shark Tank* and Chinese takeout. Conclusion—God had even crafted the man's feet to perfection.

"Soooo," I prompted, "back to my 'more.'"

"What about it?"

"Don't make me pop up into your play and then refuse to catch the ball, mister." I huffed. "Come on. Tell me what it is."

"Nope. I want to surprise you when you get here next weekend. Can you wait that long?"

"Probably not." *Good girlfriend, remember?* "But I will. I know you'll make it worth it."

One of his pleasure-filled growls resonated over the line. "You're sexy when you're amenable." He continued the sound, keeping me baited. "So be even more so and let me send the jet for you this time."

I huffed again, but there was a real smile behind it. Gee, my fabulously gorgeous boyfriend wanted to send his private jet to pick me up and then fly me to him for a weekend in his gazillion-dollar penthouse on the Lake Michigan shore. I think I could be okay with that.

But just this once.

"Yes, Mr. Stone. I would love that." A silence went by. Not one of our comfortable pauses either. "And Kil..."

"Yeah?"

"I need to...apologize to you. About earlier."

This shit never came easy for me, and the man knew it. His voice became softened with understanding. "It's okay."

"No, it's not. I let my I-am-woman-hear-me-roar run a little too wild over the tundra. The housekeeper is great, and I was ungrateful. I hope I can make it up to you?"

I tried to finish off with playful and sexy, hoping he caught on to my hint. Who was I kidding? The man made innuendoes off my boring media spreadsheets.

"Hmmm. Maybe a little more begging is in order—on your knees in particular, in something small, black, and scandalous. Maybe you can...coax out my forgiveness."

Hell. He'd gone from sultry to throaty, melting my panties by corresponding degrees right here on the beach. What his words alone were capable of doing to me... Yeah, I had every right to be scared. If he truly knew what kind of putty I became in his thrall...

God, I was in such danger. And I wasn't sure I ever wanted to be safe again.

"So, tell me where you are." He purposely jumped onto a more innocent track. "What beach did you head to?"

"Torrey Pines," I supplied. "I usually don't come here since it's a little farther from home, but since Christina is taking care of the chores, I had some extra time." I paused, sensing him smiling through the phone line. He warmed my skin more than the sun itself. "I wish you were with me, though. You could rub lotion on my hard-to-reach spots."

His groan was low and telling. "Oh, I know all about your little...hard spots."

So much for innocent. I was certain the man had secretly taken euphemism courses at MIT. I was about to laugh off his tease but realized I didn't want to. Today's events—facing the paparazzi, our tiff on the phone, doubting my capability to be the compliant partner he needed—made the distance between us feel like galaxies instead of miles.

And the shadow that fell across every star in those galaxies? The secrets he was still keeping from me. The double meanings in conversations I would sometimes overhear. The distance that sneaked into his eyes when he spoke about himself sometimes, as if looking at in from an outsider's viewpoint...

How could I feel so close to him yet so far?

I fell back on the easy stuff. The lust. After covering my legs with a towel, I pushed them together and then slid one foot up the opposite leg. The friction on every tissue between my legs was enticing, exquisite...

And just like him.

A dark, unattainable pleasure.

"Claire?"

"Yes," I rasped. "I'm here. Sorry."

"Why are you apologizing? What's wrong?"

"Nothing." Everything. Oh, hell. Maybe I really wasn't cut out for this role...this being Killian Stone's damn girlfriend. I second-guessed every other thought in my head and comment from my mouth because when I didn't, I flew off the handle and pushed all his buttons anyway. He said he loved me this way.

Even called me adorable and exciting and claimed he liked living life *on his toes*. I loved him more for it but wondered if the toe talk came from how far in the deep end we both were with this thing. And what would happen if we both drowned. And if I needed to check for a life preserver before it was too late.

"Well, that's bullshit if I heard any," he muttered.

"I just miss you." My voice was sloppy and thick with emotion. "I know it's only been six days. I'm just...sad." And lonely. And pathetic. Was being in love supposed to make you sound so morose?

"Only six days?" He repeated it like I'd told him the earth was really a square. "You mean the one hundred and forty-four hours of sheer hell we've just endured? Because I wasn't counting or anything."

I let a watery laugh spill out before waving my hand, actually thinking I could dismiss my gloom like a pesky fly. Sure. That was going to be effective. "Go back to work, Chicago. Forget all this. I'm just being a dumb girl. I'll be okay by tonight, and—"

"No."

"No...what?"

"I'm not forgetting about it." He expelled a hard breath. "We've been apart too long."

"But it's only been a week."

"And it's been too long."

I really felt silly now. "Killian, come on. I just need to chill out, and—"

"No. You need me near you, just like I need you near me. You need me pulling you off your feet and kissing you until you're dizzy from it. You need my hands tearing off your clothes and then all over your naked skin...every fucking inch of it...until my fingers find their way inside you and spread you, getting you ready for my cock. Why don't you tell me what you need after that, baby?"

"You." Thank God for my sunglasses and sun hat. I pulled the brim lower, hiding the way I panted for every breath and shut my eyes, fantasizing all the images he painted. "Inside me, Killian. With me."

"Yeah, my sweet fairy. That's exactly right. And that's exactly what I want. I'm so hard, so hot, so miserable. I need to be near you, holding you, a part of you—reminding you who you belong to, where you belong. With me. Nowhere else." His breaths were just as rough and fast as mine. "Does that sound about right?"

Damn him. How I love him.

"Why can't it be next weekend already?" It was a needy, desperate whisper, and I didn't care. "I wish I were wrapped in your arms..."

"Done."

"Huh?"

"You heard me. Go home and pack. Bring your work clothes and files with you because you're working from the headquarters office this week. And you'll spend every night in my bed, damn it."

"All week?" I should have been miffed. Instead, my heart sang.

"I'm sending a driver and the plane. I'll text you the details. Don't bother arguing." The line went rough, as if he'd adjusted his grip on the handset again. His voice had thickened with pure command. "I need you. Not just with my body. With—" He grunted as if trying to talk himself into saying something.

My heart tripped over at least ten beats. "I'm done with this bullshit, Claire. Two weeks is too damn long. By tonight, we'll be together."

"I love you." I sounded loopy and lovesick, even to my own ears. It didn't matter. Nothing did, except the idea of getting to see him for more than forty-eight consecutive hours.

"I'll see you soon. Now go get packed."

I threw all my stuff back into my striped beach bag and headed for the car. A quick dusting of baby powder made sure the sand stayed at the beach, and I'd be ready to hop right into traveling clothes. As I drove home, the songs on the radio sounded happier, the breeze seemed lighter, and even the traffic seemed more agreeable.

Killian Stone made everything in my world better.

So, was it such a horrible thing that he preferred to keep some things in his world private?

I turned the question over in my mind during the flight.

How bad could the damn secret be, anyway? Wasn't there a good chance I already knew all the major issues his family had thanks to the research I'd helped pull during Trey's sex scandal last year as a member of the PR cleanup team? It wasn't like Andrea, my boss, had allowed that file to grow cold, either. Killian's brother was already showing signs of pulling the black fleece out of the closet again. He'd frequented a few clubs that had been his bad-boy candy stores, showed up late to meetings, jetted to Miami for long weekends. Oh, yeah, he was back on everyone's radar.

I actually smiled while enjoying a sip of the champagne the flight attendant had opened before takeoff.

Trey's addiction to fun was extra stress for everyone, but after all that, how huge a bomb could Killian have to drop?

And was it possible I'd created that bomb in my mind, bracing myself for an explosion that was never to come, just because I couldn't trust in the good of what we had?

I had to stop constantly pushing back. Had to trust that Killian would open the door and let me see the secrets of his tower when the time was right. I'd fallen this hard for him without the invitation. I could certainly wait a little longer.

Until then, I vowed to be less his adversary and more his girlfriend. Be more gracious about the extravagances, even if I didn't need them.

I had to stop being tempted to run again.

Because one day, he'd refuse to give chase.

Then I would truly know what devastation was. If being apart two weeks at a time was doing this to me, not having Killian at all was...

Unthinkable.

I directed my thoughts to another path. A viable action plan.

Maybe it was time *I* chased *him* a little.

Maybe it was time to rethink a permanent move to Chicago.

I had a week to look at things with new eyes...and perhaps at the end of it, to surprise my Prince Charming with a sparkling surprise of his own. Finally, I could hit him with something he'd never see coming.

★ ★ ★ ★

Around eight o'clock CST that night, I deplaned the Stone Global private jet at Midway Field.

The world's most stunning man waited for me on the

tarmac next to the Stone Global town car, the wind kicking at his thick dark hair and his long leather trench.

With each step I took down the stairs, my heart leaped one notch higher in my throat. Hoping this feeling never went away, no matter how long we were together, I scurried into the strong haven of his arms, burying my face in his neck while he pressed every inch of my body against his.

I was home.

I was his.

While I never wanted the embrace to end, I finally pulled away enough to kiss him, grabbing his neck to keep him close. When we dragged apart, the night became day again with the brilliance of his smile.

"Hi there, San Diego."

My grin couldn't be contained. *San Diego? Maybe not for much longer, Mr. Stone.*

"Hi there, Chicago."

"How was the flight?"

"Unbearable without you." I giggled as he rolled his eyes but sighed when he moved in for a deeper kiss. His tongue rolled against mine, tasting like a little Scotch and a lot of lust. We'd be lucky to make it to the penthouse if this kept up. "Thank you for this," I murmured. "You spoil me rotten, and I promise I'll start to love it more."

He brushed away the hair that had escaped my wool cap, his gaze raking my face with intensity. "That sounds really nice, fairy—because you haven't seen anything yet."

I was happy to know his surprise hadn't slipped his mind. It sure as hell hadn't escaped mine. I grabbed his hand with an expectant grin, but the man returned an evil smile before ushering me into the car. He didn't say a word as the driver loaded my bags into the trunk. Still nothing as we pulled away from the airport.

"We probably should feed you first." His statement was all business, but his gaze was pure mischief. "Did you eat on the plane? Before you left?"

"Aggghhh." I whacked his chest, but that only fed his mirth. I straightened, folded my arms, and drawled, "You want to know what I did do on the plane?"

Inside a second, his stare turned to sensual velvet. "Does it involve you sprawled on the bed with your fingers in your panties?"

I smacked him again but let my hand linger on his coat. The mix of the night wind, his cosmopolitan cologne, and that thick leather...*wow*. "I don't use the bed unless you're in it with me. You know that."

He curved his palm over mine, making me stay close. "I'll be good. For now. Tell me."

"I worked on new affirmations. I'm going to be better about accepting surprises from you."

A rare, soft smile lifted his lips. It was the look he didn't use very often, reserved for occasions like visits to the no-kill animal shelter he championed and Sunday dinners with his mom. "I really like the sound of that."

"Me too." Since he had his animal rescue eyes on, I put on my best matching stare, along with a corresponding pout. "So...?"

"So?" He slid the smile back into a smirk. "What?"

"Damn it," I groaned. He chuckled. "Are you going to make me beg? I'm not above it, Mr. Stone."

That ended the smirk. His face took on a thousand angles of lusty possibility, concentrated most fiercely in the sensual sweeps of his lips. As he tugged me against his chest, he let them part in heated promise before quietly ordering, "Yeah. I do want to hear you beg."

I didn't need another cue. While pressing closer and lifting my face, I whispered, "Please don't make me wait any longer. I'll do anything you want."

His panther's growl took greater force in his throat. "Anything? Hmmm. You may regret that promise, fairy."

"Try me," I challenged.

"You know I would've told you anyhow, right?

"But making a deal with the devil is so much more fun."

As he laughed, he readjusted our positions, setting me back by a bit—and clearly trying to wrestle his crotch to a less conspicuous swell. I bit my lip hard, gazing at that bulge. It was just as difficult for me to hold back from grabbing a good feel.

"Okay...here goes." He actually seemed a little nervous, and that made my heart pound again. "You know how you've been moaning about your passport gathering dust?"

"Ummm...yeah?" I didn't hide the questioning lilt to it.

"Does three weeks sound like ample time to do some dusting?"

Forget the pounding. My pulse took off at a gallop. "Wh-What do you mean?"

"I mean three weeks. You and me. Your birthday is coming up, and I thought we could celebrate with a splash. Italy and France, maybe Spain if we have time. Rome? Venice? Marseilles? Paris? What sounds good?" His gaze narrowed when I could do nothing with mine but gawk. "We leave in ten days, so I can have the travel girls tweak the arrangements. I know you've also lusted after Tuscany. It's harder to get to, but we could work in a small side trip if you—" He halted, staring at me with a hint of panic. I could count on one hand how many times I'd seen that look on his face. It stunned me just as much as what he'd said. "Claire?" He tapped a nervous thumb on his thigh. "For God's sake, say something."

I swallowed, forcing myself to comply. "I...it's...well... whoa. Three weeks. Wow."

"Which means what in English?"

I felt like an ass. Shock had me going for the nonstop stammer, and it all seemed to be the wrong damn thing.

"I'm sorry. No, wait—I mean, I'm not sorry, not about—oh, hell. Did Andrea really agree to this? How pissed was she when you—?"

"You're worried about Andrea?" He looked as furious as a wildcat stuck in a barrel over Niagara Falls—with my words as the rushing water.

"I'm ruining this," I muttered. "Again." When Killian's jaw clenched so hard his chin nearly formed a V, I dropped my head and fell into silence, knowing if I said anything else it would emerge in a tearful blubber.

Killian yanked me close again. "I have Andrea handled, baby. She's Barney compared to the T-Rexes I've taken on in my life."

I giggled at the image of my boss's elegant face poking out of a purple Barney costume. But what the hell did he mean by T-Rexes? And wasn't I not supposed to care anymore, anyway?

That handled my resistance to the tears. Perfect. Now I was slinging the waterworks at him too. And, oh, how he loved that. Not.

I pushed away, burying my face in my hands. "Please. I need a redo, okay? I'll get this right, I promise."

Killian growled. Hard. Right before clutching the back of

my neck and forcing my face into the command of his mouth-mashing kiss. A whine tore up my throat, thick and needy. I clawed at his arm, making it my anchor during my ride into blissful surrender.

"You're getting it right already." His voice was as coarse as the steel in his stare. "Understood?"

I started bawling harder.

Would he ever stop being amazing? Ever?

"Oh, baby." He rubbed my cheek with a big thumb. "Don't cry. I just wanted to make you happy. We don't have to go. I can just have the girls cancel and—"

"Don't. You. Dare." Though my order spurred him to more laughter, I added, "I'm crying because I'm happy. And..."

"And what?"

"And because of my own stupidity." I returned his caress, pressing a hand to the magnificent, high plane of his cheek. "You are amazing. And perfect. I'm just not used to all of it...to your generosity, to you filling all my dreams like this. I'm not used to trusting it, to trusting any kind of happiness, so I don't. Instead, I turn on the soundtrack of suspicion, unwilling to believe that this is really happening."

He blinked hard. For a moment, the clarity in his gaze was replaced by dark-gray clouds, as if only half his thoughts were still here and half had jumped to the moon. "I know." His words were so full of commiseration, I felt it to the marrow of my bones.

I pressed my hand a little tighter to his skin. "You do know, don't you?" When he reacted simply by kissing me softly, I went on, "I love the surprise. I really do. Thank you, Mr. Stone. Now I just need to pinch myself to assure I'm not dreaming."

"Hey." He threw a mock glower. "If there's any pinching

going on around here, I'll be the one doing it." After a quick kiss to my nose, he grinned again, obviously pleased with himself for blowing my mind. "Now, no more crying, Miss Montgomery. Let's get you some food."

"Okay." I giggled and sniffed. "That sounds really good. Maybe a big salad—and an even bigger glass of wine."

"Fuck." He rolled his eyes. "No way. You're getting a burger. And some goddamn fries. And then the wine." He finished the look by letting his stare darken back to sensual velvet. "And then me."

As usual, the man knew exactly what it took to make my world perfect.

And for once, I chose to believe that it wouldn't all disappear tomorrow.

This story continues in
No More Masquerade: *Secrets of Stone Book Two!*

ALSO BY ANGEL PAYNE

Secrets of Stone Series:
No Prince Charming
No More Masquerade
No Perfect Princess
No Magic Moment
No Lucky Number
No Simple Sacrifice
No Broken Bond
No White Knight

Honor Bound:
Saved
Cuffed
Seduced
Wild
Wet
Hot
Masked
Mastered (Coming Soon)
Conquered (Coming Soon)
Ruled (Coming Soon)

The Misadventures Series:
Misadventures with a Super Hero

**For a full list of Angel's other titles,
visit her at angelpayne.com**

ABOUT ANGEL PAYNE

USA Today bestselling romance author Angel Payne loves to focus on high-heat romance starring memorable alpha men and the women who love them. She has numerous book series to her credit, including the Suited for Sin series, the Cimarron Saga, the Temptation Court series, the Secrets of Stone series, the Lords of Sin historicals, and the popular Honor Bound series, as well as several standalone titles.

Angel is a native Southern Californian, leading to her love of being in the outdoors, where she often reads and writes. She still lives in Southern California with her soul-mate husband and beautiful daughter, to whom she is a proud cosplay/culture con mom. Her passions also include whisky tasting, shoe shopping, and travel.

Visit her here:
angelpayne.com

ABOUT VICTORIA BLUE

International bestselling author Victoria Blue lives in her own portion of the galaxy known as Southern California. There, she finds the love and life–sustaining power of one amazing sun, two unique and awe-inspiring planets, and four indifferent yet comforting moons. Life is fantastic and challenging and every day brings new adventures to be discovered. She looks forward to seeing what's next!

Visit her here:
victoriablue.com